Critical acclaim for the marvelous romances of Jude Deveraux

The Summerhouse

"Deveraux is at the top of her game. . . . [She] uses the time-travel motif that was so popular in *A Knight in Shining Armor,* successfully updating it with a female buddy twist that will make fans smile."

—*Booklist*

"Entertaining summer reading."

—*The Port St. Lucie News* (FL)

"[A] wonderful, heartwarming tale of friendship and love."

—America Online Romance Fiction Forum

"A wonderfully wistful contemporary tale. . . . With *New York Times* bestselling author Jude Deveraux, one thing that's guaranteed is a happy ending."

—Barnesandnoble.com

"Thought-provoking, entertaining, and downright delightful."

—Amazon.com

"Jude Deveraux's writing is enchanting and exquisite in *The Summerhouse.*"

—*BookPage*

"Once again, Deveraux gives us a book we can't put down."

—*Rendezvous*

"Jude Deveraux takes a fascinating theory and runs with it. . . . A very compelling and intriguing story."

—Romantic Times

Temptation

"An exciting historical romance that centers on the early-twentieth-century women's rights movement. . . . Filled with excitement, action, and insight. . . . A nonstop thriller."

—Harriet Klausner, Barnesandnoble.com

"[A] satisfying story."

—Booklist

"Deveraux['s] lively pace and happy endings . . . will keep readers turning pages."

—Publishers Weekly

High Tide
A *Romantic Times* Top Pick

"*High Tide* is packed full of warmth, humor, sensual tension, and exciting adventure. What more could you ask of a book?"

—Romantic Times

"Fast-paced, suspenseful. . . . [A] sassy love story."

—Publishers Weekly

"Exciting. . . . Fans of romantic suspense will gain much pleasure."

—Midwest Book Review

"[A] fast-paced escapade . . . as mysterious and sultry as the Everglades themselves."

—BookPage0

"Jude Deveraux not only keeps you guessing but mixes crime and human morality with humor in the most unexpected moments. . . . [A] fantastic read."

—Rendezvous

The Blessing

"Plenty of romance, fun, and adventure . . . fans won't be disappointed."

—San Antonio Express-News

"[A] fun and entertaining love story. . . . A must for Deveraux fans."

—The Advocate (Baton Rouge, LA)

An Angel for Emily

"All sorts of clever turns and surprises. Definitely a keeper. . . . Wow!"

—The Philadelphia Inquirer

Legend

"First-rate reading. . . . Only Jude Deveraux could mix romance with tongue-in-cheek humor and have it all come out so perfectly right."

—Rendezvous

Books by Jude Deveraux

The Velvet Promise	Wishes
Highland Velvet	Mountain Laurel
Velvet Song	The Conquest
Velvet Angel	The Duchess
Sweetbriar	Eternity
Counterfeit Lady	Sweet Liar
Lost Lady	The Invitation
Twin of Ice	Remembrance
Twin of Fire	The Heiress
River Lady	Legend
The Temptress	An Angel for Emily
The Raider	The Blessing
The Princess	High Tide
The Awakening	Temptation
The Maiden	The Summerhouse
The Taming	The Mulberry Tree
A Knight in Shining Armor	Forever . . .

Jude Deveraux

Forever...

A Novel of Good and Evil,
Love and Hope

POCKET BOOKS
New York London Toronto Sydney Singapore

An *Original* Publication of POCKET BOOKS

 POCKET BOOKS, a division of Simon & Schuster, Inc.
1230 Avenue of the Americas, New York, NY 10020

Copyright © 2002 by Deveraux, Inc.

ISBN: 0-7394-2912-4

POCKET and colophon are registered trademarks of Simon & Schuster, Inc.

Front cover illustration by Lisa Litwack
Front cover photo by David Perry/Photonica

Printed in the U.S.A.

Forever...

Prologue

BENDING OVER THE CHILD, the woman began to ask her questions. What had she done that day? Had she told the truth? Who had she seen? What had she learned that day?

All in all, it could have been a scene in any of a million homes, but there was a difference here.

The room itself was plain, sparsely furnished, no soft, cuddly toys, no dolls, no games. There were iron bars on the windows. There was a desk with neatly arranged books, papers, and pens on top of it. There was a small bookcase against one wall, but there were no childish titles in it. Instead, the books were about runes and symbols, about Druids. And there were many books on women of the past who had conquered countries and ruled nations.

Three of the walls were covered with displays of weapons: old ones, new ones, knives, swords, weapons that needed gunpowder. They were arranged in perfectly symmetrical patterns on the walls, in circles and diamonds, rectangles and squares.

Over the child's narrow bed was an enormous painting based on the tower card of the tarot deck: the card of death.

After a few minutes of questioning, the woman sat on a chair by the child and, as she did every night, she started to tell her the bedtime story. She told the same story every night, never varying it by so much as a line, because she wanted the child to memorize the story and to learn from it.

"Once upon a time," the woman began, "there were two sisters, one named Heather, and the other one named Beatrice. Actually, they weren't really sisters, not by blood. Heather's father had died when she was twelve, and Beatrice's mother had died when she was only two. When the girls were both thirteen years old, their parents married each other, and Beatrice and her father (who had been alone together for a long time) moved into the house that Heather's rich father had left to his wife and only child.

"But even though the girls were only three months apart in age, they were very different. Some unkind souls (and there were a lot of them in that little town) said that Heather had received everything, while Beatrice had received nothing. And it did seem that way. Heather had beauty, brains, talent, and even a bit of clairvoyant power that she had inherited from her great-great-grandmother. It wasn't enough psychic ability to make her a freak, just enough to put her in demand at every party. Heather could hold someone's hand, close her eyes, and tell the person his or her fortune—which was always good. If Heather ever saw anything bad in someone's future, she kept it to herself.

"On the other hand, Beatrice was quite plain-faced, of average intelligence, had no known talent, and certainly no psychic abilities.

"All through school people loved Heather and ignored Beatrice. In their final year in high school, Heather went to France on a school trip, and she returned a different person. Whereas before she'd been a friendly, sociable young woman and had dated many boys, after she returned from France, she would lock herself in her room for hours at a time and she turned down all invitations. She gave up the lead in the school play; she stopped taking singing lessons. And she stayed away from boys as though they were the enemy.

"Whereas other people thought it was commendable for Heather to become so studious, Beatrice thought it was just plain odd. Why would her sister, who had everything that Beatrice dreamed of having, give it up? Beatrice asked her sister what was going on. 'Boys can't be trusted to behave themselves' was the only answer that Heather would give before she slipped back into her room and locked the door. Beatrice thought this was a very strange answer because she didn't want the boys to behave, but then she was never asked out. 'Too weird' is what the boys said about Beatrice.

"So one day, Beatrice decided to find out what was going on. When she knew that Heather was alone in the house, Beatrice ran in the front door screaming that their dear mother had just been run over by a truck and was right now bleeding to death in the emergency room of the hospital. As Beatrice knew she would, Heather ran out of the house, grabbing the keys to her stepfather's car (he took the train to work), and drove off in a flurry of gravel and tears. Of course Heather hadn't taken the time to lock her bedroom door, so Beatrice knew that she would have a long, uninterrupted opportunity to see what was so very interesting in her 'sister's' room.

"After an hour of searching, Beatrice had found nothing particularly interesting or new—and Beatrice knew everything in Heather's room, even where she kept her diary under the loose floorboard.

"The only thing new in Heather's room was an old mirror that Beatrice guessed she'd bought in an antique shop in France. All those beautiful French clothes and those beautiful French men, and Heather had probably spent her time poking about in antique shops—that would be just like her, Beatrice thought.

"But look at it as hard as she could, Beatrice could see nothing interesting about the mirror. But then, sighing—annoyed that, for once, Heather had defeated her—Beatrice said aloud, 'I wonder when she'll get back?' As soon as she said the words, there in the mirror was an image of Heather in the car, driving back to the house, her face furious. Not that Heather's anger about the lie worried Beatrice. No, long ago, Beatrice had learned that there were ways to deal with Heather; for, you see, Heather was one of those stupid people who loved. And Beatrice had found out that people who loved could be manipulated. All you had to do is take away—or threaten to take away—whatever they loved and that person would become your slave.

"So now, as Beatrice looked into the mirror, she at last

knew why Heather had been spending so much time alone in her room. What had she been looking at in the mirror? 'Show me my father right now,' Beatrice said, and immediately there was the image of her father and his pretty secretary in bed together. That made Beatrice laugh, but then she'd always known that her father had married Heather's silly mother for the money her husband had left her.

"Beatrice didn't get to ask any more questions because she heard Heather's mother enter the house downstairs, and Beatrice knew that she had to go down and pretend to be glad to see her. Actually, she had to pretend to have thought that she'd actually been run over by a truck. (Beatrice was careful to make her stepmother think that she was a loving child.)

"It was two nights after Beatrice had discovered the mirror that Heather was found hanging from a beam in the basement. It seemed that she'd climbed onto an overturned bucket, put the noose around her neck, then kicked the bucket away.

"In the town's misery that followed the death of someone so well loved, the town gave Beatrice, for a little while, all the attention she'd dreamed of having. But then Beatrice began to see a couple of people looking at her and whispering, so she asked the mirror to show her the future. It seemed that the undertaker had become suspicious when he'd seen red, raw marks on Heather's wrists and suspected that they were rope burns. It almost appeared as if Heather's hands had been tied behind her back when she'd stepped onto that bucket.

"What Beatrice saw in the mirror was herself being put into a police car, handcuffs about her wrists.

"The next day Beatrice disappeared. No one who'd known her ever saw her again. At seventeen years of age, she began a life of hiding and disguise that would never end.

"What Beatrice had seen in her short life was the power of money. She and her father had been quite poor, but she'd seen how he'd lied, cheated, and borrowed to get good clothes and a good car (he'd stolen that) so he could present himself as an eligible suitor to a rich widow. Beatrice had seen the difference between herself, who had grown up in poverty, and Heather, who had grown up in wealth.

"So for the next years Beatrice used the mirror to amass money. She soon found out that the mirror would show her whatever she wanted to know, whether past or future. But what did she care about the past? Did it matter to her to see her father push her mother out a window? She wanted to see what stocks and companies were going to do well. Eventually, she paid cash for many acres of land in Camwell, Connecticut, and she moved into the small house set on the edge of the acreage.

"But here's where the story turns. You see, the mirror can be tricky. When it comes to viewing the future, the mirror shows what can—and probably will—happen, but it makes no comment as to what's good or bad. You have to look far ahead to see that. But since Beatrice had used the mirror only for obtaining money, she didn't know this.

"Eventually, it came to pass that Beatrice was twenty-six-years old and very rich, but she was still a virgin. But because she'd never looked far ahead in the mirror, she didn't know that her virginity was a requirement for seeing the visions in the mirror.

"But her sister, Heather, had known. I told you, didn't I, that Heather was the smart one?

"So one day, Beatrice was looking at the stock market in the mirror when she looked out the window at the beautiful spring day and whispered, 'I wonder if there will ever be a man in my life?' The mirror's vision of the stock market report was replaced with a vision of herself under a flowering pear tree, and she was being made love to by a handsome man. Since by this time Beatrice had somewhat satisfied her craving for wealth, this young man appealed to her. So that day, Beatrice left her isolated house and looked about the countryside until she found the pear tree that she'd seen in the mirror, and for days she spent from early morning until late evening sitting under it and waiting.

"And during those days, she did not look in the mirror, which was a very bad thing, because if she had, she would have seen the result of her tryst.

"Finally, on the morning of the fourth day, the handsome young man showed up. He was hitchhiking across the U.S., as young men sometimes do, but he'd had no luck in getting a ride that morning. He was hungry and thirsty and in a bad temper, when he came around a corner and saw a plain-faced young woman with a full picnic basket sitting under a flowering pear tree. So he stopped, and after his belly was full, he began to make love to her.

"However, something odd happened to Beatrice. While the young man was making love to her, something that she'd wanted for a very long time, she thought, I can't wait to get back to my mirror and to making money. She also thought that the whole process of 'lovemaking' had been highly overrated, and she vowed there and then never to do it again. So, as soon as she could get away from the young man, she ran back to her house and to her beloved mirror.

"But because she was no longer a virgin, she couldn't see the images in the mirror.

"Poor Beatrice. The mirror had finally been something she could love, and it had betrayed her. The rage of the tantrum she threw was so violent that the mirror rocked until it almost fell off the table.

"For weeks after that, Beatrice was ill, and she didn't know what to do to make herself well. It was true that she had more money than she could ever spend, but it was then that she realized that it was the power that she liked, not the money. So she began to think, How can I get the power back? I still have the mirror and maybe *I* can't read it, but perhaps someone else can.

"That's when Beatrice found that money could buy *anything*. She easily found men who would kidnap young, virginal girls for her. One by one, Beatrice would set them before the mirror, but if the girl saw nothing, Beatrice 'got rid' of her. She couldn't send her back to her parents, not after what she'd seen, now could she?

"Finally, after a year or more, Beatrice found a little girl who could see visions in the mirror, so Beatrice kept the child for quite a while. But the girl's visions were vague; she couldn't see half as much as Beatrice had been able to see. 'Who can see better than you?' Beatrice demanded of the frightened child. The little girl thought that if she worked really hard—looking into the mirror made her head ache—and found someone else to look into the mirror for 'the witch,' as she referred to Beatrice in her mind, then 'the witch' would be sure to send her home. And, indeed, that's what Beatrice promised the trusting but not very bright little girl every day.

"So the child looked and asked, and asked and looked, and, one day a clear vision came to her. Beatrice wrote down every word the child told her.

"The child said that the one who would be able to see clearly into the mirror was a girl whom Beatrice would kidnap. She saw Beatrice stealing a child from a store and told her in detail what the child looked like, where the store was located, what the child would be doing, and how Beatrice could trick the mother. She told her everything she saw. She even saw Beatrice branding the child with a mark on her chest. 'Branding?' Beatrice said, then shrugged. Why not?

"So Beatrice sent the child 'away' because she'd seen much too much, then Beatrice did everything that had been seen in the mirror.

"However, it wasn't until after she'd branded the screaming brat that she was told by a follower that she'd kidnaped a male.

"Once again, the rage that Beatrice felt was horrifying. She couldn't get that wretched child who had seen the vision to clarify it, because that girl was 'gone.' This time, protecting herself in case she should need him again, Beatrice had the worthless boy put into a metal box while she considered what to do next. It took her a whole day to figure out that the boy she'd kidnaped must have a sister. Hadn't the mirror shown that the kidnaping would lead to the girl who could read the mirror? But how to get the sister? It took only one trip into New York to see that the boy's parents were now surrounded by police.

"Since Beatrice was so very plain, no one seemed to notice her. She was only twenty-seven now, but she was stooped from years of bending over the mirror. She easily slipped into the service entrance of the fancy apartment building with a few maids and soon found out which one of them worked for 'his' parents.

"It was also easy for her to 'dispose' of the regular maid, then put on her uniform and go to the apartment. But it was in the elevator on the ride up to the apartment that she found out that the boy she'd taken was an only child. For a few moments of panic, Beatrice thought that the mirror had lied. But then she smiled because she realized that the mother must be pregnant with a daughter. *Her* daughter. The female child that was Beatrice's, the one who could read the mirror.

"So Beatrice went to the apartment and said that her cousin, their regular maid, was too upset to work because she loved the little boy so much. The boy's father had looked at Beatrice hard, too hard for her liking; then he'd nodded that it was all right for her to come in. He seemed to know that Beatrice had something to tell him, and he wanted to hear what she had to say.

"After that, it was very easy. When Beatrice finished cleaning—and she didn't do a very good job—an opportunity presented itself and Beatrice handed the father a note. It told where he and his wife were to go the next day. She left the apartment as unnoticed as if she'd never been there.

"The next day, as directed, the plane carrying the little boy's parents landed on Beatrice's private airstrip. The man was dispatched instantly, as he was of no use for anything, and the plane was taken apart, piece by piece, and buried or burned. But the woman, who was indeed pregnant, was kept in relative comfort—although she did not appreciate it, Beatrice thought—until after the child was born; then she, too, was sent to join her husband.

"And, in the end, Beatrice was left with a pretty little female child whom she raised in luxury and comfort. And, true to the predictions, the child could see the visions in the mirror as clearly as though she were watching television.

"And Beatrice knew that, if she could not read the mirror herself, she had the next best thing. The only flaw in her plan was that the brat of a boy child had escaped from the metal box where she had put him. Who would have thought that a child that young would be clever enough to be able to unfasten a catch that intricate and strong?

"For months after the boy escaped, Beatrice followed in the newspapers and on television what she could about the child who had been found wandering in the Connecticut woods. He had been covered in deer ticks and running a fever and had been hospitalized for a while. But when Beatrice learned that the brat remembered nothing that had happened to him, she relaxed and turned her attention to the little girl who now belonged to her.

"She soon found out that the little girl, whom she named Boadicea, after a warrior queen that Heather had written a paper about but that Beatrice had turned in as her own, was very intelligent. She thought of seeing things in the mirror that Beatrice had never tried to see. Gradually, Beatrice began to use the mirror, through Boadicea, as a way to gain power, not just as a way to make money. Beatrice began to control people and businesses.

"And, most of all, she used the mirror to look for other magic items, because what Beatrice had decided that she wanted was immortality. If it could be had, she was going to get it."

That had been the story she told to the child, and all had gone well for many years. Beatrice had a sizable following of people who lived for nothing more than to do her bidding. She owned several important people, and she'd found a formula for immortality. Beatrice had collected six of the nine objects needed when the mirror showed a snippet of a girl, a skinny little thing with blonde hair and blue eyes and a left hand with nine moles on it, who was going to be the end of her.

After that, Beatrice's only goal in life was to get rid of that skinny little girl.

1

DARCI LOOKED OVER the job application again, checking that she'd been absolutely truthful on every line, with no "imagination" added. Her mother said that Darci's "imagination" was like a family curse. "Must have come from your father's side of the family," Jerlene Monroe would say whenever her daughter did something she didn't understand. "Whoever he may be," Uncle Vern could be counted on to add under his breath—then there'd be a fight. When it got to the part where Uncle Vern was shouting that his niece wasn't "full of imagination" but was just a plain ol' garden variety blankety-blank liar, Darci would silently leave the room and open a book.

But now Darci was in beautiful New York City, she had a fabulous college education under her belt, and she was applying for what had to be the best job that anyone had ever seen. And I'm going to get it! she said to herself, closing her eyes for a moment as she clutched the folded newspaper to her chest. I'll apply my True Persuasion to this and I'll be *sure* to get the job, she thought.

"You okay?" asked the young woman in front of her in what Darci recognized as some type of Yankee accent.

"Wonderful," Darci said, smiling. "And you?"

"Feeling like an idiot, actually. I mean, can you really believe this thing?" she asked, holding up the same newspaper that Darci was clutching. She was a tall young woman, much taller than Darci, and, compared to Darci, she was downright fat. But then people were always describing Darci as scrawny. "She's 'fashionably thin,'" her mother would say. "Jerlene!" her sister, Thelma, would snap, "you ain't never fed that girl nothin' but Jell-O and sugar cereal. She's probably starvin' to death." This statement would produce a lot of anger from Darci's mother, then a torrent of words about how hard it was to raise a daughter single-handedly. "You ain't raised her; the neighbors has," Uncle Vern would say; then the fight would escalate.

Now Darci smiled at the woman in front of her. "I think it's a miracle," she said. Darci was pretty in a fragile sort of way, with wide-set blue eyes, a tiny nose, and a little rosebud mouth. She was only five-feet-two and weighed so little that her clothes always hung loosely on her. Right now, her little black skirt with the shiny seat was fastened at the waist with a big safety pin.

"You don't think you're really going to get this job, do you?" the woman in front asked.

"Oh, yes," Darci said, taking a deep breath. "I believe in

thinking positively. If you think it, you can achieve it, is what I truly believe."

The woman opened her mouth to say something; then she gave a sly smile. "Okay, so what do you think the job is, exactly? It can't be sex because it pays too much money. I can't imagine it's for running drugs or that they need a hit man, because the announcement is too public, so what do you think they *really* want?"

Darci blinked at the woman. Her aunt Thelma had washed Darci's only suit in soap powder that she'd bought on sale, then had taken it out of the washer before the rinse cycle began. "Saves money that way," Aunt Thelma had said. Maybe it was cheaper, but now the dried soap in the fabric was itching Darci's bare arms inside the unlined sleeves of the suit, as her pink, ruffled blouse was sleeveless.

"I think someone wants a personal assistant," Darci said, not understanding the woman's question.

At that the woman laughed. "You really think that someone is willing to pay a hundred grand a year for a *PA* and that *you* are going to get the job because you.... What? Because you *believe* you're going to get it?"

Before Darci could reply, the woman standing in line behind her said, "Give her a break, will you? And if you don't think you're going to get the job, then why the hell are *you* standing in line?"

Darci didn't approve of cursing, not in any way, and she meant to say something, but the woman three down in the line spoke up. "Does anybody here have any idea what this job is about? I've been waiting for four hours and I can't find out anything."

"Four!" a woman several people ahead said loudly. "I've been here for *six* hours!"

"I spent the night on the sidewalk," a woman standing half a block ahead yelled.

After that, all the women began to talk to each other, and since the line was nearly four blocks long, that made quite a noise.

But Darci didn't participate in speculating on what the job was really for, because she knew in her heart, in its deepest part, that the job was for *her*. It was the answer to her prayers. For the last four years, all through college, she'd prayed every night for God to help her with the situation she was in with Putnam. And last night, when she'd seen this ad, she'd known it was the answer to her prayers.

"Sure has your qualifications," Uncle Vern had said when Darci showed him the ad. His face was twisted into the little smirk Darci had come to know too well.

"I'll never understand why your mother let you choose that highfalutin fancy school," Aunt Thelma said yet again. "You coulda gone to a secretarial school so you could get yourself a real job—not that you'll need one after the weddin'."

"I . . ." Darci began, but then she'd trailed off. She'd long ago learned that trying to explain was useless. Instead, she just let Uncle Vern and Aunt Thelma run down; then she went to the converted closet in their apartment that was now her bedroom and read. She liked to read nonfiction because she liked to learn things.

But Uncle Vern had been right: The ad was written with Darci's qualifications in mind.

PERSONAL ASSISTANT

No computer skills necessary. Must be willing to travel, so no family attachments. Must be young, healthy, interested. Starting salary $100,000 a year, plus medical, dental. Apply in person, 8:00 A.M. 211 West 17 Street, Suite 1A.

"What d'you mean that she's right for this job?" Aunt Thelma had said last night. "It says 'no family attachments.' If it's one thing Darci's got, it's family."

"On her mother's side," Uncle Vern had said, smirking. Aunt Thelma wasn't a fighter as her sister, Darci's mother, was, so she just tightened her lips and picked up the remote control on the TV and switched from the Discovery Channel program that Darci had been watching to QVC. Aunt Thelma knew the life stories of all the presenters on all the shopping channels. She said that the shopping channels made her feel at home even in a place as big and busy as New York. She'd often told Darci in private that she should never have left Putnam, should never have married an ambitious man and moved all the way to Indianapolis ten years ago. And when, three years ago, Vern's boss had asked him to go to New York to supervise a crew of lazy welders, Thelma said she should have refused to go with him. But she had gone and she'd suffered through every minute in the city she detested.

Now, waiting in line, Darci tried not to listen to the angry words that were floating around her. Instead, she closed her eyes and concentrated on the image of her being told that she had this perfect job.

As the day wore on, information trickled down the line.

Once they entered the building, they were allowed into a waiting room, and, finally, they were allowed into the interview room. There was a heavy wooden door leading into the interview room, and it became known as "the door." As for what went on inside that room, they heard little, probably because no woman wanted to jeopardize her chance at such a great job.

It was nearly four P.M. when Darci was at last allowed inside the building. There was a woman standing in front of the doorway into the waiting room, and she only allowed into the room exactly as many women as there were chairs. Hours ago everyone in the line had seen that men weren't really being considered for the job. The men would go up the stairs, but they'd go back down just minutes later.

"Told you," a woman near Darci said. "Sex. This is for sex."

"And what do you have that's worth a hundred grand a year?" a woman asked, holding her shoe and rubbing her foot.

"It's not what I have so much as what I can do with it."

"*Done* with it, more likely," someone else said loudly, and for a moment Darci thought there was going to be a fistfight. There would have been had those words been said in her hometown of Putnam, Kentucky, but she'd learned that Northern women fought with words rather than fists. "Be a lot kinder to punch 'em in the nose," her mother had said after she'd heard a couple of Yankee girls arguing.

"Next!" the woman said sharply as the wooden door opened and out came the young woman who had first spoken to Darci while they were in line. Darci looked up at her in question, but the young woman just shrugged, as though to say that she didn't know if she'd done well in the interview or not.

When Darci stood up, she suddenly felt light-headed. She hadn't eaten since she'd left Uncle Vern's apartment early that morning. "I want you to have a good, solid breakfast," Aunt Thelma had said as she handed Darci a Pop-Tart and a plastic cup full of warm Pepsi. "Fruit's better for you than those cereals your mother gives you. And you need caffeine and sugar and somethin' warm inside you when you go job huntin'," she'd said kindly.

But now, when Darci stood up too quickly, the breakfast seemed a long time ago. She took a couple of deep breaths, put her shoulders back, and, controlling the urge to reach inside her jacket and claw the itchy place on her shoulder, she walked through the open doorway.

One side of the room was lined with windows so dirty she could barely see the building across the street. On the floor under the windows was a messy heap of metal folding chairs, most of them broken.

In the center of the room was a big oak desk, the kind that all used-furniture stores seemed to have an unlimited supply of. A man was sitting behind the desk on one of the metal chairs, and to his left, off to one side, sat a woman. She was in her fifties, dressed in a pretty twinset and a long cotton skirt, and around her neck and on her hands sparkled gold and diamonds. She had a perfectly ordinary face, one that no one would notice in a crowd, except that she had the most intense eyes that Darci had ever seen. Now, as she watched Darci enter the room, those huge brown eyes didn't blink.

But after only one glance at the woman, Darci looked away, because the man behind the desk was the most gorgeous person she'd ever seen in her life. Oh, maybe he wasn't movie-star beautiful, but he was the kind of man that Darci had always liked. For one thing, he was older, at least in his midthirties. "You can't get a father by marryin' one," her mother had said more than once, but that didn't stop Darci from being attracted to men past thirty. "Past thirty and they may as well be past seventy" was her mother's philosophy, but then Jerlene's boyfriends seemed to get younger every year.

"Please have a seat," the man said, and Darci thought he had a lovely voice, deep and rich.

He was a tall man, at least he looked as though he would be tall if he stood up, and he had beautiful black hair, lots of it, with wings of gray above his ears. Like a lion's mane, she thought, staring at the man with her eyes so wide open they were beginning to tear. But she didn't want to blink in case he was a product of her imagination and didn't really exist.

Besides his beautiful hair, he had a strong jaw with a lovely square chin with a little cleft in it (just like Cary Grant, she thought), small flat ears (she always noticed men's ears) and deep-set blue eyes. Unfortunately, they were the eyes of someone who seemed to be carrying the weight of the world. But then, maybe he was just tired from asking so many women so many questions.

"May I see your application?" he asked, holding out his hand to her across the desk.

May I? Darci thought. Not "Can I?" but a proper "may," as in asking permission. With a smile, she handed the paper to him, and he began to read it as she sat down. While she was waiting, Darci tucked her hands under her knees and began to swing her legs as she glanced about the room, but when she looked at the woman to the man's left, she stopped swinging and sat still. There was something about the woman's eyes that were a bit unnerving. "Nice day," Darci said to the woman, but her face gave no indication that she'd heard Darci, even though the woman was staring at her hard.

"You're twenty-three?" the man asked, drawing Darci's attention back to him.

"Yes," she answered.

"And college educated?" At that he looked her up and down, and his eyes said that he didn't believe her. Darci was used to that. She didn't quite understand it, but it often happened that people looked at her machine-washed suit and her fine, flyaway hair and thought that she didn't look like a college girl.

"Mann's Developmental College for Young Ladies," Darci said. "It's a very old school."

"I don't think I've ever heard of it. Where is it?"

"It's anywhere, actually," she said. "It's a correspondence school."

"Ah, I see," the man said, then put down her application. "So tell me about yourself, Darci."

"I'm from Putnam, Kentucky, and I've lived there all my life. I'd never been more than fifty miles out of Putnam until two weeks ago when I came here to New York. I'm staying with my aunt, my mother's sister, and her husband, until I can find a job."

"And what do you want to become when—" He

stopped himself, but she knew he'd been about to say, *When you grow up?* The smallness of her often made people mistake her for a child. "And what did you study to be?"

"Nothing," Darci said cheerfully. "I studied a little bit of everything. I like to learn about different things." When neither the man nor the woman responded to this, Darci said meekly, "I know nothing about computers."

"That's fine," the man said. "So tell me, Darci, do you have a boyfriend?"

Alarm bells started ringing in Darci's head. Had she given herself away already? Had this beautiful man seen that Darci was attracted to him? Was he thinking that he wasn't going to get a worker but some love-struck girl mooning over him all day?

"Oh, yes," Darci said brightly. "I'm engaged to be married. To Putnam. He's—"

"The same name as your town?"

"Yes. Putnam owns the town." She tried to laugh in what she hoped was a sophisticated, big-city way. "Although Putnam's not much to own, what there is, belongs to Putnam. Or to his family, anyway. All of them own it, the town, I mean. And the factories, of course."

"Factories? How many factories?"

"Eleven, twelve," she said, then thought. "No, I think there're fifteen of them now. Putnam's father builds them at a prodigious rate."

"'Prodigious,'" the man said, then bent his head down, and Darci wasn't sure, but she thought he smiled a bit. But when he looked back up, his face was once again solemn. "If you're to marry a rich man, then you don't need a job, do you?"

"Oh, but I do!" Darci said fiercely. "You see—" she began, but then she broke off and caught her lower lip between her teeth. Her mother was constantly warning her not to tell everybody everything there was to know about her. "Leave some mystery," her mother said. If there was ever such a time, Darci was sure that *now* was the time to leave a bit of mystery. And maybe it wouldn't hurt to add a little "imagination." "Putnam won't inherit for years, so we have to make it on our own. I came here to New York to earn as much as I can so I can return to my beloved home and marry the man I love." She said all this in one breath, while behind her back, the fingers on her right hand were crossed.

For a while the man looked at her hard, and she stared back at him just as hard. As for the woman, she had neither spoken nor even blinked as far as Darci could tell.

"If you're in love with a man, you won't be able to travel. And if you have relatives here in New York, you'd miss them if you were away for weeks at a time."

"No, I wouldn't!" Darci said too quickly. But she didn't want the man to think that she was an ungrateful person, certainly not after all her aunt and uncle had done for her. "They, uh . . ." she began. "They have their own lives, and as much as I love them, I think they'd do quite well without me. And my mother has. . . ." What could she say? That her mother had a new boyfriend twelve years her junior and she probably wouldn't notice if Darci fell into a hole? "My mother also has her own life. Clubs, charities, that sort of thing." Could Putnam's Spuds and Suds be considered a "club"?

"And your young man?"

She had to think for a moment to know whom he meant. "Oh. Putnam. Well, he has lots of interests, and he, uh. . . . He wants me to have a whole year of—" She almost said "freedom," which would have been close to the truth. "He wants me to have a year to myself before we begin on our lifelong journey of love together."

Darci thought this last was a rather nice turn of phrase, but she noticed there was a teeny tiny curl of the man's upper lip that made him look as though he were going to be ill. She wasn't sure what she was doing wrong, but she knew that she was blowing this interview. She took a deep breath. "I really do need this job," she said softly. "And I'll work very hard for you." She knew that her voice was pleading, almost begging, but she couldn't help herself.

The man turned to the woman who was sitting slightly behind him. "Do you have what you need?" he asked, and the woman gave a tiny nod. As the man turned back to Darci, he picked up her application and put it on top of a pile of others. "All right, Miss, uh—"

"Monroe," Darci said. "No relation." When the man looked blank, she said, "To the other one."

"Oh, I see," he said. "The actress." He didn't pretend to think the joke was funny but kept his solemn expression. "As you have seen, we have many applicants, so if we'd like to interview you again, we'll call you. You wrote your telephone number on here?"

"Oh, yes, but don't call between eight and ten. That's when my uncle Vern watches TV, and he. . . ." Her voice trailed off. Slowly, she stood up, then paused as she looked at the man. "I do need this job," she said again.

"So do they all, Miss Monroe," the man said, then

looked back at the older woman, and Darci knew that she'd been dismissed.

It took all her willpower to keep her shoulders erect as she left the office and looked into the hopeful eyes of the women sitting in the little waiting room. Like all the others she'd seen leave the office, she shrugged in answer to their silent inquiries. She had no idea how she'd done in the interview. Once she was on the street again, she opened her handbag and checked her wallet. How much food could she get for seventy-five cents? Sometimes the greengrocers would charge her very little for bruised bananas that they couldn't sell.

With her head up, her shoulders back, Darci started walking. Maybe she *was* going to get the job. Why not? She had all the qualifications, didn't she? They wanted someone who had few skills, and that certainly fit her. The spring returned to her step, and, smiling, she began to walk faster, occupying her mind with planning what she'd say when the man called and told her she had the job. "That's how I'll act: gracious," she said aloud. "Gracious and surprised." Smiling more broadly, she picked up her step. She needed to get home so she could apply her True Persuasion to this problem.

Adam signaled to the woman at the door to hold the applicants for a while. He needed to stretch and to move around. Walking to the windows, he clasped his hands behind his back. "This isn't working," he said to the woman behind him. "We haven't found one woman who's even close to being right. What do I have to do, canvass the elementary schools?"

"The last one was lying," the woman behind him said softly.

Adam turned to look at her. "That one? The little Kentucky hillbilly? Poor thing. That suit she had on looked as though it'd been washed in a creek. And, besides, she has a boyfriend, a rich one. Is that what she was lying about? Those factories she says his family owns? He probably has a twenty-year-old pickup with a gun rack in the back."

"She was lying about everything," the woman said, staring up at Adam.

He started to speak, but he'd learned long ago that Helen used her mind and abhorred normal human ways of communication—which meant that she hated to talk. Many times she'd said to him, "I told you that." Afterward, he'd racked his brain until he'd finally remembered that she had indeed said one short sentence that had told him everything.

But now Helen had repeated this one sentence, so he knew it was *very* important. Tired as he was, he nearly leaped across the room to grab the girl's application off the top of the stack and handed it to the woman. Staring into space, she took the paper and ran her hands over it, not reading it, just touching it. After a while, she smiled; then the smile grew broader.

She looked up at Adam. "She's lying about everything there is to lie about," she said happily.

"She doesn't have a boyfriend, no aunt and uncle? Doesn't need the job? Exactly *what* is she lying about?"

Helen waved her hand in dismissal, as these questions weren't important to her. "She's not what she seems, not what she thinks she is, not what you see her as."

Adam had to work to keep his mouth shut. He hated the

convoluted, cryptic talk of clairvoyants. Why couldn't the woman just say what she meant?

Helen, as always, read Adam's thoughts, and, as always, they amused her. What she liked about him was that he wasn't in awe of her abilities. Most people were terrified that clairvoyants could read their innermost secrets, but Adam was trying to find out his own secrets and those of others, so she held no fear for him.

"You want to tell me what you're really saying?" he asked, glaring down at her.

"She's the one."

"That undernourished waif? The Mansfield girl?"

Puzzled, Helen glanced down at the paper. "'Darci T. Monroe,' it says. Not 'Mansfield.'"

"It was a joke," Adam said, knowing he'd not be able to explain. Helen could tell you what your dead grandfather was doing at any given moment, but he doubted if she'd ever watched a TV show or movie in her life.

Taking the application from Helen, he looked at it, trying to recall all that he could about the tiny girl who'd sat before him just minutes ago. Since he'd seen hundreds of women today, they were all blending together in his mind.

Small, delicate, with an air of poverty hanging about her. But, still, she was a pretty little thing, like some tiny bird. A goldfinch, he thought, remembering her blonde hair that hung limply about the shoulders of her cheap suit. She'd had on sandals, no stockings, and he remembered thinking that she had feet the size of a child's.

"I'm not sure—" he began as he looked up at Helen. But she had "that" look on her face, the one that meant that she was in a semitrance as she looked deep into something. "All right," he said with a sigh, "out with it. What're you seeing?"

"She will help you."

Adam waited for the woman to elaborate, but then he saw the smile play on her lips. Lord help him! It was clairvoyant humor. The woman was foreseeing something that amused her. From his experience this could mean something as good as winning the lottery or something as bad as being stranded in a snowdrift for three days. As long as everyone survived, Helen thought that such miserable experiences were amusing. In fact, any adventure that one survived delighted her. So who needed movies and TV when such things were running through a person's head?

"That's all you're going to say?" Adam asked, his mouth set in a firm line.

"Yes," Helen answered; then she gave one of her rare full smiles. "She's hungry. Feed her and she'll help you."

"Shall I name her Fido?" Adam asked, trying to be nasty, but his tone just made Helen smile more as she stood up.

"It's time for me to go to work," she said, for she spent the darkest hours of every night in a trance looking at the lives and futures of her clients.

For all that she annoyed him, Adam felt a sense of panic as she was about to leave. "Are you sure about her? She can do this? *Will* she do this?"

Helen paused at the door, and when she looked at him, her face was serious. "The future is to be made. As it stands now, you could fail or succeed at this. I won't be able to see the outcome until you're there with this Mansfield girl and—"

"Monroe," Adam snapped.

Helen gave a bit of a smile. "Remember. You must not touch her."

"What?!" Adam said, aghast. "*Touch* her? Do I look desperate? That poor little girl? She probably grew up in a sharecropper's cabin. What was that school she went to? Mann's something or other? *Touch* her! Really. I'd rather—"

He stopped talking, because Helen had left the room, closing the door behind her, but her laughter wafted about him. He'd never before heard her laugh.

"I hate clairvoyants!" Adam said when he was alone; then he looked down at the application again. Wonder what the *T* stands for? he thought, shaking his head in dismay. Today, every time some gorgeous, long-legged beauty from South Dakota or wherever had walked in, Adam's heart had nearly skipped a beat. If she was "the one," then he'd be spending day and night with her, sharing meals, sharing what might become an adventure, sharing. . . .

But, each time, after the beauty had left the room, he'd looked at Helen, and with a mocking expression, for she'd seen every one of his lascivious fantasies, she'd shaken her head no. No, the beauty was not "the one."

But *this* one! Adam thought. This Darci T. Monroe—no relation to the other one—didn't look strong enough to help him accomplish anything. Maybe it was true that she was, well, physically qualified—he could certainly believe that—but how could she . . . ?

"Oh, the hell with it," he said, then picked up the phone and called the number she'd written on the application. As the telephone was ringing, he thought, I still have two weeks. Maybe someone else who has the proper qualifications will show up, he told himself as a woman's voice answered.

2

THE GROVE IN CAMWELL, Connecticut, was the most beautiful place Darci had ever seen in her life. The inn and its grounds had once been a rich man's farm. Like George Washington's Mount Vernon, she'd thought when she'd first seen it. The main house, with its deep porch and many windows, had been built in 1727. Inside, the floors were of wide oak planks, and to the left of the entrance hall, where she registered at a pretty little desk, was a large room with fat, overstuffed chairs and two sofas, all facing a massive stone fireplace.

"It's beautiful," she'd said to the young man carrying her one small suitcase.

"You're in the Cardinal guest house, you and Mr. Montgomery together," he said as he looked her up and down.

"Oh?" she asked. "Does Mr. Montgomery come here often?"

"Never been here before as far as I know," the young man said as he walked through the main house and out the back.

When Darci saw the area, with the flower-lined pathways leading to several small houses nearly hidden under the trees, she smiled. "Dependencies," she said.

"Right on," the man said, smiling at her. "Not too many people know that word. You like history?"

"I like a lot of things," Darci said. "Is Mr. Montgomery here yet?"

"Checked in hours ago," he said as he turned down the left path. "All the guest houses are named for birds, but between you and me, yours used to be the icehouse. I shouldn't tell you this, but. . . ." His voice lowered. "Look under the bed and there's a trapdoor to a cellar. They used to keep ice under there."

"And is there a stream too? Something to keep the ice cold?"

"Used to be, but I don't think it's there now," he said. "Here it is." He opened the unlocked door and walked into the little house.

It was a small version of the big house, with two bedrooms, two bathrooms, a tiny, fully equipped kitchen, and a very pretty sitting room. The furniture was a mixture of old and new, but everything was beautifully kept, exquisitely decorated. "It's beautiful," Darci said softly. "You must love working here."

"Pays the bills," he said. "Which room?"

"Oh, uh, I don't know. The one that's vacant, I guess," she said, then saw the young man smile a bit before he turned toward the bedroom on the right. Darci sighed.

Darci knew about small towns, so she was sure that everyone in the tiny town of Camwell was soon going to know that she and her new boss were not there for a sexual rendezvous. Too bad, she thought, because she would have liked for people to think that she was doing something sexy.

The young man plopped her bag down on a little stool at the foot of the bed, then turned to her in expectation, and it took Darci a moment to realize that he wanted a tip. Slowly, she opened her handbag, withdrew two quarters and handed them to him.

For a moment the young man stared down at the coins in his hand in astonishment; then he looked back at her and smiled. "Thanks a lot," he said, seeming to be greatly amused about something.

When she was alone in the guest house, Darci sat down on the bed. Now what? she thought. Since the last two weeks had been the oddest of her life, she wasn't sure what she was supposed to expect next.

First of all, it had been Aunt Thelma who'd told her that she had the job, as she had been the one to answer the telephone.

"What did he say?" Darci'd asked. "When do I report to work? Where?"

Aunt Thelma hadn't known any of these things. Her only thought was of the pleasure she was going to feel when she said, "I told you so," to her husband. But when Uncle Vern got home, his only concern had been to try to calculate how much room and board he was going to charge Darci for the privilege of staying with them.

As for Darci, she didn't hear a word of the argument

that went on around her. All she felt was a sense of satisfaction, because her belief that everything would work itself out had come true.

But for the next two weeks, the only thing she'd heard from the man she'd met so briefly was a request for a social security number and other pertinent information needed so he could send her her first paycheck in advance. By the time two weeks had gone by and Darci had heard nothing else, Uncle Vern had started telling Darci that he'd known all along that the job was a come-on to girls like her.

"And what does that mean?" Aunt Thelma had snapped. Since her sister's daughter had landed a hundred-thousand-dollar-a-year job, she felt that her place in life had escalated, so she was standing up to her husband more. "What does 'girls like her' mean, Vernon?" Thelma had asked, her mouth in a tight line. Uncle Vern had replied, "Like mother, like daughter," and that's when Darci had left the room.

But finally, an envelope had arrived and in it had been a letter and a check for more money than Darci had ever seen in her life.

And it was in that moment that Uncle Vern found out that there was indeed something of Jerlene Monroe in Darci—but not the trait that he thought she'd inherited. The instant Vernon saw that check, he came up with a scheme to deposit all of it in his own bank account. "You'll get more interest that way," Uncle Vern had said in a voice that dripped sincerity.

"I tell you what, Uncle Vern," Darci said with a smile. "Why don't I open an account and you deposit your money into *my* account?"

There'd been a lot of sputtering, and Darci had had to listen to a lot of words thrown at her, but she was used to that. If she hadn't had a need for the money, a need that would determine the entire course of her life, she would have been more than willing to share her good fortune with him. But she couldn't share a penny with anyone.

"You know what debts Darci has," Aunt Thelma had said, but Darci could tell that her aunt wasn't too pleased that her only niece was going to keep all that money for herself. Besides, Darci knew only too well that none of her relatives, by blood or marriage, thought Darci's "debt" was the intolerable burden that Darci did.

In the end, Darci had told them that she was going to give Uncle Vern's request some serious thought and that she'd let them know her answer tomorrow. What she didn't tell them was that the letter included with the paycheck had been from one Adam Montgomery, who Darci assumed was the man she'd met at the interview and who was now her boss. His letter had given her a date and time when he said he'd be sending a car to meet her to drive her to the Grove in Camwell, Connecticut. There was also a telephone number, but when Darci called it, all she got was a machine. She left a message asking that the car meet her, not at her uncle's apartment, but sixteen blocks away in a much nicer part of New York.

On the morning of the day she was to start her new job, Darci had packed all her belongings in her one old suitcase and carried it the sixteen blocks to the place where the car was to meet her. Since the car wasn't to arrive until two P.M., she'd stayed there all morning and early afternoon, so afraid that she'd miss the car that she'd only left the corner once to purchase a tuna salad on toasted whole wheat; then she'd run back to the corner. The black Lincoln, with its tan leather seats, had met her exactly at two.

For the entire trip to Connecticut, Darci had sat on the edge of the backseat and asked the driver questions. By the time they arrived in the remote area of northern Connecticut where the town of Camwell was located, she knew more about him than his last two wives had.

So now she was here, but Adam Montgomery was nowhere to be seen. She was much too full of energy to want to stay in the guest house and unpack her suitcase. Besides, that would take all of five minutes. Instead, she wanted to go exploring—and the first place she planned to explore was the other bedroom.

His room was quite a bit larger than hers, and it had two queen-size beds in it. She ran her hand over a bedspread and wondered which bed he used; then she went to the closet. It was full of clothes. It was autumn in New England, and the wardrobe inside Mr. Montgomery's closet looked as though it had been made for the season and the place. When she ran her hand over one of his corduroy shirts, she couldn't help but notice that the only label inside bore his initials. In other words, they were clothes custom-tailored just for him. There were flannels and corduroys and woolens, and cotton shirts that were impossibly soft. On the floor of the closet were six pairs of shoes, all with wooden shoe trees inside them.

"Imagine that," Darci said aloud. "Six pairs of shoes."

She snooped through the drawers in the room, then went into his bathroom and looked through everything. She opened every bottle, smelled the contents, touched every item. When she left his room, she knew that she would be able to recognize him just by the smell of him, if she had to.

The problem now was, where was he? At six P.M., she walked back to the hotel's main house and wandered into every room that wasn't locked. She said hello to the kitchen staff and asked them their names. She introduced herself to the housekeeping people, and they let her explore the basement of the house. At eight, she went back outside, pulling the jacket of her suit close about her as it was quite cool. She checked the guest house again, but Mr. Montgomery still wasn't there, so Darci went out again. He had a heavy flannel shirt jacket in his closet that she would have loved to put on, but she thought that that might be overstepping the bounds, so she buttoned her jacket and walked faster.

A couple of times, she stood still, closed her eyes, and let her mind concentrate on the image of the man she'd met. Where was he? When she heard someone walking, not on the pathway but through the dried leaves on the ground, Darci stopped walking and inhaled. She had found him. Without another thought, she began to follow him.

He didn't use the town's sidewalks but moved from lawn to lawn, and she followed him around Camwell for nearly an hour before she spoke. "What are you looking for?"

Adam nearly jumped out of his skin at the sound of her voice so near, but he recovered himself as soon as he realized who she was. She was standing under a streetlight, wearing the same thin, worn suit that he'd first seen her in, and she looked so fragile that he thought that if he sneezed, she'd probably go flying backward. "Why aren't you at the hotel?"

"I wanted to find you and ask you what you want me to do. For my job, that is," she said, smiling up at him. He looked great, she thought. He had on a fashionably stressed leather jacket over an Aran sweater, and his jeans were perfectly faded.

"I planned to talk to you about your job when I saw you," he said, his voice full of annoyance.

"So what were you doing out here?"

It was on the tip of Adam's tongue to tell her that it was none of her business, but if he was going to have to spend time with her, he didn't want to anger her. In fact, it would be better to get on her good side. He forced a smile. "I'll tell you everything all in good time."

"If you're searching the town for available sex, I'd be willing," Darci said, then batted her pale eyelashes at him.

For a moment Adam wasn't sure that he'd heard her right, so he just blinked at her.

Then, as he looked down at her, clasping her arms about herself to keep warm, the idea of intimacy with this shivering girl suddenly seemed very funny. He couldn't contain his laughter. And as he laughed, his annoyance fled. What she lacked in other areas, she obviously made up for in having a good sense of humor, he thought.

"Come on," he said good-naturedly, "there's a diner down the street. Let's go get something to warm you up."

Minutes later, they were inside a bright coffee shop and he'd ushered her to a booth. The waitress, a tall, thin woman in a blue uniform with a little white apron, asked what they wanted. "Coffee?" Adam asked Darci and she nodded.

"Anything to eat?" the waitress asked, bored.

"No," Adam said, then he looked across the table at Darci. "Actually, you could bring us a couple of pieces of pie, apple if you have it."

"This is New England, it's October, and you ask if we have apple pie," the waitress said as she went away, chuckling.

Adam turned to Darci. "Thanks. That was the best laugh I've had in a long time."

The waitress set two thick green mugs in front of them and filled them with coffee. Adam sipped his black as he watched Darci put three teaspoons of sugar in hers, then empty four tiny paper cups of cream into it. When she had the coffee to her liking, she drank deeply, then held the mug in her palms to warm them.

"Glad to be of help," Darci said, looking up at him with big eyes. "So, what were you looking for tonight?" When the waitress set two big wedges of pie in front of them, Darci dug into hers, but that didn't stop her from looking up at Adam in question.

"How did you find me?" he asked, avoiding her question.

"I applied my True Persuasion to you."

"Oh," he said, his lips twitching in a smile. "And what is that?"

"If you think about something hard enough, you can make it happen. I just thought really hard about your coming close to where I was and you came."

"I see," Adam said, his smile broader.

"So what *were* you looking for?"

"Actually, I can't tell you yet," he said, smiling in what he hoped was a fatherly way. "At least there's no reason to tell you yet."

"Are you going to eat your pie?" she asked.

Still smiling, he shoved his untouched plate toward her.

"You want me to work for you, but you don't want me to know what it is that you're doing. Not yet anyway. So what has to happen before you're allowed to tell me? Earthquake? Hurricane? Microsoft buys China?"

He chuckled. "Very funny. Nothing has to happen. I just need to find something first then I'll be able to tell you."

"Ah. I see," she said.

"You see what?" he asked, feeling more annoyed than he wanted to feel. Why wasn't this snippet of a girl backing off?

"The hero myth. You have to find the treasure first, then you stand on it and beat your chest in triumph while the heroine swoons at your feet."

"Beat my—" For a moment, all Adam could do was blink at her. Women didn't usually talk to him like this. Usually women . . . well, women had never been a problem in his life. Forcing himself to relax, he smiled at her. "All right, I guess you'll have to be told sooner or later." Standing up, he looked around the restaurant to make sure that there was no one who could hear him near their booth. When he was sure that he wouldn't be overheard, he sat back down, leaned toward her, and said quietly, "There's a witches' coven in this village, and I'm trying to find out where it meets."

Calmly, Darci continued sipping her coffee. Her lack of reaction annoyed him. There wasn't so much as a flicker of interest in her eyes.

"Have you asked anyone where it is?"

"Didn't you hear what I said? It's a witches' coven. Evil. This one is particularly bad. A coven is not exactly something that's held out in the open."

"But this is a small town," Darci said as she used the side of her fork to scrape her plate. She'd eaten both pieces of pie.

"What does the size of the town have to do with anything?"

"It's my experience that in a small town nobody can keep a secret about anything. If I wanted to know what my mother was up to—not that I ever would, mind you—I could call anyone in Putnam over the age of seven and find out."

"Remind me never to visit that hometown of yours. However, I doubt very much if there's anything going on in your town that comes near the evilness of this coven."

"Well, there was—"

Before Darci could finish her sentence, the waitress slapped the check down on the table. "Anything else?" she asked as she looked at the two scrubbed-clean plates in front of Darci. "We got a slice of cherry left."

Darci's eyes lit up. "Oh, that would be—"

"Actually, we have to go," Adam said as he handed the waitress some bills.

"Are there any witches' covens around here?" Darci asked, her head turned away from Adam's look of shock.

"Sure. There's a big one over at the Grove."

"You mean where we're staying?"

"Yeah. You're in the Cardinal House, right? Go out the back door, turn left, then follow the path to the old slaves' quarters. Can't miss it."

"I hardly think—" Adam began.

"Is it a really *evil* coven?" Darci asked.

"Excuse her, she doesn't—"

The waitress acted as though Adam hadn't spoken. "It's real nasty. Four people have disappeared around here in the last four years—none of them locals, of course—and we all think they're doing some folderol with blood down there in the tunnels. The sheriff laughed it off, but his ugly sister-in-law owns his house and everyone knows she's deeply involved in the thing. Listen, you two be careful, 'cause it's nearly the end of the year and they'll probably want to make it five strangers that have disappeared instead of just four. So have a good night and hope to see you again. Ha-ha. Just kiddin'," she added before she picked up the money and turned away.

When Darci turned toward Adam, she saw that he was leaning back against the bench and staring at her in open-mouthed astonishment. But he recovered himself soon enough.

"Are you ready to leave?" he asked, and Darci could see that he was angry at her.

Once they were outside, he walked so fast, with such long strides, that she had to run to keep up with him. "Are you going to fire me?" she asked.

"I ought to!" he snapped. "I didn't want anyone to know why we're here, but you. . . . You. . . ." He threw up his hands in a helpless gesture, as though he couldn't think of anything horrible enough to describe what she'd just done.

"But everyone would know anyway," Darci said, still running beside him. "She knew we were staying at the Grove, didn't she? She even knew the name of our guest house."

"You are obviously not taking this seriously."

"You wanted to know where the coven is, and I found out for you. What else is a personal assistant supposed to do except help wherever help is needed? But the truth is, I don't know what *is* required of me, and, when it comes to that, why *did* you hire me? Except that you were the answer to my prayers, so maybe— Oh, thank you," she said as he opened the door to the cottage for her.

Once inside, she turned to him and waited.

"I have no idea which of those questions I'm supposed to answer first," he said stiffly.

"Do you want to follow the path and go see the witches' coven right now?" she asked, and there was eagerness in her voice.

"No, I do not. In fact, I may never want *you* to go with me. I may. . . ." Trailing off, he turned away from her.

"May what?" she asked softly.

"Nothing," he answered, then gave a fake yawn. "It's late and I'm tired. And tomorrow I have to—" Breaking off, he looked down at her.

Darci waited, not saying a word, because she wanted him to tell her whatever it was that she sensed he was hiding.

But Adam wasn't going to tell her more than he had to before he had to. "Well," he said slowly, then he remembered the way she'd made him laugh tonight. "Good night, Miss Mansfield." When she didn't so much as smile at his joke, he thought she didn't understand. "Monroe? Mansfield?" he said. "Get it? Marilyn. Jayne."

"I understood it the first time I heard it when I was four," Darci said seriously. "What exactly is it that you're hiding?"

Adam gave a sigh, both because his joke had fallen flat and because she was so blasted perceptive. "We'll talk in the morning, but for now, I think we should sleep. Good night, Miss Monroe."

"Good night, Mr. Montgomery," she said loudly when he turned his back on her.

Instantly, Adam turned to her, and for a moment he looked as if he were going to say something. But, as though he could think of nothing else to say, he turned away, went into his bedroom, and shut the door.

Darci also went into her room, and ten minutes later she was in bed and asleep. But she was awakened by the sound of a door opening and closing. Looking at the clock beside the bed, she saw it was three A.M. Had Mr. Montgomery been awake all this time?

Turning onto her back and closing her eyes, she began to True Persuade him into feeling sleepy. Within moments, she saw the light that was coming in under her door go out and she could feel peacefulness settle over the little cottage. Smiling, she went back to sleep.

3

"So what do we do today?" Darci asked brightly the next morning.

Since she was wearing the same clothes that she'd worn the day before as well as the day of the interview, Adam frowned. "Did you sleep? Don't tell me that you're an insomniac, too?"

"I could sleep on a bed of needles," she said, smiling. "Isn't it beautiful out there?" Outside the window, the New England foliage was a patchwork of brilliant reds and oranges.

But Adam had never paid much attention to scenery. "Why do you have on that thin suit?" he asked. "You need a jacket or at least a thick sweater."

"Don't have one," Darci said, never losing her smile. "Don't worry about me, I don't mind the cold. My mother says that I move around too much to feel it."

Adam opened his mouth to reply but then closed it. He

had on corduroy trousers, a cotton flannel shirt, and a heavy sweater over it. "Come on," he said, biting his lip on his comment about Darci's mother. "Are you hungry? Let's get some breakfast, then go to work."

"Always," she said as she walked through the door he held open for her. "I'm pretty much always hungry. So what are we going to do today?"

Adam didn't reply because he hadn't yet thought of an errand that would keep her busy while he did what he had to do. But first, he thought, as he watched the autumn wind whip her thin clothes about her, she needed something warm to wear.

At breakfast in the sunny, cozy dining room of the Grove, she ate twice as much as he did. But what startled him was that she seemed to be on friendly terms with everyone in the hotel, both guests and staff. "Thank you, Allison," she said to the girl who poured the coffee. "Thank you, Ray," she said to the young man who put their plates in front of them. "How's your back this morning, Mr. Dobbs?" she asked the guest at the next table.

"Have you told *all* of them what we're here for?" he asked quietly as he reached for another piece of bread from the basket in the middle of the table. But Darci had eaten all of the bread, plus a four-egg omelette and three sausages.

"Haven't had time," she said. "I didn't know until last night."

She was smiling, but Adam wasn't sure if she was joking or not, and that worried him. How could he impress upon her the seriousness of what he was trying to do? "You ready to go?" he asked, then led the way into the entrance hall. But he halted at the door to the outside because Darci had stopped to talk to a man behind the desk. He was a very old man, his skin as brown and thin as an onion's, but Darci was smiling at him as though he were the man of her dreams.

"So tell me, Miss Darci T. Monroe, what does the *T* stand for?" the old man asked.

"It's an old-fashioned name," she said. "I was named after a silent-movie star, but I'm sure you've never heard of her. Theda Bara."

At that the man gave a dry laugh. "She was sexier than anything on the screen nowadays."

Darci leaned across the desk. "Why you naughty old man," she said in a voice that fairly purred. "Those were the days before censorship."

The old man laughed so hard that Adam feared that he was going to expire right before their eyes.

Smiling, Darci left the desk and followed Adam outside.

"Do you always do that?" he asked when they were in the cool air.

"Do what?"

"Flirt and tease," he said, sounding priggish even to himself.

When she looked up at him, he was frowning. "I do no such thing!" she said. "I just like. . . ." Pausing, she thought for a moment. "I like to make people feel good. I think it's like a mirror. If they feel good then it reflects back to me. Don't you feel the same way?"

"No," Adam said curtly as he halted, then reached into his pocket, withdrew his wallet, and handed her three one-hundred-dollar bills. "I want you to go into that store across the street and buy yourself a jacket," he said. Then, aware of the modern woman's pride in paying her own way, he added, "You can deduct the money from your pay."

Darci handed the bills back to him. "No, thanks. So what do we do today?"

"Is it the money, or do you have some other reason for not buying a jacket?"

"I don't want to spend the money," she said, smiling up at him; then she gave an involuntary shiver as a cold breeze went through her thin clothing.

Cocking his head to one side, he looked down at her. "I have never seen a woman who didn't love to buy herself clothes. So why didn't you take your first paycheck and buy yourself a whole new wardrobe?"

"I'm saving for something," she said as she turned around and started walking down the sidewalk. "Let's see if there's a library in town. Maybe we can find out something about the local history. Maybe we should check the local newspapers too and see what we can find out about the four people who've disappeared. I'd like to know if they were male or female."

"Female," he said, but he didn't take a step forward. "What are you saving for?"

"Freedom," she answered as she turned and started walking backward, moving farther away from him.

Adam gave a sigh. Maybe he was a snob, but he couldn't bear to be seen with someone dressed as poorly and as inadequately as she was. "All right," he said with a sigh and held up the bills. "It's yours. I won't take the money out of your pay."

At that Darci gave a big smile, walked toward him at a surprisingly quick pace, snatched the money from his fingers, then ran across the street, barely missing being hit by two cars, and entered the clothing shop. Adam stood still, his mouth quirked up at one side. "Didn't take her long to get over her reluctance, did it?" he mumbled as he went toward a park bench to sit and wait. He really hoped she wouldn't take too long.

But he had no more than sat down when Darci ran back across the street, dodging the light traffic in a way that made him catch his breath.

She had on what had to be the ugliest sweater he'd ever seen in his life. It was thick and probably warm, true, but it looked as if a child had spilled a dozen tubes of acrylic paint on it. And it was so big on her that the sleeves fell below her hands.

"What is *that?*" he asked.

"A sweater," she answered, pulling up the sleeves, then running her hands down her arms. "It's warm."

"Please tell me that you didn't pay three hundred dollars for that thing."

"No, not at all," Darci said brightly. "Twenty-nine ninety-nine on third markdown. Plus sales tax, of course. That means that I have $268.21 left to put into my savings account."

Adam didn't want to argue with her, but his conscience wouldn't allow someone in his employ to be inadequately clothed—not to mention that he would have to look at the ugly thing. "Follow me," he said sternly, then led her to the street corner. When the one and only traffic light in Camwell turned red, he walked across the street, Darci running to keep up with him.

Adam opened the door to the little shop. In the window were beautiful, expensive clothes, shoes, and boots. The saleswoman inside looked up, and the moment she saw

Adam, wearing his expensive clothes, she smiled warmly, but when Darci entered behind him, her expression changed to a look of disdain. The way Darci was dressed, combined with the fact that she'd bought such a cheap item only moments before, made the woman look down her nose at Darci.

In all his life, Adam had never had anyone look at him the way this woman was looking at Darci, who, as far as he could tell, was oblivious of the saleswoman's scornful gaze.

With a voice that barely concealed his anger, he held up a platinum credit card and said, "Run this through the machine."

"I beg your pardon," the saleswoman said, her eyes still on Darci, who was looking at a rack full of blouses. The woman looked as if she thought Darci was going to shoplift.

"Run this through with a credit card slip," Adam growled as he nodded toward a pile of old-fashioned slips stacked behind the counter.

That voice got her full attention, and she jumped to obey him. Puzzled, she handed the imprinted slip to him, then Adam signed it. There was no amount on it, just his signature.

"Now dress her from the skin out, and from the feet up," he said in a low voice meant only for her ears. "And take that hideous sweater back. If you foist another item like that on her, I'll buy this damned store and burn it down—and I hope to hell you're not in it when it goes. Do I make myself clear?"

"Yes, sir," she said meekly.

4

IN HIS ENTIRE LIFE, Adam had never seen anyone as pleased about anything as Darci was about her new clothes. When she walked out of the store carrying three shopping bags in each hand, it was on the tip of his tongue to make a sarcastic remark about how she was obviously good at spending money that wasn't her own. But the look Adam saw on her face made him withhold his remark. Her eyes were huge and filled with a wonder he'd only seen in toddlers on Christmas morning. Adam had spent a great deal of his life bumming around the world, and he'd seen a lot. "Jaded," his cousin Elizabeth called him. "Seen it, done it, bored by it" was the family pronouncement about their black-sheep cousin.

But Adam didn't think he'd ever seen anything like Darci's face now. She was looking straight ahead, her eyes seeming to see nothing but some inner vision that was making her sublimely happy.

"Want me to carry those?" he asked, unable to keep the amusement out of his voice.

When Darci didn't answer, he reached down to take one of the bags from her, but her fingers were so tightly clenched about the string handles that he would have had to break her fingers to make her release the bags. "Maybe I should just carry you instead," he said, but that gibe didn't get a response from her either. She was still staring into space, her eyes full of wonder.

"Come on," he said good-naturedly, "let's go back to the hotel. It's time for lunch. Hungry?"

When the mention of food didn't get a reply from her, he waved his hand in front of her face. Darci didn't blink.

For a moment Adam contemplated throwing Darci over his shoulder and carrying her; the bags probably weighed more than she did. But they were on a public street and he really didn't want to cause more gossip than need be. Putting his hands on her shoulders, he turned her toward the sidewalk, then gave her a bit of a push to make her legs move; then he steered her toward the street corner.

When the light changed, Adam had to give Darci a harder push to make her start walking again and he had to catch her to keep her from falling as she stepped off the curb. There was one car waiting at the light, and the woman inside put down her window and stuck her head out. "Is she all right?"

"Fine," Adam said. "New clothes." He nodded down toward the six shopping bags that Darci was clutching as though they were her life-support system.

"I understand that," the woman said as she put her head back inside the car, and Adam heard her say, "Why don't you ever buy *me* anything new?" to the man beside her.

When they reached the other side of the street, Adam couldn't get Darci to step up, so he put his hands about her waist and lifted. He was used to women who weighed more than Darci, so when he lifted, she came up about a foot above the curb, her head nearly hitting him in the chin. Once she was on the sidewalk again, he was able to steer her back to the driveway that led to the Grove, then around the main house to their bungalow.

Once inside the door, Darci stood there.

So now what do I do? Adam thought. For all that he'd traveled quite a bit in his life, for all that he'd seen and done many things, domestic situations were not something he was familiar with. What did . . . well, what would a husband do in this situation? On the other hand, did normal, ordinary women act this way after they'd been shopping?

Hangers, was his only thought. Maybe he could get her to hang up her new clothes. Maybe that task would bring her out of her trance. With that in mind, Adam went into Darci's bedroom and opened her closet door. There were hangers in the closet but no clothes. Absolutely none. Where *were* her clothes?

Curious, Adam went to the chest at the opposite side of the room and opened a drawer. Inside was a pair of often-washed white cotton panties, a pair of socks that were thin at the heel, a pair of neatly folded blue jeans, and a long T-shirt that he assumed was a nightgown. Adam began to frown as he went into the bathroom. On the countertop was a toothbrush that had to be five years old—the bristles were so worn that they were nearly flat to the handle—and a box of baking soda that he figured she used for toothpaste. And there was a plastic container of deodorant that looked as though it had been a hotel freebie.

As Adam walked back into the sitting room, he was cursing under his breath. He'd sent her money, so why hadn't she bought herself something decent to wear? Why hadn't she—

She was standing exactly where he'd left her. Shaking his head in disbelief, Adam again gripped her shoulders and turned her toward her bedroom. When she was standing at the foot of the bed, he began pulling items from her bags; he wasn't about to try to loosen her grip on the handles.

As he took the clothes out of each bag, he thought about the fact that he'd had money all his life, so nice clothing wasn't unusual to him. He'd never given much thought to new shirts and trousers. But what did these clothes mean to someone who had so little?

As he unpacked her new items, he was glad to see that the clothes were top quality. For a tiny town like Camwell to support such a store, it was obvious that the residents had to have money. Cashmere seemed to be the predominant fiber in the clothes. There were soft sweaters, tweed skirts that were lined and had pockets (one of his cousins said that a skirt wasn't worth having if it didn't have a lining and pockets), and there were trousers that looked to Adam to be too small to fit a child. The label inside them said they were size two. There was also a navy blue blazer with silver buttons, two thick pullover sweaters ("hand knit in Maine," the label read), and a cardigan dense and heavy enough to keep an orchid warm in a snowstorm.

Inside a smaller bag was tissue-wrapped jewelry. The jewelry wasn't real, of course, just gilt and nickel silver, but he could see that it had been chosen to match the clothes. The bag was also full of what looked to be underwear, but he just closed that bag, taking nothing out of it.

Once he'd laid out all the clothes on the bed, he turned to Darci. She was still holding the bag handles in her white-knuckled grip, still staring straight ahead sightlessly. So now what did he do?

Without giving it another thought, he picked her up and tossed her onto the bed on top of all the clothes.

That woke her up! She was off the bed in a second. "You'll hurt them. You'll crush them. You'll. . . ." Her voice faded away as she bent down to touch one of the cashmere sweaters. It was a deep purple, and there was a plaid skirt whose pattern contained the same color.

As Adam watched her touch the clothes with a reverence that he'd only seen people use with holy objects, he found that he was a bit annoyed. Well, maybe it wasn't annoyance he was feeling but, well, just maybe it was a tiny bit of jealousy. After all, *he* was the one who had bought the clothes for her, shouldn't she be. . . .

"You ready to go to lunch?" he said, then further annoyed himself because his voice sounded harsh and almost angry.

"Oh, yes," Darci breathed. "Yes, yes, yes. I'll be ready in a minute."

"Oh, yeah, sure," he said as he left the bedroom to wait for her in the living room. Ten minutes later she emerged, and once again she was clutching her six shopping bags. It was obvious she had put her new clothes back into the bags. "You aren't returning them, are you?" he asked, aghast.

"Of course not," she said, smiling. "I'm just going to show everyone in the hotel my new clothes, that's all."

"You're going to show . . . ?" he began, then had to shake his head to clear it. "You don't even know these people. What do they care whether you, a stranger, got new clothes or not?"

For a moment Darci blinked at him in disbelief. "What an odd person you are," she said; then she slipped past him and out the front door, using just her fingertips to turn the doorknob, never loosening her hold on her six bags.

For a few minutes, Adam stood still, debating whether or not he should follow her. She was a child, he thought, as his whole face drew down into a deep frown. What she didn't know about people would fill a library.

But a few minutes later, when Adam reached the dining room of the main house, he stood to one side of the doorway for a few moments and listened.

"And this sweater can go with that skirt too," he heard a woman say.

"I hadn't realized that," Darci said. "And aren't you clever for seeing it?"

"For me, I like this necklace with this blouse," said another woman.

"And, oh, that skirt is my favorite color," said the first woman.

"That's because your eyes are exactly that shade of blue," said a man's voice.

"Oh, Harry, get on with you," the woman said in a flirty way.

She's making everyone feel good, complimenting every-one, Adam thought as he stepped through the doorway.

"And here's the man who did it!" a tall, dark-haired woman said when she saw him. "What a great boss you are. Look at that! He's blushing."

Adam wanted to snap at them, at what looked to be the entire population of the hotel, staff included, that he had never in his life *blushed*. He wanted to inform them that he was a man with a mission, a mission of great secrecy, and that he was not a man to blush over a passel of new clothes.

But Adam didn't say any of that. Instead, he grabbed Darci's elbow and pulled her toward the doorway. "We're going out to lunch," he mumbled.

But Darci leaned back on her heels in such a way that if Adam was going to get her out of the room, he was going to have to drag her or carry her. At first he thought she didn't want to leave the other guests, but then he realized that it was her new clothes that were keeping her there.

Laughing, one of the women patted Darci's shoulder. "You go on, honey. I'll see that all your clothes are put away in your room." It was only when Darci heard that that she began walking again and followed Adam into the entrance hallway.

Just as they were leaving, two women came in and stopped in front of Darci. They were both dressed like men, in heavy work boots, jeans, and Barbour coats. "Have we missed the fashion show?" one of the women asked, and Adam wondered how they could have heard of it if they were outside.

"Hello, Lucy and Annette," Darci said as though the women were old friends. "No, my new clothes are still in there." There couldn't have been more longing in Darci's voice if she'd been a nursing mother leaving her newborn baby.

"Oh, good," the shorter woman said. "We raced back to see them. By the way, I've been meaning to ask you. What does the *T* in your name stand for?"

"Tennessee," Darci said instantly. "For Tennessee Claflin, the suffragette."

"And proponent of free love," the taller woman said. "Good for you, girl!"

Laughing, both women went into the hotel, and Darci started walking again. "Where do you want to go for lunch?" she asked, then stopped when she saw that Adam wasn't beside her. He was still standing by the doorway.

"So what *does* the *T* stand for? Theda or Tennessee?" His eyes were narrowed at her, but when Darci opened her mouth to reply, he put up his hand. "No, I don't want to hear. I'd probably get a third answer."

Turning away, Darci smiled. "Want to go to the diner?" she asked.

"Sure. Why not? I don't think there's much choice in Camwell."

"We could have stayed at the Grove."

"And be ogled at by everyone? No, thanks," he said.

When he opened the diner's glass door for her to enter ahead of him, the waitress said, "Back already?"

"We couldn't stay away, Sally," Darci said as she went to the same booth they'd had the night before.

"And how do you know *her* name?" Adam snapped as he slid onto the seat on the opposite side of the table and picked up the menu.

"It's on a badge on her chest," Darci said. "I read it."

Adam had to laugh at the way she'd answered him. "All right, point taken." He handed her the menu, as there seemed to be only one on the table. "See anything you like?"

"All of it," Darci answered truthfully. "But I guess I'll just have the special."

"Okay, so what'll it be?" the waitress asked as she put glasses of water before them, then took her pad and pencil out of her apron pocket.

Adam knew that the special was the cheapest thing on the menu, and it was his experience that "special" meant that the cook wanted to get rid of it. "You have any steaks? Filet mignons, maybe?"

Sally was chewing gum, and her black hair looked as if it hadn't been washed recently. Also, the black was in stark contrast with the extreme whiteness of her skin. She didn't look like the type for outdoor sports. "No steaks in here, but there's a grocery next door. You want somebody to run over there?"

Adam looked at Darci. "Steak for lunch too heavy for you?"

Mutely, Darci shook her head no.

"Two of the best," Adam said. "With everything that goes with it. Can you microwave a couple of potatoes?"

"Microwave?" Sally said, chewing on one side of her mouth and looking bored. "Naw, we don't need microwaves in Camwell. The cook's a warlock, and he uses his magic wand to—" Adam's look made her cut off her sentence, but she went away laughing.

"So, do we go to work this afternoon?" Darci asked as soon as they were alone.

"Actually," Adam said as he picked up the menu again and began to read it with all-consuming interest, "I have to do something personal this afternoon, so you can start your job tomorrow."

When Darci didn't say anything, he looked up at her. "Personal?" she asked quietly, her eyes boring into his. "What you mean is that you're going out snooping again, so you want me to sit and wait in the hotel room."

"No," Adam said slowly. "I meant that I have some personal business to take care of, so you have the afternoon off. You can spend time with all the friends you've made here. I know! Why don't you go to the local library and research those women who disappeared. Or maybe you can find 212 words to tell people that the *T* in your name stands for?"

Darci had had a lifetime of people who loved to start arguments so she wasn't about to take his bait and defend herself, or even explain. "If all you want me to do is wait in a hotel room, why did you hire me in the first place?"

Adam picked up his water glass and drank deeply.

Darci narrowed her eyes at him in speculation. "Are you being so nice to me because you plan to sacrifice me to these witches?"

At that Adam nearly choked, and his water spewed all over Darci. She didn't move, but he grabbed a handful of napkins from the dispenser and reached across the table to blot water off her chest, but then he thought better of that idea and handed the wad of napkins to her. She wiped her chin, then tossed the napkins onto the table.

"I'm on to something, aren't I?" she said, her voice

barely above a whisper, her eyes never leaving his. "You're going to do something about witchcraft this afternoon, aren't you?"

"What I do with my time is none of your concern," he said, leaning so far toward her that his head almost touched hers.

"You hired me as your personal assistant, so if you're going to do something personal, then I'm going to assist you."

"You got the 'hired' part right," he said, glaring at her. "*I* hired *you,* which means that you go where I want when I want and—"

"You two wanta give me some room?" Sally asked. She was standing at the end of the table, big platters and a basket of food on her arms.

"That was fast," Adam said as he sat back on his seat.

"We gotta couple of fire-breathing dragons back there. Makes everything cook faster."

As she set the plates before them, Adam glared at Darci to let her know that it was her big mouth that was causing this ridicule. But Darci's eyes were on the plates of food.

"I doubled everything," Sally said to Adam. "I've seen her appetite so I thought you'd need the extra. And I know that if you can spend what you did today at the Dress Place, you can afford it." With that, she left the table.

"Everyone knows everything about us," Adam muttered as he picked up his knife and fork, and by the time he'd cut his first bite, Darci had eaten half her platter full of steak, potatoes, green beans, and coleslaw. There was a basket full of slices of pumpkin bread and two tubs of butter, and another platter contained cranberry tarts and slices of acorn squash dripping butter and brown sugar.

"It was my minor, wasn't it?" Darci said, her mouth full.

"Your what?"

"My college minor. You hired me because of my college minor, didn't you?"

Adam blinked at her in consternation for a moment before he resumed eating. "Yeah, sure, you're right. That's exactly why I hired you. That was a great course of study. It was . . . ?" He put a huge piece of steak in his mouth, then waved his hand for her to talk while he chewed.

"Witchcraft."

"What?" Adam said, then made himself continue chewing calmly. He was going to murder that psychic Helen! Is this what she meant when she'd said that Darci wasn't what she seemed? "You took college courses in witchcraft?" He hadn't known schools offered such courses.

Darci was looking at him in speculation. "You don't remember reading that on my application, do you? So if that's not why you hired me, then why did you?"

"I'm sure it was your True Persuasion," he said, smiling. Lifting his hand, he spread his fingers, then made a pulling motion, as though he were a sorcerer casting a spell on her. "You persuaded me to hire you."

Darci didn't smile. "You called before I had time to apply my True Persuasion to getting the job. When you called my aunt, I was sitting on a park bench eating bananas. Are you going to tell me the truth or not?"

"What do *you* know about the truth?"

"I know that you didn't read my application so you must have another reason for hiring me."

"Of course I read your application. I just forgot the details for a moment, that's all. I think this coleslaw might be the best I've ever had. What do you think? Or what did you think?" he added when he saw her empty plate.

"You're here to search for a witches' coven, you've hired an assistant who minored in witchcraft, but you 'forgot' what she studied. 'Forgot.' 'For a moment.'"

"So what *did* you study about witchcraft in college?" he asked, smiling. "By correspondence, that is? And where did you buy your newt's eyes in Putnam?"

"At Putnam Drugs, of course," she shot back at him, not smiling. "So when do we start searching for witches?"

"You're not going with me," Adam said, his mouth set in a hard line. "I work alone."

"I see. And what will you do when a witch puts a zenobyre spell on you?"

"A what?" he asked as he reached for a slice of pumpkin bread, then waited for Darci to take one. He ate his plain while she put a layer of butter on top of hers.

"A halting spell," she said. "It won't let you escape."

"That's bunk. No one on earth can do that."

"Of course not. The continued failure of witchcraft is why the practice has persisted over the centuries."

Adam pushed a cranberry tart around on his plate. Maybe this is the real reason he'd been told by the psychic to hire her, he thought. Maybe she did know something.

He looked up at her. "You don't have anything appropriate to wear for where I'm going."

"Under the underwear you wouldn't touch is a black Lycra leotard. It's called a cat suit." Smiling, Darci ate the last piece of pumpkin bread in two bites. "You think they have any dessert today?"

5

"SO HOW DO I LOOK?" Darci asked as she emerged from her bedroom wearing the one-piece stretchy black cat suit.

Adam was annoyed, feeling that he'd been manipulated by two women, first the psychic, and now this scrap of a girl. He'd thought about trying to slip away from Darci, but he had no doubt that she'd do something like call the local police to search for him. And they'd already been told that the local police turned a blind eye to what was going on in Camwell. I'm going to send her home tomorrow, he thought. It was the only way. Later, when he needed her, he could get her to return.

With a ferocious frown, Adam turned to look at Darci; then his mouth fell open. The clothes he'd seen her in previously had been too big and so down-at-the-heels that he'd not seen much else except her clothes. But now she was wearing a one-piece leotard that was as tight as her skin. She was curvy. No, she was very, very curvy, with round thighs, a little rear end that curved outward, a tiny waist, and small, round breasts.

"You look like my ten-year-old cousin," he said as he turned away from her.

"Girl or boy?" There was a full-length mirror on the back of the door to the little coat closet in the living room, and she was twirling in front of it, looking at herself. Not bad, she thought. Not much up top, but the rest of her seemed to be in the right places.

"What?" Adam snapped.

"Is your ten-year-old cousin a girl or boy?"

"Girl."

"You know, I think the Andersons' boy is about twelve. Think he'd like me?"

Adam laughed. "Come on, let's go. If you can stop admiring yourself, that is."

"I can if you can," Darci said brightly, and Adam snorted in answer to that as he handed her one of his jackets to put on over her cat suit.

"If we see anyone, just act as though we're out for a walk. And please do me a favor and don't announce to anyone where we're going."

"Since I have no idea, I can't tell anyone anything, now can I?" she said as she walked out the door before him, then followed him once they were outside. "Left," she said a moment later. "Sally said to go out the back door then turn *left* to reach the path."

"Right," Adam said as he turned. "And it's too bad you don't know where we're going."

She smiled at the back of him as she followed him down

the path, and she buried her face in his coat, rubbing her cheek against the soft wool. The jacket smelled of him. He was the most generous man she'd ever met in her life, she thought, as she remembered all the beautiful clothes he'd bought for her.

The path was almost obscured by the deep pile of multicolored leaves that had fallen from the canopy of trees overhead. After several minutes of walking, Adam stopped before a row of small buildings that had been restored.

"Slave quarters," Darci whispered, then quieted at a look from Adam. He didn't say anything, but he made a gesture with his hand that she knew meant for her to stay where she was while he went into one of the cabins. After three minutes had passed and he still hadn't returned, she went in after him. She was just in time to see his foot disappear behind a hidden door. If she'd obeyed him, he would have gone without her, she thought. But she caught the door and slipped into the darkness behind him.

He had a flashlight, a tiny thing that threw little light on the stairs that led down into darkness. At the bottom of the stairs, he moved the light about. Before them was a tunnel scooped out of the black Connecticut earth that was filled with thousands of rocks, some of them sticking out of the walls. Every few feet the tunnel was shored up with heavy beams and posts. The tunnel curved to the right about a yard ahead, so they couldn't see very far ahead of them. "Leave your coat," he whispered. "You might need to move quickly, and it'll hamper you."

She slipped out of the warm coat, handed it to him, and he stashed both his and hers out of sight under the wooden stairs. Then Adam started to walk down the tunnel, Darci close behind him.

She didn't want to admit that she was nervous about doing this. What she wanted to do was sing and dance loudly, anything to break the ominous silence. She tried hard to think about the men and women, probably slaves, who had carved this tunnel out of the rock-filled earth. "They were carving a passage to freedom," she whispered up to Adam. "What do you think they used for digging? Clamshells? Or their bare hands?"

"Quiet!" he said over his shoulder.

As Darci looked at the dark walls, she was sure that she could hear mice scampering about. Or maybe it was rats. Every one of Edgar Allan Poe's stories seemed to fill her mind. She was so close behind Adam that her nose kept bumping into his back. "No," she whispered, trying to distract herself. "I'm sure they used their own chains to scrape and claw the pathway to the freedom of their very souls."

Halting, Adam turned and she could see by his flashlight his fierce look of warning for her to be quiet.

Darci clutched Adam's belt, and her silence lasted about two minutes. As the tunnel began to widen, she started thinking about its present use. "But maybe the witches did this. They must have worked in the black of night, under a cover too secretive even for lanterns, as they carved out this tunnel with axe and adze."

Suddenly Adam stopped short, making Darci slam into the back of him. "Ow!" she said, rubbing her nose. There was light around them now, not enough to read by, but enough to see Adam's face.

"Stay here!" he ordered. "And not a word out of you."

Darci nodded, but she took a step when he did.

He stopped again. "You want me to find some of those slave chains and a hook?" he whispered down to her.

She didn't think he'd do something like that, but then, one time her cousin Virgil had. . . . She nodded up at Adam, then watched as he disappeared around a curve in the tunnel.

He was gone probably for only a few seconds, but to Darci it seemed like eons. When at last he came back around the corner, he was smiling at her in an odd way. "What?" she asked, rubbing her nose.

Still smiling in that odd way, Adam stepped back to let her go down the tunnel ahead of him. His flashlight was off, but there was enough light for her to see the way. After about ten yards, the tunnel opened up into a big underground room that was ringed with electric lights and to one side was one of those little earthmovers that all of Darci's male (and some of her female) relatives so passionately wanted: a Bobcat. No clamshells, no chains had been used to dig this tunnel. Instead, it had been dug out with a modern machine.

She looked around the rest of the big, empty room. There were no chairs, no furniture, just the Bobcat, and, oddly enough, against the opposite wall were a couple of vending machines. The far wall had three big black holes in it, three doorways into other underground passages.

So now Darci understood his odd look. It was nothing but a smirking, laughing-at-the-silly-female look—a look she decided to ignore.

But she could also see that Adam was as shocked as she was at the obvious size of this coven. That a room the size of this one could have been dug, the dirt discarded somewhere, meant that many, many people were involved in this.

Once again, Darci wanted to turn tail and run, but instead, she forced herself to pretend to be brave. She wasn't going to say or do anything that would make Adam think about sending her away.

With a smile of her own and a devil-may-care set to her shoulders, Darci walked toward the vending machines. "Do you have any change?"

"No, I do not have any—" he said, then broke off because they both had heard a noise. One second Darci was standing in front of a vending machine and the next she'd been pulled through the air to land in a crouching position behind the Bobcat—and Adam had wrapped his body protectively around hers. Her back was pressed against his chest and all Darci could think about was his heart beating against the back of her. For a moment she closed her eyes and thought that if she died right at this moment, she would die happy.

But all too soon a black cat came strolling into the room, looked around, then walked out the way they'd entered.

Darci could feel Adam's body relax, and she knew that the moment of intimate physical contact was about to end. But before he fully took his arms from around her, she stood up. "I've never been so frightened in my life," she said as she swayed on her feet. She put the back of her hand to her forehead. "I feel soooo. . . . Oh, my goodness," she said, then her knees buckled under her.

But Adam stepped aside just as Darci fell—which caused her to land hard on her derriere.

"People who faint usually turn white beforehand," he said, looking down at her. "They do not go bright pink with excitement."

"I'll try to remember that," she said as she rubbed her bruised posterior, refusing to look up at Adam. She didn't want to see that smirk again.

When Darci got up, she saw that Adam was studying the three openings to the other tunnels. Looking like a scout for a posse, he had one knee on the floor, the other supporting his elbow as he examined the floor for tracks and any markings that might tell him which way to go. To find whatever it was he was looking for, Darci thought with a grimace because he hadn't told her anything. Yet, she thought. He hadn't told her anything *yet*.

Again, she walked over to the vending machines. Her fear, the activity, and the nearness of Adam had combined to make her *very* hungry. In fact, she thought that if she didn't have some chocolate and have it *now*, she just might die. "Are you *sure* you don't have any change?"

"Is it possible for you not to eat for ten minutes?" Adam said, not looking up from the tunnel floor. He was examining the second opening now.

Darci looked from him to the vending machine then back again. She knew that it was daylight outside, and what self-respecting witch practiced during the day? And of course Adam knew this, too, or he wouldn't have been snooping around here now. All in all, she thought it was highly unlikely that they'd encounter anyone down here at this time of day.

With that in mind, she walked around to the back of the candy machine and gave it three sharp kicks in exactly the spot that her cousin Virgil had shown her. Unfortunately, her kicks and the resulting thud of the dropping candy bars made quite a noise inside the underground room.

"What the hell?" Adam said as he jumped up just in time to see half a dozen candy bars slide into the trough on the front of the machine.

"I knew I shouldn't have let you come with me," Adam said as he grabbed Darci's arm and started pulling her away from the machine.

But Darci's other arm was inside the trough, her hand latched onto three candy bars that were stuck up inside the machine, so she let out a yelp of pain.

Instantly, Adam released her arm. "Go!" he hissed at her through clenched teeth as he pointed toward the third tunnel opening.

Darci grabbed the candy bars and cradled them to her as she ran toward the opening. The fact that no one had appeared to investigate the noise made her relax. She was sure that no one else was in the tunnels. But then, maybe Adam had heard something that she hadn't.

Obeying Adam's order, she hurried down the tunnel, with him close behind her, but when one of the candy bars dropped, she stopped to pick it up. When she rose, she saw that Adam was glaring at her in a way she understood too well: Angry Male.

She gave him a tentative smile, but his face didn't soften. Instead, he raised his flashlight and pointed silently toward the blackness ahead of them, and Darci started walking.

But it wasn't easy to walk on the uneven dirt floor while carrying nine candy bars. Also, the tennis shoes she'd bought that morning in the shop were a tiny bit too big, so they were slipping up and down on her heels. Between the candy and the shoes, she again fell behind him, but, as quietly as she could, she hurried forward until she was beside him.

"Could I put some of these in your pockets?" she whispered up at him.

"No," Adam said curtly.

"But cat suits don't have pockets," Darci said, her voice coming out as a whine.

"That's because women who have the figures to wear cat suits don't eat candy bars," Adam said out of the side of his mouth.

When Darci came close to losing yet another bar of chocolate (a Snickers, her favorite), she pulled down the front zipper of her cat suit and shoved all of the candy bars down the front.

When Adam heard the noise, he turned back to her, ready to strangle her if she didn't keep quiet. But when he saw her lumpy chest and her with her arm reaching down inside as she fished about for a particular candy bar, he lost his anger. Shaking his head in disbelief, he said over his shoulder, "Are all people from Kentucky like you?"

"No," Darci said, still searching for the Snickers inside her tight suit. "Even in Putnam I'm unique." She looked up at the back of him. "That's why Putnam's so mad for me," she added.

"Makes mad passionate love to you, does he?"

She didn't like his tone, which implied that it was impossible to believe that someone would make mad, passionate love to *her*. "The maddest, the wildest. All day and all night. He's quite young, you see." At that last remark, Darci saw the tiniest movement of Adam's shoulders, as though he'd been hit with an arrow right between his shoulder blades.

"Hmph!" he said. "Does this child have a first name?"

When Darci was silent, Adam stopped walking and turned to look back at her.

She still had her hand down the inside front of her suit, and had this been another time and another place, he would probably have found such a pose to be interesting, but now there was such a look of deep thought on her face that it intrigued him.

"You know," Darci said, "I don't think I ever asked. If Putnam does have a first name, I'm not sure I've ever heard it. It's just so easy to put that one word on everything."

"Oh, yes, you're the one who has the boyfriend with the factories, aren't you? Fifteen, wasn't it?"

"Eighteen," she said as she pulled her hand out of her suit, then smiled when she saw the Snickers bar and began to peel back the wrapper. "I had a letter from him, and his father's built some more," she said as she took a bite. "Want some?"

"Of Putnam?" Adam asked. "Or the candy?"

"Either," Darci said seriously. "There's enough of both to go around. Putnam played all-star football. He's six-two, three hundred and fifty pounds."

"But you're—" Adam broke off as he looked her up and down. He doubted very much, even with the candy bars, that she weighed a hundred pounds.

"Oh, don't worry about us," she said blithely. "We manage." She hoped she sounded worldly, or at least knowledgeable.

"You have chocolate on this tooth," Adam said, pointing at his own incisor, then he turned back around, smiling.

For a moment, Darci had a vision of transforming herself into Awesome Woman, creature of massive strength, and pulling stones from the walls and bombarding his head with them. But when Adam turned back to look at her, she smiled sweetly and finished her third candy bar.

When Adam stopped abruptly a few minutes later, he put his arm behind him to keep Darci from plowing into his back. And when she opened her mouth to speak, he put his warm hand over her mouth. This so delighted her that she didn't say a word.

Bending down so he was eye to eye with her, he put his finger to his lips for silence, then raised his eyebrows in question. Did she understand?

Darci nodded; then, with a frown, Adam took the half of the candy bar she hadn't yet eaten and slipped it down the front of her leotard and silently zipped it up to her neck. Pointing to the far wall, he motioned for her to stand against it and stay there.

Darci didn't want to admit that his manner was scaring her, but it was. In fact, her heart was pounding in her chest as she watched Adam disappear around the corner of the tunnel. When he was out of sight, she did just what he'd told her to do and stood there in silence and waited. And waited. Then she waited some more. Nothing. No sound whatever. Maybe if she recited some poetry. . . .

On a dark and gloomy night, she thought, then made herself stop. Maybe he was in trouble, she thought. Maybe he had been captured by evil beings. Maybe he. . . .

All in all, she thought it was better not to think along those lines while standing in a dark tunnel. There was some light coming from the direction in which Adam had headed, but she couldn't see his flashlight. Had he abandoned her? Had he—

With her hands on the rocky dirt wall, she inched along in the direction he'd gone, her shoes making no noise on the dirt floor. Slowly, she moved along, and with each step she took, she dreaded what she was going to see at the end of the tunnel.

But when she did come into the dim light and was able to see, she wanted to yell at Adam Montgomery that he had no right to scare her like that.

Carved out of the earth along one side of the tunnel was a room with an iron fence across the front of it. Inside the fence were shelves covered with cardboard boxes that had words like *cups* and *plates* written on them. It was an ordinary storage closet. True, it was underground and, true, it had a strong iron fence across the front of it, but it was, otherwise, quite ordinary. Against the wall, just past the fence, was a table and some shelves holding more boxes, but nothing that she could see was unusual or even very interesting.

So what was her esteemed boss doing in front of the gate? He had bent his body into an awkward position as he leaned toward the fence on the left side, and he had half his left hand inside the fence. She couldn't see what he was holding, but it looked like a broom handle. Appropriate, she thought, considering where they were. So what was he trying to reach?

Silently, she walked over to stand beside him. "What are you—" she began, but she didn't have a chance to say another word because suddenly the air was filled with a deafening screech from a high-pitched siren. Putting her hands over her ears, Darci looked up at Adam. She could see that he was shouting at her, but she had no idea what he was saying. Oh, yes, now she could read his lips: "You set off the alarm," he was saying. There were some other words added to the phrase, but she preferred not to try to decipher those.

She wanted to apologize, but behind him she could see a small round light coming toward them: a flashlight, and by the look of it, whoever was holding it was moving fast. She pointed, and, turning, Adam saw the light. In the next moment, he grabbed Darci's hand and pulled her toward the end of the tunnel from which they'd just come.

But Darci didn't move. Her feet moved, but her head stayed where it was. She yelled in pain, but even she couldn't hear herself above the siren's screeching.

In an instant Adam saw what was wrong: Darci's hair was caught in the lock on the gate.

Adam moved without thought. Thrusting his arm through the bars of the cage, he grabbed the dagger he'd been trying so hard to get without setting off the alarm, and in one whack, he cut Darci's hair from the back of her head, leaving a big piece attached to the lock. In the next moment, he picked her up and tossed her onto one of the high shelves outside the fence among some boxes. Darci curled into a ball, making herself as small as possible. But the problem with her position was that she could see nothing. She couldn't see what Adam was doing or where he was. He wouldn't do something dumb but heroic, would he? she wondered.

When the alarm stopped, it took all of Darci's willpower to stay curled up where she was and not move. She very much wanted to rub her ears, rub her jaw, and stretch her legs out straight. But, most of all, she wanted to see where Adam was.

"I hate that thing!" said a man's voice. "Why don't they get it fixed? Damned thing goes off twice a night."

"It is fixed. That's the way she likes it. Sensitive."

"Sensitive, hell," the first man said. "A sneeze sets it off. And I swear those cats do it on purpose."

"Look at this," the second man said.

"What is it? I don't see anything."

"Get your glasses changed. It's a couple of long strands of hair. It was in the lock."

"Somebody's doing a spell, no doubt."

There was silence for a while, and Darci desperately wanted to know what they were doing, but she didn't dare move and draw attention to herself. As long as they didn't find her or Adam, everything would be fine. But why did they have only a few strands of her hair? When Adam had freed her hair, it felt as though half of it had been cut away.

"You know something," the second man said softly. "I think this hair is from a natural blonde. I don't see any dark roots."

"What a great sense of humor you have. A natural blonde. You've been drinking too much of that stuff they brew over in the east tunnel."

"Maybe," the second man said thoughtfully, "but, all the same, let's take these strands to the boss."

"Suits me. Maybe she'll give us a pay raise."

"Yeah, well, don't hold your breath. She didn't get what she's got from being generous. You ready?"

"Yeah, sure. This place gives me the creeps."

"That's because you know too much," the second man said, then chuckled deep in his throat at his own joke.

Darci heard the men leave, but still she didn't move from her perch on the shelf. She didn't lift her head or move her legs, even though both of them had gone to sleep.

She didn't move until Adam reached up and pulled her down from the shelf and set her on the floor. But when her numbed legs gave way under her, Adam put his hands under her arms and pulled her upright. With a little smile, Darci pointed down at her legs to show him that there was no blood in them. He gave her a look of appraisal to see if she was faking it or not, then he tossed her over his shoulder and began to jog down the tunnel they had entered from.

By the time they got to the big room with the vending machines, Darci could have told him that her legs were fine and she could walk by herself, but she kept her mouth shut. Instead of protesting, she put her arms around his waist—upside down, true, but it was his waist and it was her arms—and she was resting her head on the small of his back. It wasn't his shoulder, but it was better than nothing.

He put her down when they reached the staircase. With his finger to his lips, he warned her to say nothing; then he thrust her arms into the too-large jacket and that was when she realized he was angry. Probably very angry, if she knew men.

He put on his own jacket and gave her a little push up the stairs. When she came out into the relatively bright light of the restored slave cabin, she took a deep breath, then ran out the door into the clear, clean air.

6

"OF ALL THE STUPID, asinine things I have ever seen in my life," Adam Montgomery said from between his teeth when they were just a few yards from the slave cabins. "These people are dangerous, but you treat all of this as if it were a game. Vending machines! Candy bars! And talking nonstop. I told you to stay where I put you and to wait for me, but what do you do? You stick your head in the path of a laser beam and set off an alarm! Do you have any idea what could have happened to you if you'd been caught?"

Darci couldn't suppress a yawn. Maybe she should go to bed earlier tonight, she thought.

When she heard nothing more from Adam, she looked up at him. He was staring at her angrily.

"I can tell my words are having no effect on you," he said coldly.

"Sure they are. You're scaring me to death." Once again she had to work to suppress a yawn.

For several minutes they walked side by side, him a foot taller than she, both of them silent.

Suddenly, Adam didn't want to be angry. He didn't want to lecture Darci on the seriousness of what they'd just been through and what could have happened. From the time he was three years old he'd been angry, and it sometimes seemed that his anger hadn't let up since then for even seconds.

But there was something about Darci that made him see only the present. When he was near her, she seemed to drain away the past and the future.

Yes, the witches' tunnel had been hideous. To think that evil could have carved out such a place. . . . To think of what he knew sometimes went on in such places. . . .

But now, at this moment, the air was clean and fresh, the leaves beautiful, and he knew that this little woodland sprite of a woman near him was ready to laugh. He'd already learned that Darci was *always* ready to see humor in any situation.

"If they'd looked up at that shelf," Adam said softly, "I wonder what they would have thought you were? One of their cats?"

With eyebrows raised, she looked up at him. "Where were you?"

"Hiding under the table behind a box. But I didn't fit very well, so my feet were on one side of the box, my hands on the other, and my head was. . . ." He turned his head to an uncomfortable-looking angle, which perfectly showed how it had been wedged below the table.

Darci laughed. "At least you could stretch your legs out. Mine went dead asleep. I couldn't even stand up."

Adam put his hand to the small of his back as though in pain. "Tell me about it," he said with a grimace.

"Are you saying that I'm too heavy for you?!" Darci said in mock outrage.

"I think it was the candy bars." He gave her a one-sided grin. "I'm not sure, but I'd be willing to bet that the inside of that black thing you have on is covered with chocolate."

Darci didn't have to look because she could feel it. The candy bars had burst their wrappers and been squashed when Adam had carried her out. She batted her lashes at him. "Wanta bite?"

"Do you always have your mind in the gutter?" he asked.

She smiled at him. "If you're not interested I think that that nice young man in 4B might be," she said as she took a couple of long strides ahead of him.

Catching her arm, he pulled her back. "You can't think of going after—" he began, but then he saw something in her eyes that made him know that if he took that line, he'd regret it.

"You know, I could stand something to eat," he said. "How about if we go to the grocery and see what we can find, then take it back to the guest house and have a feast?"

For a moment, Darci only blinked at him. "You mean, buy anything we want?"

"Anything," he said, smiling. "From the bakery, the deli, whatever. There's a fridge in the house so we can put leftovers in there."

"'Leftovers'?" she asked. "Is that a Yankee word?"

"It's—" Adam began, then realized she was teasing him. "We could even buy a couple of bags of Hallowe'en candy."

"Race you!" Darci yelled, then took off running.

Smiling, Adam followed her. It didn't take much speed to keep up with her as she ran down the path past the main house of the Grove, then out to the street. Once again, she ran across the street, right in front of two cars, in order to get to the Camwell grocery.

Adam went to the corner and waited for the light to change before crossing the street. Through the big windows of the grocery, he could see her pushing a cart and looking at the items in the store. She made him feel . . . well, grateful, he thought. She took so much pleasure from the simplest things in life, such as food and clothing, that she made him see how much he'd taken those things for granted.

But while he was smiling beatifically, Darci turned around and he saw the back of her head. A big chunk of her hair was missing! From what he'd seen of this town, if anyone saw her hair, it would take about five minutes for everyone in town to know who had been snooping in the tunnels today.

When the light changed to WALK, Adam was already halfway across the street, and he was inside the grocery in four long strides. He caught Darci just as she was picking up a can of something called deviled ham. And there was a woman coming down the aisle. Knowing Darci's propensity for talking to anyone anywhere, Adam had no doubt that Darci would start a conversation with the woman.

Having nothing else to use, Adam slapped his hand over the back of Darci's head to cover the missing hair. "There you are," he said loudly. "I was looking for you every-where."

He had to give it to Darci: She didn't miss a beat. Any other woman Adam knew would have demanded to know what he thought he was doing with his hand holding her head in what had to be a painful grip.

"I'm so glad you found me," Darci said cheerfully, then smiled at the woman as she pushed her cart past them. Reaching up, Darci put both her hands over Adam's. "He can't stand being without me for even a minute," she told the woman. "Really, it's most annoying. Every minute it's, 'Where's Darci? Has anyone seen Darci? I need my Darci!' I can't get a moment's peace."

The woman gave Darci a tentative smile; then she steered her cart to the farthest side of the aisle. When she was past both of them, she nearly ran to the end and turned.

"Would you stop that?" Adam hissed down at her as he forcibly pulled his hand out from under hers. "Why do you have to tell everyone everything about us?"

"Then it's true? You really can't stand to be without me?"

Rubbing his hand, for Darci had held it so tightly that she'd cut off circulation, Adam shook his head in frustra-tion. "No, it's not true. I was covering your hair. There's a big piece of it missing and I don't want people to see that."

Darci felt her hair. "Right. The blonde strands that the man is going to give to some witch. Did he really only get 'strands'? It feels like a huge piece is missing." Right away Darci saw that Adam had clamped his mouth shut in a way that meant he wasn't going to answer that question. I'll find out later, she promised herself; then, lowering her voice, she fluttered her eyelashes at him. "You know, I really am a natural blonde."

"And therefore too easy to recognize," Adam said. "Come on, let's get out of here. We'll do something with your hair tomorrow. What is this stuff?" he asked, looking into the grocery cart.

"Food," she answered, puzzled.

"No, this." He held up a package of cheese with individually wrapped slices and another package of "pizza snacks."

"It's—" she began.

"I know what it is," he said impatiently. "I can *see* what it is. I just meant. . . ." He didn't say anything else, but scooped up everything she had in the cart and shoved it onto a shelf in front of the canned peas.

"You shouldn't do that," Darci said, frowning. "I'll put everything back in its right place."

"And let everyone in this town see your hair? I'd tell you to go back to the guest house and wait for me there, but I don't think you'd obey. Go find some of those tie things that girls use and pull your hair back so it covers that missing piece. I'll do the shopping."

"You'll—?" Darci said, eyes wide, as though that were the most extraordinary thing she'd ever heard in her life.

"Let me guess," Adam said under his breath. "Underground tunnels don't surprise you, but the idea of a man buying groceries does?"

Darci could only nod in silence.

"Go," he said. "And don't let anyone see the back of your head. I'll meet you outside. Stand somewhere where people can't see you, and don't talk to anyone. Understand?"

Darci didn't move. "I'd have to pay for the hair ties."

Adam started to say something sarcastic about how little they would cost but then he gave a sigh and handed her a ten-dollar bill.

Holding the bill, Darci just looked up at him, not moving. "How will I get your change back to you?"

"I'll trust you until we get back to the room."

Darci still didn't move.

"Keep the bloody change!" he said much louder than he meant to; then Darci ran down the aisle so fast that he thought of Road Runner cartoons, with the bird leaving a cloud of dust behind him.

"I have never seen anyone so in love with money as she is," Adam muttered as he pushed the cart to the deli section of the grocery and began filling it, starting with Brie cheese and a carton of hummus. "What's she saving her money for?" he muttered. "A wedding gift for her big, strong, *young* Putnam?"

"Sorry. I couldn't hear what you said," the man behind the counter said, and Adam was embarrassed to have been caught talking to himself. He ordered three fresh salads and a quarter pound each of four different kinds of meat. "On second thought, better make that a half pound each," he added.

In the end, he bought twice as much food as he should have. But then he found himself thinking, I wonder if Darci has ever eaten a pomegranate? As he went up and down the aisles of the small grocery, he kept tossing things into the cart, all the while thinking hard. I must send her away. She doesn't understand how dangerous this could be. Oh! Wonder if she'd like smoked oysters? She treats all of this like a joke. We can drive to Hartford tomorrow and find a good hairdresser there. I've got to send her away until I need her. Maybe if she had some really good chocolate, she'd give up those dreadful candy bars. This last thought came to him as he dropped a twenty-five-dollar box of Godiva chocolate into the basket. Then he found himself grabbing six bouquets of autumn-colored flowers from the selection along the wall as he wheeled the cart to the checkout stand. Maybe if they went to Hartford, they'd have time to see Mark Twain's house. Darci would probably like that.

"Credit or cash?" the woman at the register asked, and Adam had to bring himself back to reality.

"Is there a liquor store near here?" he asked. "Somewhere I can get a bottle of wine?" He smiled when he was told that a liquor store was two doors down.

When they got back to the guest house, Darci disappeared for a few moments to remove the squashed candy bars from inside her cat suit, and Adam was hoping she'd put on something less revealing. Instead, when she reappeared, she still had on the clinging leotard. Her only concession to modesty was to take a sweatshirt of his out of the closet and pull it on over the suit, but her Lycra-covered legs were still exposed beneath it.

"You couldn't find anything of your own to wear?" he asked, sounding more snappish than he meant to.

"Don't want to wrinkle anything," she said as she picked up the bags of groceries and carried them to the little kitchen.

Adam had planned to make sandwiches with as little fuss as possible, but Darci shooed him away and she took over. She didn't set the food on the little table in the corner of the room, but instead, cleared the coffee table of its fabric flowers in a pot and set out plates, knives and forks, and glasses from the kitchen cabinets. In the kitchen, she began unloading the food from the plastic bags. She rummaged inside the cabinets until she found a vase and he watched in surprise as she took a pair of scissors from a drawer and expertly snipped the stems of the flowers. Within seconds, she had arranged them, making the flowers form a perfect oval above the vase.

"Where'd you learn that?" he asked.

"Putnam Flowers. I worked there for a few months."

"Handy thing to know," he said. "My cousin Sarah would like to be able to do that. She has thousands of flowers in her garden but not a clue as to how to arrange them."

"'Thousands,'" Darci said as she took the flowers into the living room.

"Yeah, well, it's a big house," Adam said, feeling embarrassed. He didn't like to reveal things about himself, and he was grateful when Darci didn't ask him any questions. Instead, he stood back and watched as she pulled long loaves of French bread from the bags, then opened the containers of food and carefully put them into dishes that she carried from the kitchen. For his part, he would have eaten from the cartons but Darci seemed to want to make as elegant a table as possible.

When she was finished, she motioned for him to take his seat on a couch cushion on the opposite side of the coffee table, and immediately, Darci began asking questions about each item he'd bought. When he didn't have a sharp knife to cut open the pomegranate, she jumped up and got him one; then she watched intently as he cut it open and began to extract the seeds. Without hesitation, she dropped a handful of the seeds into her mouth and declared them delicious.

She tasted everything, exclaimed with delight over every item, and Adam found himself talking more and more about the food. She wanted to know where each cheese had been made, how oysters were smoked, and why the water crackers were called that. Adam tried to answer her every question and when he didn't know the answer, he handed her the food container and she read what was printed on it to him. And there was a lot of discussion about vineyards and how wine was made.

In the end, the meal took over two hours, and afterward Adam realized he'd enjoyed himself a great deal. And to his disbelief, the two of them had eaten everything. But still, he found that he somehow had room for the Godiva chocolates, and for a moment, he watched Darci close her eyes and let the rich chocolate melt down her throat.

Adam knew that he'd better say something or he'd find himself reaching for her. "Why don't you get fat?" he asked.

Darci opened her eyes. "No fat cells. I never developed any as a kid, and my metabolism is very fast. My mother says I must get it from my father, because she says that if she eats a piece of lettuce, she gains weight."

"What does your father do for a living?"

Darci looked into the big box of chocolate and made no answer.

"I was just curious," Adam said. "You often mention

your mother but never your father. Does he live in Putnam, too?"

"I don't know," Darci said quietly. "Sometimes you *can* keep secrets in a small town because I don't know who my father is." Her head came up and she smiled at him. "What about yours?"

"My father? Dead. Both my parents are dead. They died when I was three so I never really knew them."

"How did they die?" she asked, but as soon as she asked the question, she saw that closed-down look come over Adam's face. She was already learning that when she got too near a spot that he didn't allow people into, he turned as mute as a rock.

So now, if she didn't want him to get up and leave the room, she knew she'd better change the subject—and find out what she wanted to know in a less direct way.

"Me neither," Darci said. "Know my mother much, that is. She was always at work or . . . well, she was busy."

"So who raised you?"

"Everybody in town, is what Uncle Vern says. They passed me around from one to another. Mostly I heard, 'Could you watch Darci this afternoon and give me a break?'"

She was looking at him as though she expected him to smile at her joke, but Adam didn't see any humor in what she was saying.

"Don't look at me with pity in your eyes," she said, still smiling. "I was a conniving little demon. By the time I reached eight, I knew every secret of every person in town. Whenever I wanted to see a movie, all I had to say was, 'You want me to wait outside while you and Mr. Nearly spend the afternoon . . . talking?' And *bam!* Movie money was shoved into my hand. Or clothes or slices of pie. Whatever I needed was given to me."

Adam didn't smile at this attempt at humor either. She was trying to make light of it, but he saw the loneliness of her childhood. She'd learned to blackmail people into giving her food, clothing, and shelter by the time she was eight years old. But he didn't say anything. As she'd just said, she didn't want to see pity in his eyes.

"So what made you decide to spend your life fighting evil?" she asked.

At that, Adam did smile. "Does Superman have a reason for what he does?" he asked, an eyebrow raised.

"Sure. He wants to run around in leotards and a cape," she said quickly, making Adam laugh.

She was on her third piece of chocolate. "So when are you going to show me the knife?"

"The what?" he asked, stalling for time.

"You know, the knife you stole from behind that iron fence down in the tunnels. The one you used to cut my hair. And by the way, what happened to the big piece of my hair? Those two men said they found strands, not a piece the size you cut off."

"That was clever of them to see that the hair was from a natural blonde, wasn't it?" Adam said quietly. "I was thinking that tomorrow we'd drive into Hartford and get your hair cut properly, something that would cover up the hole at the back. Maybe we should have it dyed too. Maybe you should become a redhead."

Darci didn't so much as smile at him. Instead, she looked into his eyes hard, letting him know that his changing the subject wasn't going to work.

"In my coat pocket," he said with a grimace. Why couldn't she have forgotten about that knife?

Darci was on her feet in seconds and nearly ran to the coat closet. When she returned to the table, she was holding the dagger in her outstretched hands. Adam had to work to keep from grabbing it from her because he was dying to have a good look at it. But his plan had been to look at it alone in his bedroom, after Darci was asleep.

As if she knew what he was thinking, she handed the knife to him, then began to clean up the remains of the meal. She was giving Adam time to examine the dagger by himself. Moving from the floor to the couch, he held the knife under the lamp on the end table. The dagger wasn't very big, only about seven or eight inches, with a steel blade with several pits of rust on it. The handle was gold and black, and as he turned it about in the light, he realized that the raised gold part was writing. The writing had been cleverly twisted around the handle so that it looked more like a design than writing, but Adam felt sure that it was a language of some sort.

Too quickly, Darci was sitting beside him. Actually, she was sitting so close to him that she might as well have been sitting on his lap, and the sweatshirt she'd purloined exposed much too much of her.

"Don't you ever wear any of your own clothes?" he snapped. "You couldn't have cleaned up that fast, and why don't you sit on that side of the couch?"

"I told you that I don't want to mess up my new clothes. Dishwasher. The light's better on this side," she said, smiling at him; then, after a moment, she held out her hand, palm up.

With a sigh, Adam gave her the dagger. He would have moved away from her, but his right side was squashed against the arm of the couch and there was no room to move. You're acting like a high school boy, Montgomery! he scolded himself, then forced himself to relax.

"You studied witchcraft. Do you recognize any of the symbols from your studies?" he asked.

For a moment Darci held the dagger up to the light, turning it around in her hands. "Evil. Great evil."

"I hope you didn't pay too much for that education of yours," Adam said.

"Not a penny."

"You went on a scholarship?"

"No. Actually, Putnam paid for my education," Darci answered, smiling, then she yawned. "You know, as fascinating as this thing is, I think I'm going to have to go to bed."

For a moment Adam was annoyed. Part of him wanted to discuss this knife with her. Tonight when they'd talked about food and wine, he'd found that he enjoyed talking to her. She always had a quick answer for every question.

"So where do you want me to sleep tonight?" Darci asked, then yawned so wide that he heard her jaw pop.

"'Where?'" Adam said. But then he laughed, all his bad humor gone. "In your own bed. Go on, get out of here. I'll see you in the morning."

Darci paused at the doorway to her bedroom. "Mr. Montgomery, I had a good time today," she said softly.

He started to say that he would have had a better time if she'd stayed behind and not talked all the way down the tunnel, then faked a faint, then nearly got her arm broken trying to pull candy bars out of a machine, then disobeyed him again and set off an alarm. But he couldn't say that because it wasn't true. Instead, he smiled and said, "It's Adam. Good night, Miss Mansfield."

Darci hiked up the sweatshirt to her waist and stuck out her hip in the pose of a 1950s bombshell. "Good night, Adam," she said in a breathless way that was an astonishingly good imitation of Marilyn Monroe.

Again, Adam laughed, then he waved his hand in dismissal, and she went into her bedroom and closed the door.

When he was alone in the living room, he saw that she had set out a little tray of cheese and crackers for him, with a full glass of red wine. Smiling, he took the wine and sipped it as he pulled paper and pencil out of his briefcase and began to make a rubbing of the raised characters on the knife blade. When he'd finished, he went to his bedroom and faxed the paper to a friend of his in Washington, D.C., with a cover sheet that said, "See what you can find out about this, will you? If it's writing, what kind and what does it say?" and was signed, "A. Montgomery."

After he'd showered and put on a pair of pajamas, he was tempted to open Darci's door to check and see if she was all right. But he thought he'd better not do that. Instead, he went to bed, and, like the night before, he was asleep instantly.

7

"WELL, WHAT DO YOU THINK?" Darci asked as she looked up at Adam, her hand on her newly cut and colored hair. "Like it?"

But Adam's astonished look said it all. She was wearing some of her new clothes for the first time: a dark green wool skirt, a burgundy cashmere sweater, and a jacket in a plaid of the two colors. The dark brown boots she had on were lined with sheepskin and were wonderfully warm and comfortable.

When Adam got up this morning, Darci had already been dressed and waiting for him, eager to drive to Hartford and visit a hairdresser. While he dressed, she ran to the main house and returned with croissants, coffee, and fruit, which she fed him in the car on the way. "You're going to make me fat," he said, with his mouth full.

"To whom did you send the fax last night?" she asked as he held the coffee cup to his lips.

At that, Adam spilled coffee down the front of his sweater, and while he was mopping it up with the napkins that Darci handed him, she took the steering wheel of the rental car.

"Do you snoop into everything?" he asked.

"I have very good hearing," she answered. "So whom did you send a fax to?"

"My girlfriend," he said, still brushing at droplets as he took the steering wheel back from her.

That statement silenced Darci so effectively that he almost regretted it. "All right," he said after several minutes of silence. "I made a rubbing of the markings on the dagger and I faxed them to a friend of mine in D.C. She knows a lot about languages so maybe she'll know, or can find out, what's written on that knife. If it is writing, that is. I'm not even sure that it is."

"Maybe it's a magic knife and it'll give the holder three wishes." Darci said that nonsensical sentence to cover the annoyance she'd felt when he'd said "she." But Adam's silence made her look at him closely. "Hmmm," she said.

"What does that mean?" he snapped.

"I see that Mr. Bad Mood is back."

Adam sighed. "All right, out with it. What's in that little Kentucky mind of yours?"

"Nothing really," she said slowly. "But every time I mention certain words, you go bananas."

"I do not go 'bananas,' as you so inelegantly put it. In fact, I can assure you that I have never in my life gone 'bananas.'"

"Of course not. But you do react rather, well . . . strongly when I say words like *sacrifice* and *magic*."

"Of course I do. Yesterday we went inside the underground tunnels of a witches' coven. Did you forget that? There are certain words associated with witches, and it's to be expected that—"

"Broomstick!" Darci said loudly. "Cauldron! Black cat! No, no, I can see that those words have no effect on you. But the idea of a *magic* knife and a sacrifice, specifically a sacrifice of *me,* nearly sends you over the edge." She was looking at him intently, obviously waiting for his answer.

"I've been meaning to ask you why you have very little southern accent. In fact, you almost sound as though you came from this part of the U.S."

Taking her eyes off him, Darci turned around in her seat and looked out the window. "Okay, so you don't want to tell me. Yet. You don't want to tell me *yet.* I can wait." She took a deep breath. "Elocution lessons. Mann's Developmental College for Young Ladies had elocution lessons. I listened to tapes and imitated them."

"How interesting," Adam said. "Why don't you tell me all about your school?"

She narrowed her eyes at him. "I'd rather hear all about what you're after and why you hired *me* over all those other young women."

Adam let out his breath in a long sigh. "Aren't the trees beautiful at this time of year?"

After that there had been no more talk of any importance between them, and when they got to Hartford, Adam had gone into a hairdressing salon and ten minutes later came out and told Darci that they were ready for her. She didn't ask how he got her into such an exclusive-looking salon without an appointment, but she'd already seen in Camwell that he was able to make people do things.

So now, hours later, her hair was finished, and she thought it looked good. In fact, one of the other hairdressers had said to the woman who did Darci's hair, "I think that's the best cut you've ever given." "Me too," the hairdresser had said in wonder as she looked at Darci in the mirror.

"Do you like it or not?" Darci asked Adam.

Adam was looking at her as if he'd never seen her before. Her lank, shoulder-length blonde hair had been cut short and layered in such a way that it hugged her face. And it had been dyed a strawberry blonde that perfectly complemented her pale skin. And her eyes were different, too. He couldn't see any makeup on her face, but her eyes were definitely different.

"It's called a pyxie cut, with a *y* instead of an *i;* that's how they spelled it. And my hair's been downlighted. That means that they darkened parts of it instead of lightening it, which is what they usually do to women's hair. Are you listening to me?"

"Every word," he said, still staring at her.

"As soon as I got into the chair, I applied my True Persuasion to the beautician—I mean, the hairdresser—and I told her to give me the best cut she had ever given anyone in her whole life." Darci ran her hand through her hair, and it sprang back into place perfectly. "I think maybe she did. She said that the long part of my hair, the part she cut off, was in poor condition, but that the new growth was thick and healthy. Feel."

"No."

Darci gave Adam a little smile. "Are you afraid that touching my hair will drive you mad with passion?"

"Give me a break, will you?" Adam said, frowning; then as she continued to look up at him, he sighed in capitulation. Darci bent forward as Adam put his hand on her head.

"Nice."

"You mean that?"

Adam smiled. "Yeah, I mean that," he said as he turned and started walking toward where the car was parked.

But when he realized that Darci was no longer beside him, he halted and looked back. She was reading a menu posted outside an Italian restaurant.

Adam didn't bother pointing out that they could drive back to Camwell and eat there. Nor did he mention that it had been only three hours since they'd eaten breakfast. Besides, the truth was, he was feeling a bit hungry himself.

Walking back to her, he opened the door to the restaurant and followed her inside. After they'd placed their orders (Darci ordering eggplant Parmigiana, saying that she'd never eaten eggplant before), she told him that she'd been told all the gossip at the hairdresser's.

"Everyone in this town and maybe everybody in the state, considers Camwell a scary place. And the Grove is haunted. No one who lives within a hundred miles of that town would stay there overnight. And the waitress in Camwell was telling the truth: Every year for four years now someone has disappeared."

Darci was keeping her voice so low that he could hardly hear her. When he asked her why she was speaking so softly, he was told that "big city" people couldn't be trusted. It took him a moment to digest this statement. In tiny Camwell, a place that people called "evil," Darci blabbed to everyone about everything. But here in "big city" Hartford, Connecticut, she acted as though everyone in the restaurant were a spy.

Adam wasn't going to try to understand her "logic." Instead, he reached into the inside pocket of his jacket and pulled out a sheaf of papers. "While you were hexing the hairdresser, I went to the library and made some photocopies of articles about the four women who disappeared."

Darci smiled warmly at him. She liked that he said "photocopy" and not "Xerox." She reached out to take the papers, but Adam drew back. "No, not now," he whispered. "Our table may be bugged. You never know what these Hartfordites can get up to."

"Very funny," she said, but her eyes glanced sideways for a moment. When she didn't ask him for any more information about the papers, he put them away.

Because of Darci's belief that they shouldn't discuss anything important in the "big city," they confined their lunch talk to one of Darci's favorite topics: food.

"You've been to Italy?" she asked, and when he nodded, she fired off questions at him. How did the food in Italy compare to Italian food in the U.S.? Did he get to know any Italians? How did they differ from Americans? Her questions and his answers kept them busy throughout lunch.

The only time there was a silence between them was when she asked him *why* he'd traveled so much in his life. "Didn't you want to have a home? Kids?" she asked. But as so often happened, Adam stopped talking and looked down at his food in silence.

She waited, hoping he'd explain something about himself, and twice he did look as though he were about to speak, but then he looked down again and said nothing.

After several awkward moments, she asked him if he'd ever been to Greece.

As for Adam, he was coming to the point where he wanted to tell her something about himself, but he couldn't bring himself to do it. He liked the laughter they often exchanged, and he didn't want to risk changing that.

When she stopped staring at him and asked about another country, he smiled in relief, then lifted his head and looked at her.

The clothes, the hair, and whatever she'd done to her eyes had changed her. He couldn't believe that this pretty young woman was the same person who'd sat on the edge of her chair and swung her legs at their first meeting.

Later, in the car on the way back to Camwell, Adam couldn't keep himself from asking, "What did you do to your eyes?"

"They dyed my eyelashes so they're sooty black," she said as she turned and fluttered her lashes at him. "Like them?"

"They're artificial looking," Adam said stiffly. Her manner was playful, but at the same time it was seductive.

His coolness hurt Darci's feelings. "Oh?" she said, her lips tight. "And I guess you like natural women: the outdoors type with scrubbed skin, a fishing pole over one shoulder and a shotgun over the other."

Adam smiled at the image she conjured. He couldn't

imagine a type of woman he liked less. "That's exactly my type. How did you guess?"

"Is that what *Renee* is like?" Darci shot back.

At that Adam nearly swerved off the road. "Where the hell did you hear her name?" he said when he got the car under control.

"Don't curse. It's not nice."

Adam glanced at her, then back at the road. "Where did you snoop out her name?"

"You talk in your sleep."

"And how would you know that?"

"You talk in your sleep very *loud.*"

For a moment Adam was silent. "What else did I talk about?" he asked softly.

"Not much," she said, smiling, obviously enjoying his discomfort. "Just Renee."

He glanced at her, trying to ascertain if she was telling the whole truth or just part of it. "What did I say?" he asked, very serious.

"Well. . . . Let's see. . . . If I remember correctly . . . you said, 'Oh, Renee, my darling, I love you with all my heart, and I miss you *sooooooo* much.'"

Adam's lips twitched in suppressed laughter. "I'm sure you heard me correctly because that's just the way I feel about her."

Darci's enjoyment faded. "So what's she look like?" Her arms were folded tightly across her chest and her lips were in a rigid line.

"Long silky hair, huge brown eyes, cute little nose," he said happily.

"Educated?"

"Better yet, she's obedient."

"She's what?!" Darci exploded; then, as she watched him, she smiled. "I see. So how long are her ears?"

"At least half a foot," Adam said, and they laughed together.

"Your dog?"

"Irish setter. And I do miss her very much."

"If you want someone else—besides your dog, that is—to keep you company at night. . . ." Darci said softly.

Adam didn't dare look at her. The colorless little girl who'd sat before him in a New York warehouse held no interest for him. But between his memory of the sight of Darci in a cat suit and now her pyxie haircut, she was beginning to make him, well . . . nervous. He'd better get this back on the right track. "I have a little black book," he said, "and *you* are supposed to remain faithful to the man you love with all your heart. Remember? I bet Putnam's being faithful to *you.*"

That statement made Darci laugh so hard that he thought she was going to choke. But, try as he might, he couldn't get her to tell him what was so extraordinarily funny about what he'd said. His repeatedly asking, "Putnam *isn't* faithful to you?" gained him as many answers as her earlier questions had elicited from him. It was annoying to think that she might have as many secrets as he did.

A few minutes later, Adam turned off the highway onto a small country road. "I hope you don't mind if we return to Camwell by the back way, do you?" he said in what he hoped was a normal voice. "These trees are just so beautiful that I want to see more of them."

But Darci wasn't fooled. She looked at him in speculation. If she'd learned nothing else about Adam Montgomery, she knew that scenery did not interest him. "Did any of the women who disappeared do so around here?"

At that Adam shook his head in disbelief at the accuracy of her guess. "If I ever want to get information out of anyone, I'm going to send you to do the interrogation. Yes," he said with a sigh. "Two of the women disappeared along this road."

"Did you find this out before you went to the library today or after?"

"Today. I haven't known about the town of Camwell for very long or about what happened here. I—" He broke off because he didn't want to tell her anything more than he had to. The less she knew, the safer she would be, he thought. "Look!" he said as though he were seeing an unrecognized wonder of the world. "There's a store and I need . . . uh, toothpaste."

"You have a full tube," Darci said before she could stop herself.

As Adam turned off the engine, he looked at her. "And how do you know that?" He put up his hand when she started to speak. "No, don't tell me. You can hear toothpaste talking in its sleep."

Darci smiled as Adam got out of the car; then he turned back and looked inside just as she was getting out. "Maybe we should get *you* the toothpaste. Unless you *like* using baking soda."

Feeling that he'd just won a game of one-upmanship, Adam shut the door and stepped onto the wooden porch of the tiny country store. There were a couple of weathered rocking chairs on the porch, plus some packing crates that looked as though they'd been there for a while. The back wall was draped with perfectly aged leather straps that looked as though they'd been hanging there since McKinley was president. But Adam could see that everything was actually new. In fact, when he looked harder at the quaint items on the porch, he could see that they were all reproductions, and it made him wonder if the store owner had hired some New York designer to create an "authentic" country store that would attract tourists.

When Darci stepped up behind him, he said, "This look like a Kentucky store?"

"Heavens, no!" she said. "If a store has a porch, the owner covers it with video game machines. And, in Kentucky, when the leather rots on a horse harness, we throw it away."

Chuckling, Adam opened the screen door and went inside, Darci close on his heels.

"Good afternoon," called a gray-haired man from behind a tall wooden counter. In front of the counter were open bins full of hard candies and dried fruit. To the right were barrels filled with apples and oranges. All the shelves in the store were rough-sawn pine, and modern items were interspersed with old-fashioned boxes of things like Mother Jasper's Revitalizing Elixir.

"Can I help you with anything?" the man asked as he walked from behind the counter. He was wearing a denim apron and had on heavy black boots, as though, at any minute, he planned to go back to plowing.

"He probably ordered all this junk off the Internet,"

Darci mumbled when Adam bent down to look at a box on the shelves.

Smiling, Adam looked back at the store clerk. "Toothpaste," he said.

"And deodorant and whatever else you have," Darci said quickly, then looked at Adam in question.

He knew that she was silently asking him if he would pay for all of it. He gave a nod but reminded himself that he was going to have to ask her what her problem with money was. Was she just a tightwad, or did she have a reason for never spending a penny of her own money?

"Right over there," the man said, then handed Darci a basket that Adam was sure had been handmade in Appalachia and cost a fortune.

While Adam waited, he wandered about the store, looking in bins and inside cabinets. When he opened a pine door, he was momentarily startled to find a modern refrigerator unit hidden behind it. He took out a couple of Snapple lemonades, then saw Darci standing at the counter, finally ready to check out. When he got to the register, he saw that she had purchased $58.68 worth of toiletries! They were mostly hair products, including a conditioner that cost eighteen dollars a bottle.

"The hairdresser recommended all of these things to keep my hair in good condition," Darci explained as she looked up at Adam, again silently asking him if he was going to pay for such expensive items.

With a shrug, Adam handed the clerk a fifty and a ten; then he took the two big bags full of goods and held out his hand for the change.

"Keeping the ladies beautiful costs a lot," the clerk said,

chuckling as he looked at Adam's expression of resignation.

But when the clerk had the change, Darci put her hand out too. At that, the store clerk laughed out loud. "She's prettier than you are," he said to Adam as he turned to give Darci the change.

But when the man saw Darci's left hand, all color left his face. His eyes widened and his hand holding the change began to shake. He seemed to want to say something, and even though he opened his mouth several times, no words came out. Instead, the shaking increased until the money he held fell to the floor, and when it dropped, the man turned and ran through a curtained doorway.

It took Adam a moment to recover from his shock. He'd been watching the man's reactions in astonishment, and when the man took off running, Adam dropped the bags and ran after him. But since he had to leap over two barrels and a stack of artificially aged orange crates, by the time Adam went through the doorway into the back storage room, the man was nowhere to be seen. There was a back door, but when Adam opened it, there was nothing outside but an empty gravel parking area, with acres of Connecticut woodland behind it. There was no sign of the clerk.

Annoyed, Adam went back into the store; then he experienced a moment's panic when he didn't see Darci. Had she been kidnaped? was his first, wild, heart-pounding thought. But his heart slowed its pace when he saw her on her hands and knees behind the counter.

When she looked up to see Adam, she held out her hand, which had a quarter and two pennies in it. "You were

certainly right to run after him," she said angrily. "I think
he shortchanged us a nickel. Or else it's somewhere on the
floor."

Bending, Adam picked up her left hand and turned it
palm upward. As far as he could see, there was nothing
unusual about her hand. It was as small as a child's, and
her palm was pink from having been pressed against the
floor. The only thing distinctive that he could see was that
there were several moles on her palm. "What are these?" he
asked.

"I think I see it," she said as she pulled her hand from
his and began crawling toward the far end of the counter.

"Did you hear me?" he snapped. "What are those marks
on your hand?"

Darci stopped crawling, sat back on the floor, held up
her left hand and looked at her palm. "Moles. Everyone has
them. So do you. You have three little ones by your right
ear and you have another one by your—"

"That man looked at your hand, his face turned white,
then he ran out of here. I tried to catch him, but—"

"Could you lift your foot?"

"*What* are you doing down there?"

"I'm looking for the nickel," Darci said. "Either he
shortchanged us, or it rolled under something and—"

Impatiently, Adam took out his wallet, removed a
twenty, and handed it to her. "*Now* will you get up? And
don't you dare ask me if you can keep the change."

Tightly holding the twenty and the change she'd found,
Darci got off the floor, but her eyes kept moving down-
ward as she continued to look for the nickel.

But Adam didn't give her more time to search.

Grabbing her upper arm, he practically pulled her out of the store, Darci clutching the bags containing his purchases and hers. On the drive back to Camwell, he didn't say a word.

Only when they were back at the Grove and inside their guest house did Adam turn to her. "I knew there was something that kept ringing inside my head, but I couldn't remember what it was." He took the bundle of photocopied newspaper articles he'd shown her at lunch from inside his jacket, then removed the garment and tossed it onto the back of a chair. Seconds later, he'd spread the articles on the coffee table, sat down on the couch, and had started rereading them.

Slowly, without asking why he was so agitated, Darci hung up her jacket and his, made a trip to the bathroom, then returned to sit beside him on the couch and wait. Maybe if she was quiet and just waited, he'd tell her what had so upset him.

"Read these," he said, handing the pages to her.

It took Darci several minutes to read the articles carefully and slowly. But when she'd finished reading everything he'd given her, she didn't know what she was supposed to see. They were all sad articles about young women who had been in the Camwell area for one reason or another, then disappeared. One woman had been a photographer, taking photos of the old churches in the New England area; two others had been on vacation. One young woman had been staying at the Grove on her honeymoon.

Although the stories were horrible in themselves, Darci failed to see what it was, specifically, that was so upsetting Adam. She looked at him in silent question.

"Look at where the girls are from," he said.

She went over each article. "Virginia, Tennessee, South Carolina, and . . . this one is from Texas." She still didn't understand.

"Now look at the photos."

They were all pretty girls, the youngest twenty-two and the oldest twenty-eight. But then didn't all the photos of victims of serial killers and rapists and other sociopaths show pretty young women? she thought.

"Each woman is blonde, small, and southern," Adam said softly.

Darci blinked at him, understanding at last. "Like me? Is that what you're saying? Are you thinking that *I* am going to disappear next? Why would you think *that?* Is *this* why you hired me? To use me as *bait?*"

"Don't be absurd!" Adam said quickly, dismissing her exclamations as too ridiculous to consider. "Do you think I'd have brought you here if that were a possibility?" He took her left hand in his and looked at it under the light. "I'd like to know why that man nearly had a stroke when he saw your hand."

"Maybe his former girlfriend had moles on her palm, too," Darci said as she pulled away from him, then got up and went into the kitchen. She wanted a moment alone to think. She was trying her best to remain calm through all that she was seeing and finding out, but it wasn't easy. Small, blonde, southern women who'd disappeared in this area could be a coincidence, but it could also mean that, as Adam seemed to fear, *she* was a target.

Or *the* target, she thought with a shiver of fear.

Why, oh, why had Adam chosen *her?* Out of all those

talented, educated women who'd applied for the job, why *her?*

After she got herself under control, she filled two glasses with ice and Snapple lemonade and took them to the living room.

Adam was sitting on the couch, staring at the articles in front of him with that same dark, brooding look that he'd been wearing when she first met him. She wished she could think of something to say to make him laugh, but at the moment, she could think of nothing at all funny. The faces of the missing young women seemed to fill her mind. "The way the man reacted to seeing my hand could have meant nothing," Darci said quietly. "It could have been a coincidence or something unrelated to the witches. In fact, I don't see how you can jump from some man in a phony-looking little store to women who have disappeared to—"

She broke off when Adam got up, went to his bedroom, and returned with an address book. It was a little leather-bound volume that looked as though it had been around the world and back. When he opened it, she saw that the pages were worn and the addresses and phone numbers had been marked out and changed repeatedly.

Adam flipped through it to the *P*s, then picked up the phone and called someone. "Jack," he said a moment later, "this is Adam Montgomery. I need a favor. Can you find out about the disappearances of four young women over the last four years in Camwell, Connecticut?" He paused and listened. "Yes, I know that the police believe that their disappearance had something to do with the reported practice of witchcraft in this area. And, yes, I've read every-thing that was published in the papers, but I also know what kind of investigations you guys do, and you always know more about a case than you tell anyone. What I want to know is, was there anything significant about the missing women's hands? Specifically their left hands?" Again he waited and listened. "Okay, sure. Call me back on my cell phone," Adam said, then hung up and looked at Darci. "He's going to call me back as soon as he finds out anything."

"Is he a policeman?" Darci asked.

"FBI."

"Oh," she said, then paused. For the life of her, Darci couldn't seem to think of any questions to ask him. FBI? The FBI was not something she'd encountered in real life. After a moment of silence, she put on her happiest face. "So what shall we do while we wait? We need something to calm your nerves. Maybe we should go to bed together and make mad love all afternoon. We could—" But the look Adam gave her made her stop talking. Obviously, he wasn't in the mood to laugh right now. And the truth was that she was feeling a bit too nervous to talk.

She soon saw that when Adam worried, he turned into a silent man who just wanted to be left alone. Again picking up the photocopied newspaper articles, he began to reread each one carefully. Moving to the chair beside the couch, Darci picked up the three magazines that were on the shelf under the coffee table and began to look through them, just waiting for the phone to ring.

She thought that she'd been able to calm herself, but when the phone rang, she jumped so high that the magazines slid off her lap and hit the carpeted floor. Before the first ring stopped, Adam grabbed the little black phone off the coffee table, pressed the button, said, "Yes?" then listened.

While Darci watched him, his face turned pale, and she wasn't sure, but she thought that maybe there was a bit of a tremor in one of his hands. He said almost nothing, just listened and said, "Yes," a few times. To Darci, it seemed like hours before he put the phone down. But even after he did, he still didn't speak. Instead, he just sat there and looked at her.

And Darci waited for him to speak. She desperately wanted him to tell her what the FBI agent named Jack had said, but she feared that if she asked, Adam might clam up and refuse to tell her. No, it was better to wait and let him volunteer information.

But Adam didn't speak. Instead, after several long, silent moments, he got up and went into her bedroom. Darci ran after him, and, standing in the doorway, she saw him open her closet door and pull out her ratty old suitcase. But after he looked at it, he went past Darci and across the hall to his bedroom, removed his two suitcases from the closet, then carried them back to her bedroom. Through all of this Darci watched him.

It was when Adam had set his suitcases on her bed, opened them, and started putting her new clothes into them, that Darci placed herself between Adam and the open cases. "I want to know what's going on!" she said, her voice full of all the exasperation and frustration she felt at being told so very little about what was going on.

"No, you don't," he answered as he removed her navy blazer from a hanger and put the garment into the suitcase.

"I do!" she said. "I *do* want to know!" To her horror, she realized that she was about to start crying. He was sending her away, but she didn't want to return to New York, to her aunt and uncle. No, truthfully, she didn't want to leave *him*. She didn't want to be anywhere but here with Adam Montgomery. "Why are you firing me?" she asked, her voice full of the tears she was trying to hold back.

"I'm not firing you," he said calmly as he dropped two skirts into the case. "I'm protecting you."

"Protecting me? *Why* do you need to protect me?" When he didn't answer, she said, "If you're sending me away because of some moles on my hand, we could go to a doctor and have them removed. There are *lots* of alternatives to my leaving. We could stay somewhere else and just visit Camwell when we have to. We could—" When she saw that her words weren't making him stop packing, she said, "Please don't send me away." Her voice was pleading, almost desperate. "I need the money. I need. . . ." She took a breath. "You don't understand what this job means to me. I need—"

"You won't need anything if you're dead," Adam said flatly.

"Please," she said as she went to him and put her hands on his arm and looked up at him with big eyes that sparkled with unshed tears. "Tell me what the man on the phone said. At least let me know what's going on and *why* I'm being sent away. You owe me that, don't you?"

Looking down at her, Adam had to resist the urge to draw her into his arms. Maybe he could use his own body to protect her. He took a deep breath, then sat down on the bed. "All right," he said softly, not looking at her. He didn't *want* to tell her anything so the words came out with difficulty. "I'm sure you know that in most cases the police keep something back, something that they don't tell the public. That's to protect them against—"

"The Looney Tunes who admit to murders they didn't commit," Darci said as she sat down beside him on the bed.

"Yes, exactly." He gave her a weak smile. She was so very small, he thought as he looked at her; she'd be easy to subdue. "My friend in the FBI made a few calls, and he found out that in this case there's been a major cover-up. Cover-up to the public, that is. The mayor of Camwell said that there'd been enough bad publicity about his lovely town, and he didn't want any more. He didn't want his town blamed for four murders and mutilations that no one could prove had happened in *his* town."

"Murder?" Darci asked, eyes wide. "Mutilations?" Involuntarily, her hand went to her throat.

"Yes." Again Adam had to fight an urge to put his arm around her protectively. But he didn't want to soften what he was saying. She needed to feel the full impact so she'd understand the seriousness of the situation. "The girls disappeared in this area, but each young woman was eventually found. Dead." He gave her a moment to let this sink in. "Their bodies were found, one by one, over a hundred miles from here, each one in a different direction away from Camwell."

"But what about. . . ." Darci began, her right hand rubbing her left.

Picking up her left hand, Adam held it in his for a moment, then slowly turned it over and looked at the palm. "The disappearances of the women made headline news because they happened near Camwell, but their deaths got only back-page coverage because—"

"Because other places aren't tainted by an association with witchcraft so wherever the women were found wasn't as exciting as Camwell," Darci said, watching him as he held her hand in his. She wanted to put her head down on his shoulder and let him hold her. The images inside her head were frightening her.

"Yes, exactly." His voice was very soft, and his thumb was caressing her palm. "It wasn't in the papers, but all four of the young women whose bodies were found had had their left hands amputated."

At that Darci nearly pulled away from him, but he held her fast. She *must* hear everything! "Their left hands were missing," Adam continued. "*Are* missing. The hands have never been found."

Darci pulled her hand from his grasp and held it protectively in her right. "You think they were looking for something special?" she managed to say after a moment.

"I think they were looking for *you.*"

At this statement, Darci's first instinct was to leap up and run from the room and get on the first plane out of Connecticut. But, instead, she closed her eyes for a moment and used her True Persuasion as best she could on herself. She needed to stay calm right now. She needed— She *needed* to know *what* was going on!

Slowly, Darci stood up, put her hands on her hips and glared at him. "All right, Adam Montgomery, this has gone on long enough. I want to know why you chose *me*. And for *what* did you choose me? Out with it. Now!"

Adam seemed to wrestle with himself before he spoke.

"I guess I owe you that much," he said at last. "In fact, maybe if you know more, you'll be willing to leave peacefully." He said the last word as though if he told her, peaceful or not, she *was* going to leave.

"Do you remember the woman in the warehouse with me the day you interviewed for the job?"

"The woman with the big eyes?" Darci said as she sat back down on the bed beside him.

"Yes. Her name is Helen Gabriel, and she's a psychic. She told me that she could find the correct woman to help me fight these witches, and when she said you were the one, I hired you."

Darci waited for several moments, but that seemed to be all the explanation he was going to give her. That's *all?* she wanted to yell at him. That's *all* you're going to tell me? But she didn't say that because she was sure that those words would make Adam refuse to say more. Instead, she decided to use one of the words that pushed his buttons. "I see," she said as she stood up. "Then you *were* planning to sacrifice me."

"I was planning no such thing!" Adam snapped. "What an appalling idea. Do I seem like the type of man who—?"

"Then you probably just meant to let them have me, so you could plan to rescue me at the last minute. Is that it?" She looked him hard in the eyes. "Are you undercover FBI? Is that how you can get secret information?"

"If I were, I wouldn't need to go to a library to get newspaper clippings about the missing women now would I?"

"But you already knew about them, didn't you? On that first night the waitress told us about the missing people— that's what she said: people. But *you* knew they were female."

"What a memory you have!" he said, carefully not giving her any more information.

"So if you don't want me to be your bait, what do you want me for?" she asked, again glaring at him.

After taking several moments to try to formulate an answer, Adam threw up his hands in defeat. "Okay, I didn't want to tell you this yet. In fact—" He had to take a deep breath before he could continue. "The power of this coven of witches is based on . . . well, there's an object, and as long as they have this thing, they'll be powerful. My goal is to take this object away from them and thereby render them powerless." After this, Adam gave a little smile, as if to say, *There. Now you know everything.*

But Darci didn't know even one percent of what she wanted to know. "So where do I come into this?" she asked. "What do *I* have to do with this 'object'?"

"Only certain people can open it," Adam said brightly. "I can't. This psychic, Helen, told me that if I put an ad in the paper, the correct woman would answer the ad and that she, Helen, would tell me which woman to hire." Adam gave Darci another little smile. "My naive idea was that you would stay here in the guest house and wait until I found the object, then I'd bring it to you and you'd 'open it,' so to speak."

Clasping her hands behind her back, Darci began to pace back and forth across the room. She felt that Adam was telling the truth, but she also knew he was holding back a lot. She wanted to know what the object was, but she needed other information first.

"Obviously, they know that someone is going to try to take this object from them," she said. "And it seems that they know, basically, what I look like. If they know that, then there must be some prophecy or a prediction that says that a short, skinny blonde from the South with a moley left hand is going to take this object of power. I guess they're taking no chances, so that's why every short, skinny blonde from the South who gets near Camwell disappears."

Darci was quite pleased with herself for coming up with this deduction, but when she turned to Adam, he looked a bit sick. Without a word, he got up and went back to putting her clothes in his suitcase. "You're getting out of here. You're going home *now.*"

"And I guess that that man in the store hasn't already told the entire coven what he saw. *Who* he saw. So, yes, I'd better go away because I'm *sure* that whomever he told can't talk to anyone in this town and find out that I'm from Putnam, Kentucky. And they couldn't possibly find Uncle Vern's apartment in New York. And, above all else, I'm *very* sure they won't be able to find a rich guy like you and use some witchcraft spell to make you tell them where I am."

"Don't try to con me. You're getting out of here and *now!*"

"Then what?" Darci asked softly. "Some other short skinny blonde from the South disappears?" She took a deep breath. "Look, we can stop this thing. You and I together can *do* something about this. Wasn't that your plan? Isn't that why you hired me? We can—"

"No!" Adam said. "*We* can't do anything. *You* are going somewhere where you're safe."

She blinked at him for a moment. "Does this mean that you plan to stay here?"

Adam grabbed her new shoes off the closet floor and dropped them into the suitcase. "Let's just say that I have a personal interest in solving this."

Suddenly, she'd had all she could take of his secrecy. "And what is *that?!*" she half shouted. "Why are you doing this? What is your big secret? Why can't you tell me how your parents died? What demons in your mind, in your life, have driven you to go after these witches? What business is it of yours? Why is this so important that you hired a psychic to help you? And why *me?!* What did that woman see in me that says *I* am the one who can open this . . . this object?"

She waited for his answers, and he seemed to start to say something, but then he walked over to the chest of drawers, pulled open a drawer, and removed her nightgown. She could see that he wasn't going to answer her questions, and she wanted to scream in frustration. As always, he was going to tell her only as little as he could and only when he *had* to.

"I have . . . personal . . . interest," he said at last. He seemed to be calm, but she could see the vein throbbing in his temple; even this tiny admission was difficult for him.

"Well, so do I!" she shouted.

He turned to her, genuine surprise on his face. "What personal interest do *you* have?"

Suddenly, her eyes were on fire. This wasn't the joking, laughing, devil-may-care Darci he'd seen up until now. "This is my one chance to do something with my life, that's what. What's out there for me with a degree from a school that most people don't even recognize as a school? What chance do I have to compete against women like the ones I saw in New York? They have education and experience. They have skills that are valuable in the workplace. But what can *I* do? True Persuade someone into . . . into. . . ." Abruptly, she turned away, not able to say any more. If she did, she was going to start crying.

When she turned back to him, she was calmer. "Let's put it this way," she said quietly. "If you send me away, I'll return here to Camwell, and I'll spread it around town that I want to join this coven, and—"

"Are you blackmailing me?"

"Yes," she said simply.

Adam looked at her with pleading eyes. "I have relatives who could hide you," he said softly. "I could call them and they could come and get you. They'd keep you safe until this is over."

"But without me, it won't *be* over, will it?" she said. "If I am the one they want, then this thing can't be solved without me, can it?" She took a deep breath to calm herself. "Why won't you tell me all that I need to know? I haven't known you very long, but I'm sure that you're the kind of man who would only use a psychic as a last resort. I can't imagine your being involved in spells and curses. How long did you work on this . . . whatever it is, before you got so desperate that you went to a psychic and did what *she* told you to do?"

"Three years," he said softly.

Darci blinked at him. "You worked on this for three *years* before you found me?" She wanted to get him to tell her what had driven him to work on this for all those years. But she didn't want to see that closed look on his face, didn't want to risk his shutting down again. "But now you're going to throw all those years away in an instant?" she asked quietly.

"I can't put another human being in danger. These people have done. . . ."

"Something personal to you," she said flatly, and with resentment in her voice at his not trusting her enough to explain.

"Oh, yes," he said quietly. "Very, *very* personal."

"Then I must stay and help you," she said, her hands turned palms upward in a gesture of begging. "Please let me stay. You need me. You can't do this without me. Please."

Adam had to turn away from the look in her eyes. He knew that every word she'd said was right. He *did* need her. He knew that he wouldn't be able to accomplish anything without her.

But he also instinctively knew that before this year was over, another, as she described them, "short, skinny blonde from the South" would disappear. And later her body would be found far away from Camwell. And her left hand—

As Darci said, he wanted to stop this. With every breath he had, he wanted to stop this. Turning, he looked at her. "You'll have to obey me," he said at last. "And you'll have to stay near me at all times. You can't put on your cat suit and run off by yourself."

"Did I mention that I'm a coward to the very marrow of my bones?" she said softly, her eyes alight.

Adam shook his head. "There is nothing cowardly about you, Darci T. Monroe. Nothing even remotely resembling cowardice."

For a moment she stood there looking at him. "Isn't this where the hero and heroine fall on each other and make mad, passionate love?"

Adam laughed, and when he did, she knew that she'd won, really and truly won. He would let her stay. He wasn't going to send her back with her tail between her legs to have to listen to Uncle Vern say, "I knew she couldn't hold a job like that one." She wasn't going to have to hear Aunt Thelma say, "I would have been proud of you, but it looks like you're gonna be your mother all over again after all." And she wasn't going to have to face her mother looking her up and down, blowing cigarette smoke in her face, then smiling in that way that made Darci feel that no matter how many college courses she took or how well-spoken she was, she was never going to rise above where her birth had placed her.

"You know what?" Darci said at last. "I want to take a shower. Would you mind . . . ?" Pointedly, she nodded toward the doorway.

"Sure," Adam said, seeming to be glad the great emotion of the last minutes was over. "Take some time to think this over," he said. "And I will, too. Maybe we'll both decide that this isn't worth the risk. Maybe we'll decide that—"

She closed the bedroom door on him because she didn't want to hear his negativity. And the truth was that she wanted to get into the shower and cry. She wanted to cry because she was scared. Really and truly afraid.

8

AFTER DARCI SHOWERED, she dried off, put on her night-gown, slipped her arms into the thick terry-cloth bathrobe that said "The Grove" on the pocket, then walked into her bedroom. The first thing she noticed was that there were no suitcases full of clothes on the end of her bed. And when she looked into the closet, she saw that it was empty; the drawers of the chest were standing open and empty.

Immediately, panic seized her. He hadn't changed his mind, had he? He wasn't going to send her away after all, was he?

Flinging open her bedroom door, Darci ran toward the living room. But the room was dark. Confused for a moment, Darci turned back and saw that Adam's bedroom door was open a few inches and there was a light on inside. Slowly, she pushed open the door. He was sitting up in the bed nearest the bathroom door, wearing a T-shirt, the bottom half of him covered by the bedcovers, and he was reading.

"Take that bed," he said, without looking up.

"Really?" Darci asked, stepping inside the room. "You know, don't you, that I sleep nude?"

"Not anymore, you don't!" Adam said quickly, then looked up at her sternly. When Darci just stood there with a grin on her face, Adam put his book down and looked at her, unsmiling. "All in all, I think it would be better if you stopped making these . . . these overtures and these. . . ."

"Invitations?" Darci asked, smiling.

"Whatever you call them, I think you should stop them. If you're going to stay and help me with this, you're not going to be allowed out of my sight for even minutes. And I am *not* going to leave you alone to sleep in a room with windows where anyone could. . . ." Again he trailed off, as though the thought of what could happen to her was too much for him to think about. "Now, get into that bed and *stay* there," he said.

But Darci was still standing in one spot and smiling broadly. "Sure thing," she said as she took off her robe, then slipped under the covers. "Did you find out anything about the dagger yet?"

"No," he said, with his head down, still reading. "Tomorrow, we're going to spend the day researching. I'd like to know more about. . . ." He glanced at her, then involuntarily down at her left hand.

"Me too," Darci said, her smile disappearing. It was the thought of what she'd seen and heard today that took the merriment out of her. Suddenly, she was exhausted. Turning on her side, she pulled the covers up to her shoulders and said, "Good night, Adam", then she let her body relax fully. Soon, she had the soft, slow breathing of a person asleep.

Adam looked at her in disbelief. Could anyone over the age of four go to sleep that easily? he wondered. Looking back at his book, he knew that he wanted to read some more, *needed* to, but then he yawned. It had been an exhausting day so maybe he'd be able to go to sleep this early, too.

After turning off the bedside lamp, he snuggled down in the covers, closed his eyes, and was instantly asleep.

In the bed next to his, Darci smiled. True Persuasion worked every time, she thought, then did indeed go to sleep.

"Nothing," Darci said in disgust. "I found out absolutely nothing. At least not anything that was relevant to us, anyway." Her shoulders were aching, and her eyes were burning from having spent the whole day in the Camwell Library trying to find out about a prophecy that said some skinny blonde Southerner was going to be the downfall of the witches in Camwell.

Originally, they'd wanted to go to a library in another town to do research, but after a quick glance inside the Camwell Library they knew that they weren't going to find a better selection of books on the occult than in this library. "They come from all over to see our books," the librarian said with twinkling eyes. "Hardly a day goes by that Yale doesn't call and ask if we have something."

"And do you?" Darci asked.

"Do I what?"

"Have the books that Yale wants."

"Oh, my, yes. I haven't failed yet. If I don't have it, I know where I can get it. I must say that one time I did have trouble finding a book that hasn't been in print since 1736, but I *did* find it."

"Where?" Adam asked, and when the librarian just looked at him, he said, "*Where* did you find such an old book?"

"Why at—" the woman began, then broke off. "There's the telephone. Excuse me as I *must* answer it."

There was no telephone ringing.

"Probably her black cat calling her," Darci muttered.

But even in this extensive collection, Darci found nothing about a left hand with moles on it.

While Darci had been imprisoned in the library, Adam had spent the day on the Internet and on the telephone, trying to find out what information he could—on what, Darci didn't know because he put down the cover on the laptop, whenever she got near him. With the library's permission, he'd hooked his computer up to a phone line in the library, so Darci was in his sight at all times. But a good part of the day he'd been outside in the sunshine talking on his cell phone—all the while keeping watch on Darci through the window. She'd tested him once by spending ten whole minutes in the rest room. But he was standing outside the door when she reentered the library.

"It would help if you'd tell me what this magic object is," Darci had said when they'd stopped for lunch. She'd run across the street to a shop and purchased sandwiches and bottles of juice, which they ate while sitting on the library steps. Adam didn't even ask for his change. "And what about *me* allows me to open this . . . this thing?" she asked as he took a bite of turkey on whole wheat. "Whatever it is, that is? I can't keep calling it a 'thing.' And *how* do I open it?"

"You probably pester it to death," Adam had muttered.

But, pestered or not, Adam wouldn't tell her more than he already had. No matter how hard she tried, Adam would give her no more information than he had the night before.

And by the end of the day when they got back to the guest house, Darci was more than annoyed with him. "You put me in the library just to keep me where you could see me, didn't you?" she said, glaring at him. "I couldn't find out anything about any prophecy and certainly nothing about left-handed witches. Or moles. Whatever. And you *knew* I wouldn't find anything, didn't you? You knew because you know about a thousand times more than you're telling me, don't you? But you plan to give me enough busywork that I stay out of your way until you find this . . . this thing, then I what? Open it for you, you find out what you want to know, then you send me back to Putnam? Is that your plan?"

"*Putnam* the man or *Putnam* the town?" Adam asked, trying to make a joke and lighten the mood. But he wasn't as good at jokes as Darci was, and his attempt at humor fell flat.

"I think I might turn in early tonight," Darci said, her eyes cool and her jaw set in a firm line.

Adam smiled in a smug way. "Sure? How about a steak dinner at the diner? Maybe you can get some information out of Sally."

"No, thank you," Darci said, then turned on her heel, went into her own bedroom, and closed the door behind her.

Adam was left standing in the living room with his mouth hanging open. Darci had just turned down *food?*

Good, he thought. She's angry at me. Now it'll be easier to get her out of here. Now is the time to stop this whole thing. What he *should* do is get both of them on the next plane out of Connecticut and go home.

But where was home? he thought. Was home where he'd grown up with his aunt and uncle and his cousins? A place where he'd never fit in? And wasn't this trip an attempt to find out the truth about himself? To find out about his sister?

And what about Darci? Would she return to Putnam to her big strong fiancé and get married? Or would she return to her aunt and uncle and— As Darci had said, she had very few job skills. He couldn't see her as a receptionist. Maybe as a personal assistant for some fat old man who'd chase her around a desk or—

Before he had any more thoughts, Adam walked to Darci's bedroom door and raised his hand to tap but didn't. "It's a mirror," he said through the closed door. "The witches have a mirror that shows the future—and the past: what has happened and what will happen. I doubt if there is a prophecy about anyone written anywhere. Someone, whoever is now reading the mirror, probably saw you in it and saw that you would be the next reader."

He waited for a few moments but heard no sound from inside the room.

"What is it that you want to see in the mirror?" came her voice through the door. "The past or the future?"

"Don't press your luck," Adam answered.

A moment later, the knob turned and Darci came out of the room. She didn't look at him directly, but he thought she was still angry with him. And Adam's only thought was to get her back into a good humor. A quiet Darci wasn't much fun. "Did you learn anything at the library today?" he asked as he opened the coat closet and took out her jacket. It was deep burgundy, and the leather was as soft as . . . well, almost as soft as Darci's hair. "I mean, about anything besides witchcraft? I saw you reading a lot, and you asked the librarian quite a few questions. I thought maybe you'd been reading about something else." His eyes twinkled. "Did you have any movie magazines hidden under there?"

As she slipped her arms into the sleeves, she looked at him with narrowed eyes. All day long he'd known that she was going to find out nothing, because what she'd been looking for didn't exist.

As he held the door open for her, she gave him a sweet smile. "Actually, I did find out a few things," she said, looking up at him with eyes full of innocence. "I learned that your family is one of the richest in the world and has been for centuries. Your family is mentioned in at least a dozen books. They say that you can trace your family back to medieval knights who fought well but also had a knack for marrying rich women. The house you grew up in was built by one of those robber barons, named Kane Taggert, who—" She gave a little laugh when Adam put his hands on her back and pushed her out the door.

"You were supposed to be researching something that I *don't* know," he said tightly once they were outside. "You're being paid to help me, not to snoop through my personal life. And furthermore—"

"By the way, don't you owe me a paycheck?"

"If I take out all the shampoos and meals I've paid for, I don't owe you—"

At his words, Darci turned and started back to the guest house, obviously not willing to eat if it meant that she was going to have to pay for anything. But Adam grabbed her arm and pulled her back to walk beside him, and when she still hesitated, he tucked her arm into his and kept walking. "What is it with you and money, anyway? Are you saving for something? Other than freedom, that is."

When she didn't answer right away, he knew that he'd hit on one of her secrets. "Ah ha!" he said. "So now *you* are in the hot seat. Maybe I should look *you* up on the Internet instead of Putnam's car factories."

The minute he said it, he knew that he'd made a mistake. Maybe Darci wouldn't notice what he'd just said. Maybe she'd think that—

Darci came to an abrupt halt and looked up at him. "You looked Putnam up, didn't you? Somebody told me that the Internet was worse than the Doomesday Book. You can have no secrets from anyone. In fact—"

Then, before Adam could blink, Darci had flung open his jacket, stuck her hand inside, and withdrawn the sheaf of papers he had in his inside pocket.

This was too much! "Give those back to me!" he said as he made a grab at the papers.

"I was right!" Darci said, holding the paper up to the light. "Putnam's name is all over these papers. You ran a check on him!"

Reaching over her head, Adam snatched the papers out of her hands, jammed them back into his jacket pocket, then zipped up the front to his throat. "I was curious about him, that's all," Adam said tightly. "You have this obsession with money down to the penny, so I thought. . . ." He glanced at her out of the corner of his eye. He didn't want to lose this easy lightheartedness. "I thought that maybe Putnam was blackmailing you," he said, trying to make her laugh.

But once again, his attempt at humor fell flat. Instead of laughing at his nonsensical statement, Darci said nothing. She pulled away from him, then ran ahead to the corner light and pushed the button. As always, she didn't wait for the light to change before she ran across the street, making a woman in a big, black behemoth of an SUV slam on the brakes.

Minutes later, when Adam entered the diner, frowning, ready to lecture her on safety, Darci spoke before he did. "Someone's in our booth," she said, nodding toward two people who sat with cups of coffee before them.

"There are four empty booths," Adam said as he removed his jacket and hung it over his arm. "We can take one of them."

"No," Darci said quietly as she looked at the people in "their" booth. "That's where we've always sat and that's where I want to sit *now*." Her voice was getting softer, and there were pauses between her words. "I'm going to apply my True Persuasion and . . . make . . . them . . . move."

Smiling, shaking his head at her, Adam looked down to see Darci staring with intense concentration at the older couple in the booth where she and Adam had always sat.

"There!" she said after a moment, and Adam looked up to see the couple leaving. But of course they'd probably finished their coffee, so maybe that had something to do with their leaving, he thought, chuckling at her. But he wasn't going to say that and risk making her angry again.

"Good job," he said, smiling at the top of her head; then they waited until the busboy had cleared the booth so they could sit down.

"So tell me everything about this mirror," she said as soon as they were seated.

"You two want the specials, or should I just bring everything on the menu?" Sally, the waitress, said in her usual smirking way.

"We'll take whatever you recommend," Adam answered, then smiled at her in a way that made her stop smacking her gum for a moment.

Sally leaned toward Darci and said conspiratorially, "You got your hands full with this one, honey. Maybe you oughta stare at him like you did that old couple. Make him behave better." With that, she went away laughing.

"That woman is just *too* nosy!" Adam said after she left.

"Small town," Darci said in dismissal. "So now tell me everything."

"If Putnam is so rich and you're marrying him, why do you need to count every penny?"

"I already know about Putnam," Darci said impatiently. "I want to know about this mirror. How did you find out about it?"

"Long story," he said as he looked down at the cuff of his shirt sticking out from under his sweater. "Did I tell you that the sweater you have on is a good color for you? It matches your eyes."

She glared at him. "This sweater is purple, and unless you're color-blind, you're trying to change the subject."

Adam took a while before he spoke, and when he did, it was so softly that she could barely hear him. She leaned forward, as he did, until their heads were almost touching. "I told you that the mirror tells the past. It shows what *has* happened, and something happened in the past that I want to know about."

When Adam said no more, Darci leaned against the back of the booth and thought about what he'd said, and thought about what she knew about him. "Your parents," she said softly. "That's what this is about, isn't it? You said they died, but *how* did they die?"

"I don't know," Adam said so softly that again she could barely hear him. "Look, the truth is that this whole thing about the mirror is a legend. It could be a lie. Maybe the thing doesn't really exist. Maybe—" He looked down again and seemed to consider whether or not he should tell her more. "It's Nostradamus's mirror," he said in one breath.

At that Darci's mouth fell open. "This mirror is. . . ."

"Yes," Adam said. "That one. He looked into it, saw the future, and wrote about it."

Darci's eyes had a faraway look when she spoke. "But predicting the future was illegal in France in the sixteenth century, so he scrambled what he wrote so thoroughly that even today people don't know what he predicted. During the Kennedy administration, half a dozen books came out saying that many of Nostradamus's quatrains were about that family. But, of course, twenty years later, the writings were interpreted completely differently, no Kennedys at all. But then Dolores Cannon says— What?!" she snapped because Adam was staring at her as though she'd just sprouted a third head.

"How in the world do you know so much about this mirror?!"

Darci shrugged. "I'm interested in a great many things, and I read a lot. There's not a lot to do in Putnam, and, believe it or not, the town does have a public library."

"Who owns it?" Adam asked quickly.

"Putnam, of course. Senior, not junior, although Putnam does give his father lists of books that he thinks the library should buy."

"I see," Adam said thoughtfully. "And who chooses the books that go onto those lists? Junior or senior?"

"*C'est moi,*" Darci said happily, making Adam laugh.

"I might have guessed," he said. "So you get your fiancé to buy any books you want and put them in the library for you. Tell me, if he's so rich, why aren't you wearing an engagement ring?"

"Don't want one," Darci said quickly and in a way that said she didn't want to talk about that subject. "So you found the mirror," she said, her voice full of wonder. "I can't tell you how many times I've wondered what happened to it. In fact, I've wondered what happened to *all* the magic objects. Aladdin's magic lamp probably had a basis in truth. And what about the magic carpet? And what happened to the mirror that used to tell the queen she was the fairest of them all?"

"What are you talking about?" Adam asked.

"You know, in 'Snow White'? The queen?"

"Snow White. Is that the one who fell down the rabbit hole? No, that was a white rabbit. Or was it? So what does this have to do with a mirror? Did—"

He stopped because Sally set platters full of food in

front of them. There were slices of turkey with cranberry dressing, pureed squash, roast potatoes, succotash, and a basket full of tiny muffins with pieces of zucchini sticking out of them. "That should hold her for a while," Sally said to Adam. "But I'll go get the pumpkin pie ready anyway."

"Odd sense of humor that woman has," Adam said, frowning.

"She reminds me of the witch in 'Hansel and Gretel' when she was fattening up the children."

"For what?" Adam asked as he reached for a muffin. He thought he'd better get one now before Darci ate the lot of them.

"'For what?'"

"What was the witch fattening the children up for?"

Darci looked at him is disbelief. "To eat them, of course. Where did you grow up that you don't know fairy tales? You don't know 'Snow White' or 'Hansel and Gretel'?"

Adam opened his mouth to speak, then closed it and looked down at his food.

"Instead of thinking up a lie, why don't you just tell me the truth?" she suggested.

"I will as soon as you tell me about you and money and Putnam," he shot back at her.

Darci started to speak, but, instead, she put a large bite of turkey and dressing in her mouth, then waved her hand that she couldn't talk.

"I thought so," Adam said. "And as for your fairy tales, if they're about witches fattening up children so they can be eaten, I'm glad I never heard them. They sound horrible."

"Quite bad, really. I once wrote a paper on the origin of fairy tales and found out that they've been toned down considerably since they were first told. Did you know that most of the Mother Goose rhymes started out as political jingles?"

"No, tell me," Adam said, as he handed her the basket of muffins. Two nights ago he had been the lecturer about foods and wines, but tonight it was her turn to tell him what she knew. At first Adam's only intent in asking her to tell him about some ridiculous nursery rhymes was to keep her from asking more questions about the mirror and how he knew what he knew. But as he listened, Adam found that he was interested in what she was saying.

All in all, he had to admit that his conversations with her beat what usually went on when he had dinner with a woman. Most of the time, he felt as though he'd been put under a spotlight and was being interrogated. "Where did you grow up?" "What schools did you attend?" they'd ask. "Oh? Are you any relation to *those* Montgomerys?" This last was said with what his cousin Michael called The Money Look.

But today Darci had found out about his family and, except for being pleased that she'd found out something he hadn't wanted her to know, he couldn't see that her attitude toward him was any different. Smiling, he asked her to tell him more about the nursery rhymes. Meanwhile, in the back of his mind, he was formulating a Plan. Maybe they couldn't find out anything in the library or on the Internet, but there was someone who knew a great deal: the man who ran the store, the man who'd fled at the sight of Darci's left hand.

Still smiling, Adam nodded at what Darci was saying.

9

Adam didn't dare set an alarm clock for four A.M. because he was sure that Darci would hear it go off. Instead, he willed himself to wake early, and as a consequence, he woke at three forty-five. Not bad, he told himself as he glanced at the luminous dial on the clock. Very slowly, with no noise at all, he moved back the covers and stepped out of the bed.

Last night in the diner, while Darci had been talking, he'd listened to her, but he'd also planned all of this carefully. He didn't want to leave her alone, unprotected, for even minutes, but he figured that if he had to leave her, then early morning was better than nighttime. So, last night, while Darci showered, Adam had stashed some clothes in the bottom drawer in the table beside the couch in the living room. Now, he tiptoed in there and dressed silently. When there was still no sound from Darci, he smiled, feeling that he was about to pull off a major coup. She was so damned perceptive! he thought. It was a wonder she hadn't found the clothes he'd hidden and deduced what he was planning to do.

When Adam was dressed in a dark sweat suit, he wrote a note saying that he'd gone out for a morning run, then put the note on the dining table by the window. Slowly and with absolute silence, he opened the front door and tiptoed out. If luck was with him, he thought he'd be back before Darci woke up. Last night he'd managed to make up an excuse to go outside long enough that he could move the car. He wanted it farther from their guest house so the noise of the engine early in the morning wouldn't wake Darci up.

Once he was inside the car, with the engine running, Adam relaxed his shoulders and smiled. That hadn't been so difficult, had it?

The passenger door flew open, and Darci jumped into the empty seat. She was wearing her T-shirt nightgown, her clothes thrown over her arm. She didn't so much as look at him but kept her eyes straight ahead.

Adam opened his mouth to tell her that he didn't want her to go with him, that he had something personal to do, and that she *had* to stay behind. He wanted to tell her to get out of the car and wait for him. He wanted to tell her—

But he knew that he'd be wasting his breath. Instead of giving her the lecture he wanted to, he sighed and put the car in reverse. "Are you going to last without food?" he asked.

"Oh, yes," she said with a smile that let him know that she knew she'd won. "I can go for days without eating."

"I do *not* want to know how you know that," Adam said as he turned the car and headed toward the road where the country store was located.

Darci spread out her jeans, then began to pull them on under her long gown. "People forgot to feed me until I learned how to use True Persuasion on them," she said, her voice telling him how happy she was to have found him.

Adam was trying his absolute best not to look at her while she dressed. It seemed that, once again, she was making him feel as though he were a randy high school boy. "Okay," he said, "I'll bite. What exactly is your True Persuasion, and how does it work?" He needed something to distract him. Was she going to take the nightgown *off* before she pulled on that turtleneck?

"Anyone can do it," Darci said, removing the top of her nightgown under the cover of the turtleneck and therefore not exposing any skin. "When I was quite young, I read a book about how if you put your mind to something, you can make it happen. All you have to do is think really hard about what you want a person to do and you can make them do it."

"Like staring at the back of someone's head and making them turn around?"

"Yes, exactly."

"But you've developed it into an art form."

"Are you laughing at me?"

"Yes. But if I don't find some humor in this situation, I may stop the car and tie you in the trunk. Didn't you realize that if I was leaving without telling you where I was going that I didn't want you to go with me?"

"Of course I did. But if I did what *you* wanted me to, I'd

just be sitting and waiting for heaven only knows what. Do you want to hear more about True Persuasion or not? It might help you sometime. In fact, the more I know you, the more I think you *need* some True Persuasion in your life. How could you have grown up so rich and yet be such a Sad Sack?"

Against his will, Adam smiled. "I haven't heard that term in a long time. Rich isn't everything. There are other things in life besides money."

"Did you ever notice that only rich people say that?" Darci said. "The poor people are concentrating so hard on paying their bills that they can't think of anything besides money."

"Is that your problem? You have bills to pay? Is that why you scramble around looking for nickels?" When Darci didn't answer, Adam's tone changed. "Look, if you need money for something, I can help you."

She took a moment before speaking. "Do you have masses and masses of money?" she asked softly.

Turning, Adam saw that she was again staring straight ahead and the expression on her face was serious. "Yes, I do," he said. "How much do you need?"

"I don't know," she answered as she turned to look out the side window. "I'd have to add it up. But I think it's about seven million."

At that Adam pulled the car to the side of the road, turned off the engine, then turned to look at her. "All right, now tell me again. You need money. How much money do you need?"

"About seven million dollars," she said, sounding as though she were saying seven dollars. "But it's okay; there are other ways to pay back the money. I think we better go. Storekeepers get up early. That *is* where you're going, isn't it?"

Adam waited, but Darci didn't say another word. "You're not going to tell me any more about this money you owe?"

"Not if I can get out of it," Darci said, then closed her mouth firmly.

Adam started the car again and pulled back onto the road. "Sometime you and I are going to have to have a long talk."

"That would be nice," she said. "How about if you go first? I want to know all about your parents and why you don't know how they died and how you know about this mirror, and, of course, I'll want to be told the *whole* truth about why you hired me. Besides that I can look into this mirror and see the future, that is. And the past. And how do *you* know that these people have the mirror? You want to tell me all that?"

"About as much as you want to tell me your story," Adam said tightly; then he slowed the car because they were near the turnoff to the store. "Now listen to me," he said, his voice sounding urgent. "I want you to stay here in the car while I go talk to this man."

"Talk to him? If you wanted to talk to him, shouldn't you have visited him during store hours?" It was just now showing early-morning light.

"All right, so maybe I want to strong-arm him a bit. The truth is that I'm at a dead end. I thought that this mirror would be easier to find than this. I thought—" Breaking off, he gave her a sideways look.

"I see. You thought I'd be some sort of magnet for the thing, didn't you? Your psychic told you I'd find this mirror for you so you thought that I'd be like a water witch and divine where it is? You *did,* didn't you?"

"You have a very annoying way of putting things," Adam said as he opened the car door, then looked back at her. "You heard what I said, didn't you? You're to stay in this car with all the doors locked." For a moment, Adam's face paled; four young women who fit Darci's description had disappeared in this area, and later their mutilated bodies had been found far away.

"I'm not going," he said, closing the door and reaching for the key.

"Well, I am!" Darci said, then she got out of the car before he could stop her.

He had to give it to her, she could certainly run across the Connecticut woodland! She was as agile as one of those deer that roamed freely and ate everything the homeowners planted, all while leaving behind millions of deer ticks. Adam ran behind her, wanting to shout at her, but at the same time not wanting to alert anyone who might be at the store. "I will kill her myself," he said as he jumped over a fallen tree.

He caught her by the back of the neck just as she stepped onto the gravel of the parking lot behind the store. But before Adam could say anything, he heard a car approach. In one motion, he fell to the ground, taking Darci down with him. Once they were on the ground, he wrapped his arm around her body and put his hand over her mouth. For all he knew, if she saw the store clerk, she'd call out to the man and ask him what he knew. He could almost hear her asking the man about "moley hands."

But the car didn't stop. Instead, it circled the store twice, the second time slowing to a crawl as it passed them. As it did, Adam ducked his head down and tucked Darci so completely under him that there was little of her visible.

The car left the parking lot after the second pass, but Adam waited until he could see the car through the trees as it went back onto the highway. "All right," he whispered to Darci, "let's go."

"And where do you think you're going?" said a voice from behind them.

Adam rolled over, ready to kick up at the person behind them, but the man was standing too far away to reach. Obviously, he'd used the cover of the sound of the car on the gravel to keep them from hearing his approach. Even though the man's face was concealed, Adam saw right away that he was not the man from the country store. This man was taller and leaner, and even though he was clad in a loose black running suit, he looked as though he was in good shape. His face was hidden by a black ski mask, and in his hand was a semiautomatic, a .38, was Adam's guess.

"You two want to move over there?" the man said slowly, motioning with the gun toward an opening in the trees.

Adam stepped in front of Darci. "Let her go. She has nothing to do with this."

The man gave a snort of laughter. "From what I hear, she has *everything* to do with this."

"No!" Adam said. "She's not who you think she is. She's my—"

"I don't care what you do with her, that's none of my business. I'm just supposed to— Hey!" he said.

Standing where he was, Adam watched in disbelief as the man slowly lowered the arm holding the gun. Truthfully, it looked as though he couldn't help himself, as though his right arm was being controlled by something outside of himself. When Adam turned to look at Darci, he saw that she had that look of intense concentration on her face that he'd seen before. Last night, he thought. He'd seen her look like that at that old couple when she'd wanted them to move out of "their" booth. What was it she'd said? She was going to apply her True Persuasion to them.

Even as Adam was thinking these things and making these observations, he wondered why he wasn't making a move. Why wasn't he leaping forward to take advantage of whatever was causing this man to lower his gun?

But, oddly enough, Adam didn't feel as though he *could* move. It was as though his entire body from the neck down had turned into a statue and he was frozen where he was. He could slowly move his neck and look from Darci to the gunman and back again, but he couldn't seem to move the rest of his body.

After several long moments, Darci, without losing concentration, without taking her eyes off the gunman, slowly walked toward him and took the gun from his hand. She held it by the grip, her hand on the trigger, for all the world looking as though she knew how to use the thing, and she aimed it at the gunman's head. "Now take off that mask," she said.

But then Darci sneezed.

And the sneeze broke her concentration. And when her concentration was broken, the hold over both the gunman and Adam was broken. The gunman didn't try to take the gun from Darci. Instead, he took off running through the woods. "You're a witch, lady," he called over his shoulder. "And they can have you!"

It took Adam a couple of crucial moments to recover his senses, both in his mind and his body, then he ran after the gunman. But it was too late. Besides, the man knew the woods and Adam didn't. As though he'd disappeared in a puff of smoke, the gunman was gone.

Slowly, Adam walked back to Darci. She was sitting on a log, the gun on her lap, and she was white with exhaustion. Her shoulders were shaking, and she looked as though she might pass out at any moment.

Adam knew he should offer her some comfort because, obviously, what she'd just done had drained her. But, for the life of him, Adam couldn't bring himself to comfort her. Nor could he think of anything to say to her. For one thing, he wasn't sure about what he'd just seen—and felt. What he'd felt was the most unbelievable. Somehow, Darci had used her mind to paralyze two grown men.

"Your sweater is on backward," he said after a moment of looking down at her.

"Oh? Is it?" She removed the gun from her lap, set it on the log beside her, then, slowly and carefully, she stood up, pulled her arms out of the sweater, and turned it around.

Adam picked up the gun and held it behind him. "You ready to go?" he asked quietly. "I don't think we'll find out any . . . more." He added the last because, though he wasn't yet sure, he thought that, maybe, he'd just found out more than he wanted to know.

He remembered what Helen the psychic had said about Darci: "*She's not what she seems, not what she thinks she is, not what you see her as.*" And the psychic had laughed after she'd said it.

Adam walked behind Darci to the car, ready to catch her if she fell, but he didn't touch her and he didn't speak. Once she was in the car, she leaned her head back against the seat, closed her eyes, and looked as though she'd fallen asleep. But when Adam got into the driver's seat, he glanced at her and thought that she was awake but too depleted to speak.

He started the car and pulled onto the highway. Police, he thought. After all, they'd just been held at gunpoint by a masked man. But Adam knew that the police would ask too many questions. What were they doing in the woods before dawn? If they had been in a city, they might get away with the lie of saying they were out for a walk. But in this tiny town he had no doubt that every person knew what they were interested in.

As he drove, Adam glanced at Darci. If he took her with him to the police, if there was an investigation and the man was caught, then what? Would the man tell about what Darci had done to him? Adam knew in his heart that Darci was the person whom the murderer of those young women had been looking for. If they went to the police would that be putting Darci in even more danger?

When they got to Camwell, he parked in front of the grocery store and started to open the car door.

"Are you angry with me?" Darci whispered hoarsely. "I didn't mean to—"

He put up his hand to cut her off. "How about if I go in and get us some breakfast and we take it back to the guest house? I think that we should have a nice, long talk, don't you?"

"A talk about you or about me?" she asked with a tired little smile.

"You," Adam said firmly. "Definitely you. Compared to you, I'm an extremely boring fellow." He was trying to remain cool and act as though what he'd just experienced was something he'd seen a thousand times. After all, he was a man of the world, wasn't he? But, truthfully, there was part of him that wanted to get out of the car and run as fast and as far away as he could get. "You don't set things on fire, do you?" he asked softly, half as a joke but at the same time seriously.

"I haven't managed to do so with you yet," she said with such resignation that Adam laughed. And with the laughter, his feelings of, well, creepiness, left him. She was just Darci. She wasn't a sideshow freak or a character in a horror novel. She was a funny little thing who just happened to have an extraordinary ability.

Smiling, shaking his head in disbelief, he got out of the car, then leaned back in through the window. "I want you to remain in this car while I'm in there. Understand?"

Darci nodded. She was still pale, still listless.

"And I don't want you to True Persuade anything to anyone. Got it?"

Again she nodded, but she looked so glum that he was beginning to feel sorry for her. Smiling, he said, "Before you arrived, I bought some delicious cinnamon rolls at this store. How about a bag of them, some freshly squeezed orange juice, and milk? What kind of fruit do you want?"

"Something good enough to say thank you to me for saving your life," she said, but she didn't look at him.

Adam was taken aback for a moment and started to

defend himself, but then he stood up and shook his head in wonder. Maybe she *had* saved his life. He wasn't yet sure how she'd done it, but she had, somehow, stopped a gunman. And him. Ms. Darci T. Monroe could use her mind to freeze people in place.

Still shaking his head, still in a state of disbelief, Adam went into the grocery and returned fifteen minutes later with four bags, one full of buns, juice, and milk, and three bags containing one of each fruit the store had.

10

～

"NOT EVEN FOR CHOCOLATE chiffon pie with raspberries on top of it," Darci said fiercely, then added, "I saw that in a magazine once. Sounds pretty good, doesn't it? Think the diner—"

"We can ask," Adam said, annoyed. "Look, I just want to do one more test and that's all. I want to see if you can—"

"What?" she snapped. "Talk to animals? Is that what you're going to ask me next?"

"No, of course not. That's absurd. You . . . you can't, can you?" Adam asked.

Darci glared at him. "I'm going for a walk. A long walk. By myself."

"Sounds good," Adam said cheerfully. "I think I'll join you."

"I said I want to be alone."

Adam gave her a false smile. "The only places you're

allowed to go alone are to the bathroom and to get on an airplane. And even then I'll choose your destination. But if you stay here, you stay near me; no walks alone."

"And to think that I thought you were—" She decided not to finish that sentence.

"I was what?" he asked as he followed her out the door. "Handsome? Intelligent? What?"

Halting, she looked up at him. "I would have been wrong if I'd thought any of those things, wouldn't I?"

"We can't all be oddities, can we?" He'd meant his words as a joke, but the minute he said it, he regretted it.

Without a reply, Darci started walking again, faster. There was a path at the back of the guest house that led in the opposite direction from the slave cabins, and she took it. Adam stayed several feet behind her, not walking with her. The truth was, he needed some time to think about today and what he'd seen and, most important, where they went from here.

It had been only six A.M. by the time they got back to their guest house at the Grove, Adam carrying all four bags of food.

Once they were inside, cautiously, he'd said, "Would you feel better if we went to the police?"

"Sure," she said with a grimace. "Then we'd spend days answering questions. 'And how did you escape this man with a gun?' they'll ask. 'Oh,' you'll say, 'my freak of an assistant used—'"

"You want cantaloupe or mango first?" Adam asked, cutting her off.

Darci blinked at him. "Does a mango taste good?"

After that, they'd not talked anymore about the police, through silent mutual agreement.

They'd spread the food on the coffee table; Adam sat on the couch, Darci on the floor. "Now," Adam said as soon as they were settled, "I want to know exactly what you can do."

"Why are some grapefruits pink and some yellow inside?" Darci asked. "Have the pink ones been crossed with another fruit, or do you think the growers bred them to be pink because market research showed that buyers like pink grapefruits better?"

"I see," he said as he bit into a cinnamon roll. "You're changing the subject. Does this mean that you want me to find out for myself?"

"No," she said sweetly as she pierced a slice of mango with her fork. "I want to punish you. I've been trying to tell you about my True Persuasion ever since we got here, but you've smirked and patronized me every time I've mentioned it. So now if you want so much as one word out of me, you're going to have to beg." At that she bit into the mango. "Oh, my, but this is good. Where do these come from?"

For a moment Adam looked at her in consternation, having no idea what exactly to do. Didn't she realize that this . . . this "power" of hers had to be part of why the psychic had said Darci could read the mirror? Didn't she realize how important this discovery was?

Adam opened his mouth to begin his speech, but before the first word was out, he could envision Darci yawning. No, lecturing wasn't the way to get her to talk.

What was it she'd said? Before she went into ecstasies over a mango, that is? Beg? Is that what she'd said?

With a great groan, as though he were a very old man,

Adam got off the couch, then slowly, creakily, went onto his knees on the carpet. He straightened and put his elbows to his side, forearms up, letting his hands dangle in front of him, then he opened his mouth, let his tongue droop out, and he began to pant. "Please tell me," he said. "Please. I beg you. I beg with . . . with every mango and kiwi that's ever been grown."

After her initial shock, Darci began to laugh.

Finally, Adam thought, he had been able to make Darci laugh. He had—at last—made a joke that had not fallen on its face. And it was amazing how good it felt to have caused that smile on her pretty face.

"Please," he said, pushing his joke further. "Just one itty-bitty test. Just one. One test and I'll listen to every Putnam story you tell me. I'll even listen about your cousin Vernon."

"Uncle Vernon, cousin Virgil," Darci corrected him, "and you might learn something from hearing about Virgil. He's the one who taught me how to use a gun."

Adam got off his knees. "Maybe that story would be too much for me," he said as he took his place on the couch. "So, does everyone in Putnam know about this . . . this . . . thing you can do?"

"People in Putnam are as good at listening as you are," Darci said instantly.

"Ouch. But then I guess that means that you haven't had much call to, uh, use it."

"I have, but nobody noticed."

Adam blinked at her. "I see," he said, again trying to sound worldly. But then he thought, Why try to do something he was incapable of? "No, actually, I don't see. Are you saying that all your life you've been stopping people where they stand and *no one noticed?*"

Darci reached across the table and speared a slice of mango off Adam's plate. "Actually, in spite of what you seem to think my life has been like, this was the first time that anyone has ever held me at gunpoint, so I didn't know that I *could* make a person freeze." She paused to chew and swallow. "All I did this morning was think as hard as I could that I wanted that awful man to put that gun down. But at the same time I didn't want to see *you* do anything silly, like wrestle him for the gun. That's all. I thought and it happened."

"I see."

"Will you stop saying that!" she said. "You sound like Abraham Lincoln."

"You haven't met *him,* have you?" he asked, eyes wide.

"Was that a joke?"

"I wanted it to be. Unless you *can* see people from . . . from the beyond. That psychic you met, Helen, *she* talks to dead people all the time."

"That's weird," Darci said.

Adam started to say, *And what you can do* isn't *weird?* But he decided that the wiser course of action would be not to say that. "Have you explored your abilities?"

She took the last two slices of mango off Adam's plate. "Why don't you just come out and say what it is that you want from me and get it over with?"

"I want to see what you can do," Adam said honestly. "Would you mind very much if I made a few experiments?"

Darci paused with a slice of mango on the way to her mouth. "You mean like rats in a lab?"

"No," he said slowly. "More like. . . ." His head came up. "Like the first friend you've ever had who's noticed that you can do something extraordinary and he wants to know all about it. All about *you*."

As Darci sat there blinking at him and considering this, he could see her defiance melting away. "Okay," she said softly. "What do you want to do to me?"

At first Adam had no idea what he did want to do or find out about. He wasn't even sure about what he wanted to know. Actually, psychic abilities and paranormal experiences were not something he'd ever been interested in. Some of his cousins loved ghost stories, but they'd never interested Adam. The only reason he was interested in recovering the mirror was because of his parents. And because—

"All right," Adam said slowly, searching his mind for what kind of test to give her. "First I'll. . . . I know! You write something on a piece of paper, turn it over, then use your mind to see if you can make me do what's on the paper. I want to see if you can make people follow your instructions."

"I like that idea," Darci said enthusiastically as she picked up a pad and pencil off the side table.

"No sex," Adam said.

"I beg your pardon?"

"Don't act innocent with me, Ms. Monroe. Don't you write on that paper that you want me to take you to bed and spend the whole day making love to you. Or even that I should kiss your neck and—"

Darci was smiling at him in a way that threatened to make him blush. "Never entered my mind," she said. "But

it obviously entered *yours*. Never let it be said that *I* interrupted a man. Kiss my neck, then what?"

"I'm not sure this particular activity is such a good
idea," Adam said, looking away.

"Oh, no, you wanted to do this, so we're going to do it.
You can't chicken out on me now." With that she wrote
something on the paper, turned it over, then looked at
Adam with total concentration.

For a moment he couldn't look away from her, but then,
he thought, I don't like these experiments, and I think they
should stop. Maybe it was better that he didn't know what
she could do.

Wanting to give himself some time to think, he got up
and went to the refrigerator. "You want a soda?" he asked.

"Sure. Seven-Up."

Still thinking, trying to decide if he wanted to pursue
this or not, absently, Adam took a bag of pretzels from the
basket of snacks the hotel had left in the room, the two
cans of soda, then took them back to the coffee table. But
as soon as he got there, he realized that Darci would want
her drink in a glass with ice. For a country girl, she certainly had some genteel ways, he thought. As he got a glass
and ice and poured her drink, he kept thinking that maybe
he should forget the entire project.

"All right?" he asked as he set her drink on the table. "I
was just thinking that I'm not sure we should do this. In
fact, I think—" He broke off because Darci had turned the
paper over. It read, *Get me a drink, glass, ice, and pretzels,
and think about dropping this whole idea.*

"Oh." Adam said as he sat down on the end of the
couch. He didn't know whether to feel foolish, frightened,

or elated. She had just made him perform a task. Like a trained monkey, he thought.

But even more astounding, she had used her mind to make him *think* what she wanted him to think.

"If you keep looking at me like that, I'll. . . ." Darci didn't know what to say to complete that threat, but she knew she was very near to bursting into tears.

Adam had to work to get himself under control. He took a deep breath and tried to calm himself. "So why haven't you used this . . . this power on whomever you owe seven million dollars to?" he asked, amazed that he could even form words. He kept looking at the paper on the table.

Darci began to clear away the breakfast things and talked as she worked. "I did. I got Putnam to pay for all my schooling."

"So you owe him? Putnam? Your fiancé?"

"His family," she said, then changed the subject. "I thought you wanted me to make you do things."

"I want to understand all of this," Adam said seriously, dragging his eyes away from the paper to look at her. How could this tiny woman hold such a power? He was having trouble comprehending what she could do. She could use her mind to make people do—and think—what she wanted them to. Didn't she have any idea of the possibilities of that kind of power?

"What have you done with this ability of yours?" he asked softly. "How have you used this power in your life? When did you first realize that you could do this? How have you refined it? Worked on it? Who knows about it?"

"Which of those questions do you want me to answer

first?" Darci asked as she sat back down on the floor and sipped her drink. "I want to make something clear from the start. I've never used what you call my power to do anything bad to anyone. And, the truth is, until today, I didn't know that I could . . . that I could make people stop in their tracks." She looked away for a moment, and when she looked back at him, her face was pleading with him to understand. "You see, I've always believed that anyone could use True Persuasion, but people *choose* to believe that they can't. They'd rather whine that they can't do so-and-so because somebody didn't give them something, or love them enough, or whatever other excuse they have for not doing something."

"You can't possibly believe that *normal* people—" He cut himself off when Darci started to get up. "Sorry," he said quickly then she sat back down. "Look, it's nice to believe that anyone anywhere can do what you can, but they can't. And I'm *glad* they can't. If everyone could do what you do—" He ran his hand over his face to clear his mind of that thought.

Looking at her again, he took a breath. For himself, he needed to understand all of this. "Okay, so maybe you haven't explored this ability of yours fully. You're young, so you haven't had time. And you haven't shared this with anyone because you didn't grow up with a warm, loving family who could sit down with you and explain things and—"

"And you did?" she shot back at him. "I haven't heard you say anything warm and loving about *your* childhood. What happened to your parents that was so horrible that you can't speak of it? And don't tell me again that you 'don't know.' And how old are you, anyway?"

"This isn't about me," he said, louder and more angrily

than he meant to. "This is about you and how you can freeze people in place. Oh, no, you don't!" he said when he saw Darci looking hard at him. "You're not going to—" But in the next moment he leaned across the table and kissed her on the cheek.

Part of him was annoyed, but the greater part of him saw the amusement in what she'd just done. Leaning back against the couch, he looked at her. "I want you to tell me everything. I want to know what you can do, what you have done, and I want to find out what you don't know that you can do."

"Why?" she asked. "Give me a good reason why I should share my lifelong secret with you when I've shared it with no one else."

It took Adam a moment to form his answer. "When I started this search, it was personal. All I wanted to know was what happened to my parents." When Darci started to speak, he put his hand up. "Yes," he said, "that's what I want to know. But I also want to know what was done to me. No! I can't go into that now. Now's not the time. Anyway, since I started searching, I've learned a lot about some ugly things that go on in this world, and I'd like to put a stop to as much of the ugliness as I can."

"What you're saying is that you want to use me to obtain what you want."

Adam took a deep breath. Should he lie? Or should he tell the truth and risk angering her so much that she walked away? "Maybe," he said, deciding on the truth. "The idea that's coming to me is that you could stay somewhere safe and use your mind while I. . . ." He lifted his palms up as if to say he wasn't sure what he meant.

"You mean that we'd make a team," Darci said, smiling. "Almost a marriage of sorts."

Adam smiled. "I guess so."

"That makes sense," Darci said lightly. "So, where do you want to start?"

"With your history," he said quickly. "Tell me what you've done and what you know," he said as he pulled his briefcase from beside the couch and withdrew a notebook and a pen.

This time, when she started talking, Adam listened. Previously, she'd accused him of not listening to her, and he knew that she'd been correct. As she began to talk, he racked his brain to remember every time she'd mentioned her True Persuasion, trying to recall what she'd said—and what had happened. On her first night in Camwell, she said that she'd found him by applying her True Persuasion. *What can she find?* he wrote in his notebook. Darci had said that she had been surprised when he offered her the job because she hadn't yet applied her True Persuasion to it. In Hartford, she'd used it on the hairdresser to give her a great haircut. She'd used it on the people sitting in "their" booth. She'd used it to get people to feed her when she was a child.

And she'd used it to paralyze two grown men.

"You sneezed and broke the spell," Adam said, interrupting her. "How long can you hold a spell?"

"I am *not* a witch," Darci said. "I don't cast spells on people. I just—"

"Make people do what you want them to. For how long can you hold them under your"—he searched for a word—"enchantment?"

"Some people are easy and some difficult. I think it depends on how stubborn they are. But if I think really hard over many days, I can almost always bring even the most stubborn person around. But sometimes I can't persuade the person, so then I have to maneuver others around that person."

"What does that mean?" Adam did all he could to keep his feelings from showing on his face. She seemed to have no idea how truly unbelievable what she was saying was. But he knew that to express shock would make her stop talking. He held his pen ready to write down her answer. "What are you going to do with what you're writing?"

"Publish a biography on you and make millions," he said quickly. "You'll either be reviled or worshiped. You'll certainly be a celebrity."

"Very funny," she said, but she didn't laugh. Instead, she was looking at him hard.

"Are you trying to make me fetch something for you or trying to read my mind?"

"Read your mind," she said, "which, by the way, I can't do. Was that a joke about writing a bio? I can never tell about your jokes."

"Yes, it was a joke. You know, some people think I have an excellent sense of humor. They— Never mind about that. I want you to tell me about what you can do. I know. How about giving me an example? Take one thing you've done and tell me about it from beginning to end. Tell me an instance of where you worked on someone stubborn."

"All right," Darci said slowly. "There was a man in Putnam named Daryl Farnum who owned a very mean dog. Actually, Mr. Farnum owned lots of dogs and some of them were probably very nice. I guess. But then, it's not like anyone ever saw the nice dogs Mr. Farnum owned, because he kept them in back of his house where no one ever went. Except for Mr. Farnum, that is. Anyway, he kept the mean dog chained up in his front yard, and the animal snapped at everybody who walked past his house. And since he lived next door to the elementary school, there were a lot of scared kids. Also, the animal barked all day long, so the teachers on that side of the building could hardly hear themselves talk."

"So what did you make Mr. Farnum do?" Adam asked.

"Move away from Putnam."

Adam's face showed his disappointment in her answer.

"It wasn't an easy job," she said defensively. "Mr. Farnum's house and property were a pigsty so the first thing I did was think really hard in an attempt to get Mr. Farnum to clean it up. But I couldn't make him do it. If there's one thing I've learned, it's that all the True Persuasion in the world can't change character. That man was lazy to the bone, and I could have sent him industrious thoughts forever, but I don't think I could have changed him. So I had to work on the mayor of Putnam to make him want to get the place clean; then I had to work on Putnam's father—"

"Also called Putnam?"

"Yes," she said, narrowing her eyes at him. "I worked on Putnam in Putnam. Now are you happy?"

"'On Putnam in Putnam,'" Adam quoted as he wrote, then he looked back up at her. "Go on."

"Now I see why you're so old and unmarried. No woman will have you."

"Don't kid yourself," he said cheerfully. "So what did Putnam of Putnam do?"

"Paid for everything, of course. That's what Putnams do. They pay. I worked on putting the idea that Mr. Farnum's place was a disgrace to the town into the mayor's mind—I knew he was very civic-minded—then I worked on Putnam to make him want to pay for the backhoe."

"Backhoe?" Adam asked, eyebrows raised.

"I told you that the place was filthy," Darci said in exasperation. "Are you not listening again?"

Putting down his notebook, Adam looked at her in genuine interest. "Next door to the elementary school was a house that was so, uh, filthy that it needed a backhoe to clean it up?"

"Private property is a sacred concept in Putnam, so people don't interfere in a man's right to do what he wants on his own land. And the Farnums always kept dogs," she said. "Lots of dogs. Generations of them. Generations of Farnums as well as generations of dogs, all on the same acre and a half."

"I see," Adam said, but he certainly did not *want* to see. Or smell. His nose twitched just thinking about the smell. "So you got Putnam to pay for the, uh, cleanup. I bet Mr. Farnum was glad of that. All that . . . dog, uh, matter, must have been an annoyance."

"Actually, Mr. Farnum didn't want the place cleaned up. He was an old-fashioned man, and he said that what was good enough for his daddy was good enough for him, so he wanted things to stay as they were. And that attitude is why I knew that nothing good could happen if Mr. Farnum stayed in his house every day, all day, as he usually did. Besides, he had quite a few shotguns, some of them dating back to . . . well, whenever shotguns were invented, and he knew how to use them. Nobody in town ever gave Mr. Farnum much trouble so—"

"I'm curious. What did this man do for a living?"

"Sold dogs. All the Farnums had an eye for dogs. Ones that they bred won all the shows. Not that the Farnums ever showed the dogs they bred. No, they were more on the . . . the breeding side. And when out-of-towners wanted to buy a dog, Mr. Farnum sent a litter of puppies to his sister's house in Lexington. I heard that she has a nice place, so no buyer ever saw where their sweet little puppy had come from."

"So you had to get Mr. Farnum away so he couldn't shoot anyone, right? Did you send him to his sister?"

"Heavens, no! Daryl Farnum didn't speak to his sister because she'd moved up north and married a Yankee."

"But I thought you said she lived in Lexington. Lexington, *Kentucky?*"

"*North* to Lexington," she said emphatically. "North. Yankees. Get it?"

"Oh," Adam said. "So how did you get Mr. Farnum away from his house so it could be cleaned?"

"I knew that Mr. Farnum liked to drink whiskey, so I thought that if I got him drunk enough, he'd get thrown in the Putnam jail for a couple of days and that would give the town time to clean up his place."

"But isn't that illegal? Isn't that trespassing?"

"Completely. But I worked on this so hard that the people involved didn't think of that. Besides, if a Putnam was in on it, what could someone in Putnam do about it?"

"I don't know why I didn't think of that. This place, Putnam, *is* in the United States of America, isn't it? Governed by both state and federal laws?"

"Only vaguely," Darci said, then glared at him in impatience to let her continue her story.

"So you got Mr. Farnum drunk."

"That took work because, you see, Putnam is dry, so at first I didn't know how to get whiskey to the man. I was sure that no liquor-store owner was going to drive up from Tennessee and present Mr. Farnum with a case of whatever, so I had to work on the local moonshiner."

"The local—" Adam began, then ostentatiously shut his mouth.

"I had to make Mr. Gilbey, the moonshiner, visit Mr. Farnum, which wasn't easy because Mr. Gilbey's great-great-great-grandfather had impregnated Mr. Farnum's great-great-aunt when she was thirteen, so there was a lot of hostility between the two families. And before you say anything, it wasn't the age that bothered anybody, it was that the girl was so pretty that she was engaged to marry a Putnam. Mr. Farnum's family was angry because they said that Mr. Gilbey's family had taken away their one and only chance to join with the Putnams, because, well, you see, as a general rule, the Farnums don't usually produce good-looking offspring."

Adam's eyebrows were raised so high that they were nearly hidden under his hair, and he had to stamp down the urge to say, "I see." "But you did manage to get these two feuding families together?"

"Yes. I knew that Mr. Gilbey liked dogs, so I concentrated real hard and told him he absolutely, positively *had* to have a Farnum dog. He couldn't live without a Farnum dog."

"Okay," Adam said, picking up his notebook and looking down at his few notes, "let me see if I can figure this out. You first tried to get Mr. Farnum to clean up his property, but when that failed, you made the mayor think that the Farnum place was a detriment to the beauty of Putnam, what with all the dog . . . waste and all. Then you made Mr. Putnam—oops, no *Mister,* just *Putnam*—When you're talking to a local, not an outsider like me, do you ever add a *junior* or *senior* onto the names so your listener will know which Putnam you're talking about?"

Darci shook her head. "No, everyone knows."

"Of course they would. So Putnam agreed to pay for the cleanup with a backhoe and—"

"It took a bulldozer. It was worse than anyone thought."

"Ah. Yes. A bulldozer. And this cleanup was done while Mr. Farnum was in jail for . . . what? Disorderly conduct?"

"Lewd behavior in front of the windows of Putnam Elementary School."

"I won't ask," Adam said. "So what happened after they bulldozed the place?"

"Mr. Farnum was let out of jail, and when he saw his house, clean and freshly painted, he was really angry. He said that his beloved home, the home of his ancestors, had been ruined."

"But he couldn't do anything legal because a Putnam was involved, right?"

"Right. So he burned the house down, then he went away. I don't know where. He had cousins in West Virginia, so maybe he went there. But the good thing was that he took his dogs with him, so, after that, we could hear the teachers. Although, a lot of the kids said that wasn't a good thing."

"But they weren't angry at *you* because they didn't know you were the one who had done it all, did they?"

"*Ooooooohhh,* no," Darci said, looking at him as though that was the most horrible thing she'd ever heard. "I was careful that no one knew what I could do. If anyone in town had known that I could. . . . Oh, my, no. I would have been besieged."

"True," Adam said, thinking about that. "But *no one* knew? Not even your mother?"

At that Darci gave a snort of laughter. "Jerlene was the last person in Putnam who I'd want to know that I could True Persuade people into doing things. If she'd known. . . . Well, let's just say that there were some young men in town who wouldn't have been safe."

All in all, Adam decided that he'd better not pursue that line of questioning. "So how old were you when you did this?"

"Eight."

Adam's jaw dropped down. "You were eight years old when you did this?"

Darci nodded.

It was after that revelation about her childhood that Adam decided he'd heard enough about Putnam for one day. Instead, he decided to see what Darci could do, so he began to set up tests for her. She'd said that she couldn't read minds, but he wanted to know for sure. After all, just that morning she'd found she had the ability to do something she hadn't known she could do. If he looked at symbols on cards and concentrated, could she "see" what he was sending her? It took three hours of testing with the cards and symbols before he believed her. As far as he could ascertain, she wasn't any better than the average person at reading thoughts.

Then, after much talking in order to persuade Darci to try it, Adam got her to try to move a couple of objects across the coffee table. She couldn't. Or, as Adam thought to himself, she didn't want to. Darci seemed to have definite ideas of what was "freaky" and what wasn't. Being able to move a pencil across a coffee table with her mind would have been, according to her, "too weird."

But research as he might, Adam couldn't bring himself to try any more experiments that called for her to tell him what to do or put thoughts into his mind.

At one point Darci wailed in frustration, "But you're just giving me things I *can't* do!"

Her words made Adam see that the truth was that he was a little frightened of what he'd seen her do this morning. And he was more than a little afraid of finding out the extent of her talent.

Because of her frustration at trying to do things that she couldn't, at five in the afternoon, Darci decided that she'd had enough and walked out of the guest house, saying she refused to allow Adam to try any more experiments on her. Not even for "chocolate chiffon pie with raspberries on top of it."

So now Adam was following her in silence and thinking. And he didn't like what was going through his mind. They—whoever "they" were—probably knew who or what Darci was. And after seeing and hearing about what Darci could do, Adam had no doubt that the young women who had been killed had been taken because they were believed to be Darci. Even the clerk in the store knew that the "correct" woman had moles on her left hand.

And Adam had brought her here. In his pursuit of knowledge about his own past, he had brought this young woman here and put her in mortal danger.

So what did he do now? Adam was sure that as Darci had said, if they left now, they would be pursued. Already, someone had been sent to. . . . To what? What had the gunman said? *"They can have you."* Obviously, someone wanted her.

Adam's head came up and he looked at Darci walking ahead of him. If someone knew enough about her to know that she had a power that Adam thought even Darci didn't know the extent of, then. . . . He drew in his breath. Then someone somewhere knew a great deal more than that about what Darci could do. They probably knew more than Darci did. And certainly much more than Adam did.

He took another deep breath to calm himself. So, okay, maybe if he had more time, say, a year or so, he might be able to find out exactly what she could do and how her power could be used. But they didn't have any time. It was close to the end of the year. It had been nearly a year since the last woman had "disappeared." By the laws of statistics, that meant they had only a few weeks, eight at the most, to figure out what Darci could do and how to use it. And in the meantime, she had to be protected every second.

And how could he, one man, do that? Truthfully, it was stupid of them to stay where they were right now. If he had any sense, he'd put Darci on the first plane and— What?

Send her back to Putnam? As she'd said, how long would she last there? How long before she was found by whoever had sent that gunman this morning?

In exasperation, Adam wiped his hands over his face. What did they want of her? How could he find out their intentions? How could he speed up this whole process? She could defeat them. He was sure of that. But *how?* What was her power? She couldn't freeze the whole coven in place. Holding just two men for minutes this morning had drained her so much that it had taken hours for her to recover. And all it had taken was a sneeze to break her hold.

But she did have the power to defeat them, or they wouldn't be so afraid of her. But what was that power?! he asked himself again. It was his fault that she was here now and in mortal danger, so it was his responsibility to protect her. And the only way she would be protected was if her—and his—enemies were defeated.

For a moment, Adam looked skyward and gave a little prayer asking for help, then he looked at Darci's back. She had a stick and was trailing it through the fallen leaves. Surely, there was someone somewhere who knew what Darci could do, he thought. Maybe she had a grandmother who'd had this talent. Or a cousin. She seemed to have many relatives in that town of hers.

In two long strides, he was walking beside her. "Are you the only one in your family, your extended family, that is—cousins, aunts, all of them—who has this power?"

Darci seemed surprised at the question. "I don't know. I know my mother's side of the family hasn't had a true thought in their lives, but I have no idea what my father's family is like."

"I want to ask you something, but I don't want to offend you," Adam said slowly.

"Go ahead. I have a thick skin," she said, but, still, she lifted her shoulders as if he were about to strike her.

"Is it possible that your mother had dealings with an . . . an underworld figure?"

Darci relaxed, and a smile twitched at the corners of her mouth. "Do you mean, is it possible that my mother went to bed with a warlock and conceived me?"

"Sounds kind of dumb when you say it out loud," he said. "But, yeah, I guess that's what I did mean. More or less."

"It would have depended on what he looked like. My mother likes her men young and beautiful. So if he was, then she probably did."

Frowning, Adam refrained from commenting about Darci's mother's morals. "If you've been able to keep your abilities a secret, maybe your father did, too. Maybe someone else has powers like you do. But you don't know who in Putnam that could be?"

"She doesn't confine herself to Putnam. Sometimes my mother travels all the way up to Louisville in search of a 'party,' as she calls it. My mother loves to party."

"Darci, what I'm thinking is that maybe you received this talent through your father's family, so maybe there's someone on that side of your family who knows something about what you can do. These people here are afraid of you. But why? What exactly can you do that can harm *all* of them? You can't read minds. You can freeze people, but it exhausts you and you can't hold it for very long. And we don't have time to do what you did about Mr. Farnum so. . . ." He shrugged in helplessness. "So I thought maybe a relative might know something. If it's not your mother's side, then maybe your father's side would know something. But we need to know who your father is. Do you think you could persuade your mother to *tell* you?"

Darci's eyes shifted to the side. "It wouldn't do any good to ask. She doesn't remember her . . . parties. And I don't think she'd like to remember that summer when I was conceived. She had her tubes tied after I was born because she said she didn't want to make *that* mistake again."

Adam glanced down at her quickly, but he saw no sign of self-pity in Darci. "Can you call her?" he persisted.

Darci punched her stick through a pile of dried leaves near a rock at the side of the path. "I don't see any use in that. Besides, she's rarely at home."

"She doesn't have a cell phone?"

"Yes, she does, but—" Breaking off, Darci looked up at him and saw he was staring at her intently. "Oh, no," she said, backing away from him. "This job did *not* include calling my mother."

Shocked, Adam blinked at her. This young woman had the power to paralyze men, but she was afraid of calling her *mother?!*

"The sooner you ask, the sooner we can find out."

Darci was still backing up. "My mother doesn't like to be bothered. She doesn't—" Halting, Darci took a deep breath, then put her hand to her ear as though she were holding a telephone. "What am I supposed to say to her? 'Mom, I've just been told that I have some weird, strange power. Yeah, right, I can cast spells on people. Yeah, just like on *Bewitched*. Isn't that a treat? Well, anyway, this guy here, my boss— Yeah, he's beautiful, but he's too old for you, Mom. So, anyway, my boss was wondering if maybe I inherited this ability from some relative of my father's, so he was wondering if maybe you could remember who you were with that summer and who could have fathered me. Okay, Mom, it was just a thought. Mom, you don't have to yell quite that loud and you don't have to use those words. They're not nice. No, Mom, I'm not back-talking you. No, Mom, I didn't mean any disrespect. And, no, Mom, I won't bother you again. Have a nice life.'"

Darci put down her pretend telephone and looked up at Adam.

It took Adam a few moments to recover from the vision she'd put into his head. "All right," he said slowly, "if we can't go through your mother, how do we find out who your father is? You told me that no one could keep secrets in Putnam, so who would know who your mother was with that summer?"

"Her sister, Thelma," Darci said immediately. "Aunt Thelma is quite jealous of my mother, and there's always been tremendous rivalry between them. I think Aunt Thelma could probably remember every man my mother has, uh, dated."

"Shall we go call her?" Adam asked softly. "You won't mind talking to your aunt, will you?"

"Not at all. And if Uncle Vern isn't at home to hear her, Aunt Thelma will enjoy ratting on my mother."

Try as he might, Adam couldn't smile at this statement. After what he'd heard so far of the people in Putnam, he'd like to go into the town with a flamethrower. "All right," he said, "Aunt Thelma it is. Shall we call from inside? We might need to take notes." He knew was being overly gentle with her, and he expected her to snap at him that she didn't want his pity. But he couldn't get the images of Darci's childhood from his head.

As they were walking side by side, Darci tripped over a stone, and instinctively, he reached out to steady her. When he looked down at her, it occurred to him that never in his life had he seen anyone prettier than she was. She had on a big pink fuzzy sweater that exactly matched the color in her cheeks. He couldn't stop himself from reaching up to touch her hair as it swept forward on her face.

"I'm sorry I got you into this," he said softly as he tucked a strand of hair behind her ear. "It's too much for you. And it's too dangerous." As he looked down at her, her lips were very appealing, and he couldn't seem to stop himself as he bent forward to kiss her.

As his face came within inches of hers, he really looked into her eyes. The irises were closed down so small that they were barely pinpricks. She was concentrating so hard that her eyes were closing off all light. And he damned well knew *what* she was concentrating on: him!

"Why, you little brat," he said under his breath, then he looked about for a way to break her concentration. If he was going to kiss her or anyone else, he was going to do it when *he* wanted and not when he was voodooed into it.

When his words didn't break her concentration, or take away his urge to kiss her, to sweep her into his arms and *give her the best kiss you've ever given anyone in your whole, entire life, ever!*—which were the words that were flooding loud and clear into his mind—he grabbed her and tossed her over his shoulder. The second her feet left the ground and her concentration was broken, the overwhelming, undeniable "need" to kiss her left him.

"Listen to me, you brat," he said as he began to twirl her about. "Don't you ever, *ever* again use that . . . that whatever it is that you have, against *me!* Do you hear me? Do I make myself clear?"

"I think I'm going to be sick," Darci said as Adam spun her about.

He turned around faster. "I want your promise."

"I'm going to throw up," she said. "And it's going to go all down your back!"

"Then you'll give me your promise after you empty your stomach," he said, not giving in. "I mean it, Darci T. Monroe. I want your most sacred, solemn vow that you will never again use that power of yours against *me.*" He stopped twirling. "Do I have that promise?"

He heard the sound of retching, but when he looked over his shoulder, nothing had come up.

Setting her down on the ground, he put his hands on her shoulders, and looked at her. "Do I get your promise?"

Darci bent over, putting her hands on her knees. "I hate going round and round," she said as she took deep breaths. "I was the only kid in Putnam who hated those rides at the local fair." Still bending, she tilted her head to look up at him.

But Adam's face showed that he had no sympathy for her. His eyes were ablaze with anger. "I want your promise. You do not use your power against *me.* Ever."

"But you need sleep," Darci said, her head still down.

"What?"

"Sleep. You don't sleep much, so I concentrate and help you relax."

Adam didn't know why such an answer made him furious, but it did. He could forgive her for making him want to kiss her; after all, that was flattering, wasn't it? And, also, maybe he had wanted to kiss her. But when he thought of her using her . . . her abilities to make him sleep. . . . The idea made him furious!

Darci didn't need clairvoyant power to see that she'd said the wrong thing. Instantly, she stood up. "Okay, I promise," she said quickly. "I swear it. My sacred word of honor. Okay?"

Adam was afraid of what he'd say if he opened his mouth. Instead, he jammed his hands into his pockets and went back toward the guest house with such long strides that Darci had to run to catch him.

"You're just angry because you don't want to admit that you want to kiss me. With all your heart and soul you want to kiss me. You want to take me in your arms and say, 'Darci, my darling, I've never met anyone like you, and I know that I never will. I've never talked to a woman as much as I have to you. I've never revealed as much of myself to a woman as I have to you. And I've—'"

But Adam didn't smile at her words. Instead, he paused at the door and looked down at her. "If this is going to work between us, I have to know that you aren't going to be working against me. I have to be able to trust you. I need your promise. No jokes. Your promise."

"Not even—" she began, but his look cut her off. "All right," she said at last. "You can wander around all night long and I won't help you. Now are you happy?"

"More than I was," he said, then opened the door for her to go in ahead of him.

"But you *did* want to kiss me, didn't you?" she said over her shoulder. "I didn't have to put much energy into making you *want* to kiss me."

Smiling in spite of himself, Adam followed her inside. "All right, you win. I've been dying to kiss you since I first saw you. Now call your aunt."

Darci leaned over the telephone on the side table and began to punch buttons. "I'm giving you my promise, but I want you to know that this is difficult for me. I'm in the habit of—"

"I'm not part of your 'habit,'" Adam said as he walked across the room to stand near her.

"Of course you aren't," Darci said, then looked down at the telephone. "Busy," she said, then hung up the receiver. Too bad she wouldn't be allowed to put things into his mind, she thought, because right now she'd like to tell him, *Darci is such a wonderful person that I want to buy her a steak dinner and three dozen yellow roses.*

"I don't know about 'wonderful,'" Adam said, "but steak I can handle. But after the little trick you just tried to pull, you don't deserve a clump of turnips, much less yellow. . . ." He trailed off when he saw Darci's face.

As though in a trance, she looked up at him.

At first Adam didn't understand her shocked expression, but then the reason dawned on him. "You didn't say that out loud, did you?"

She could only shake her head no.

"Say something else to me. Silently."

I wish you'd take me in your arms and—

"Not that," he said impatiently. "Something for me to *hear* and—" His eyes widened. "But I just did hear you, didn't I?" he said softly. "I heard what you said. Say something else. No, wait a minute. Let's go to the diner and get some food and bring it back here. We'll call your aunt again, then we'll get on the Internet and see what we can find out about any names your aunt gives us. If she has names for us, that is. There has to be someone out there who knows something about what you can do."

Can't do much with you, Darci thought with a grimace, then was annoyed to hear Adam laugh. Was he going to be able to read *her* mind? Hear her every thought? Was she never again going to be able to have a private thought? When she looked at Adam, she could see by his self-satisfied little smile that he was thinking this very thing.

Smiling at him, she tried to shut her mind to him, then thought, *Your hair is on fire.* When Adam didn't move but just kept smiling, she relaxed. No, he could hear her thoughts only when she wanted him to—or when she was too relaxed to keep her guard up.

As they left the guest house, Darci breathed a sigh of relief.

11

"So what was that?" Adam asked in disgust. "Number twelve? Or was it number two hundred and six?"

Darci looked at the list of names that her Aunt Thelma had given her and counted. "Fourteen."

"I still can't believe that your aunt remembered all these names."

"She keeps diaries," Darci said, looking at the screen of Adam's laptop computer, which was on her legs. He'd spent about fifteen minutes showing her how to use the Internet, and she'd taken over from there. Adam typed with two fingers and a thumb, but Darci's small fingers flew across the keyboard.

"I thought you had no skills," he said when he saw her type. "And that you didn't know anything about computers."

She knew he was still annoyed because she'd figured out

how to block him from reading her thoughts. She had an idea that he'd wanted to hear her thoughts so he'd know what she was up to every second of the day. "This Internet thing isn't exactly rocket science, is it?" she said. "It's like a big mailbox. You type in the address and voilà, up it comes."

"You're not dumb, are you?"

"Did you think I was?" she shot back at him.

Adam thought it was better that he didn't answer that question.

As soon as they'd returned to the guest house loaded with food, Darci had called her aunt Thelma and told her what she wanted. "I don't know if Jerlene would want me to tell you that," Thelma said, but even Adam, who didn't know the woman and was listening in on the extension, could hear the insincerity in her voice. Thelma was dying to tell all about her sister's liaisons.

When Darci didn't bother answering the rhetorical remark, Thelma said, "But then a girl should know who her parents are, shouldn't she? That's what I told Jerlene back then and that's what I'm sayin' to you now. I said that a girl should know who her parents are. And you know what your mother said when I told her that?"

"No, but I can guess," Darci said tiredly, obviously having heard the arguments between the two sisters for many years.

Thelma ignored her niece's tone of voice. "Jerlene said, 'Then you figure out which one her father is and *you* tell her.' Never let it be said that *I* would do anything without my sister's permission. So I kept all the names of the boys that I had written down that summer. They were all hangin' around your mother, and I had a premonition that something was gonna happen, and when it did, I had those names. Not that I've ever shown them to anyone, mind you, but I knew that someday *you* might ask. The truth is, Darci, honey, I tried my best to get your mother to say which one was your father, and I was gonna try to get him to pay for your support. You know what your mother's like, so you'll believe me when I tell you that some of those young men were drivin' Cadillacs. But you know how Jerlene is, she just laughed at me and said something quite nasty about what I could do with my list. So, now, Darci, it's up to you to figure out which one of them is your daddy. You got some paper and a pen with lots of ink in it?"

Darci then spent ten minutes on the phone with her aunt as she wrote the names of the men down. The second the list was complete, Thelma said, "I know she's your mother, Darci, honey, but you tell me what you think of a woman who'd—"

"Thank you so much, Aunt Thelma," Darci said. "This is just what I needed." Then she hung up.

So now it was nearly midnight, and both Adam and Darci were tired, but, still, they kept feeding names into a couple of search services on the Internet. But it was difficult to get information because they had nothing but the names of sixteen men. They had no numbers of any sort. They didn't have so much as a state where the men could have come from. It was a long, tedious, frustrating search as one search engine after another threw the names out for "insufficient data."

At one point, Adam said, "Your mother didn't . . . you

know . . . with *all* these men, did she? I mean, not in one summer."

"I doubt it. Aunt Thelma probably wrote down the name of every man my mother spoke to that summer, and she probably accused my mother of bedding them all. And my mother loves to antagonize her sister by agreeing that, yes, she did the dirty with each man."

In an attempt to find the men, they'd had to individually try every state and every possible spelling of the names. And it took a long time for the data banks to look through the records.

"How many more?" Adam asked.

"Just one," Darci answered, yawning, wanting to go to bed. Maybe Adam was a night owl, but she wasn't. She looked at the list that was beginning to blur before her tired eyes. "Taylor Rayburn," she said, then yawned again. "Taylor is my—"

"Go to bed if you want to," Adam said, taking the computer from her. "I can do this alone. Holy sh—" he began but cut himself off from cursing.

Darci had typed in the name, spelling it "Rayburn," but the request had been redirected to "Raeburne." There were 821 sites for "Taylor Raeburne."

"Couldn't be the same guy," Adam mumbled as he clicked on the first site. "What would a superachiever like this guy obviously is be doing in Putnam? Ow! That's my foot you're on."

"Is it?" Darci asked. "And what did you say about Putnam?"

"Man, boy, or town?" Adam asked, his eyes intent on the screen; then, suddenly, he drew back and turned the computer around for her to see. He had pulled up a beautiful Web site with "Taylor Raeburne" in big blue letters that moved across the screen. On the left was a list of choices that were contained within the Web site. "Taylor Raeburne, author of forty-two books on the occult," the screen read.

"You don't think. . . ." Darci began.

"That he's a warlock and into evil?" Adam finished for her.

"Are you reading my mind again?" she asked, trying to inject some humor into the situation.

"No. That was from my own mind." He scrolled down the list, looking for a bio on the author. When he saw the word *biography* at the bottom of the list, he put the cursor on it, then looked at Darci. "Ready?"

"Sure," she said. "Why not? As you said, what would a man like him be doing in Putnam? I'm sure that all he did was stop at the filling station and my aunt put his name on the list. I can assure you that my mother isn't one to like men who write books. She likes— Oh, my goodness," Darci said.

On the screen had come up a large photo of a man. And even to Darci, her resemblance to him was clear. It was her face, older and quite masculine, but it was, indeed, Darci's face.

She fell back against the couch, her eyes wide in shock, unable to speak. All she could do was stare at the picture on the screen.

"I think we found him," Adam said, and there was elation in his voice. "You're a dead ringer for him. You know that old saying that the first child always looks like the father. In this case—" When he looked at Darci, he stopped talking. "Are you all right?"

She didn't answer but just kept staring at the photo on the screen, so Adam clicked on exit, shut down the system, and closed the computer. "I think this is enough for one night," he said, but when Darci still didn't react, he did what instinct told him to: He pulled her into his arms and held her, her face buried against his shoulder.

"A shock, huh?" he asked softly.

She nodded against him.

"You've had a lifetime with one really bad parent, and—" She started to lift her head at that, but he held her down until she calmed. "Yes, one really bad, absent parent, and now you find that, all along, you've had a second parent."

Pulling back, he turned her head so she could look at him, putting his fingertips under her chin. "You're not going to chicken out on me now, are you?" he asked. "We're going to contact him, aren't we?"

"He might not like me," Darci said in a tiny voice.

At that Adam smiled. "Not like you?!" he said. "How could he not like *you?* You're smart, something you obviously inherited from him; you have such a great sense of humor that you can make even an old stick-in-the-mud like me laugh, and you're frugal to the point of. . . . Well, anyway, you make people like you. You make friends with everyone everywhere and— Stop looking at me like that!" he said, then dropped his hand from her face and got up off the couch. "I told you that you were not allowed to use your power against me. No kissing thoughts!"

"I wasn't using any power!" Darci said. "I was merely wishing very, very hard, that's all. And why not? I thought you *liked* me. You were saying wonderful things about me."

For a moment Adam turned away from her, then he looked back at her, and when he spoke, his voice was calm. "You're lovely. I didn't think so at first, but— Please stop looking at me like that. I'm trying to be honest. You *are* a wonderful person. I've never before met anyone like you. I've bummed around the world, and never have I met anyone with your . . . your enthusiasm for life. The truth is that I like you more than . . . well, more than I should." Suddenly, he stopped talking. "Actually, I think we'd better talk about this another time."

"Are you blushing again?" Darci asked, eyes wide.

"No, of course not. Men don't blush. Let's go to bed," he said, annoyed.

"*Oooooohhh,* yes," Darci purred.

Adam laughed. "Get up and go put your pajamas on. And put on those big ones, not that little black thing you bought, but the big ones, got it? And behave yourself!"

Smiling, Darci got off the couch and went into the bedroom. The bedroom they shared, she thought. As she was in the bathroom getting ready for bed, she decided that it was better to keep her mind on Adam than on the news that she'd just found her father. A father was not something that Darci could comprehend. In school in Putnam the other kids had often taunted her by saying that any man in Kentucky could be her father. Darci had held her head high and True Persuaded the kids to go away. Now, as she snuggled down into the bed next to Adam's, she remembered that one time she'd done such a great job of True Persuading a boy into being quiet that he'd not been able to speak for three whole days. When he could speak again, he told everyone that Darci had done it to him. But, thankfully, no one believed him. People couldn't do things like that, could they? they'd said. But still, ever after that, people in Putnam seemed to sense that Darci was "different." They didn't know how she was different, but they knew she was.

And it was this difference that had made Putnam want her.

In spite of all the turmoil in her mind, Darci was asleep almost before she closed her eyes.

When Darci awoke at five A.M. the next morning, there was a light coming in through the half-open bedroom door. Was Adam already awake? she wondered. Turning, she looked at his bed and saw that it had never been slept in.

Rolling out of bed, she went into the living room, rubbing the sleep out of her eyes. The curtains were still drawn, and Adam was still bent over his laptop computer, studying the screen.

"Did you know that it's morning?" she asked, yawning as she sat down beside him.

Adam didn't answer, but nodded toward a pile of papers on the coffee table. There was now a small printer on the coffee table, and it was attached to Adam's laptop by a heavy cable.

"Where'd you get that?" she asked.

"Borrowed from 3B," he said without looking up. "Read the papers."

Yawning again, Darci picked them up.

At first she didn't know what she was looking at, as there were just lists of names and addresses. At the top of the first page was the name Taylor Raeburne, and at the bottom was the name of a company with the word *spy* in it. The title page was followed by sheets and sheets of information about people.

It was when she realized what she was seeing that she sat upright and began to read with interest. Adam had done a search on Taylor Raeburne, using the data from the Web site, and Darci was shocked to see how much information had been obtained. Mr. Raeburne's places of residence for the last twenty years were on the papers. His neighbors were listed, giving their addresses, their telephone numbers, and their occupations. There were three pages of people who "might possibly be related to or involved with Taylor Raeburne."

After the pages of addresses, her mouth dropped open further to see pages about the financial status of Taylor Raeburne.

Appalled, Darci put the papers back on the coffee table, leaving the last several pages unread. "That is an invasion of privacy," she said.

"There is no longer any privacy in the U.S.," Adam said, still not looking up from the screen. "All I had to do was give them my credit card number, wait six hours, and all that was e-mailed to me."

"I don't like that," Darci said tightly. "A person's business should be his own."

"You didn't seem to mind looking into *my* private affairs," Adam said. "So do you want to know about your father or not?"

"My . . ?" Darci said, not yet awake enough to have thought of this new idea.

"Yes, your—" Adam broke off because he had finally

turned to look at her. "I told you not to wear that black thing. I told you—"

She had on a very pretty black silk nightgown that she'd bought when she purchased the other clothes. It was a perfectly respectable nightgown and tiny robe, merely a spaghetti-strapped sliplike garment with a sheer lace jacket that covered her arms. It wasn't short or too revealing or—

Raising his arm, Adam pointed toward the doorway. "Go. Get clothes on. Do something with your hair. Go get me some food. Do it *now!*"

Smiling and very pleased with herself, Darci obeyed him. Forty-five minutes later, she'd been to the grocery and back—Adam beside her every minute, never ceasing to read his printouts—and had arranged a beautiful breakfast on the bar countertop in the kitchen. She prepared a plate of fruit, warm croissants, and coffee, and handed it to him; then she sat on the floor on the other side of the coffee table with her plate of food.

Now that Darci was decent, he was in a better humor. "So what do you want to know first?" he asked.

"Anything, everything," she answered, her mouth full.

"He writes books on psychic research, but he's not a flake. I mean, he doesn't write popular books about haunted places where the waitress saw gray smoke in a corner of a room and she was sure it was a ghost, that kind of thing. No, this man has three Ph.D.s, one of them in philosophy, and he's well respected in the academic world. What I can't figure out is what he was doing in Putnam, Kentucky, and why was he . . . ?" With a quick look at Darci, he trailed off.

"Having a tumble with my mother?" she asked.

"I wouldn't put it that way, but, well. . . ."

Darci held up her hand for a moment while she finished chewing; then she got up, went to her handbag, opened her wallet, pulled out a photo, and handed it to Adam.

Curious, Adam took the photo and looked at it. It was a picture of an incredibly beautiful woman in a white swimsuit, her long, honey-blonde hair caressing her perfect shoulders. Truthfully, she wasn't just beautiful but drop-dead gorgeous. She was tall and slim but curvy, with legs that seemed to go on for miles. As for her face, she was a cross between Grace Kelly and Angelina Jolie. She had a look of raw sex, but also the look of a pure and innocent wife left behind by a World War II soldier.

Adam was sure he—or the rest of the world—had never seen anything like her.

Adam gave a low whistle, then looked up at Darci. "Your mother?"

"That's Mom."

"How old is this photo?"

"About three weeks."

"Your *mother* looks like this *now?*"

"You're too old for her," Darci said instantly, and without a trace of humor in her voice.

Adam ran his hand through his hair. "Maybe I could cover the gray, lose a couple of pounds, and. . . ." He'd meant to make Darci laugh, but she was looking at him without humor.

"I'm sure you could try. Since she now considers herself old and ugly compared to what she looked like when she had me, you might have a chance."

Adam looked back at the photo. "Old and ugly, huh? So

now I see why a man like your father was attracted to her. I wonder how they met?"

"At the filling station, probably," Darci said.

"Your mother hung out at a filling station when she was, what, nineteen or twenty?" He was incredulous. This woman should have been immortalized on the screen. In photographs. In—

"She was seventeen when she had me, sixteen when she got pregnant," Darci said flatly. "She worked after school and on weekends in her father's filling station, which was at the junction of the off ramp to the interstate that runs past Putnam."

"Pumping gas?" he said, still unable to believe it.

"Yes. She wore pink overalls that Aunt Thelma said were so tight you could see the outline of her belly button. And Aunt Thelma said Mom used to wet the suit down twice a day so it would cling to her even more."

Once again, Adam had his eyebrows high under his hair. "To meet men? I guess that's what she wanted."

"What my mother wanted was to get out of Putnam," Darci said fiercely. "She said that the only way she was going to meet a man who didn't live in Putnam was to go where they were, which, to her, meant the cars that were traveling along the highway."

Adam shook his head, not understanding. "Why didn't she just get a job in another town and move?"

Darci shrugged. "It wasn't what was done, I guess. Her mother had told her that the most important thing in life was getting a husband, so that's what my mother was trying to do. But she got me instead, and she's never married anyone."

"I see," Adam said, then regretted it. But he spoke before Darci could again tell him that he sounded like Abraham Lincoln. Judging from the look on Darci's face and from the way her hands were now clenched into fists, he thought maybe it was better to stop talking about Jerlene Monroe. "I have your father's telephone number. Shall we call him? He teaches at a university in Virginia, and he may have classes all day, so now, in the early morning, might be a good time to catch him."

"Maybe we should wait until later," Darci said quickly.

But Adam was already reaching for the telephone, and when the call connected and the other phone started ringing, he pushed the speaker button so Darci could hear what was said.

"Yes?" said a gruff voice that obviously didn't want to be bothered.

"Are you Taylor Raeburne?" Adam asked and was surprised to hear the nervousness in his voice. It dawned on him that no matter what he found out about his own parents, he wanted to help Darci find her father.

"Is that whom you were calling?" the man shot back. "Look, I don't have time for this question-and-answer routine. I'm supposed to be in class in ten minutes. If this is about—"

"It's about Jerlene Monroe and Putnam, Kentucky, and the summer of. . . ." He looked at Darci in question.

"Nineteen seventy-eight," she said.

"And 1978," Adam said into the phone.

"I have no idea what you're talking about. I've never heard of Putnam, Kentucky, or Jenny Monroe. I have to go. You can phone my office and talk to my secretary. She—"

"Jerlene Monroe worked in a gas station off a highway that runs past Putnam. She used to wear a pink jumpsuit that her sister said was so tight that you could see her belly button. She has blonde hair, natural. . . ." He looked at Darci for verification, and she nodded. "A natural blonde. I don't think you'd forget this woman even though it may be over twenty-three years since you've seen her."

There was silence on the end of the line for so long that Adam thought the man might have hung up. "Are you there?"

"Yes, I'm here," he said softly, this time in no rush. "And, yes, I did once meet such a woman. But then every young man does things that—"

"I think that a daughter might have been produced from that union," Adam said quickly, then saw Darci draw in her breath and hold it.

"If this is an attempt to extort money from me I—" Taylor Raeburne began.

"She has seven little black moles on the palm of her left hand, and—"

"Where are you?" the man asked quickly.

"Camwell, Connecticut."

Taylor gasped. "Good lord, do you know that that town is full of—"

"Witches?" Adam asked. "I most certainly do. The problem is that these people seem to want your daughter for something, but we don't know what—not all of it, anyway. They've already killed four young women who resemble her and removed their left hands. I'm worried that your daughter is targeted to be next. I want her to leave this place, but now that they know who she is, I'm afraid that there might not be any place on earth where she can hide."

Again, there was a long silence.

If Darci and Taylor Raeburne hadn't looked so much alike that he was sure they were related, Adam wouldn't have dared say what he did next. "Yesterday, a man pulled a gun on us, and Darci, your daughter, used her mind to stop the man—and me—where we were standing. Both of us were paralyzed. Until she sneezed and broke the connection, that is."

There was no hesitation before Raeburne spoke. "I'll be there as soon as I can get there."

"We're staying at—" Adam didn't finish the sentence because the phone went dead.

Putting down the phone, Adam looked at Darci, and from the expression on her face, he didn't know if she was going to laugh or start crying.

You really think he'll like me? Darci said to him in her mind.

"Yes," Adam answered. "I really do. Look, why don't we drive down the highway today and do a little sight-seeing? Unless your father can get here on a broomstick, we have hours before he arrives."

Darci didn't so much as smile at Adam's attempt at humor. Instead, she looked at him hard. "If you want us to leave here today, then you have a reason. What are you *really* after?"

"To get us both away from here for a few hours. To get our minds off this whole thing." Darci was staring at him so hard that he knew she didn't believe a word he said. Adam threw up his hands in surrender. "Okay, so sue me. I want to get you away from here. I can't imagine why. Unless it's because someone wants to kill you. Or maybe they want to kidnap you and use you because you can do astonishing things with your mind. You have an unbelievable power, but you seem to have no idea how dangerous it could be in the wrong hands. You— Oh, the hell with it!" he said. "Get your coat. And don't you dare tell me not to curse. If we live through this, I may take up cursing as a hobby."

Darci didn't hesitate but ran to the closet and got her jacket. Ten minutes later they were in the rental car and on the highway.

12

—

"So where do you want to go?" Darci asked when they were alone in the car. "What's to see around here?"

"I don't know," Adam answered. "I just want a break from computers and research books. It's been too much of . . . well, too much of everything."

"You mean, you've had too much of me, don't you? Me and my relatives, Putnam relatives, and now my father." She said the last word at a lower pitch. She still couldn't comprehend the idea that she was soon going to meet her *father.*

Adam's laugh brought her back to the present. "I haven't been so entertained in all my life. If someone made up that town of yours, no one would believe it. Why don't you quit worrying about meeting your father and look at the scenery? It's beautiful in New England in the autumn."

Instead of looking out the window, Darci opened the

glove compartment and looked inside. "What makes you think that I'm concerned about meeting my father?"

"How many nails have you torn off in the last hour?"

Darci curled up her fingertips out of sight. "I always tear at my fingernails. Nervous habit. It doesn't mean—"

"Ha! You file your nails every night. They're always perfectly shaped into little pink ovals with not a ragged edge on them. And they're—" He broke off because Darci was staring at him in speculation. "What is that!" he snapped when she pulled something out of the glove compartment.

"It's a map of Connecticut," Darci said, smiling as she opened it. "You like my fingernails, do you?"

"Why are you looking at a map?" Adam asked, frowning. "I know this area. You do *not* need to look at a map."

"What is wrong with my looking at a map?" she asked, starting to look up at him, but something on the map caught her eye.

"What's wrong?" Adam asked quickly.

"Nothing's wrong," she answered quietly, her eyes fastened to the map.

"How about if we go to Bradley?" he said loudly. "It's a pretty little town, and I believe there are some nice antique shops there. Do you like antiques?"

"I like *you*, don't I?" Darci said distractedly, still studying the map, her fingers tracing the distance from Bradley to another town.

"Very funny," Adam said. "What is it that you're so enthralled with on that map?"

"Nothing," she answered quickly, then folded the map and put it back into the glove compartment. "Bradley's fine with me. In fact, since it's straight ahead, I could almost believe that's where you planned to go."

"Caught," Adam said easily. "I've been there before, so I know it's pretty. It'll be good for us to have a whole day with nothing whatever to do with witches, and. . . ."

Darci didn't hear the rest of what he was saying because she was looking at his profile and concentrating. All she needed to do was to get rid of him for a few hours. If she could make him want to go off by himself for a while. . . .

"Stop it!" Adam said without taking his eyes off the road. "I didn't notice it at first, but when you do that, I get a tiny pain under my left shoulder blade. It's not really a pain, just a feeling, but it's enough that I know when you're . . . when you're trying to manipulate and control me," he said, giving her a glance that told her what he thought of her action. Then, giving her a fierce glance, he said, "Your 'sacred word of honor' doesn't mean much to you, does it?"

Darci smiled, unperturbed at his attempt to make her feel guilty. "I didn't *do* anything. But it seems that when I think about things really hard, you feel it. Maybe *you* are psychic. Anyway, that tiny pain you feel, I can make it a lot worse. I can even give you a headache. Wanta see?"

"You do and I'll make you sorry," he said instantly.

Turning away to look out the window, Darci hid her smile from him. It was odd, it was awful, and it was wonderful, all at the same time, to have someone know what she could do. But it was nothing but . . . delicious to have someone know and not think she was a freak—the thing she'd always feared and why she'd never told anyone about what she could do. She knew that the people in her hometown considered her "different" even though they hadn't an inkling of the depth of the truth. Over the years Darci had almost convinced herself that what she could do, anyone could. But now it was out in the open and this man who knew about her was acting as though her "power" was something almost normal.

Within minutes, they were in Bradley, and Darci could see that it was indeed a pretty little New England town, especially since it was all dressed up in autumn leaves of fabulous colors. There were several quaint little shops that she would have loved to visit, but she knew she couldn't. After she'd looked at the map and seen a name that jumped out at her, she'd known that there was something else she had to do today.

Adam parked the car on the street, and they got out.

"I have to go to the ladies' room," Darci said abruptly, then, before he could say a word, she ran across the street to a gas station.

Annoyed, because she had again ignored traffic, Adam remained on the opposite side of the street and waited for her. Looking at his watch, he saw that time was moving quickly, and he knew he needed as much time as he could get to do what he had to today. But now he was wasting precious minutes while he waited for Darci to—

Good heavens! he thought as he looked across the street. What was she doing now? She was standing by the pumps talking to a young man who was putting gas in a customer's Volvo. Did she have to talk to every person she met? he thought, annoyed. Couldn't she—?

No, wait, he thought, this was good. He looked at the boy she was talking to. He looked to be in his twenties and was passably good-looking. Could Adam make Darci believe that he was jealous of such a child? No, she'd never fall for it, he thought. She'd never in a million years believe that he, Adam Montgomery, would be jealous of that scrawny, bad-complexioned boy.

But as Adam again looked at his watch, he knew that he didn't have time to come up with another reason to start an argument. When he saw Darci turn away from the boy, Adam drew a deep breath. He hoped he didn't hurt her feelings too much when he started an argument with her. But he had to get time alone and he knew from experience that he couldn't just ask Darci for that time. No, he'd have to start a fight between them, then storm off so they would separate for the day. The good thing was that they were many miles from Camwell, so he didn't think there'd be much danger if she was unprotected for a few hours.

"Who was he?" Adam demanded as soon as Darci returned.

"Someone I met," she said. "What do you want to see first? There are a couple of antique shops over there."

"Why were you talking to him so long?"

Darci looked up at him, her face full of fury. "You know something? I'm sick of your jealousy, just plain *sick* of it! I can't talk to anyone. You won't even let me eat in the dining room at the inn because you don't want me to see the other people."

"I do no such thing," Adam said, surprised. "You can eat anywhere you want. I thought you liked the diner and that you liked our . . . our picnics in the guest house."

"But you never asked me what *I* want, did you? For your information, I'd much rather eat in the dining room. At least there *I* can give orders. When I eat alone with you, I just get ordered about. 'Get me food,' you say. Is it because you think you're superior to me because I come from the South? Is this a racist thing?"

"Racist?" Adam asked. "What are you talking about? You and I are the *same* race! And you can eat wherever you want! I had no idea that eating alone with me offended you." He was holding his back so rigidly that his muscles were beginning to ache.

"I can assure you that I'd much rather eat with people who don't order me about. In fact, I'd have more fun anywhere than with an old, humorless, puritanical, stick-in-the-mud like you," she said. "I could have more fun at a convention of dead monkeys than I do with you."

"With— At a—" he said in a voice that was little more than a whisper. "All right then, might I suggest that we separate? In fact, I suggest that when we return to Camwell, we separate permanently, but for today, I'd like to see Bradley. Alone. Actually, I want to buy someone a gift." They were standing in front of a jewelry store. "Maybe diamonds," he said. "For a female."

Darci didn't say anything, just glared up at him in anger.

And Adam couldn't believe that the words of this snippet of a girl could hurt so much. It wasn't that he hadn't been called a downer before—it was the favorite appellation from his cousins—but he hadn't thought that Darci believed him to be a. . . . He didn't want to think of what she'd just said about him.

"All right," Adam said through clenched teeth, "you're free of my company for the day. I'll meet you back here at this spot at five o'clock. Do you think that will give you enough time to have 'fun'?" He said the last word as though it were something vile.

"Yes," Darci answered. "Plenty of time."

He would have thought, after what she'd said to him, that she'd run to get away from him, but instead, she just stood there looking up at him. Maybe he shouldn't move either, he thought. Maybe he should give her time to apologize.

"Check your watch," he said, "and make sure it has the right time."

"I can figure out what time it is," she said, hostility in her voice, as though what he'd just said was a further slur on her character.

"All right then. I'll see you here later."

But neither of them moved; they just stood there staring at each other. After all, for days now, they hadn't been apart for even minutes, and Adam was thinking that he was going to, well, maybe miss her company. But no, he told himself. He was responsible for her. She *needed* him.

"Do you have money?" Adam asked tightly. "Cash? Because I know that you'd starve rather than spend any of your own money, and I can't have anyone say that I don't feed my employees."

Darci didn't answer but just looked at him.

Taking out his wallet, Adam handed her a ten. When Darci didn't take the money, he removed a fifty. Darci took both bills, then turned on her heel and walked away quickly. As Adam watched her leave, he had an impulse to run after her. Would she be all right? Who was going to take care of her if he wasn't with her every minute? Who was going to make him laugh?

But then he remembered what she'd said to him, that she wanted to get away from him and his "puritanical" ways. He'd like to show her "puritanical"! he thought. If he weren't under constraints right now, vital constraints that included no touching of Darci, he'd show her—

But Adam didn't have time to waste in thinking about what he'd like to do to Darci. If he was going to do what he set out to, then he had to hurry in order to get back to Bradley by five. But when he looked at his watch again, he knew that the reason Darci hadn't checked hers was that she didn't have one. When he turned, the glittering jewelry store window was right in front of him. As he opened the store's door, he didn't think about what he was doing or why, but fifteen minutes later Adam emerged with a small box containing a gold Piaget watch. Then, feeling quite self-righteous that he'd bought her such a lovely gift even after what she'd said to him, he walked back to the car, all the while looking for Darci and making sure that she didn't see him leave the little town of Bradley.

"I can't thank you enough," Darci said through the car window to the young man sitting in the driver's seat.

"Sure you can," he said, his voice oozing with suggestion. "I can think of lots of ways that you can repay me. We could—"

With a smile, Darci stepped back onto the sidewalk. "Thanks again," she said in a voice that had finality in it. "You better go now or your boss will be worried."

"Nah," he said. "My uncle owns the station, and— Hey! Maybe you're right. Maybe I *should* get back."

As he pulled away from the curb in his noisy car that

was covered in rust and paint primer, Darci breathed a sigh of relief and rubbed her temples. She'd had to True Persuade him so hard that her head was hurting. But then, she thought, it also might be hunger, as it had been hours since she'd eaten.

Reaching into the pocket of her skirt, she pulled out a little piece of paper and looked at the address she'd written on it. "Susan Fairmont, 114 Ethan Way," she read, then the telephone number. But Darci didn't want to call the woman for fear that she'd say no to Darci's request.

She walked two blocks, then took a left. The young man had said that Ethan Way was just down the street. He'd wanted to drive her to the address, but Darci had taken one look at the shady, tree-lined street and had politely said, no, thank you, she could walk. She'd had quite enough of his hands that had "accidently" strayed from the gearshift to her knee.

What time was it? she wondered, glancing up at the sun as though that would help. She had to be back in Bradley by five and heaven only knew *how* she was going to get there. Her plan—if anything concocted that fast could be called a "plan"—had been to pay the young man twenty-five dollars for a round-trip fare. He'd wanted fifteen to drive her one way to Appleby, but she'd thought that once they were in the car, she'd be able to True Persuade him into taking twenty-five for returning for her. But his hands and his confirmed belief that it wasn't a ride she wanted but him had made it impossible for her to concentrate enough to True Persuade him into anything.

So now she was in Appleby, but she had no way to get back to Bradley. But then, maybe she could use this as an excuse to knock on Susan Fairmont's door. "Instead of using a pay phone," Darci muttered. "Oh, yeah, that's a great idea. I'm sure she'll allow a stranger into her house."

At the corner she saw the street sign of Ethan Way. Turning, she looked at the house numbers. One thirty-two was the first house. Looking down at the paper in her hand again, she checked the number of the house she wanted.

It was because her head was down and her attention on other things that she didn't see the man step out from behind a six-foot-tall hedge until she'd run smack into him.

"Excuse me," she said, then looked up to see Adam Montgomery.

And Darci knew that she was in for it.

"You planned this," he said under his breath. "Why, you scheming, conniving little—"

"Me?" she said in the same quiet but urgent tone. It was a warm day and some of the houses had their windows open. "You're here, too, so that means that you're after the same thing that I am! And you—" She looked at him in speculation. "You planned this *last night,* didn't you? That's what you did when you stayed up all night." Her voice changed to falsetto. "You just wanted to 'get away from here for a few hours,' didn't you? Isn't that what you said? You wanted to 'get our minds off this whole thing.' But here you are—"

"You said that being with a bunch of dead monkeys was more fun than being with me," he said stiffly.

"And you believed that?!"

Adam opened his mouth to reply, closed it, then opened it again. "Of course not, but it . . . it wasn't a nice thing to be told."

Darci blinked at him. "Nice? These people are murdering women and—"

With his hand firmly on her upper arm, Adam pulled her a few feet down the street, away from the corner. "All right, you've played your little game so you can go sit in the car and wait for me."

"Now, that's a good idea. I think I'll do just that," she said sweetly.

Adam dropped her arm, counted to ten, then took a deep breath. "All right, what's your plan?"

"I didn't have time to come up with one. Unlike you, I don't stay awake all night planning devious, underhanded things to do to someone I'm supposed to be working *with*. And, besides, that kid in the car had so many hands that I couldn't think, and before that, you were so awful that I couldn't think then either."

"*I* was awful?" Adam asked, looking at her in disbelief. "Don't tell me that you got into a car alone with that grease jockey and—"

"You *are* jealous!" she said, wide-eyed.

"I am not—" Adam began, then stopped. They were standing in the shade in a nice residential neighborhood, and behind them was a low concrete wall, tall hedges above it. Backing up, Adam sat down on the wall. "All right, you're here, so at least I'll be able to see that you don't get into trouble. So maybe we should work together and—"

"Excuse me?" Darci said, not yet willing to forgive him for being so sneaky. It was one thing to do something on the spur of the moment, but to make a plan, then deliberately lie. . . . Well, it was the difference between manslaughter and murder one. "What was that word you just said?"

she asked, putting her hand to her ear. "I didn't catch it. It starts with a *t. Together?* You and me?"

"Very funny," Adam said. "You want to help me, or you want to make jokes?"

"I'll have to get back to you on that."

Adam narrowed his eyes at her.

"All right," she said, giving a sigh. "What do you propose we do? What were you planning to do *alone?*" She couldn't resist one last jab.

"I thought I'd wing it, but now that I'm here, I have no idea how to go about this. Unless. . . ."

"Yes?"

"You're the same age, more or less, as the girl who died, so maybe you could tell her sister that you were a friend of the dead girl's. You could act as though you hadn't heard that she was dead, then you could ask questions. Think you can act that well?"

"I had *you* going this morning, didn't I?" Darci asked, smiling. "You believed every word I said, didn't you?"

"Of course not," Adam said, but he was looking over her head and not meeting her eyes. "I just. . . ." When he looked back at her, she was smiling smugly. "You keep up with that attitude and I'll call your little octopus boyfriend and tell him to come and pick you up."

For a moment, Darci paled. "You're kidding, aren't you?"

"You *believed* me?" he asked in the same tone that she'd used when she'd asked if he'd believed her about his being boring.

"Okay," Darci said, "that's one for you. So what do we do? I'm to pretend to be the girl's friend. And you? Who are you? My father?"

"Keep this up and I won't give you the present I bought you."

At that Darci closed her mouth and kept it shut.

Smiling, Adam outlined the plan he'd come up with in the last few minutes. Actually, now that he thought of it, it was much better that Darci was here, as he thought that the sister of the dead girl would more likely talk to Darci than to him.

"You ready?" he asked when he'd finished outlining the plan.

Darci nodded, and they started walking toward the corner to turn down Ethan Way. "Did you really get me a present?" she asked softly.

For a moment Adam was embarrassed. Why had he purchased her a gift? At the time he'd bought it, he thought it might be a parting gift. He'd been thinking that Darci was going to walk out of his life forever—not that he would have allowed her to do that. There was too much danger for her to be unprotected. But he'd thought she *wanted* to get away from him.

"Actually, I got it for me," he said gruffly. "Out of self-defense. There may be occasions when I have to arrange to meet you at a specific time, so you have to know what time it is."

"You bought me a watch?" she asked softly, looking up at him.

Shrugging, as though it were no big deal, Adam pulled the little box out of his jacket pocket and handed it to her. They kept walking, with Adam watching Darci out of the corner of his eye.

When she opened the box and saw the beautiful gold

watch inside, she halted. Standing there, she looked down at the watch in its case and didn't move. She didn't walk, but she also didn't seem to continue breathing. If she'd been frozen, she couldn't have been more still.

"Like it?" Adam asked, smiling, as he stopped to look down at her. When she didn't answer, he said, "Darci?" his voice full of amusement. Still, she didn't answer but just stood there staring at the watch. "Darci, are you all right?" he asked, this time with concern in his voice. Then he saw that the color was draining out of her face. He'd once told her that people turn white before fainting, and that's what Darci was doing now. As he watched, her knees seemed to give way; she was sinking to the ground!

In one swift gesture, Adam picked her up before she hit the ground. His arms went under her legs and back; then, as he was holding her, he looked in disbelief as her head lolled to one side in a faint.

But she was still clutching the box that held the watch in a grip of death.

"Is she all right?" came a woman's voice, and Adam turned to see a woman of about his age standing there— and, instantly, Adam knew who she was. The photos of the girls who'd been reported missing in Camwell were burned into his mind, and this woman was an older version of one of the missing girls.

"You're Susan Fairmont, aren't you?" Adam asked quietly. "You're Laurie's sister." He nodded down to Darci, lying limp in his arms. "She and your sister were friends, and she just found out about Laurie's death."

The woman seemed to consider this for a moment, and Adam could see that she was considering what to do—and a wave of guilt swept over him. How many sensation-seekers had tried to get close to her, to ask her questions about her dead sister?

"Come inside," the woman said at last; then she led the way up the path into her house.

"The police said it wasn't murder. They said that Laurie may have committed suicide," Susan Fairmont said with bitterness in her voice, and her soft accent showed her southern origins. "Or maybe she fell asleep at the wheel of her car and that's why it slammed into that tree."

It was twenty minutes later, and they were inside Susan's house, and surrounded by her Early American antiques. Darci and Adam were sitting on a sofa that could have been used in Williamsburg. In a wing chair across from them sat Susan, a cup and saucer in her hand. She had made them tea, serving it in a pretty floral pot. Darci was still white and still seemed a bit shaky on her feet, so Adam was sitting close to her in case she decided to pass out again. She was holding her cup of tea with one hand, but he knew that her left hand, tucked under her skirt, was still tightly clutching the box containing the watch he'd given her.

"You look a bit like Laurie," Susan had said to Darci as soon as they were seated, and when all Darci did was nod, Susan had seemed satisfied with that—which furthered Adam's feeling of guilt. They had lied to this nice, trusting woman.

"It was horrible," Susan said, putting down her tea. "Laurie disappeared while photographing an old church in that odious town of Camwell, and, right away, the world assumed that it was witchcraft."

"You don't think it was?" Adam asked.

For several long moments, Susan sat there and looked at them in silence. She seemed to be considering something. "I don't say what I think because, you see," she said so softly they could barely hear her, "I've been warned. I've been warned to keep my mouth shut."

"Who told you to do that?" Darci snapped, indignity in her voice, and at last coming alive.

"The police and a man from the FBI."

"FBI?" Darci asked. "What did they have to do with this? Especially if the local police said they believed it was a suicide?" There was such a sneer in Darci's voice that Adam looked at her in speculation. Was it real, or was she acting?

"I think the FBI's been investigating the witches in Camwell for years, and—"

"Then why haven't they done anything about them?" Darci asked quickly. "How many more people have to die before they actually *stop* them? Did you know that they have underground tunnels where they meet? *Huge* tunnels."

Adam wanted to put his hand over Darci's mouth.

"Yes, of course I know," Susan said. "Anyone who lives this close to Camwell knows that. It's a big organization, and they recruit people to join them. The prospect of great power is a strong enticement."

"So why doesn't the FBI—"

It was Susan's turn to interrupt. "Why don't they go in there with bulldozers and level those tunnels and stop all this?"

"You can destroy the hive, but if you don't get the queen, they'll just rebuild," Adam said softly.

"Are *you* an FBI agent?" Susan shot at him.

"He just thinks like one," Darci said. "So what were you told not to say?"

Once again, Adam was astonished at Darci's audacity. But this time he wasn't shocked when Susan answered. He'd already seen that Darci had a way of getting close to people.

"I was told that my theories were my own personal opinions and that if I spread them around, it could cause a lot of problems. One of the sheriff's deputies from Camwell asked me if my taxes were in order. The hint was that he'd see that I was audited."

"Yeow!" Adam said. "Blackmail of the lowest kind. What American isn't afraid of the IRS?"

"Exactly," Susan said. "So I've kept my mouth shut for the whole two years since Laurie disappeared. And I've kept it shut since my sister's body was found months later mangled in her car that was wrapped around a tree. They said that she'd probably met a man in Camwell, run off with him, and later she'd been driving and fallen asleep at the wheel and crashed."

"Or maybe she'd broken up with the man and killed herself in despair," Darci said softly.

"Exactly. That's exactly what I was told. But I know Laurie. She was my *sister!* The evening she disappeared, she was planning to come here to my three-year-old's birthday party. Laurie loves . . . loved her niece, my daughter, very much, and she wouldn't have missed the party for anything. The party was hectic, sixteen three-and-under kids here, but, even so, I'm ashamed to say that I didn't realize that my sister wasn't here. Later, after my husband and I had cleaned up, I went in to check on my daughter in bed and she was crying. When I asked her why, she said it was because her Auntie Laurie hadn't come to her party."

When Susan stopped speaking, Darci asked softly, "What did you do?"

"I calmed my daughter down by making some promises that I haven't been able to keep, but inside I was panicking. I knew that something was wrong. You can't imagine how much Laurie and my daughter loved each other. I knew that only something horrible would have kept Laurie from being here on that special day. I grabbed the phone and called Laurie's cell number, but there was no answer. That's when I nearly went hysterical. John, my husband, said that maybe she'd left the phone in her car while she was in a hotel somewhere sleeping."

"But you knew that wasn't true," Adam said.

"Yes. Laurie was a creature of habit. She loved schedules, and she knew where she was going to be when four months ahead of time. But then, she had to live like that if she was going to be the photographer that she wanted to be. She—" Breaking off, Susan got up, walked to a bookcase behind her and withdrew a tall, thin book, then turned and handed it to Darci. "You might have seen this."

It was a big book called *Time and Place,* with photography and text by Laurie Handler.

"She said it was being in the right place at the right time," Susan said, "and doing that took timing and it took giving up any thought of a personal life. My daughter and I were all that Laurie had outside of her work."

Putting the big book down on the coffee table, Darci opened it. Inside were large black-and-white pictures, and each one told a story. The first one she opened to was of a couple holding each other in front of a house that had been destroyed by a hurricane. But in spite of the tragedy of the subject matter, there was a tiny sparkle on the man's wedding ring, as though a ray of sunshine were hitting it and nothing else. The ring cut into the man's flesh, showing that he'd had the ring on for a very long time. The ring led the viewer's eye to the way the man and woman held each other, their faces hidden in shadow, with complete trust in each other, with complete familiarity.

Somehow, Laurie Handler had made the photo of a disaster into a portrait of love, real love, not lust, but the kind of love that endures forever. When Darci looked at it, she thought—and couldn't resist sending to Adam—*I wish someone loved me like that. Someone who loved me all of the time and forever.* But when she looked up at Adam, he had that look on his face that told her to behave herself and tend to what they were there for.

All the pictures in the book were the same. No matter what the circumstances, no matter how bad the subject matter and the background, Laurie seemed to be saying that there was still love in the world, deep, enduring love.

"My goodness," Darci said as she closed the book. "The pictures made me feel. . . ."

"Like love conquers all?" Susan said bitterly.

"Well, yes, I guess so," Darci said. "Is that bad?"

"It is if you're an FBI agent. They said that these photos were proof that Laurie was a romantic, which was proof that she probably ran off with some man; therefore her disappearance probably had nothing to do with whether or not there's a witches' coven in Camwell."

"But you know that isn't true, don't you?" Adam asked. "Do you know that just because Laurie wouldn't have missed her niece's birthday, or do you have some other reasons for believing there was foul play?"

"Laurie wasn't a person to 'run off' with someone," Susan said, then looked at Darci. "You knew her. Tell him what she was like."

At that Darci was speechless. Turning, she blinked at Adam. *Help me,* she said to him in her mind. *What do I say?*

"Darci is—"

"Oh, don't bother to lie," Susan said, waving her hand in dismissal. "I know neither of you knew Laurie. You're not her type. Both of you are too pretty, too clean-cut, too average American. And you," she said, looking at Adam, "reek with money. Am I right?"

At that Adam's back went ramrod straight, but Darci laughed. "Masses of it," she said happily. "He has loads and loads of it. Old money, and he—"

"Would you mind!" Adam said stiffly.

"It's all right," Susan said. "I don't know exactly why I let you in except that you are *my* type. I figure that if you've performed this little charade to get in to see me, it must be personal." She paused for a moment. "So what are you really after?" Susan asked.

Darci spoke first. "He wants to break up the witches. He has some personal reason that makes him want to do this, but he won't tell me what it is. I haven't been able to get it out of him yet, but—"

Adam cut her off. "What Darci means is that, yes, this is very personal to me. To us, actually, and we'd appreciate any help you can give us. If you could tell us anything that you know, or even something that you think might have had anything to do with Laurie's death, we'd appreciate it. Anything at all." He gave Darci a quelling look to tell her not to give away too much.

Darci ignored him. "Was there anything odd about Laurie's left hand?"

At that Susan's eyes widened and she drew in her breath sharply. "Her left hand was . . . cut off in the car wreck. The police said that her hand went through the windshield and was severed. But they couldn't find the hand. The police said that since the accident happened on a country road and it was hours before anyone found her, they thought that . . . that . . . maybe wild dogs had. . . ."

"I see," Adam said.

Ask about the moles, Darci said in her mind.

"I'd like to ask you an odd question. Was there anything unusual about your sister's left hand?"

"No," Susan said, frowning. "She didn't have an odd-shaped birthmark, didn't have an extra little finger, if that's what you mean. There was nothing strange about my sister at all. Except her talent, that is."

"I didn't mean anything bad," Adam persisted. "I meant—"

"Like this," Darci said, as she held out her left hand, palm upward.

For a moment, Susan just sat there blinking, looking at Darci's palm uncomprehendingly. Then she understood. "Yes," she whispered. "Laurie had moles on her hand just like that. They made a duck."

"What?" Adam asked.

"When we were kids, we used to take a pencil and connect the moles on Laurie's hand, and one way we connected them, they formed a duck. We used to. . . ." Trailing off, Susan's eyes filled with tears. "It was silly, but we used to call her Ducky Doodle and she used to make a little duck noise like—" Susan stopped talking because she was choked by tears.

"I think we better go," Adam said as he stood up, and Darci got up too. "Thank you," he whispered, then he looked down at Darci and saw that she was staring hard at Susan, who had her head bent, a tissue to her eyes. Adam knew that Darci was using her power, her True Persuasion, on the woman, and his first thought was to do something to break her concentration to make her stop. But his intuition told him that whatever Darci was doing, she wouldn't hurt Susan.

A moment later, Susan looked up and she was smiling, the tears still in her eyes, but the smile was real. "You're going to think I'm crazy, but I just had the oddest thought that Laurie was here with me and she was telling me that she was all right. I wish I could believe that, and that. . . ."

"What?" Adam asked as Darci was still staring hard.

"I wish that this could be stopped. Did you know that in the last four years some children have disappeared in the Camwell area as well as adult women? No one can prove that the witches had anything to do with them, but when I think of my little daughter and— Are you all right?" Susan asked Adam.

"Fine," he said, but his voice was harsh. "Thank you for your time. Thank you for everything." Abruptly, he turned and walked out the front door, leaving Darci behind.

13

~

"YOU WANT TO TELL ME what that was all about?" Darci asked when she joined him outside on the sidewalk. "You left a bit abruptly, didn't you?"

"The kids," Adam said. His voice was so harsh that she could barely understand him. "I didn't know that they were still using children."

"'Still'?" Darci asked. "What does that mean? Still? You never mentioned that these people 'used' children. What do they use children *for?*"

"Only they know. Once the children disappear, they're never seen again. Or if they are, they don't remember what happened to them. You ready to leave this town?" he asked as he started off in a stride too swift for Darci to be able to walk beside him.

Running, she moved next to him. "*What* children forget? How do you remember this? I don't remember reading anything about any children in the research I saw."

"Probably wasn't in there," Adam said, still walking so fast she had to run to keep up with him. "Do those moles of yours connect into a shape?"

"I have no idea. To tell the truth, I've never paid much attention to them. It was more, 'There are moles on my hand,' not, 'Wow! I can't believe that I have moles on my hand!' Will you *please* slow down?"

"Sorry," Adam said as he slowed his pace. "It's late so you must be starving. What do you want to do for lunch?"

"Eat and talk. I want you to break down and tell me absolutely everything you know about these witches, and about Camwell, and especially why you were so upset when Susan Fairmont said that some children had disappeared. Don't you read what's on milk cartons? Don't you get those flyers in the mail that show photos of missing children? Children go missing every day."

"And that should make me callous to what happens to them?" he said, his face and voice showing barely controlled rage. "Because thousands disappear every year, should I not *care?*"

Darci was looking at him hard, and he could feel that she was using her mind to calm him down. Part of him wanted to yell at her that she'd given her word of honor not to use her power on him, but another part of him was grateful for the soothing effect she was having on him. He didn't even mind the sharp pain her concentration was causing in his left shoulder blade.

They didn't speak again until they reached the rental car. By the time Adam started the engine, he was feeling much calmer and he wanted to lighten the mood. "I saw a little tavern on the way here. The sign said that the building had been there since 1782. Like to go there for lunch?"

"Love it," Darci said, leaning back against the headrest. "Maybe it will look like a pub in England. Have you ever been to England?"

"Many times," Adam said as he backed out of the parking space. Right now she was looking drained. Had what Susan told them done that to her? Or had calming him down taken her energy? He knew he should lecture her about breaking her word, but he couldn't think clearly when he was consumed with rage. He knew that because he'd spent a great deal of his life too angry to be able to think.

So maybe not mentioning that she'd just broken her word was the cowardly way out, but Adam couldn't bring himself to chastise her.

"Putnam says he'll take me to England after I give him a son," Darci said. "One week in England. But he said that if I have a girl first, I get two weeks in Nebraska. In August."

Frowning, Adam pulled onto the road. "When this is finished, *I* will take you to England. For six weeks. And I'll spring for country-house hotels. They cost a fortune, but they're worth it."

"Tell me everything about the country," Darci said, her eyes closed as she leaned back against the seat.

Adam saw that she was still holding the watch case in her left hand. Would she release it to take a shower? "What do you want to hear about first?"

"About Cambridge. I heard it has fabulous bookstores and the colleges there are beautiful. And I want to hear about Bath. I'd like to see— Oh!" she said, sitting upright. "Could we stay one night at Clarendon? It's terrifically expensive."

"Yes," he said. "Clarendon. For three nights. The best room will be yours." Smiling, he pulled into the gravel parking lot of the little tavern, and they went into the restaurant.

But once they'd ordered the prime rib and had been told that it would take a while, Adam was feeling so much better that he made yet another attempt at a joke. Darci was thinking really hard, not with that look that she wore when she was subjecting him to her True Persuasion, but as though she was thinking about something with all her might.

"I'll show you mine if you show me yours," he said in a jovial manner.

Darci looked up at him. "I don't have any hope that you're talking about sex, so you must mean that I'm to show you or tell you my thoughts."

Adam gave a sigh. Had he always been this bad at humor? He seemed to remember having made people laugh in the past. So why did most of his jokes fail to make Darci laugh? "Darci, about this . . . this sex business," he began awkwardly. "It's not that I'm not attracted to you, it's just that. . . ." He trailed off.

"That what?"

"I think it's better if we keep a strictly employer-employee relationship between us. We should make every attempt to keep personal feelings out of this."

"That makes sense," she said. "So, tell me, does sleeping in the same room together come under this employee-employer relationship? What about picking me up and twirling me about? How about—"

"Okay, you've made your point."

"There's another reason you keep me at arm's length, isn't there?" she said, squinting at him as though she were trying to read his mind.

"Just ten minutes ago you were talking about the children you and Putnam are to have together, and now you're—"

"I have to marry Putnam, yes," she said. "But that doesn't mean that I can't—"

"What does that mean?" Adam snapped. "Why do you 'have' to marry him?"

"Why else does a woman have to get married?" she said, looking up at him and batting her lashes. "I'm carrying his child."

Adam didn't smile. "You don't want to tell me the truth, do you?"

"And what makes you so sure that I'm *not* telling you the truth?" she snapped at him.

"Because you're a. . . ." Trailing off, he looked away.

"I'm a what?" she asked, cocking her head at him, very much wanting to know what he wasn't saying.

"You're a real pest, is what you are. Why don't we confine our talk to the business at hand and stop getting personal?"

"Sure," Darci said, then looked down at her silverware on the table.

They were in a booth that was a bad copy of something from England, what an American thought an English pub should look like, and the tables and seats were out of scale for Darci. The table was so high it was level with her collarbone. Right now, with her chin down, she looked about ten years old.

On the other hand, her hair was beautiful, and Adam very much wanted to take her hand in his. Actually, he'd like to kiss the soft white skin and—

"So when do you think your father will get here?" he asked to get his mind off that train of thought.

Darci's head came up and she was smiling, as though he'd finally made a joke that she could laugh at.

"What?!" he asked.

"You just said that we were to have no more personal talk between us, but in the next sentence, you ask about my father. It just struck me as funny."

"You know me, Make-a-Joke-a-Minute Montgomery," he said, then when Darci gave a good laugh, he wasn't sure whether to be pleased or annoyed. But something about Darci's laughter was infectious and he found himself laughing with her.

"Okay," Adam said. "No more talk of a personal or business nature. Let's talk about travel. Where else do you want to go besides England?"

"Isn't that personal?"

"Only vaguely. Are you going to argue about words, or are you going to talk to me about countries? I've been everywhere."

"Sure. Right," Darci said, then thought for a moment. "St. Lucia. Know where that is?"

"Been there three times. Slow and easy. The conch soup is divine. Did you know that after they pull the conch out of its shell, they have to beat it strenuously to soften up the meat? The islanders have a saying, 'She beat him like a conch.'"

"He probably deserved it," Darci said. "How about Tibet?"

"Peaceful place. I have a prayer wheel from there back in the room. I'll show it to you when we get back."

"Egypt."

"Lived there for three years. Loved the Egyptians. Great sense of humor, very intelligent people. Actually, the Egyptians are very much like Americans."

After that, Darci was insatiable in her wish to hear every word that Adam had to say about his travels. Their platters of food came, and they kept talking. She soon found out that he'd answer any questions about where he'd been, but no questions about *why* he'd traveled so much. "Bummed around the world" was all she could get out of him.

"You didn't want to settle down, have a real *home?*" she asked, incredulous.

"No," was the curt answer he gave, so she went back to asking impersonal questions about where he'd been and what he'd seen.

"Tell me more," Darci said when Adam seemed to slow down.

"On one condition," he answered. "You have to put that watch box down, open it, take out the watch, and put it on your wrist. Isn't it difficult cutting that beef using only one hand?"

"No," Darci said. "It's very tender meat." At that she lifted a bite she'd cut using the side of her fork and the whole piece came up. She put the meat back on her plate. "Okay, watch on the arm."

For a moment Adam paused in eating as he observed her opening the box and removing the watch. She held the watch as though it were a holy object—just the way she'd looked at the clothes he'd bought her.

"You're not going to faint on me again, are you?" he asked, and it was yet another joke that fell flat. Quit while you're ahead, Montgomery, he told himself; then he reached across the table, took the watch from her hand, and slipped it onto her wrist.

Darci fell back against the booth, holding her left arm with her right hand, and staring at the watch. "It is the most beautiful thing I've ever seen in my entire life," she said quietly.

"Ah, well," Adam said, looking down at his food and feeling his cheeks pinken.

Darci leaned across the table toward him. "And when we get back to the room I'm going to thank you with wild sexual acts. I'm going to. . . ."

"Yes?" he asked, one eyebrow raised. "Go on. Fill in the details."

Darci sat up straight, put her arm with the watch on it on her lap, then started eating with one hand again. "Maybe we should stop by the library on the way home," she said. "I have something I need to research."

"And what would that be?" he asked, his voice teasing. "Wild sexual acts, maybe? Are you trying to tell me that you and Putnam haven't done any creative and innovative sex acts together?"

Smiling, she looked back up at him. "No, we haven't, but then we're just kids. Maybe an old guy like you would be willing to teach me so I can teach him. Think of it as doing something to help the younger generation. A philanthropic act, so to speak."

Adam was saved from having to answer by the ringing of his cell phone. It had been Darci's experience that when a person had a cell phone, they were always on it, but Adam had rarely used his.

Instantly, he took the phone out of his jacket pocket and answered. "Yes," he said, then listened. "Thank you for calling and telling me."

As Adam folded the phone up and put it away, he kept his eyes on Darci. "Your father has arrived and has checked into the Grove. I asked them at the desk to call me if he showed up."

"That's nice," Darci said as she moved a bit of beef around on her plate. After a while she put her fork down and looked at him. "You know, I really would like to see more of Connecticut. You were going to show me Bradley, but that was all a trick, one of your schemes to—"

"You are not going to be able to start a fight with me," he said calmly. "One argument per day is my limit. I suggest that we go back to Camwell immediately and meet your father. Obviously, he wants to meet you. Do you think he took a private plane to get here this quickly?"

"Don't know," Darci said, leaning back against the booth and looking at her new watch.

"Come on, then, eat the rest of your lunch and we'll go."

"I'm not hungry," she said.

"Should I take you to a doctor?"

She glared at him, not laughing at his attempted joke.

"I'll be right there with you," he said.

"Is that supposed to make me feel better? You'll probably tell him I'm a Kentucky hillbilly and that I freeze people with my mind. You'll probably tell him you were surprised to find out that I can read, much less—"

"Go ahead and say any insulting thing you want to me,

but you are not going to goad me into an argument. So if you're finished, let's go. I'm sure your father's a very nice man, and he wants to meet you."

"What kind of man impregnates a sixteen-year-old girl then leaves her?"

"Let me guess: Aunt Thelma said that?"

"Actually, all of Putnam said it."

"How about a man who was never told that he was leaving a pregnant girl behind? The man stopped to put gasoline in his car and there was this gorgeous *woman*"—he emphasized the word— "in pink overalls who was. . . . Well, what comes to my mind is that movie *Cool Hand Luke,* where the well-endowed girl is washing her car and driving all the prisoners insane with— Well, anyway, did you see that movie?"

Silently, Darci nodded. "My mother would do that. She'd do most anything to get the attention of a man. She says that male attention is the only thing in life that matters."

"But you know that that isn't true, don't you?"

Looking up at him, Darci thought for a moment. "No, I'm not sure that I do know that. And how long are you going to talk to me as though you think you are my father?"

At that Adam threw up his hands to signal that he was giving up, grabbed the check, waited for her to get out of the booth, and paid on the way out.

On the short drive back to Camwell, he could feel Darci's tension, and he wanted to make her relax. "Too bad you can't True Persuade yourself," he said, smiling. "You could calm yourself down, as you did me today after we left Susan's house." He couldn't resist letting her know that he knew what she'd done.

"It is," she said, without much interest. "Do I look okay?"

"Darci, you are beautiful!" Adam said, and his words were so heartfelt that he was a bit embarrassed.

"Good. I guess," Darci said without much energy. "If he likes beautiful women. What do you think our meeting will be like?"

"I think it'll be cautious at first," Adam said, trying to prepare her for what he imagined was ahead. "Neither of you know each other. When I spent the night on the Internet, contrary to what you seem to think I was doing, I was reading about Taylor Raeburne. There's very little about him personally. He's a professor at a university, and—"

"That right there! What's he going to think of a daughter whose degree is from Mann's Developmental College for Young Ladies?"

"Are you asking me honestly?"

Darci looked at him in disbelief. "What does that mean?"

"I just want to say that if the other young ladies who got degrees from that school are half as well educated as you are, then I'd say that that school may be in the top five in the country."

"Oh," she said but still with no energy. "But he doesn't know that, does he?"

"Nor did I when I first met you. At least now you have on decent clothes and you no longer have that hungry-waif look." The minute it was out, he wished he hadn't said it.

"Is that what you thought of me? I bet you were upset when that psychic friend of yours said, 'She's the one.' I bet you said, 'Not that starving girl! Oh, no! Why couldn't I have some tall, gorgeous girl with a degree from Yale?'"

What she said was so close to exactly what Adam had thought that he could feel the blood creeping all the way up into the tips of his ears.

"You did!" Darci said under her breath. "That's just exactly what you *did* think. Adam Montgomery, you are the biggest snob who ever lived on the face of this earth. You think that because you were born rich that you—"

"Do you think that's him?" Adam asked.

Darci had been so busy ranting at Adam that she hadn't realized that they'd reached Camwell and were pulling into the parking lot of the Grove. Glancing out the front window, Darci saw a man standing under a tree that was festooned with dark red leaves. Since he had his back to them, she couldn't see his face, but she knew she hadn't seen this man in his perfect navy wool topcoat at the inn before.

Putting her hands over her face, Darci dropped her head onto Adam's lap. "I can't do it," she said. "I can't do it. He won't like me. What do I say to him? He'll want proof that I'm his daughter. He'll think—"

When she'd first put her head on his lap, Adam had felt such a charge of electricity go through him that he'd immediately wanted to grab her, pull her up, and . . . well, he thought, probably ravish her on the car seat. But after a moment of keeping his hands raised and forcing himself not to touch her, he began to hear her words.

He put his hand on her head, on her soft, silky hair, and after exhaling a couple of times to calm himself, he stroked her hair. "Come on, be brave. I told you that I'll be there to protect you."

Darci's head came up so quickly she almost hit his chin. Her face was level with his, her lips near his. "Promise me?"

"Sure," he said, but his voice came out raspy.

"Swear it." She grabbed the sides of his leather jacket and pulled on them, drawing his face even nearer to hers.

Her breath smelled so good that for a moment Adam was dizzy.

"Swear it!" she said. "Swear it on. . . . What do you hold sacred?"

"At the moment, my sanity."

"None of your dumb jokes now. This is important."

"I swear on my sister's life that I won't abandon you."

That statement made him curse under his breath, because he'd revealed something that he hadn't meant to. Maybe she wouldn't notice his slipup.

But Darci's eyes widened until he could see white all around them. "The Internet said that you're an only child, so who is your sister?"

"She—" Adam looked around Darci's head. "The hotel people must have told him what kind of car I'm driving, because your father is coming this way."

"No!" Darci half squealed, and Adam nearly wept with relief when she rolled away from him to go to the other side of the car. Her anxiety about her father had made her stop asking questions about his sister. For a moment, Adam closed his eyes and tried to regain his equilibrium.

When there was no sound from Darci, he looked at her sitting in the passenger seat. Her face was as white as a marshmallow. She wasn't going to faint again, was she? he thought, and at the same time he wondered how much time he was going to have to spend acting as mediator between these two strangers. All he wanted to do was work on the problem at hand, but now he'd have to be a family counselor. The truth was, he'd been hoping that this man Taylor could baby-sit Darci for a day or two so he could go back into those tunnels. On his own, he could make a map. On his own, he could—

When he heard Darci open the car door, he stopped his thoughts and looked at her. She was staring, with a look he'd never seen before, at the man walking slowly toward them. The man certainly did look like Darci, Adam thought. There'd be no need for DNA tests to prove paternity.

Darci started to get out of the car.

"Wait a minute and I'll go with you," Adam said. "I'll—Damnation!" The seat belt lock was jammed, and though he pushed as hard as he could on the red button, the thing wouldn't release. But after a moment, he stopped pushing the button and looked out the window at what was happening.

Looking as though she were in a trance, Darci had gotten out of the car, leaving the door open, and slowly begun to walk toward the man as he walked toward her. His eyes were intent on the young woman coming toward him, and the closer they got to each other, the faster they began to walk. By the time they were thirty feet from each other, they were running.

A car had pulled in beside Adam's in the parking lot, and half a dozen people had climbed out, their arms laden with shopping bags, but when they saw Darci and the man walking toward each other, they halted and watched also.

Adam had to admit that it was a sight to see, these two people who looked so much alike running toward each other, their arms outstretched.

When Darci was about a yard from the man, she leaped off the ground.

For a moment, Adam held his breath; then he jerked hard against the seat belt and it released. In one quick movement he was out of the car, ready to run to Darci's rescue if this man didn't catch her.

But he needn't have worried, because the man caught her against him and enveloped her in his arms. Darci's legs went about his waist and her head buried itself into his shoulder, as she curled herself against him in complete and total submission.

And love, Adam couldn't help thinking as he watched them, and a white-hot emotion ran through him. The feeling was something like anger, no . . . actually, it was more like rage. But it also felt like. . . .

His thoughts were interrupted by the people standing by the car next to his. They were applauding! One of the women was wiping tears from her eyes; a teenage boy put his fingers to his mouth and gave a loud whistle, then he clapped some more.

Adam was quite annoyed. His inclination was to snap at the tourists that this was a private reunion between a father and daughter who had never met each other, and therefore—

But Adam didn't say any of that. In fact, he didn't say anything at all to the people, even though they were gushing about how "romantic" what they'd just seen was. After closing his car door and locking it, Adam went around to the passenger-side door, closed, and locked it. When he thought he'd delayed as long as he could, he turned and started walking slowly toward father and daughter, who were now standing close together, Taylor Raeburne's arm around Darci's shoulders, hers about his waist.

Taylor Raeburne was only about five-foot-six, maybe seven, inches tall, Adam saw as he drew closer. From the photo, Darci's mother had seemed to be rather tall, so he'd wondered why Darci was so short. At the time, he'd figured that it was malnutrition. But now he saw that it was heredity. In fact, looking at them together, he didn't think he'd ever seen a parent and child more alike than these two.

"You're Montgomery?" Raeburne asked when he saw Adam.

When Adam looked into the man's eyes, he knew that there weren't many people who'd called Taylor Raeburne short and lived to tell about it. He reminded Adam of a gladiator of old: small but powerful. This man had an air about him that would make people notice him wherever he was.

"Yes," Adam said, trying not to look at Darci as she clung so closely to this man. "There's no need to ask who *you* are."

At that, Raeburne just stared at him, blinking, as though he hadn't understood the language Adam was speaking.

"Don't mind him," Darci said. "He's always trying to make jokes and failing. He just meant that he could see that you're my father." Darci gave the man such a look of love that again that feeling went through Adam, this time so hard that he had to look away for a moment.

"So where do we begin to work on clearing out these witches?" Taylor asked.

Adam looked back at the man, glad to be on familiar territory. "I thought that maybe you and Darci could spend some time together and get to know each other while I do a little . . . well, mapping."

"Of the tunnels?" Darci snapped, taking her arm from around her father's waist. "You can't go without *me!*"

"I'd do a great deal better without you!" Adam snapped back. "Look at what you did last time!"

"I got you your dagger, that's what I did. You couldn't reach it, but I set off the alarm and that gave you time to reach in and grab the thing. Not that finding that knife has helped us any."

"You act as though you *planned* that," Adam shot back at her. "You act as though—"

"You two haven't become lovers, have you?" Taylor asked, interrupting the two of them.

"With him?" Darci said, almost sneering. "No, he's saving himself for Renee."

"Very funny." Adam looked at Taylor. "Renee is my dog."

Taylor Raeburne didn't smile. "It's a good thing that you haven't become lovers because as I'm sure you know, my daughter must remain a virgin if she's to read the mirror."

When Taylor said that, Adam could feel Darci staring at him. *That's why you hired me!* she screamed in his head. *You hired me because I'm a . . . a. . . .* Even in her mind she couldn't say the word.

"Darci, I—" Adam said, turning to look at her. "Ow! That hurt!" he said when a sharp pain shot through his head. A pain like an ice pick went in one temple, straight through his brain, and out the other temple. "Stop it," he whispered, putting his hands to the sides of his head.

Through this Taylor had been standing in silence and watching, but now he understood what was going on. Grabbing his daughter's thin shoulders, he stepped between her and Adam. "Darci," he said, but the expression on her face didn't change. Her eyes were big, the pupils enlarged, and they were sightless. "Darci!" he commanded, then he gave her shoulders a shake. "Stop it! Stop it now or you're going to kill him!"

In an instant, Darci came out of her spell, looked at her father as though she didn't know who he was; then she saw Adam behind him. Adam was on his knees on the grass, the palms of his hands pressed to his temples. There was a trickle of blood from his right nostril.

"I did that?" she whispered, holding on to her father's strong arms, because if she didn't hold on to something, she was going to fall down. Her entire body was weak, drained. There was no more energy left inside her.

"Yes," Taylor said, looking at her intently, seeing the way the blood was draining from her face. "You didn't know you could do that, did you?"

She looked back at him. "That I can kill people with my mind?" she asked, because she felt that if she'd kept on blasting Adam with her rage, she could have made his head explode. Her voice was barely a whisper. "No. I didn't know that I could do that. I don't want to know it. I don't want to be a freak. I don't even want to be a . . . a. . . ." Her eyes filled with tears, choking her.

Taylor drew her to him, hiding her face in his shoulder. "Are you all right?" he asked Adam.

Adam had bent over to put one hand on the ground, the other was pressed to his bleeding nose, but he nodded at Taylor that he was okay.

"What I'd like more than anything is to go somewhere and talk, but I don't think we have time," Taylor said. "Tonight's the thirtieth."

Both Darci and Adam looked at him in question.

"Please tell me that you two know what that means," Taylor said.

"He tells me nothing," Darci said angrily.

"And she tells me even less," Adam said hoarsely, still unable to stand up.

"I'm not sure of this," Taylor said slowly, looking from one to the other, "but it's my guess that neither of you knows much to tell." He looked at Adam. "Did you tell my daughter"—Taylor had to pause, as those words made a catch come into his throat— "why you're doing this? Did you tell her about the kidnaping?"

"No," Adam said, slowly standing up. He hadn't yet looked at Darci. Part of him wanted to protect her, but part of him wanted to run away from her. Could she really *kill* a person with her mind? But, worse, she had turned her power against *him.*

"And you?" Taylor asked, moving Darci to stand at arm's length so he could look into her eyes. "What do you know about what you can do?"

"I don't think I know much of anything," she said, also not looking at Adam. She could feel his anger, but worse, she could feel that he was afraid of her.

For a moment Taylor stepped back and looked at the two of them. "Good hearts," he muttered. "You two have good hearts but not many facts." He gave a sigh, then said louder, "All right, let me spell it out for you: We have until the thirty-first, tomorrow, to get what you're seeking." He was looking at Adam. "Is it the mirror or the reader you want most?"

"*She* is a rumor. No one is sure that she exists," Adam said, eyes wide.

"Oh, she exists, all right, and— Show me your chest. I want to see that you're who you claim to be."

"How do you know about this?" Adam asked.

"I have a woman who works for me, a Mrs. Wilson. The woman can find out anything about anybody in less time than it takes you or me to read our driver's license. I drove up here from Virginia, and by the time I got here and had plugged in my fax machine, she had already found out a great deal." He looked hard at Adam. "There's been quite a bit written about you. If you're the man you say you are, that is."

Adam took a moment to consider this. Right this second he had to decide whether or not to reveal who he was and what he was after to this man, to this stranger. But he had seen that Darci was part of this and by looks alone he could see that this man was part of Darci.

And the man knew about the mirror. And about "the reader."

"Shall we go to the guest house?" Adam asked. "I think we've received enough public attention for one day."

"Yes," Taylor said, "let's go somewhere private."

As Adam walked past Darci, she whispered, "I'm sorry. I didn't mean to hurt you."

But Adam wasn't ready to forgive her.

14

ONCE THEY WERE INSIDE the guest house, Adam pulled his sweater over his head, then unbuttoned his shirt. On the left side of his chest, directly over his heart was a scar. No, Darci, thought as she looked at the place. It wasn't just a scar, it was a brand. It had become distorted over the years, as it was obviously an old scar, but she could still see that it had originally been a shape. But she couldn't identify the shape.

Right now she could feel that Adam was still so angry with her that he didn't want her near him, so she didn't step forward to look closer at the scar.

"Do you know what it is?" Taylor asked, not touching Adam but looking hard at the old scar.

"A tower," Adam said. "From the tarot deck. It's the card of death."

"Yes. It's her personal symbol. She must hate you a lot if

she branded you with that," Taylor said, then looked at Adam in speculation. "But you're still living. How old were you when she did that to you?"

"Three," Adam said as he buttoned his shirt. "And it's no use asking me what happened because I don't remember. And, before you ask, I've been hypnotized several times— or people tried to put me under, anyway—but I still don't remember what happened."

"If she couldn't wipe that memory from your brain, she wouldn't be worth much, would she?"

"She! She! She!" Darci said. "Who is this *she?!*"

Taylor looked shocked at Darci's question. "The hotel staff said you two have been here for five nights. Have you even spoken to each other?"

"She never stops talking," Adam said, but he didn't look at Darci. "But what she talks about is mostly Putnam— man, boy, town."

"And my True Persuasion," Darci shot back. She wanted to feel sorry for Adam, for what had been done to him when he was only three years old, but right now he was so angry at her that she couldn't feel anything at all for him.

Taylor was looking from one to the other, then back again. "I'm guessing that neither of you has any idea what's going on. It seems that what little bit you do know, you've kept to yourselves and not shared it. I guess that you don't even know the connection between you two, do you?"

"If you mean that she shouts things into my head, yes, we found that out last night." Even to himself, Adam sounded like a sulky little boy.

"Darci, dearest, hold out your left hand to me," Taylor

said as he took a pen from his jacket pocket. "Seven moles. Didn't you tell me that she has *seven* moles on her hand?"

"Yes, that's how many I counted. I don't think she's ever counted them."

Holding his daughter's hand, Taylor gently rubbed her palm with his fingers. "I didn't think I'd ever have children of my own," he said softly. "I was in a car accident about two years after I met your mother. Like all men, I thought I had all the time in the world to have a family, but I was injured in that accident, not horribly, but enough that something was damaged, and even though I've been married twice, I've had no children. One wife left me because of it. But then, this morning, that call came, and. . . ." When he looked into her eyes, he sent love to her.

Still holding his daughter's hand, Taylor looked at Adam. "My daughter is descended from a long line of powerful women. I've written about my female ancestors and what they could do, but I thought that there would be no more of these wonderful women. I thought that I'd stopped the line. Did you know that she can sense people's happiness or their unhappiness? She can feel what you feel about her right now."

Darci pulled her hand out of his grasp. "I don't like this. I don't want to be some weird, strange—"

"Then don't try to *kill* people!" Adam snapped at her, but when he saw tears gather in Darci's eyes, the anger went out of him. "Oh, hell," he said.

"Don't curse," she said, beginning to sob.

Adam took a step toward her, his arms open, ready to comfort her, but Taylor stepped between them. "Not yet," he said. "Two more days, then I'll walk her down the aisle to you, but not yet."

"Aisle?" Darci said, her eyebrows raised.

"She's engaged to somebody else," Adam said, "and, besides, she and I aren't— I mean, we don't—"

"I can see that," Taylor said, and he was obviously highly amused at Adam's statement. He couldn't keep himself from openly chuckling. "Yes, I can definitely see that you two are 'not.'" Still smiling, he turned and picked up Darci's left hand again and began to draw on it. He was connecting the moles on the palm of her hand.

"Ducky Doodle," Adam said softly, making Darci smile.

When Taylor looked at her in question, she said, "Sometimes his jokes aren't so dumb," then she let out an "Oh!" of surprise.

"That's what I thought," Taylor said. "It's nine moles, not seven. The second two are lower down on her wrist. See?"

You better catch me, Darci said in her mind to Adam as she looked down at her palm, because her knees were giving out on her once again. On her palm was the exact same shape, the tower, that had been branded on Adam's chest.

Pushing Taylor aside, Adam swept Darci into his arms and placed her on the couch. "Get her some water," he ordered the older man—and was ashamed at how good it felt to put himself between Darci and her father. "In a glass. With ice."

When Taylor returned with the glass of water, he said, "Are you sure she's not just hungry? She's awfully thin. Do you ever feed her?"

It was what was needed to break the tension. Adam

looked at Darci lying on the sofa, once again halfway to a faint, and he started to laugh. And his laugher started Darci's. As Adam plopped down on one end of the sofa, Darci pulled herself up to a sitting position and began to laugh harder. And the more they laughed, the more they kept on laughing, until they were reaching for each other and were soon collapsing in each other's arms.

Taylor stood there watching them in speculation; then, after a moment, he walked about the guest house. When he saw that the clothes of both of them were hanging in one closet and that they were obviously sleeping in the same room together, he picked up the phone, called the desk, and told them to repack his luggage and move his bags into the Cardinal House. With Taylor's voice and his air of authority, the young man who answered the phone didn't say that repacking and moving was not a normal service of the hotel. All the young man said was, "Yes, sir. I'll see that it's done."

Thirty minutes later, Taylor answered the knock on the door and admitted what looked to be every staff member at the Grove into the guest house. Each person was carrying a suitcase or a cardboard box or an odd-shaped case.

"What in the world—" Adam began as he watched the parade.

"I decided to stay here—in this house," Taylor said pointedly, looking hard at Adam. "The staff will need to be tipped, and I'm sure you can afford it better than I can."

Adam started to speak, but, instead, he opened his wallet and passed out several bills to the waiting staff. "Like father, like daughter," he said under his breath. The staff left smiling. "You want to tell me what this is about?" Adam asked as he turned back to Taylor.

Taylor sat down on a chair across from the sofa. "I didn't have much time to plan so I brought everything that I thought we'd need. Tonight we have to try to get the mirror. Tomorrow is the thirty-first, so—"

"Hallowe'en," Darci said. She was sitting on one end of the sofa, Adam at the other end. She realized that she'd paid no attention to the date.

"Yes, exactly," Taylor said. "If we wait until tomorrow, it will be too late, if she keeps her power past tonight, her power will double. She will use children in the ritual," he said softly. "But I don't know where she keeps the mirror. She—"

"The boss?" Darci asked, trying not to think about what her father had just said. "That's what we've heard her called."

"And when was that?" Taylor asked, then put up his hand. "No, don't tell me. There's no time. She won't be expecting us tonight. I'm sure she's seen Darci in the mirror, so she—"

"Me?" Darci asked. "Why me?"

"You can read it," Taylor said before Adam could speak.

"Oh, yeah, I forgot," Darci said bitterly. "I was hired because I'm a . . . a. . . . Wait a minute! If this witch is reading the mirror, then does that mean that she's never . . . ?"

"That puzzles me," Taylor said softly. "Has she made herself a nun to the mirror? Or is it just a legend that only a virgin can read it?"

"This doesn't make sense. Nostradamus was certainly no virgin. He had a couple of wives and children," Darci said. "So why does the reader have to be . . . chaste?" She swallowed, too well remembering all the times she'd talked to Adam about sex. Yet he'd known all along that she knew *nothing*. How he must have been laughing at her!

"But then maybe the mirror was made for him," Adam said softly, and the way he said it made Darci turn to him sharply.

"What else are you hiding?" she asked. "Besides hideous scars and knowledge of a person's most intimate secrets?"

Adam took a deep breath. "There's a possibility that my sister is the one reading the mirror," he said. "My mother was pregnant when she . . . when she disappeared. I've been told that three people were on the plane that my parents disappeared in and that one of them is still alive. My sister would be about thirty-two now."

At this revelation, all Darci could do was stare at Adam. No wonder he was so fierce about finding this mirror. If he found the mirror, maybe he'd find his sister. Maybe he'd find a woman who had been held captive her entire life.

"Ah," Taylor said. "This makes things even more imperative." He was looking from Darci to Adam and saw the way they were gazing at each other. Taylor's mind was moving quickly. Because of his ancestresses, he had dedicated his life to the study of some of the ugliness that was going on in the world. Twice he'd been able to infiltrate covens and bring them down. But each time, the things that he had seen had sickened him.

When Adam Montgomery had called early this morning, Taylor hadn't given himself time to feel the joy of finding out that he had a daughter—a daughter who had the power that had been in his family throughout remembered time. Instead, he'd flown into a frenzy of activity. He'd grabbed his case files on Camwell—boxes of them—all while dictating to his longtime assistant, Mrs. Wilson.

It was she who remembered the rumor about the mirror. Taylor had heard about the mirror years before from a student of his whose sister had joined the cult. In an attempt to get her sibling to join the coven, stupidly, the girl had told her of the mirror. "It's going to let us conquer the world," the sister had said. "She has an old-maid virgin—she *has* to be a virgin—who can see the past *and the future* in the thing."

These few sentences had been told to Taylor, and he'd spent as much time as he could finding out what the girl had meant, but he could find out little.

He had been on his way here to Camwell when Mrs. Wilson had called to tell him what she'd found out about Adam Montgomery and what had happened to him when he was a child.

Mrs. Wilson said, "And here's an interesting fact: This man's mother was pregnant when she disappeared." It had taken Taylor several moments to put two and two together. "Old-maid virgin," the girl had said. "How old would her child be now?" Taylor said into the speaker phone. Mrs. Wilson was prepared for the question; they had worked together for many years. "The child would be about thirty-two now."

Taylor'd had to take a few moments to calm himself. No matter how much he heard about the evil on earth, he was never quite prepared when he heard more. Had the girl been raised in captivity? Been raised so she could read a magic mirror?

By the time Taylor reached Camwell, he had several pieces of information, but he wasn't sure how they all fit together. He wouldn't reveal the information under torture, but he was often consulted by the FBI when there was a possibility of so-called witchcraft in a case. Because of this connection, Mrs. Wilson had been able to find out about the shape of the brand the doctors had seen on the chest of a small boy found wandering in the woods years ago. Taylor even knew that the FBI—with the approval of Adam's guardians—had ordered the doctor to repair the wound in a way that scar tissue would cover the brand. Adam's guardians didn't want him to have a visual reminder of what he'd been through.

And Taylor had been called into the case when the first young woman had disappeared near Camwell years before. He was the one who'd figured out about the moles when the second woman disappeared.

But it was only while driving in the car today that Taylor had made a guess—a guess based on years of research and experience—about the shape on Darci's hand and the brand that had been put on Adam's chest when he was a child.

So now Taylor knew more than he wanted to. This "boss," this evil woman who had kidnaped an unborn baby and held the child for thirty-two years, was now after Taylor's beautiful—and very *precious*—daughter.

Taylor had heard an abbreviated version of what this Adam Montgomery had been through, but was Adam truly prepared for what might be ahead for him?

Was Adam ready for what he might find? Was Darci, who seemed to be the personification of innocence, ready for what she might see?

Part of Taylor wanted to spend time talking to them, warning these two innocents. He wanted to talk to Adam about that young woman who had been held prisoner all her life. Would she be worth saving?

But Taylor didn't have time to give a lecture on philosophy, or to recount the horror he'd seen in his lifetime of fighting these evil people. And he didn't have time for squeamishness. If they were going to do it, then it had to be done *now*. If they didn't try, or if they tried and failed, then, tomorrow, yet another person—or persons—would be killed.

Taylor took a deep breath. "First Darci has to find where the mirror is; then we have to go there and, somehow, try to get inside and get the thing. I'm sure that wherever it is, it's heavily guarded, so I brought night-vision goggles. I don't think there's a spell yet that can stop those things," he added, because Adam and Darci were looking at him in disbelief.

Taylor sobered. "Adam, I think you have to be prepared for the fact that if it is your sister who's reading the mirror, she may have turned . . . the other way."

"Evil, you mean?" he asked.

"Yes." Taylor was looking hard at Adam, trying to read his thoughts, and Adam was looking back just as hard, as though something was passing between them.

"I hate to interrupt this lovely male-bonding session," Darci said, "but could we go back to the part where you said, '*Darci* has to find the mirror'? 'Darci' as in *me*? Or maybe you have someone else named Darci in mind?"

Adam looked at Taylor, and Taylor looked at his daughter. "You don't know that you can find things?"

"When I met her, she believed that anyone could do what she does if the person would just put his mind to it," Adam said.

"Are you making fun of me?" Darci asked, narrowing her eyes at Adam. "Because if you are, I'll—"

"You'll what?" Adam asked.

"Children!" Taylor said, but he was smiling. "Darci darling—"

"Don't you love the way that sounds?" she asked, clasping her hands and holding them to her heart, her eyes closed in ecstasy. "Darci *darling.*"

"Too bad the word doesn't begin with the letter *t*," Adam said as once again *that* feeling had flashed through him. "If it did, you could say it was your middle name. And, no, she doesn't know she can find things. I spent an entire day trying to find out what she can do, but, obviously, I didn't ask the right questions."

Taylor smiled lovingly at his daughter. "I think that when one has a talent, it's difficult to imagine that others don't have that extraordinary ability. I only know what she can do because I've spent so much of my life researching my ancestors and learning what they could do. Each generation of our family—and considering that a generation could be only thirty years, there have been a lot of them—produced a girl who had Darci's gift. But the gift didn't descend in a straight line. Sometimes a woman who had it could have multiple daughters who didn't inherit the gift. Or she could produce a daughter who had it, but the child died an infant so it would seem that the talent skipped a generation.

"What I'm saying is that while some women grew up

with a mother who could teach them what they could do, many of them were like Darci and grew up without having any idea what power they had. And the intensity of the gift differed from one woman to another. Only some of the women could project their thoughts to another person, as Darci does to you."

"She can do that, all right," Adam said with a frown, then rubbed his temple.

I told you I was sorry! What else do you want? she said to him in her mind.

"How about begging my forgiveness?" Adam answered, and Darci smiled, knowing he was referring to the time he'd gone on his knees and acted like a begging dog.

Not in this lifetime, she said, but she was smiling.

"I see," Taylor said, leaning back against his chair and watching the two of them. "She can talk to you very clearly, not just in visions or ideas, but in words. I must say that I'm jealous. It's always only one person my relative can talk to. She can make people feel things and think things, but she can only talk, in words, to one person—and most of them couldn't do that."

In spite of himself, Adam was pleased at this. "Have any of these women ever used their power for good on a large scale? Or for bad, for that matter? And how have they kept it a secret all these centuries?"

"Yes to both," Taylor said. "Some of my ancestors have been horrible creatures. One woman terrorized a whole town with her power, until someone dropped some poison in her soup and that was the end of her. And I believe that there have been some positive things on a grand scale done by my ancestors, but I can't prove it. I truly believe that an aunt of mine was heavily involved in the halting of the Vietnam War, but, as I said, I can't prove it. Others have used their power to soothe people, and to change things for the good."

"Darci's done that to me," Adam said softly. "And she sorts out that town of hers, that Putnam."

"As for keeping secrets, it has depended on the town where the woman was living. Sometimes her neighbors knew; sometimes they didn't. Sometimes only one or two aspects of her talents were known and used. One ancestress found sheep. She lived in Scotland and all she did was find lost sheep."

"Which brings us back full circle," Adam said. "You said that Darci could find things, but I haven't seen any evidence of that."

"No? Didn't she find *you*? Isn't that how you two met?"

Darci was smiling. *Me. I found you. Not you found me.*

"She found me the first night," Adam said quietly. "I was looking about the town, in the dark, without even a flashlight, but she found me."

"Yes," Taylor said as he got up. "Come with me. I want you to look at something."

Taylor led them into the bedroom that was to be his, but as he looked at it, he wondered if he'd ever sleep there. If they made this invasion tonight, they wouldn't be able to return here. He tossed a couple of cases about until he came to a small black one. He pulled it onto the end of the bed, then twirled the dials on the combination lock until it popped open, then unzipped the case. Slowly, as though what was inside was precious—or perhaps horrifying—he withdrew a small red leather box. Turning, he held it out to Darci.

But Darci wouldn't touch the box. Instead, she backed

out of the room, backed all the way into the brightly lit living room, Taylor and Adam following her.

"I don't like that thing," Darci said, still backing up. "Whatever you have in there is bad. Putnam has a collection of guns from famous murderers, and I won't touch them either. Whatever you have in there is the same as those guns."

"No," Taylor said. "What's in here is much worse. It belonged to her. It took me years to find something that belonged to her, but I did it. Darci, if we're to stop this, if we're to find Adam's sister, you *must* help us."

Slowly, Taylor opened the red leather box, and Adam held his breath, preparing himself for what he was about to see. Would it be some evil amulet? Or "just" something old and hideous? Would it be a body part?

But when Taylor opened the box, all Adam saw inside was an old-fashioned pin, a simple, childish thing, with a little enameled picture of a pretty girl in a gold frame, surrounded by seed pearls.

"Is that the witch?" Adam asked, for the girl didn't look to be evil. She had lots of dark brown hair, big brown eyes, and a small, full-lipped mouth. Even in the picture she looked as though she were about to start laughing. All in all, Adam had never seen a less evil-looking object than that little pin.

But Darci wouldn't get near the box. And after one glance at the pin, she looked away.

"Tell me what you see, Darci," Taylor said softly.

"I don't want to see anything," Darci said. "I didn't ask to be able to see or do things that other people can't." There were tears in her voice.

"I know," Taylor said in a quiet, soothing voice. Over the years he'd worked with many clairvoyants, and all the good ones had voiced these same words. It was the ones who were the self-declared "most powerful," those who could see too little to be frightened by what they saw, who were glad of their small gift. "I know that you don't want to see things, and that's why you've stamped your powers down all these years. But, Darci, baby, you're not a freak, not a mutant. You're talented. What you have is a gift from God, and—"

Embarrassed, Darci put her head up and looked at Adam. "No, that girl in the picture isn't a witch. The girl in that picture was killed by a very evil person. And. . . ." Breaking off, she blinked at Adam. "I've met her murderer."

"Who?!" Adam and Taylor said in unison.

"The woman who runs the clothing store is my guess," Darci said quickly. "A nasty piece of work, she was."

Neither Adam or Taylor could figure out whether Darci was joking or not, and judging from the look on Darci's face, neither did she. And when Darci said no more, both Taylor and Adam saw that they were going to get no more out of her.

In answer to Taylor's questioning eyes, Darci said, "Yes, I'm joking. I don't know who murdered her, but I feel that I've met her." She put her hands to her temples. "That makes no sense. If I can feel evil from a pin, how could I meet an evil person and not recognize her?"

"She can block things, disguise herself," Taylor said, then turned away so his face couldn't be seen. If he'd known he'd had a daughter who had the power of the women in his family, he could have trained her. He could have explained to her about what she could do. She would *never* have felt that she was a freak.

But he'd not known about a daughter, never in his life thought that a quickie with a stunningly beautiful girl inside the men's rest room of a service station had produced a child. At the time, Taylor couldn't get away fast enough. He had been disgusted with himself for having done such an out-of-character thing. And his major concern had been that he might have contracted a disease from the woman who'd begged him to take her away with him.

What if I had taken her with me? Taylor thought now. Darci would have been his all these years. His to love and to—

He turned back to look at his beautiful daughter. "Do you think you could find something on a map for us?" Taylor asked softly. "We need to know where to start looking for the mirror."

"I don't know how to do that. I've never . . ." she began, then cut herself off as she looked at the faces of the two men. They looked like children who'd been told they couldn't have dessert. "But I could try," she said at last.

"That's all we can ask," Taylor said and breathed a sigh of relief.

15

"ARE YOU SURE?" Adam asked, looking at the very ordinary house in front of them. True, the house was old, but then this was Connecticut and there were a lot of old houses in the state. And, true, this house was surrounded by acres of mowed lawn, with no shrubs or trees where intruders could hide, but many houses in the state were surrounded by lawns. It was a two-story farmhouse, big and rambling, looking as though it had been added on to several times in the hundred or so years since it had been built. The house did not look as if it was a place of evil. And it certainly didn't look like a prison. There were no high walls or fences surrounding the property, nothing that a person would expect when thinking of witches and covens and a woman who had been held prisoner all her life.

"Yes," Darci said, swallowing. "This is the house."

Couldn't they *feel* it? she thought. Couldn't they feel the evil that surrounded the house? To her, the evil was something she could *see*, like colors. No, the malevolence was more like flames leaping about the old house. "Yes, I'm sure," she repeated. "Adam, you can't go in there. You can't." She tried to keep the tears out of her voice, but she couldn't.

Darci had easily been able to close her eyes, run her fingers over a map of the Camwell area, and find a place that matched what she had felt coming from the little enamel picture of the slain girl.

"You've done this before," Taylor said, looking at her hard.

"Yes," she answered in resignation.

"Darci, you know much more about what you can do than you let anyone know, don't you?" her father asked.

"Yes," she answered. "It's just that I've never wanted to find out what I could do. I've never wanted to be different, and I especially haven't wanted others to know about me. I've never—"

"It's okay," Taylor said, pulling her into his arms, her head down on his shoulder. "It's all right. Once this is over, you can go home to live with me in Virginia. I have a very nice house, and—"

"No," Adam said. "She's going home with me."

"We're going to England," Darci said to her father, moving away from him. "Adam's promised me a six-week trip," she said over her shoulder as she walked out the door of the guest house.

"You take her anywhere without marrying her first and I will kill you," Taylor Raeburne said under his breath to Adam as they left the guest house.

At that, Adam smiled but made no answer. The truth was that he wasn't ready to think about what he felt for Darci. He knew that he'd never met anyone like her, and he knew that she had the ability to get to him in a way that no one else ever had. With others from the time he was three years old, he'd kept a protective shell around himself. No one had been able to make him love, or hate, for that matter. After he'd been branded by that evil woman when he was so very young, it was as though he'd closed himself off from all emotion, both good and bad.

But since he'd met Darci, he'd been able to laugh. He'd been able to tease. And he'd thought of things other than the black side of life. She'd made him want to buy her gifts and show her things. He wanted to show her the world. As he'd told her, he'd bummed around the world, had seen a lot of things and met a lot of people. But he'd never felt any joy in his travels. Once an old man had said to him, "Boy, I think you're lookin' real hard for somethin'. But I don't think you know what it is you're lookin' for."

The old man's words had seemed to sum up Adam's life. And he hadn't known what he was looking for until one fateful summer day a few years ago when he was watching his cousins play tennis. That day and a casual remark had set him onto a road that led here.

Here, to Darci, he thought and smiled as he followed Taylor out the door.

Darci pulled things from Adam that no one else had ever been able to. And, in return, he'd wanted to give back to her.

He'd tried to make her laugh, and the few times he'd succeeded, he'd felt as though her laughter had been a rare and precious gift. He wanted to protect her and. . . .

And he wanted to make love to her, he thought with a smile. She'd been angry that he'd known she'd been lying when she told him about her past sexual experiences, but he liked that she'd never known another man. He liked that she could belong to him and only him.

But all that would come later, he thought. First they had to finish the onerous task that had brought Darci and him together.

So now the three of them were lying on their bellies in the fallen leaves on top of a little knoll, several hundred yards from the house that Darci said was full of evil. Taylor passed out night-vision goggles to each of them, but they saw nothing unusual. They could see no people anywhere. There were no guards outside, no dogs, nothing that could be thought of as a barrier to their walking into the house. There was only one light on in the house and that was at the top of the third floor in what was probably the attic. There was a round window in the gable end of the roof, and a warm yellow light glowed from there.

"I don't like this," Taylor said, sitting up. "This lack of protection scares me more than anything I've seen before in this business. Do you think the town knows that this house belongs to the woman and therefore they leave it alone?"

"Probably," Adam said, also sitting up. "But still, it's spooky, isn't it? I thought the place would be a prison, with walls and guards carrying guns. If she owns something as valuable as this mirror, wouldn't she be protecting it?"

"Do you know who else knows she has the mirror?" Taylor asked.

"Besides me," Adam said, "I think there are a number of

psychics, and, from what I've seen, probably half of Camwell knows. How do you know about it?"

"A student of mine has a sister who joined the cult, and, as far as I can tell, the mirror is what they base all their hopes of attaining power on."

"Psychics and hearsay," Darci said as she sat up beside Adam. "What you two are saying is that you aren't completely sure that this thing exists."

There wasn't much light, but Darci saw Adam open and close his mouth a couple of times as though he were preparing to defend himself. But then he looked at Taylor. Finally, Adam looked back at Darci. "Right. That's about it. I'm not sure about much of anything. I spent years trying human methods to find information, but I couldn't find out much of anything. So I went to the inhuman side. Or the paranormal side, I guess." While Adam had been saying this, he had been looking upward into the trees. Near them was an oak tree that had to be several hundred years old. It had thick, sprawling branches.

"Taylor, old man," Adam said, "think you could give me a boost up? I'd like to climb up there and see what I can of the inside of the house. Maybe I could see someone or something."

"Old man," Taylor said with a snort. He was only seven years older than Adam. "Come on, child, and I'll help you up." Cupping his hands, he looked at Adam.

Adam stepped into the older man's hands, then up onto his shoulders until he caught the lowest branch of the oak tree and he began to climb upward.

Not too far, Darci said to him in her mind. *Please don't fall. I don't want you to get hurt. If you get hurt—*

"Quiet!" Adam hissed down at her. "I can't think when you talk so much." Carefully, he walked out onto a thick branch while holding an upper one, then stretched out on his stomach, put the night-vision goggles to his eyes, and looked.

What do you see? Darci called up to him, but Adam didn't answer.

"Well?" Taylor asked his daughter.

Darci shrugged. She could only project thoughts to Adam, not receive them; she couldn't hear what he was thinking.

Minutes later, Adam came down from the tree, swinging on the last branch and dropping to the ground. "There's someone in that room at the top of the house. It's a woman, and I can see her pacing back and forth. She moves as though she's young."

"That's not much to go on," Taylor said.

Adam looked hard at Darci. "When I'm up there and with these on, I can see laser beams across the lawn. From this angle you can't see them. You can't even see them from only fifteen feet up. You have to be up where I was. It's a state-of-the-art protection system," he said. "I'll give that to her. She has some technology that I've never even heard of before." He paused for a moment, his eyes drilling into Darci's. "But I can get through it."

"How can you do that if you can't see where the beams are?" Darci asked instantly. "You know what *I* think we should do? We should call the police and let them handle this. Or, better yet, let's call your friend in the FBI. The FBI has experience at these things."

"And you don't think that she'd see that in the mirror?" Adam asked softly.

"If she sees them coming, then she must have seen us too," Darci said in exasperation, then, "Oh. We have been seen in the mirror," she said and thought of Susan Fairmont and her dead sister who looked like Darci.

"Time-wise, Nostradamus's predictions were never really right on the mark," Taylor said. "Even the quatrains that people have been able to figure out were off by years. I'm sure that the mirror has shown you to her, Darci, but I don't think they know the exact date when you'll show up. And it's my guess that they expect you at the tunnels."

"I think the tunnels might be safer than this place," she said. "We were in them, and I didn't feel anything horrible in them." She rubbed her arms as chills ran up them. "But then, I've never felt anything as . . . as unhappy as that house is." Neither man replied to this but just kept looking at her. She knew they wanted something from her, but she didn't know what. She ignored them as long as she could, then said, "What?!"

Adam looked at Taylor, and they silently agreed that her father would tell her. "Darci, you can direct Adam around the laser beams. You need to climb that tree, put on the goggles, and tell him with your mind how to step around them."

She set her mouth into a rigid line. "I don't like high places. I don't climbing trees, and I especially don't like anyone going into houses full of very bad things."

Adam frowned. "What if you had a sister and she were—"

Taylor put his hand on his daughter's arm. "What if Adam were trapped in that house? What would you do to get him out?"

Darci was embarrassed that her father, this man she had so recently met, could see so much about her. "Nothing," she said, trying to keep her dignity intact. "I wouldn't so much as lift a finger to get him out of anywhere. I just met him a few days ago and, all in all, he's a pain in the—"

She broke off because Adam put his arm around her lower back, pulled her up toward him so that her feet came off the ground, and kissed her. He kissed her with everything that he had come to feel for her. He kissed her in memory of the first time he'd seen her in her little cat suit. He kissed her in memory of all the times she'd made him laugh. He kissed her for every time he'd wanted to touch her but hadn't allowed himself to. And, most of all, he kissed her for . . . well, he wasn't yet sure, but he thought maybe he kissed her for love.

When he set her back down on the ground, Darci's body swayed and Adam put a hand on her shoulder to steady her.

"Want a boost up?" he asked, and his voice was husky.

All Darci could do was nod.

But instead of a boost, Adam removed her jacket, so that she was standing there in just her little black leotard, then he lifted her up to the lowest branch. But as he lifted her, his hands ran up her body, touching the sides of her breasts, moving down her ribs to her waist, then down the side of her little derriere and down her legs. "You ready to help me?" he asked when she was sitting on the lowest branch.

All Darci could do was nod silently.

"Good girl," Taylor said, but he was frowning at Adam. "If you—" he began under his breath.

Adam turned a cold face to Taylor. "You researched my family. Did you find any history of dishonor anywhere in my family?"

"None," Taylor said. "A few tragedies, some failures, and a lot of success, but no stories of betrayal by a Montgomery."

"Right," Adam said, "and I can assure you that I won't be the first." He turned back to look up at Darci. "Now, baby, climb up to where I was. Be careful, go slowly, and don't fall. But, remember, if you do fall, I'll be here to catch you. All right?"

Again, Darci nodded; then slowly, she began to climb the tree. She didn't move with the assurance that Adam had, but she was able to find her way and put her feet where she needed to.

"That's it," came Adam's soothing voice from below, but she didn't look down at him, afraid that her fear might overwhelm her. Right now the feel of Adam's lips on hers, and his hands on her body, were keeping her strong and brave. But if she looked down and saw reality, saw that the ground was about twenty feet below, she wasn't sure that any memory on earth would hold her.

Once she was at the branch that Adam had been on, she slowly and carefully stretched out on her stomach, put the big goggles on, and looked toward the house. Sure enough, she could see the crisscrossing red beams of laser light that surrounded the house and protected it. What happened if someone walked through one of those beams of light? she wondered. Did dogs come out and attack the trespasser? Or, did the fire-breathing dragons Sally the smart-mouthed waitress mentioned rush out to devour the intruder?

"Stop it!" Adam hissed up at her. "You're thinking out loud—and I do *not* like what I'm hearing!"

Darci took a deep breath. It took concentration to avoid sending her thoughts to Adam, and when she was thinking of something else, her thoughts just seemed to go to him naturally.

"Ready?" he said up to her.

Yes, she told him, then took a deep breath to steady herself so she could concentrate on the job ahead of her.

Right away, she realized that it wasn't going to be easy. There was no pattern to the red beams of light, and, worse, it was very difficult to tell how far they were from the ground. From her perch high up, it was close to impossible to tell if the beams were two feet off the ground or ten feet.

Stop! she yelled at Adam in her mind. He had taken only two steps and already he was half an inch from the first beam. *Left, now right. Now. . . . Wait.* Darci had to take the goggles off and close her eyes for a moment. Give me strength, she prayed. Give me knowledge. She put the goggles back on, then looked again at the beams. They were different shades of red! she thought. Maybe it was the way she'd first put on the goggles or maybe, she thought, it was her prayer, but now she could see that the beams were different shades of red. The ones high off the ground were lighter than the ones that were close to the ground. Now she could tell Adam which ones to step over and which ones to snake under.

Down, she said. *Down now. Lower. On your belly.* Darci was spitting out orders to Adam, short, staccato orders that she could send to him with a force that made his head ache. *Up!* she ordered. *Stand up and step over. Leg higher.*

Now stick out your leg. Follow it. Turn left. Sharper. No, go back. Down on your belly. Up. Now! Over. Watch your foot. Slowly!

On the ground, Taylor could hear nothing. Standing on the little hill, he used the goggles to watch Adam as he did what looked like a contortionist's dance across the front lawn. Taylor was a bit in awe that Adam could hear Darci's directions so clearly in his mind. First Adam would stand up and take a high step over an invisible line, then he'd drop down and crawl. He would go forward for three feet, then turn back toward them for four feet. For Taylor, watching, it was exciting and terrifying at the same time.

He had been involved in the supernatural for all his adult life. As a child he'd heard the whispered tales of his ancestors and what the women in his family could do. In his family it was something to be proud of, but, at the same time, it was something to keep hidden at all costs. In 1918, many members of his family had been wiped out in the flu epidemic, and the family had never recovered their numbers from it. They had never been prolific at best, but after the losses of the epidemic, it seemed that the number of members in each generation had grown smaller. His mother had told him a thousand times that it was up to *him* to produce a daughter with the "gift."

It was when Taylor had found out that a car accident had rendered him infertile that he'd become interested in the occult professionally. But over the years he'd developed a theory that the most talented of the clairvoyants and other psychically gifted people stayed away from people like him, who wanted to study them and categorize what they could do. In all his years of research, he had never seen anything like what he was seeing at this moment, with this lovely girl stretched out on a tree branch and using her mind to direct a man through a field of laser beams.

It took Adam nearly forty-five minutes to get through the field, and when he reached the front porch of the house, Taylor was so relieved that he had to sit down. But now what? he thought. How did Adam get inside the house? Did a witch hide a key under the doormat?

Adam, standing on the porch at last, seemed to be thinking the same thing. Turning, he looked back at the tree where Darci was hiding and lifted his hands and shoulders as though to say, What now? The next second, he nodded, so Darci must have said something to him.

Taylor could see Adam's shoulders rise, as though preparing for a blow, as, slowly, he put out his hand toward the doorknob. Then, even more slowly, he began to turn the knob. So far, no alarms had gone off. But as Taylor watched Adam continue to turn the knob, his heart began to beat faster and he held his breath.

When the door opened, Taylor let out his breath. With a glance up at the tree toward Darci, he wished he could share a shout of triumph with her. But he couldn't. Turning back, he watched Adam disappear into the house.

"I can't see him!" came Darci's cry down from the tree, and Taylor could hear the agony in her voice. What was going on inside the house?

Taylor wanted to reassure her, but he couldn't. He wanted to tell her that everything was going to be all right, but he couldn't. Over the years he'd seen more horror than anyone should have to see in a lifetime so he knew, better than they did, what *could* happen.

All they could do now was wait. Who was inside the house? Was someone waiting in ambush for Adam? The witch had bungled her first attempt to imprison Adam so many years ago, but Taylor doubted that she'd miss her second chance. She wasn't going to lose him a second time.

It took all Taylor's self-control to calm down and make himself wait. And wait. Time passed. He couldn't tell if it was minutes or hours. He watched the house until his eyes ached. Up in the tree, Darci was silent.

Suddenly, Taylor's head came up. Something was wrong. He knew it. Something had gone wrong. Adam was taking too long. But there was something else wrong, too, something that he couldn't identify, but he could *feel* it.

He readjusted the goggles and looked about the house and grounds. Nothing. He could see nothing wrong.

"What is it?" Darci whispered down to him, feeling her father's rapidly growing fear.

Taylor put up his hand for her to be quiet. There was nothing that he could see, but the hairs on the back of his neck were standing on end. Quietly, he walked down the hillside toward the house. He couldn't see the beams, and if Darci saw him get too close to one, she couldn't warn him with her mind as she did with Adam. All she could do would be to shout at him, and he knew that might create a commotion that they couldn't afford. They couldn't risk anything while Adam was in the house.

"There!" Taylor said aloud when he saw it. It was so dark that he hadn't seen anything at first. Yes, the witch had been expecting them. And, yes, she had known what they were going to do. Very, very slowly, coming down over the windows and the doors were steel bars. Their slow descent was to prevent whoever was watching from noticing the bars and shouting a warning, either by voice or thought. The woman must have known that someone would be watching and that their attention would be on those red beams of light and the unlocked front door.

"Darci!" Taylor said as loudly as he dared. "The windows! Look at the windows!"

At that moment a cool burst of wind sent thousands of autumn leaves cascading down. "What?" Darci asked, not able to hear him.

"The windows!" he said again. "Look at the windows. Get Adam out of there *now!*"

When Darci was finally able to hear her father, she looked back at the windows, and saw that the bars were already halfway down. The bars were moving so slowly that she couldn't actually see them moving. No wonder the movement hadn't caught her eye! *Out! Out! Out! Out!* she screamed to Adam as loud as she could, but when she saw no movement inside the house, she sat upright.

In her panic, she had forgotten that she was in a tree and that just above her was another branch. Darci's head slammed into the branch, and for a moment she looked at the world going round and round. In the next second, she fell back down onto the branch, her cheek smacking hard into the rough bark.

"Oh, God," Taylor said, having seen everything from below. Think! he commanded himself. It was up to him now, so what could *he* do? All the gates coming down were now so low that with another inch or so and Adam would not be able to escape the house. If Taylor could run across the beams, if he could wedge something strong under a window, if he could—

In the next moment, Taylor was running down the hill and thanking God that they had decided to bring his Range Rover instead of Adam's cheap rental car. The Range Rover was an odd vehicle. It was a draft horse compared to the racehorses that most cars on the road were. The Range Rover was slow and sluggish; it was a pain to try to drive on highways. It was big and cumbersome and as heavy as a dump truck. Its true four-wheel-drive gearing made it difficult to turn even with power steering, and at stop lights, a child on a tricycle could probably speed away faster.

But what was magnificent about the Range Rover was that it could climb a glass mountain. A wet one. Taylor had traveled with his Rover into the backwoods of Virginia, North Carolina, and Kentucky, and there was nowhere the vehicle couldn't go. It could go straight up, over rocks, across dry gullies. It could ford rivers deep enough to run a boat on. It could cross logs that had fallen across steep mountain roads. As long as the Rover had one wheel touching the ground, it would go.

But right now, what Taylor needed most was the weight of the Rover. It was a heavy, heavy car. Thousands of pounds of steel, with a motor that would keep on going no matter what.

Grabbing the keys out of his pocket as he ran, Taylor leaped up into the seat of his red Range Rover, started the engine, and put it in low gear. He'd owned three Range Rovers in fifteen years, and no matter that he'd climbed mountains with them, he had never, ever put the car in its low gear, the one that the Range Rover people said he might need for "really tough terrain."

"How about a really tough *house?*" he said aloud as he put the big car in low and hit the gas. Range Rovers never leaped, no more than a bull elephant ever needed to leap. When there was that much torque and pulling power in a vehicle, it didn't need to leap.

The driveway to the house was about a quarter of a mile down the road; they had stayed away from the front entrance, but Taylor didn't want the driveway. He turned the dial for the headlamps, pushed the button for the flashing emergency lights, then started up the hill that lay between him and the house where Adam was slowly becoming imprisoned.

Easily, the Range Rover went up the hill, and when Taylor topped it, he knew that if he was going to make a hole in that house, a hole that would have no steel cage in front of it, he had to hit the wall hard. When he came over the top of the hill, the Rover was on two wheels, and it hit the ground at the bottom of the hill so hard that Taylor went flying upward, but, thankfully, he was short enough that his legs were under the steering wheel and that kept him from slamming into the roof.

The moment Taylor had started down the side of the hill, he prepared himself to hear the screech of alarms going off when he hit the laser beams. But there was no sound. Either they were phony or Adam had somehow disconnected them once he'd entered the house.

But Taylor had no time to think because he was fast approaching the house—and he tried to prepare himself for the coming impact. He knew he wouldn't be able to get out of the car before the collision. If he let up on the gas, the Rover would stop in its place and he'd not make an escape hole for Adam. In his headlights, he could see that the steel bars were now only inches from the windowsills. Adam was trapped inside!

Taylor went through the side of the house, the big car tearing a hole all the way through it, and try as he might to keep his head upright, when he hit the staircase at the far side of the room and stopped, Taylor's head hit the steering wheel and the blow knocked him unconscious.

Adam had been standing at the top of the staircase when the car hit it. Over his right shoulder was slung the wrist-and-ankle-bound body of the young woman he believed was his sister. Over his left shoulder was a leather pouch that contained an old, beat-up, and very ordinary looking mirror.

The impact of the car coming through the wall of the house, then hitting the staircase, knocked Adam off his feet. He did the best he could to protect the woman he held as he went down, but he still heard her muffled, "Uff!" when Taylor and the car slammed into the staircase and the two of them hit the floor.

Adam didn't know what was wrong. He'd heard Darci yell that he was to get out, but at that moment, he couldn't leave because he hadn't finished securing the woman.

Earlier, when Adam had turned the doorknob to the house and found it unlocked, his breath had caught in his throat. He was so sure that alarms were going start screeching that, for a moment, the silence was deafening. As he stepped inside the house, his breath was held, his every sense alert, and he held at arm's length a gun that he'd had concealed under his sweatshirt.

But he saw no one, heard no one. After a moment of standing still and listening, he stepped out of the little entrance hall and looked into the room to his right. He was looking for would-be attackers, but he couldn't contain his curiosity about the interior of the house. How did a woman of such evil live?

Adam had grown up in a house full of museum-quality antiques, but, even so, that house had been a home. But, right away, Adam saw that this house was not a home. The contents of the living room had been bought off a show-room floor and set inside the house without much concern for homeyness. There was no lived-in look about the room; there were no personal artifacts, no photos on the mantel, no pictures on the walls that seemed in any way personal.

In spite of himself, Adam shivered at the sight of the room. There was something eerie about the place, even though there was nothing overtly sinister within sight.

With his gun still held out, he moved to the dining room. It was the same: nothing personal, nothing that looked as though it had ever been used by any human. Was the house a front for the woman? Did she live elsewhere in a house that was protected by walls and gates? Was this house a decoy to lure Darci to her?

For a moment, Adam felt panic rise in him. He'd left Darci alone, with only Taylor for protection. At that thought, his panic grew stronger. What did he really know about Taylor? The man had written many books on the occult. Maybe he knew so much because he was inside the system. Maybe he—

Adam had to take some deep breaths to calm himself, or he'd never be able to accomplish what he'd set out to do. For all that he'd talked about the mirror, his true purpose was to get the woman at the top of the house and get the hell out of there.

There was a kitchen at the back of the house, and Adam took a moment to fling a couple of cabinets open. Empty.

If this house was a front, if it was unused, then why had Darci said it was "full of evil"?

Quietly, his shoes making no sound on the hardwood floor, Adam made his way upstairs. The woman was on the top. Was that where the traps lay? Is that where the evil that Darci had sensed was hiding?

At the top of the stairs, Adam halted. Down the hallway were four closed doors. Should he continue up the next flight of stairs and ignore the doors? Would an army jump out from behind the doors as soon as he started up?

Slowly, silently, he crept down the hall toward the first door and opened it, pushing the door all the way back to the wall. It was a bedroom, again an impersonal place, its contents bought in their entirety from a furniture store's showroom. The curtains didn't fit the windows, and there'd been no attempt to make them fit. The chest of drawers was too big for the room and overlapped a window. Again, there was not so much as a hairbrush in the room.

The next room was a bathroom, with white tile and white towels that looked as though they'd never been used.

Another bedroom followed, but this room was different. It had nothing personal in it, nor did the adjoining bathroom, but it did look as though it had been used. The bedspread, a plain white cotton one, looked as though it had been washed many times. The furniture was that fake-antique stuff that manufacturers did so well, but it had a glossy look to it that no true antique ever had. After making a quick reconnaissance about the room, Adam left it.

The next door was to a room that made Adam's stomach turn over. It had a single iron bed in it, like a child's bed. There was a desk and a few bookcases against the walls. It might have been a normal room except for the walls. The one over the bed was painted with a picture of the tower from the tarot deck—the shape that had been branded on his chest, the shape that could be formed from the moles on Darci's hand.

On the facing walls were arrangements of weapons in patterns, something that had obviously been copied from similar collections he'd seen in medieval castles in Europe.

What was sickening about the room was that Adam knew in his heart that this was a child's room. And he had no doubt that it was the room his sister had been raised in.

Adam made a quick run through the adjoining bathroom, glanced at the sterile place, then left as quickly as he could. His mind was racing, full of what he'd just seen, and full of what Taylor had asked him. Could his sister have joined forces with the woman who was the head of this evil coven?

For all that Adam desperately wanted to get his sister away from this place, he knew that he couldn't trust her from the start. He'd have to make her prove herself to him. He couldn't—

As Adam put his foot on the bottom stair step in preparation for going up, he suddenly stopped. He'd seen something that was itching at the back of his mind. What was it? For a moment he closed his eyes and let the visions of what he'd just seen run through his mind. What had he seen? Something was wrong; something was out of place. Where? he shouted inside his head. *What* was wrong?

He couldn't figure it out, but when he put his foot on the second step, he knew. Everything in the house, except for the weapons on the walls, was new and impersonal. There wasn't an antique or even anything old anywhere. Many things had been cut and grooved and speckled by the manufacturers to try to imitate antiques, but Adam knew they were fakes.

But not all of them, he thought, then turned and nearly ran down the hall to the bedroom with the white bed-spread. On the far wall were three pictures, each of them those ubiquitous Redouté roses that designers so loved. But as Adam paused in the doorway and looked at the pic-tures, he knew that the frame on the end wasn't a fake antique; it was real. All the artificial aging in the world couldn't make wood look like that.

In one leap, Adam was across the bed and he'd grabbed the picture off the wall. As soon as he held it, he knew he was right: It was an antique, at least fifteenth century, was his guess. With hands that were close to trembling, he turned the picture over and tapped the back of it. The glass fell out into his hand, the print of the roses attached to it.

When Adam turned the frame over, he saw that he was holding a mirror—and when he looked into it, he could see nothing.

He had no time to congratulate himself on his clever-ness, but he stuck the frame with its mirror inside his sweatshirt, tied the waistband of his pants tight around it, then practically ran up the stairs.

There was only one door at the top of the stairs, and he knew that she waited inside for him. With a weapon? he wondered. Would he open the door and be felled by a shotgun? Or a crossbow?

He flung open the door as he hid to one side, then waited, but there was no sound from inside. Cautiously, he put his head around the door frame.

She was sitting in a chair, facing the doorway, and for all the world, she looked as though she were waiting for him. The chair was one of those wicker ones, with a tall, round back that made it look like a throne.

He would have recognized her anywhere. She had the look of his family, with her green eyes and cleft chin. Her hair was pulled back into a loose braid that hung over one shoulder, across her chest, and onto her lap, making him wonder if her hair had ever been cut.

For a moment he leaned back against the wall. Now was not the time to let sentimentality rule him. This woman might be related to him by blood, but she had been raised in a way that he didn't want to think about it. It had to have affected her.

With the pistol held at arm's length, Adam entered the room, keeping her under surveillance at all times.

There was little expression on her handsome face. She just looked up at him as though she knew what was in his mind. No, Adam thought, she looked at him as though she knew what he was about to do. When she silently held out her hands toward him, her wrists held together, he had a momentary feeling of eeriness. It was true, he thought. Everything he'd been told was true: She had been kidnaped so she could read a magic mirror, and in the mirror she'd seen the future. She knew better than he did what he was going to do.

He didn't waste more time thinking about how or what she knew. There were several silk scarves draped over the arm of the big chair. After slipping the gun into his pants' pocket, he quickly used the scarves to tie her hands and wrists. She did not speak to him, and he was glad for that.

It was while he was tying her ankles that he heard Darci screaming inside his head that he had to get out *now!* What had she felt? he wondered. Or seen? Was it that she felt danger coming from this woman?

Quickly, Adam tied a scarf over the woman's mouth; he couldn't risk her giving a warning to whoever might be hiding and waiting for him.

But it was when he had her bound and gagged that he turned and saw a small wicker desk and stool against the wall. On the desk was a small mirror in a frame. The frame was gold—real gold, he could see that—and it was set with uncut diamonds, rubies, and emeralds. He knew that the frame was worth many hundreds of thousands of dollars, at least, if not more.

Adam wanted no such gaudy prize as this, but he knew that it had been placed there for his benefit. But by whom? If it had been put there by this woman, his sister, had she done it with the intent of tricking him? If so, then he was right not to trust her.

With a little smile at her, a smile that he hoped would make her think he believed he'd just found the real mirror, he picked it up and looked into it. But he could see nothing whatever.

"Which proves that *I'm* not a virgin," he said aloud, then he heard a sound from the woman from behind her gag. He must be going mad, he thought, because it had almost sounded like a laugh. Couldn't be, he thought. Not a laugh at one of *his* jokes.

But Adam had no more time to dawdle. In what he was sure was preparation for his taking of the mirror, there was a leather satchel draped from a hook on the wall. Grabbing the bag, Adam dropped the gold-framed mirror into it; then, with his back turned to her, he surreptitiously removed the other mirror from under his shirt and dropped it also into the bag. When the satchel was on one shoulder, he bent and slung the woman over his other shoulder—no mean feat, considering that she was nearly as tall as he was.

He had been at the top of the staircase down to the first floor when all hell broke loose as a big red car came tearing through the house.

Adam gathered up the satchel and the woman, then stood up again and looked down, seeing the top of Taylor's head leaning on the steering wheel. Such an act by Taylor could only mean that time had run out. The staircase was ruined, so Adam couldn't get down that way. He had no time to hesitate. With one great leap, he jumped onto the top of the Range Rover, then carefully put the woman down on the roof. She was glaring at him hard and desperately trying to say something. But Adam didn't want to hear what she had to say. Was she telling him that he'd be sorry for taking her? Or was she going to thank him for rescuing her? Right now Adam didn't have time to find out.

He scrambled down the side of the car, opened the door and roughly pushed Taylor into the passenger seat. Right now he didn't have time for niceties.

But what was going on? Adam wondered. Even though the side of the house had been smashed, there were still no alarms going off. But, worse, there was no Darci shouting in his head that he had to get out. No Darci telling him what he needed to do to get out. Where was she?

Adam pulled the woman off the roof and put her across the backseat, then he got into the car behind the wheel. Please go, he prayed. The engine was still running, so maybe there was a chance. He put the car in reverse and it moved. "Thank You," he whispered, eyes skyward, then he backed the car over the debris and out of the hole as fast as it would go. The tires were scraping something in front that had been smashed, and he could see smoke coming from under the hood, but the big car was still going.

When he reached the top of the hill, Adam leaped out. There was no longer any need to remain quiet, so he shouted up into the tree, "Darci!"

Here, came the weak reply. *I'm*—"Eiiiiiiiiiiii," she screamed as she fell. She had awakened at Adam's call, but she'd lost her balance and slipped off.

Adam caught her, but the force of her hitting him made him fall back against the ground hard.

"Adam, darling," Darci said as she put both hands on the sides of his face and began kissing him. "Are you all right?"

"Fine," he managed to say. "But we have to go. Can you get in the car?" He was woozy from the impact of her hitting him, but he didn't want her to know that. But when he stood up and took a breath, he thought that a couple of ribs might be broken.

"You're hurt," she said.

Adam saw the way she was listing to one side. She, too, was hiding injuries. "Can you get into the car?" he repeated. "We need to get out of here. Fast."

"Yes, of course," she said.

"In the back," Adam said, holding his side as he opened the door for her. "And be careful. *She* is in there."

For one horrifying moment, Darci thought Adam meant the boss, the witch, but then she looked into the car and saw the bound-and-gagged woman lying across the seat. Instantly, Darci knew that there was no evil coming from this woman. She didn't think twice before gently lifting the woman's head and putting it on her lap. Darci knew evil when she was around it, and this woman was *not* evil.

As quickly as he could, Adam got into the driver's seat. Taylor had regained consciousness and was sitting up. "Where are you going?" he asked hoarsely.

"As far away from here as I can get," Adam answered. "I have what I came for, so I'm leaving."

"She will retaliate," Taylor said in a voice barely above a whisper. "Let me out here."

"What?!" Adam said. The car was badly damaged and wouldn't last much longer, so they needed to get away as fast as possible.

"She will want someone to take revenge on, so let me out *now!*" Taylor said more forcibly. But the effort took his strength, and he leaned back against the leather seat and closed his eyes.

"I'm getting us all out of here," Adam said quietly.

"She knows who Darci is now," Taylor said, his voice barely a whisper but urgent. "Darci will never be safe again in her life. No matter where she goes, the woman will come after her."

"And *you* are going to stop her?" Adam asked. "How can you do that? You don't even know what she looks like. And you're injured."

"But *I* do," came a voice from the backseat, a voice that neither Adam nor Taylor had heard before.

"You took the gag off of her?" Adam said in horror, looking at Darci in the rearview mirror.

"It was hurting her," Darci said defiantly.

"We don't know anything about her. She could be—"

"But you know everything about me, don't you, brother?" the woman said, then, with Darci's help, she pulled herself upright and looked at Adam in the rearview mirror. "I can help," she said. "I can help bring her down, but I cannot do it alone. It is nearly dawn now. We must rest. Is there somewhere we can go to rest? Tonight is the time. If she is not stopped tonight, her power will double." The way she spoke was odd, every word carefully pronounced, as though she'd learned to speak by reading, rather than by hearing other people talk.

"Why?" Taylor said, turning around to look at the woman. But he was in too much pain to turn fully, so he couldn't see her face. "How? What has she planned?"

"She knew of this. She has seen some of it. I saw all of it, but I lied to her, as I often do. But she has others who can see in the mirror now, so she validates me. You do not have the true mirror. She has it. She has children locked up, and tonight she means to sacrifice them. I must stop her."

"You won't be alone!" Taylor said, then had to lean back against the seat to get his breath.

"And I will help you, too," Darci said softly.

"Oh, hell!!" Adam said angrily.

"Don't curse," Darci said at the same time that the woman said, "Do not curse" then the two women looked at each other, and in spite of the situation, they smiled.

In the front seat, Taylor smiled too, but Adam didn't. If he had been alone, he would have readily agreed to go back there after that evil woman, but now he had Darci. And, he thought as he looked into the rearview mirror, he had a sister. And, glancing at Taylor, who was obviously in pain, Adam acknowledged that, with Darci's father, he now had a family, his own family, not one where he was an outsider, an intruder.

Now that he had everything he'd ever wanted in his life, he was going to have to risk losing it all in one night.

16

"I GUESS THIS IS AS SAFE as we're going to get," Adam said in resignation as he pulled the severely damaged Range Rover into the back of the parking lot of a cheap motel. He parked off the gravel, under a tree, where the car could not be seen from the road or even by someone driving through the parking lot. Leaving the others in the car, he woke the owner of the motel and paid cash for one room with two queen-size beds.

While he was doing this, he was thinking about what he could say to Darci to persuade her to not participate tonight. Adam knew that he would be going into the tunnels or wherever "it" was to be held tonight—the mention of the children had decided him—but he didn't want Darci involved. As long as he had breath in him, he'd do what he could to prevent another child being hurt, but he didn't want Darci or Taylor or even this new person, his sister, involved.

As for his sister, all he could see when he looked at her was that room with the tower painted over the bed. Considering how she had been raised, for all he knew, the woman could be as diabolical as the witch she'd grown up with. She'd admitted that the mirror she'd seen him take was not the true mirror, but Adam couldn't bring himself to show her the other one he'd found. He'd already seen that he couldn't see any visions in it. Maybe Darci could; maybe she couldn't. The only way to find that out was to show it to her—and right now he couldn't do that in secret. Not yet, anyway. Maybe tonight, after they'd rested, he'd find a way to show Darci the mirror in private.

When Adam returned with the key to the room, the others were standing beside the car waiting for him. He studied them in the harsh yellow motel light. Taylor looked bad. There was a huge, darkening bruise on his forehead, and he was holding one arm awkwardly. Darci's eyes were red, and she looked a bit dazed, disoriented.

Beside Darci was the woman Adam was sure was his sister. He had to admit that she was a heroic-looking figure as she stood there with her hands bound in front of her. She was extraordinarily tall, and during the fracas, her thick black hair had come loose. It now fell in huge waves past her waist, cascading over a loose white blouse that was gathered at the neck. She had on a long cotton skirt and sandals on her bare feet.

She was looking at him with such defiance that Adam thought that he'd not like to be pitted against a woman such as she was. For all that, so far, her words had been right, and for all that she was his sister, and for all that she hadn't fought him when he'd taken her, in his mind, she had yet to prove herself.

Opening the door to the motel room, Adam let the others go in ahead of him, but as this woman passed him, he couldn't stop himself from saying, "I do not trust you."

"You are the fool then," she said, then walked past him, her head held high.

Once they were inside the room, Adam closed the door. "I think we should get some sleep," he said, looking at the two beds. In other circumstances, it would have made sense to put the two women in one bed. But he was not going to let Darci get near this woman who was nearly six feet tall.

Abruptly, Darci turned on him. "Adam!" she said angrily. "You're being a jerk."

"I must agree," Taylor said as he sat down on one of the two chairs in the room. "I think your sister has been through enough in her lifetime without the barbarian treatment that you are according her. Really! Just look at her!" he said, turning to gaze at the woman standing in front of the door. She was tall, beautiful, regal, dressed in an old-fashioned way, and her hands were bound before her. She looked like a romantic heroine from a story about clans and warfare and honor.

"She reminds me of someone," Taylor said in an odd voice that made Darci look at him. Since he'd first seen her, he hadn't seemed able to take his eyes off this proud, statuesque woman.

"Me too," Adam said, "but I can't think who it is."

"A queen," Darci said, smiling warmly at the woman. "She looks like a queen."

At that the woman smiled a bit at Darci, but she didn't bend her neck—and she didn't lose the arrogance of her glare at her brother.

"Boadicea," Adam said. "The warrior queen. That's who she reminds me of."

At that the woman's haughty look left her and she smiled; then she began to laugh. In fact, she laughed so hard that she had to sit down on the edge of one of the beds.

"Someone laughed at one of *your* jokes," Darci said to Adam in wonder. "If you had any doubt that she's blood kin, there's your proof."

Adam couldn't help but be pleased at his sister's laughter, but for the life of him, he couldn't see the joke. Boadicea was a first-century queen who led the British to fight the Romans, but *what* was so amusing about *that*?

Turning, the woman looked up at Adam. "Boadicea is my name."

"Aptly given," Taylor said, his eyes never leaving the woman.

At that moment Darci relaxed. Maybe Adam was being unreasonable about his sister, but if she could laugh at Adam's humorless jokes, then Darci was sure that soon he'd come around. "Is anyone besides me hungry?" she asked.

The men didn't answer her. Adam was staring at Boadicea in speculation, as though he was trying to figure her out. And Taylor was looking at the woman as though he'd fallen in love with her.

But Boadicea's attention was given to Darci. In a way, it was as though she was dismissing the men as of no importance. "Do you think we could buy what you people call junk food? I have a great desire to try such a thing."

"It's what I grew up on," Darci said cheerfully. "There's a grocery across the street, and—"

"I'll go," Taylor said. "I'll get you whatever you want."

"No, I'll go," Adam said. "I think it's my duty."

Turning, Darci looked at the men in surprise. It was almost as though they were fighting over who could fetch food for this extraordinarily beautiful woman.

Darci grimaced, then looked at Boadicea. "Have you ever heard the expression, 'Men are slime'?"

"Worse," Boadicea said. "*She* says they are useless."

At that the two women shared laughter.

Refusing to comment on what the women were laughing about, Adam looked at his watch. "It's four A.M. and I think we should all get some sleep. Later we can make plans about . . . about what we're going to do tonight. And as for food, we'll have to wait until the grocery opens. For sleeping, I think. . . ." He trailed off. If this woman was his sister and she wasn't the enemy, then it made sense that Darci should bunk with her.

But the truth was that Adam wanted to hold Darci in his arms. He just didn't know how to obtain that goal without saying that's what he wanted.

Standing up slowly, Taylor knew what Adam wanted, and he also knew that it was too late for subtlety. "I think that Boadicea is an unknown and therefore should not be trusted." When he glanced at her out of the corner of his eye, he could see the anger that was starting in her. "Therefore I think that a man should sleep between her and the door."

"Him?" Boadicea said, holding up her bound hands to point at Adam. There was a sneer in her voice.

"No!" Adam said. "I should. . . ." For the life of him, he couldn't think of a reason why he should be the one to sleep with Darci. After all, wouldn't it make sense to have father and daughter in one bed and brother and sister in the other?

"The two of you wouldn't fit in one bed," Darci said to Adam. "Look at her. She's as big as you are. You'd be hanging over the sides of the bed all night."

For a moment all three of them looked at Darci in puzzlement. The beds were quite big. But then they all smiled in understanding.

"Yes," Adam said. "That's a perfect solution. Okay, who gets the bathroom first?"

"Me!" Darci yelled, then ran.

Darci awoke from a sound sleep snuggled in Adam's arms. At first she was too tired and too disoriented to understand his muffled cries. Hours ago, when she'd first climbed into bed with Adam, she'd been sure that she was going to die of ecstasy. Never, ever would she be able to fall asleep.

"If we were very, very quiet," she whispered to him as she slipped into his arms, "you could make love to me right now."

Adam put his lips to her ear. "I give you a promise, Darci T. Monroe," he said. "If we get out of this alive, I swear by all that's holy that you won't be a virgin for more than five minutes after you tell me what I want to know from that mirror. Hey! You aren't going to faint on me again, are you?"

"Maybe," she said. "Would fainting get me more kisses?"

"I can't kiss you and keep my sanity. Just holding you is making me go"—he smiled—"bananas. And stop that! No wiggling allowed."

She stopped moving, but she kept her body pressed close to his. He'd never said that he loved her, but she felt that maybe he did. Truthfully, maybe she'd felt his interest in her from the first. He'd always looked at her as though she were someone unique.

"You want to take your watch off?" he whispered. She was still in her one-piece leotard, still wearing the beautiful gold watch he'd given her.

"No," she said. "I plan to wear it every day for the rest of my life. I'm going to be buried with it."

"By that time I'll have bought you a dozen watches, and this poor thing won't interest you anymore."

Darci had to take a deep breath before she replied to that. She knew that he was hinting at . . . she hardly dared think the word . . . marriage. She wanted to believe in that dream, but she also wanted to be honest with him. She took a deep breath. "Under different circumstances you might not like me. Now you need me to read a mirror, so I'm important to you. But I grew up in less-than-fortunate circumstances and there are things about me that might make you change your mind. I'm—"

She broke off because Adam kissed her. He didn't kiss her deeply, as he had before, because with the circumstances as they were now, he didn't know if he'd be able to stop. But he kissed her enough that he kept her from finishing her sentence. "Don't ever let me hear you say anything like that again," he said. "I liked you long before I knew you had any ability to boss people around with your mind. And as for where you come from, remember that I've been all over the world and I've met a lot of people. Trust me on this, Darci: You are unique no matter where you grew up."

"Is that good or bad?" she asked seriously.

"It's good. By the way, do you think you could teach me how to cast a zenobyre spell?"

"What's that?" she asked sleepily.

"A halting spell," he said. "You learned about it in college, remember? In your witchcraft minor."

Darci smiled as sleep began to overtake her. "I didn't study witchcraft. I studied poetry."

"Why, you rotten, low-down, lying . . ." he said, parodying her earlier words, but he could feel that Darci was asleep, so he kissed her hair and closed his eyes.

But Darci wasn't asleep. She wasn't sure, but she thought that, maybe, he planned to wait until she was asleep, then go to the tunnels himself. She wouldn't put it past him to lock them in the motel room and leave them without transportation. She knew that Adam had always been a lone soldier, and this time was no different. She couldn't risk his trying to save everyone by himself. Snuggling closer to him, she used her True Persuasion to soothe him and make him sleep.

But now, hours later, he had wakened her with his thrashing and his moaning.

"Is he all right?" Taylor asked as he leaned over the bed. "Can you calm him?"

"No," Darci said, frowning. "I've tried, but he's in some sort of deep trance, and I can't reach him."

"Adam," Taylor said, leaning across his daughter and trying to wake him. He could see that Darci was concentrating, trying to reach Adam with her mind—whether to soothe him back to sleep or to wake him, Taylor didn't know. Behind them, Boadicea stayed silent in the other bed, not stirring in spite of the commotion.

Adam suddenly struck out with his fist and barely missed hitting Taylor on the jaw.

"Wake him!" Taylor commanded his daughter. "What he's reliving must be horrible."

Darci had spent her life using her power in only the most superficial of ways. Making the moonshiner want to buy a dog hadn't taken any seriously deep concentration. But now, reaching Adam inside the sleeping trance that he was in took great effort. Her head was already aching from where she'd banged it on the tree—not that she'd told anyone that—and using her True Persuasion made it hurt more. But she stamped down the pain as she reached deep inside herself and concentrated until the room seemed to disappear. She was no longer in a body but was only energy, the energy of her mind, and this energy could move where it wanted, do what it needed to do. She found Adam's mind and entered it as best she could. Even though the pain in her head was increasing from this great effort, she pulled away from the discomfort for fear that Adam would feel her pain. Instead, she concentrated on soothing his tortured mind. She thought of a golden light covering his body and making him tranquil.

"Darci!" her father said. "Darci! Come out of it."

Slowly, she opened her eyes to look up at her father. He had her by the shoulders, and he was shaking her. When she opened her eyes, he embraced her and pulled her close to him. "I thought I'd lost you. Darci, you looked as though you were dead. I couldn't feel your pulse. You didn't even look as though you were breathing."

Turning slowly, for her neck hurt, Darci looked at Adam. He was sleeping peacefully now, but she sensed that he was close to waking up.

"Are you all right?" Taylor asked, looking at her in concern. "I've never seen anyone go into a trance as deeply as you just did. I think a train could have run over you and you wouldn't have felt it."

"I'm fine," Darci said, trying to smile and alleviate his worry. "But I need to go to the bathroom."

"Sure," Taylor said, pulling back the cover to allow her to get out of bed.

It took all Darci's strength and concentration not to fall down as soon as she put a foot to the floor. But she didn't want to add to her father's worries. The bruise on his forehead was very dark now, and he was holding his left arm closely to his side. "Really, I'm fine," she said again. "Just. . . ." She made a gesture toward the bathroom door, and he stepped aside.

Darci had to control herself to slowly close the bathroom door, and when she was alone, she fell to her knees and emptied her insides into the toilet. And when there was no more to come up, she gave dry heaves that racked her body, making her stomach contract until it felt as though it were next to her backbone.

She took her time washing out her mouth and trying to clear the air of the smell of her vomit. She didn't want the others to know that she'd thrown up. Nor did she want them to know how hard she'd hit her head on the tree branch last night. In the car, while Adam was driving and arguing that he didn't want to go on, Boadicea had sat silently next to Darci, and she was glad that his sister's presence had distracted Adam. He didn't see Darci blotting blood from her head with a box of tissues she'd found in the back of her father's car. And when they'd entered the motel room, Darci had been the first to go into the bathroom so she could wash the blood from her hair and scalp. But now, hours later, the cut was still oozing blood and still causing her a lot of pain.

But she wasn't going to let an injury stop her from participating tonight any more than her father was going to let his arm stop him. And, even though Adam pretended he was all right, Darci knew that Adam's ribs were injured. Of the four of them, only Boadicea seemed whole.

When she went back into the room, Adam was sitting up in bed. "Sorry to make such a pest of myself," he said, and she could see that he was trying to sound lighthearted.

In the other bed, Boadicea was lying quietly, eyes open, and Darci had an idea that she was used to being quiet and listening.

"I want you to tell us what happened to you when you were a child. I want you to tell us how you got that mark on your chest," Taylor said. "I think we all deserve that much." When he said this, his eyes included Boadicea in his statement, and the way she nodded made Darci wonder what had gone on between them during the night. Had her father told Boadicea about himself? About Darci? Adam?

Whatever had gone on between them, Darci could now feel that a bond had been formed between this beautiful woman and her father. Darci wanted to ask him about what she was feeling, but her father was right: Now there was a need for a different type of information. It would help all of them, give them courage, perhaps, if Adam told the whole story of what had happened to him when he was a child.

At first Adam protested, but one look at Taylor's eyes and he stopped. Even after he agreed to tell, it took Adam a moment to begin because he had never told anyone the whole story.

"When I was three years old," Adam began, and his voice was weak, shaky, and full of emotion, "I was told that my parents had died in a plane accident, so I was sent to live in a huge house in Colorado with my noisy, prolific Taggert relatives." He took a deep breath. "But the truth was that when I was three, I was kidnaped, and as a result of that, my parents died."

Here Adam had to pause, and Darci had to work to keep from saying something about how he must have felt carrying such a burden of guilt for his whole life. No, she wasn't going to interrupt him. But she used her mind to try to comfort him, to tell him that he was safe and among people who loved him.

"To this day, no one knows what actually happened," Adam continued. "I'd always been an independent child who loved to play hide-and-go-seek, and I'd hidden from my mother while she was buying me clothes in New York. Later, my mother told the police that she could see my shoe sticking out from under a rack of clothes, so she'd felt safe. She could *see* where I was, so she kept shopping. But after about ten minutes or so, when she was ready to check out, she tiptoed over to the rack, flung the clothes back, and said, 'Boo!' But only my shoe was there."

Darci could only imagine the hysteria his mother must have felt, the terror. Reaching out, Darci took Adam's hand in hers.

"After an hour or so of the entire store being searched, the police were called in, then the FBI. But a couple days went by and nothing happened. There was no ransom request, nothing. No contact was made by the kidnappers.

"But after three days of waiting, my parents sneaked out of the apartment and disappeared. To this day, no one knows why. Did they receive a message from someone? If so, who?"

Both Darci and Taylor waited in silence for Adam to continue, both of them feeling the many years of agony that Adam had felt in so desperately wanting to know who? Why?

"After my parents' disappearance, everyone on the police force was questioned. A policewoman said she remembered my parents stepping into their bedroom and closing the door for a few minutes. When they came out, she said they looked grim, as though they'd decided something. She said that at the time, she hadn't thought anything about the incident. It was only later that she remembered the looks on their faces.

"A couple of hours after my parents were alone in their bedroom, my father told one of the FBI men that he'd given up smoking years ago, but now, like he needed to breathe, he needed a cigarette, so he was going down to the local store to buy a pack. The FBI man offered my father one of his, but my father said they weren't his brand. Later, the agent said that my father seemed very nervous, but that was to be expected under the circumstances.

"No one knows when my mother slipped away. Minutes after my father left the apartment, the telephone rang and everyone jumped up and ran to it, ready to trace the call if it turned out to be the kidnapers. But on the fourth ring, when my mother didn't appear to answer it, they found that she wasn't in the apartment. Everyone searched for her, but no one could find her in the halls, the elevator, the stairs, anywhere. And when they went looking for my father, they couldn't find him either.

"Later, the FBI tried to piece what had happened together. My parents went into the bedroom and my father went down the fire escape to my cousin's apartment, where he called a helicopter company he sometimes used in business. When it was time for the helicopter to arrive, my father left the apartment, supposedly to get cigarettes. The FBI figured that he took the elevator upstairs to the roof, then called his apartment from the phone in the elevator. The second the phone rang, the FBI people ran toward it, while my mother slipped out the front door and ran up the stairs to the roof. She and my father were aloft in the helicopter by the time the FBI realized she was gone.

"It was easy enough to find out that the helicopter landed in upstate New York at a small airfield where my father kept his own four-seater plane. The helicopter pilot, who had no idea anything was wrong, waved good-bye to them as my father taxied down the runway and took off.

Adam closed his eyes for a moment. "My parents were never seen again."

"What about *you?*" Darci asked. "How did you get away from the kidnaper?"

"I don't know," Adam said. "Three days after my parents disappeared, a woman in Hartford, Connecticut, called the police. She was very upset, saying she'd found a little boy wandering in the woods behind her house."

"You," Darci said, squeezing his hand in both of hers.

"Yes. Me. I was naked and covered in deer ticks, and later I had the high fever of what was probably Lyme disease."

Darci and Taylor watched him in silence, waiting for him to continue.

"I remember nothing about what happened while I was kidnaped. I know children aren't supposed to remember much before their third birthday, but I do. In fact, I remember so much about my parents and our life together that, years later, the shrink I ended up going to didn't believe me. He called my cousin to verify what I'd told him."

"But you were right," Taylor said softly.

"Every word. I remember—" Breaking off, Adam took a deep breath. "Let's just say that if my parents walked in that door right now, I'd recognize them."

"What did the FBI find out when they investigated your disappearance?" Taylor asked.

"Nothing. They think my parents somehow received a message that hinted at my whereabouts. It probably said, 'Tell the cops and the kid is dead,' that sort of thing. They can only speculate because they don't know. They can't even figure out how a secret message was sent to them."

"Where did your parents go after they got into the plane?" Taylor asked.

"No one has any idea. The FBI thinks the plane went down over water. No one saw anything or has ever found anything, not so much as a piece of wreckage that could be from their plane."

"And what about you? You were so very little," Darci said. Lifting his hand, she held it to her cheek for a moment.

"I was a . . . mess," Adam said. "I was cold, hungry, dehydrated, and running a high fever when I was found. And I had an oozing sore on my chest that had become infected. At the time I was found, there were hundreds of people searching for both me and my parents." He looked at Taylor. "The FBI had managed to keep the kidnaping quiet, but when my parents disappeared, all hell broke loose and the media picked it up."

"So, after their disappearance, you were sent to live with relatives," Taylor said, disgust in his voice. "And it would be my guess that your family decided that it would be better for your peace of mind if they told you nothing."

"Yes. I'm sure they meant well. They thought I was young enough that I'd forget everything, especially if I didn't continue to live in a place that would remind me of my parents. And I was considered too young to have an opinion about where I wanted to live."

"But you did, didn't you? Even at three you had an opinion," Darci said fiercely.

"Oh, yes. I remember crying and saying that I wanted to get on a boat and go look for my mom and dad."

Me too, Darci thought to him as she held Adam's hand tighter. *I used to want to go look for my mother. My real mother. The one who loved me madly.* When Darci saw her father looking at her in curiosity, as though he was wondering what thoughts she was sending to Adam, she cleared her throat and released Adam's hand. "So you went to Colorado to live?"

"Yes. I lived with my cousins the Taggerts in an enormous house built in the 1890s. A beautiful house."

"But you got lost," Taylor said.

"I got lost," Adam said. "There were eight kids in the family, none of them haunted by grief. Their mother, my cousin Sarah, tried to make me part of their family, but she couldn't. No. That's not fair. I wouldn't allow myself to become part of them. I know that most people consider being an only child lonely, but I didn't." He gave a little one-sided grin. "I loved having a hundred percent of both my parents' attention."

Darci didn't smile. She knew about loneliness, both as a child and an adult. "So what happened to you?" she asked. "After you went to Colorado, I mean?"

"Nothing. I grew up. My cousins soon learned to leave me alone. I wasn't like them. I wasn't a team player. In fact, too many people around me makes me . . . well, nervous. And small spaces. . . ."

Adam took a moment to quiet himself. "Anyway, when I was twelve, I began to have nightmares. They were . . . pretty bad. I used to scream so loud that I woke the whole household, and when Sarah—I could never call her Mother—tried to hold me, I fought her, kicking, clawing. She once had a bruise from here to here," he said, running his hand along his jaw. "After that, only the men came when I started screaming. And when the dreams wouldn't stop, I was sent to a psychiatrist."

"Was he able to help?" Taylor asked.

"Not really. He tried to hypnotize me, but I wouldn't go under. But he did make my relatives tell me the truth about the kidnaping and tell me what little they knew about my parents' disappearance. But that made me feel worse. If it hadn't been for me, they wouldn't have died."

Taylor wanted to stop Adam from these thoughts; he could hear the anguish in Adam's voice. "So what happened with the psychiatrist?"

"After a year of trying, the man gave up. He couldn't get anything out of me because I didn't—and don't—remember what happened after I was taken. And the nightmares stopped as abruptly as they'd started."

"So you went back to your family and lived a normal life," Taylor said, smiling at his own jest.

"Not quite. I never told anyone—until now, that is—but after the dreams stopped, I was haunted by memories of my parents. I seemed able to remember my every moment with them." Adam closed his eyes for a moment, and Darci could feel that he was fighting back tears. "And I *missed* them. I missed my mother's laughter and the way she used to—"

He took a deep breath. "Anyway, I missed them, and I—"

"—wanted to know what happened to them," Taylor said.

"No, not then I didn't. During those years, I . . . drew into myself."

"You realized that you were different from other people, so you created your own world inside yourself," Darci said softly. "You wanted to avoid the outside world."

For a moment Adam looked at her in silence. She was blocking her mind from sending him any thoughts, but he knew what she was thinking: *Like me.* Adam didn't have power, or a "gift," as Taylor called what Darci could do, but the horror of Adam's early years made him as different from others as she was.

"Yes. Exactly," he said after a while. "I went to college, and while my relatives were becoming doctors or lawyers or majoring in business, I studied ancient history. I didn't know what I was going to do with such a degree, but I was drawn to read about civilizations of long ago. Then, after I got out of school, I drifted. I was offered a couple of teaching positions thanks to family connections, but what I really wanted to do was. . . . Does it make any sense to say that I wanted to disappear? I wanted to run away from myself."

"Yes, very much," Darci said before Taylor could speak.

"I have family money, but I didn't touch it. In fact, I didn't tell anyone where I was or where I was going—not that I knew. I took jobs wherever I could find them. I was a deckhand on a tramp steamer for four years. I worked on a ranch in Argentina for a couple of years. I just wandered around the world, living here and there, but not really living at all. For a while I thought I wanted to write, but what I put on paper seemed to tap into some black part of my soul that I didn't want to look at, so I stopped that."

"What made you start this? This looking for evil. And involving yourself in witches' covens?" Taylor asked.

"One of my Taggert cousins spilled a cup of tea on me. Ironic, isn't it? I traveled all over the world seeking . . . I'm not sure what I was looking for, but I know that I didn't find it. Then I was on one of my rare return visits to Colorado, and several of us were outside by the tennis court. They were laughing and talking, but I was just sitting there watching them, there but not with them. All of us had cold drinks, but my cousin Lisa drank hot tea all year round. She stood up to cheer her brothers on in a tennis match, and the hot tea spilled down the left side of my chest. It was nothing really, but Lisa made a big fuss about it and had me take off my shirt so she could see if I was injured."

Adam took a deep breath. "But the tea hadn't hurt me much because there was thick scar tissue across that area of my chest."

"From the 'oozing sore,'" Taylor said softly.

"Yes. It was a scar I'd had as long as I could remember, and I'd thought little about it. My cousin Sarah said she guessed that I'd fallen against some rocks, but she didn't know for sure. Since there was a big chunk of my life that I didn't remember, the scar seemed the least of it. It was tight, and sometimes when I moved my arm over my head, it would pull a bit, but I never really paid any attention to it."

"Until that day," Taylor said.

"Right," Adam answered. "On that day, one of my cousins, who was a year younger than me and so didn't remember anything about the kidnaping, said it was an ugly scar and I ought to get a plastic surgeon to fix it. Then her brother, who is six years older than I am, said, 'Maybe he should see what's under it.'"

"The brand," Darci said. "It had been hidden by the scar tissue."

"Yes. As soon as my cousin said that, his mother told him to go into the house and get her a sweater even though it was eighty-five degrees in the shade."

"Did you ask your cousin what he meant by that?"

"No. I could see by his mother's face that she didn't want to talk about the kidnaping and what had happened. I've always felt sorry for her because she tried really hard to make me part of her family, but she couldn't. I know she blamed herself for. . . ."

"For your sadness?" Darci asked.

"Yes. My sadness and my feeling that I never belonged."

"So what did you do?" Taylor asked.

"The next day I left and flew to New York, where I consulted a plastic surgeon. I told him I wanted the scar tissue removed carefully because there was something under there that I wanted to see. It was more than a brand. The skin"—he sounded as though he was talking of someone other than himself—"had been deeply cut first, and the branding iron had a black pigment on it. When the scar tissue was cut away, the black design could be seen clearly."

"And that's when you realized that there was more to this than you'd been told," Taylor said, sitting back in the chair and looking at Adam in speculation.

"Yes. First I started searching for the information the 'normal' way. I went to private detectives, and I even got into the FBI files, but there was nothing there. Finally, when I'd exhausted every other route, I went to see a psychic. But all she said was that my parents were dead and that their death was surrounded with evil. It was very annoying to hear such silliness. I wanted to know who, how, and most of all, *why*.

"Why were my parents killed before a ransom could be

paid? My father started liquidating stocks the moment he heard I was missing. But nothing was paid. What happened to their plane? Thousands of questions ran through my mind.

"But the psychics I consulted had no answers for me, and I was left feeling more frustrated than I'd been before I went to them.

"I had decided not to see any more psychics when one of them called me and said that Helen Gabriel wanted to talk to me. Since I'd never heard of the woman, the name meant nothing to me, but the psychic on the phone said that I *had* to call Helen. As far as I could get out of her, this Helen Gabriel was a psychic's psychic."

"Real as opposed to hype," Taylor said from experience.

"Yes," Adam answered. "It seemed that this woman didn't take on clients. I mean, you can't make an appointment to see her. You have to be *invited* to go to a session with her." Adam looked at Taylor. "You've met people like her?"

Taylor smiled and looked as though he was considering whether or not he should tell what he knew. "There are twelve women . . ." he said softly.

"Who can change the world with their minds," Darci said, her eyes alive with excitement. "Avatars."

When Taylor smiled at his daughter, there was such love—and pride—on his face that Darci blushed with pleasure. "Later, when this is over, I want you to tell me about your marvelous education that has allowed you to know such an obscure piece of information as that one."

Extremely pleased, Darci looked at Adam, who had an I-told-you-so look on his face. He'd said her father would see that she was educated.

"So what did Helen tell you?" Taylor asked, and from the way he said the name, Adam was sure that Taylor knew of the woman.

"At first, she was a disappointment because she told me that she wasn't sure what had happened to my family. But then she threw me for a loop because she said that one of my family was still alive."

"I bet that made you crazy," Taylor said.

"Oh, yes. I wanted to hire mercenaries and attack whoever was still holding one of my parents, but I didn't know where to start looking or whom to attack. And that's when Helen told me that there was only one way on earth for me to find out the truth about the past. She said there was a woman in Camwell, Connecticut, who had in her possession a magic mirror. When she told me that, I nearly walked out. I've always been a realist. Even as a kid I hated those stories of magic this and magic that."

"That's true," Darci said, smiling. "He knows nothing about fairy tales."

"I think Helen read my mind, because she then said there was some magic that was real. She told me that the mirror had once belonged to Nostradamus. Truthfully, I couldn't believe what she was telling me. But she said that if I could get that mirror, then it could be seen what had happened to my family. I want you to notice that she always said 'family,' and not 'parents.' I didn't realize this until later."

"And the mirror is where Darci came into it, right?" Taylor asked.

Adam couldn't look directly at Darci because he didn't want her to hear what else he'd been told. When he did finally speak, his voice was barely above a whisper. "I was told that I could steal the mirror, but that only a virgin past two-and-twenty could see the visions in it. If I didn't have the virgin, the mirror would only be an old piece of glass. So she told me to put an ad in the *New York Times* and I'd find the virgin who could read the mirror."

"You mean that not one of those women you interviewed was . . . ?" Darci said.

"Not one of them," Adam answered, smiling at Darci, but he wasn't about to tell her that she was the oddity, not them.

"Amazing," she said.

Adam turned to look at her. "Not that I'm complaining, but why haven't you . . . ? You know?"

Darci shrugged. "I've never met anyone who even tempted me," she said honestly. What she didn't say, either aloud or in her mind, was, "until I met you."

"Then *why* are you engaged to *marry* Putnam?" Adam said with more anger than he meant to display.

"Oh," Darci said. "That's business."

"What kind of business makes you engaged to a—?"

"How did you find out you had a sister?" Taylor cut in. He didn't like the anger, and he didn't want them to lose track of Adam's story. There would be time to tell about Darci's problems in Putnam later. Since what Adam knew might be able to help them tonight, his story was more important.

Reluctantly, Adam quit questioning Darci. "As I said, I didn't notice that Helen kept saying 'family' instead of 'parents,' but then one day she mentioned 'the three of them.' I asked her if she meant me as the third person. Helen looked surprised and said, 'No, I mean your sister.' I thought she'd lost her mind. It took me a while to get it out of her that, to her, just because the girl was a fetus when the kidnaping took place, didn't mean that the child wasn't viable. And it still angers me that no one in my family bothered to tell me that my mother was pregnant when I was kidnaped."

Adam took a breath. "And that leads us to today." For the last few minutes, he hadn't looked at Darci, as he was afraid that what he was telling them would again make her angry. He'd hired her under a pretext, saying he wanted a personal assistant, but instead, he'd involved her in something where people were murdered. He'd hired her because of her "qualification," her virginity.

Darci knew what he was thinking, and she knew why he wouldn't look at her. "And people have accused *me* of being a liar," she said under her breath; then, before he could reply, she said, "Do you think that grocery store is open yet? Bo and I are starving."

At that Boadicea sat up in bed and looked at Darci with an odd expression. "'Bo,'" she whispered. "This is what is called a nickname?"

She's seen less of the world than I have, Darci sent to Adam, wonder in her statement.

"I think your father wants to show her the world," Adam said into Darci's ear, then nodded toward Taylor, who was leaning over Boadicea solicitously. Her hands were no longer tied, and she was looking at Taylor with wide eyes, eyes that seemed to say that she'd follow him anywhere.

"I'll have to tell her about men," Darci said in disgust.

"And what do *you* know?" Adam asked. It was odd, but he suddenly felt lighter—and even happier—than he had in years. He'd just told his hideous life story, and no one was feeling sorry for him. No one was looking at him with eyes that said, *Poooooor Adam. Poor, kidnaped, orphaned Adam. If he hadn't run away from his mother when he was a toddler, his parents would be alive today.* No, instead, in this room were three other people with backgrounds as harrowing as his own.

Darci had been left by her beautiful mother to be raised by anyone who'd take her in. And she'd spent her life hiding her extraordinary power.

Adam didn't want to think about how Taylor had felt when he was told that he was infertile. His mother had pounded it into his head that it was up to him to pass on the family "gift," but he had failed. He'd spent his life trying to make up for breaking the line of inheritance.

Then Adam looked at this woman who was his sister, and he couldn't imagine what her life of imprisonment had been like, really and truly couldn't imagine it.

It was selfish of him, he admitted, but being with these people made him feel good. When he was with these people, he wasn't the black sheep. He was one of them, part of them.

"Did you hear me?" Adam asked. "What do *you* know about men?"

Darci looked at him in puzzlement. Was he serious? Or was he teasing her? With Adam and his unfathomable sense of humor, it was impossible to tell.

"Hmm?" Adam asked; then he started walking toward Darci, a menacing look on his face.

Instinctively, she backed up. "I don't know anything—" In the next moment, she let out a squeal as Adam grabbed her about the waist, picked her up, and dropped her onto the bed. Looming over her like some great monster, he bent over her, his hands made into claws.

And he began to tickle her.

At first Darci didn't know what was going on, because no one in her entire life had tickled her. She had been a solemn child, and no one had bothered to get past her solemnity in an effort to make her laugh.

But Adam did, and within minutes he had Darci rolling about on the bed screaming with laughter. "And what are you going to tell my sister about men?" he asked her.

"That they are good and wonderful," Darci said, drawing up her knees into her chest and squealing.

"And kind and loving?" Adam asked, his hands running all over her ribs.

"Oh, yes. Yes, yes, yes," she said.

"All right, then," Adam said seriously, stepping back from her. "I think we've cleared that up."

Boadicea, who, until now, had kept apart from the others, was now standing at the foot of the bed and watching this spectacle with the fascination of an anthropologist observing natives in their natural habitat. "Interesting," she said when Adam quit tickling Darci. "But now perhaps we can get food," she said as she turned away toward the door.

Mrs. Spock, Darci sent to Adam, making him laugh out loud as they all went toward the door. He took off his sweatshirt and slipped it on over her cat suit. "If you think that you're going out in public looking like that, you have another think coming," he said.

"And what is wrong with what I have on?" she said over her shoulder as they left the motel room.

"Nothing is wrong with the garment," Adam said. "It's what's inside that bothers me."

"Really . . . ?" Darci said, smiling at him. "Bet you can't

catch me," she tossed at him as she began running, making Adam's heart nearly stop as she ran across the busy highway.

Inside the little grocery store, all of them had a good time watching Boadicea's awe at what she saw. And each of them tried to imagine what it would have been like to have never seen a grocery. Each of them wanted to ask her questions, but when they did, all Boadicea would say is, "Not yet. Now is not the time to tell of me." Already, they could see that she was an odd combination of extreme innocence and great age. She annoyed Adam, and fascinated Darci. Only Taylor seemed to accept her just as she was, asking nothing more of her than what she wanted to give.

In spite of their troubles and in spite of what they would be facing tonight—or maybe because of it—they were a happy, laughing group as they bought bags and bags of food, food that they knew they'd never eat. Whatever happened tonight, they wouldn't return to this place.

Because they were laughing so much and only interested in each other, they didn't see the old woman come out of the back of the store and look at them. And if they had seen her, they wouldn't have thought much about her. Not even Darci would have felt the evil of the woman, for the old woman had long ago learned to block the vibrations she emitted. To nearly everyone on the planet, she looked like just an ordinary old person. No one noticed when she slipped back behind a curtain. No one saw her pick up a telephone and call a number known to only three other people in the world.

And no one heard her say, "They are here."

17

THEY SPREAD THE FOOD out on the bed nearest the door. Adam and Darci sat close together, cross-legged on the bed, while Taylor pulled up a chair to the bed. Boadicea sat apart from them on a chair a few feet away. But after a few minutes, Taylor moved his chair so that he and Boadicea were seated across from each other, eating together at a narrow table set under the window.

As Darci sat on the bed, her legs curled under her, eating and feeding Adam bits of food, she thought that she'd never been happier in her life. Now Adam's eyes were teasing her and hinting at wonderful things to come. And Darci kept thinking about last night as she lay snuggled close to him, his arms around her.

Never in her life had she dreamed of finding someone like this man, she thought. This man was someone who would, could, love her forever and always, as she'd always dreamed of.

Now, sitting here with him, she thought of the life she'd thought she was going to have when she'd arrived in New York; in spite of what she'd tried to make Adam believe, she hadn't been a very happy person. The people in Putnam hadn't seen Darci's future as bad—but *she* had.

But now, maybe, because she'd answered an ad in a newspaper, her life was going to change. Forever.

"You're looking at me strangely," Adam said. "Trying to decide which side I'm *really* on?"

As always, she didn't laugh at his attempt at humor, but instead, she just looked at him. She studied his dark hair and blue eyes, looked at that cleft in his chin. To her, he was such a beautiful, beautiful man. She had had more actual *fun* since she'd met him than she'd had in all the rest of her life put together. He was generous and kind and—

"Hey!" Adam said softly, "stop looking at me like that. You're making me think very naughty things." He was tearing off a piece of bread from the loaf (she'd already discovered that Adam hated bread that had already been sliced, so she'd asked at the grocery if they had a loaf that wasn't sliced). "I was wondering if I could persuade you to. . . ." Adam hesitated.

"Have sex with you before tonight so I'd lose my virginity and not be able to read the mirror?" she asked, eyes alight with hope.

For a moment Adam seemed to consider that. "Even if you couldn't read the mirror, you'd still have your power, and *you* are the person who was seen in the mirror. It's *you* she thinks will be her downfall."

"So you're saying that we might as well wait until we have the real mirror before we. . . ."

"Yeah," Adam said, then gave her a look through his lashes. "Besides, I like to take my time."

"That sounds—" She cut herself off because she thought she heard a noise outside. Turning sharply, she looked at the big window, which had a curtain drawn across it.

When she saw Darci's face, Boadicea dropped the food in her hand and jumped up to look out the window. "There is no one," she said, but she was looking at Darci very hard.

"Maybe it was a car," Darci said softly.

"Speaking of which," Taylor said, looking at Adam. "Do you have any idea how we're going to get back to Camwell tonight? I don't think my Rover's going to make it."

Adam didn't want to think of tonight. He wanted to leave both women where they were safe. He wanted to—

"And do we go into this unarmed?" Taylor asked.

"Adam has a gun that he took from a man who tried to kidnap us," Darci said. "Where did you put it?"

For a moment Adam was silent. He knew he could trust Darci and Taylor, but he didn't know about Boadicea. Yes, she was his sister, and, yes, she acted as if she was on their side. But, still, he wasn't certain this woman could be trusted. His eyes locked with hers. She could have told the others that Adam had entered her room with a gun in his hands, but she didn't. And Adam didn't tell them that the pistol was now on the window ledge behind the curtain where he could grab it easily.

"You have a knife?" Boadicea said softly. "It is hers. She was angered that you took it. It has some power."

"Adam made a rubbing of the handle," Darci said, obvi-

ously unambiguous about Boadicea's trustworthiness.
"And he sent the rubbing to a woman somewhere, but she
never replied," Darci said; then she looked at Adam, who
had his face down. "Why you rotten, low-down, lying—"
Darci began. "She *did* tell you what was written on the
handle, didn't she? But you didn't tell *me*."

Adam moved to sit on the other bed. This practice of
revealing what he knew was strange to him, and, as a
result, it was very difficult. But now there were three people looking at him expectantly. "It . . ." he began hesitantly,
"it is a knife that was once used for making sacrifices. It's a
blood knife. Darci," he said, looking at her, his eyes pleading. "I don't want you to go with us tonight."

"Just me," she said flatly. "The others can go with you,
but I can't. Is that right? Is that what you have in mind?"

"The danger is to you and you alone," Boadicea said in
her solemn manner. "We may be killed, but you would be
sacrificed."

That statement effectively stopped the others from
speaking.

"Pardon my stupidity, but what the hell's the difference?" Adam finally snapped, then shot a look at Darci that
she wasn't to tell him not to curse.

At Adam's hostile manner, Boadicea closed her mouth
and looked as though she might never say another word.

"Duration," Taylor said quietly. "Dying quickly is different from dying slowly."

Adam stood up. "Darci is *not* going," he said flatly.

Come to me, Darci heard in her head. "What?" she
asked, looking up at Adam.

"I said that you aren't going and that's final. Look, I

made arrangements with the owner of this motel to use his car tonight. It'll get us to Camwell and back, but I think we can do what we need to without Darci. You," he said to his sister. "Do you know your way around the tunnels? That is, assuming that's where she's planning to . . . to . . . with the children."

"Yes," Boadicea said, "she uses the tunnels for that. I have never been to them, but I know them in my head."

With every thought that passed through his mind, Adam grew angrier—and his anger was directed toward Boadicea. "Couldn't you have done something to stop her? You were with her for years. Couldn't you have at least *tried* to escape during that time? Couldn't you have—"

He broke off because Boadicea stood up; then she pulled her skirt up to expose one long, shapely leg. But it was a leg that bore many scars, some of them long, some of them round and raised.

"Shall I show you more?" she asked, with no anger in her voice. "Perhaps you would like to see my back. I gave up trying to escape her when she stopped taking her rage out on me and began to take it out on others. She presented me with the body part of a child and told me that there would be another one given to me every time I tried to escape. After that I asked the mirror if I would ever get away from her, and that's when I saw the three of you. I have waited for you three for six years. I have waited quietly, and therefore no more children were killed because of me."

She cocked her head at Adam. "Did I do wrong? If you had been in my place, would you have run away again, knowing that if you did, an untold number of innocent children would be tortured, then murdered because of you? Tell me, I am interested in your answer."

The three of them didn't know if Boadicea was being sarcastic, or if she was actually asking a question, but, whichever, no one had an answer to that horrible question.

"He's sorry," Darci said. "He has a very bad temper, and he sometimes says things that he doesn't mean. Please forgive him." *Come to me,* she heard again in her head. *Leave them and come to me.* Darci put her hand to her forehead as she realized that the words were coming inside her mind and not from anyone in this room.

"You are not well," Boadicea said, looking at Darci.

"No, it's nothing," Darci said. "I'm fine. I just had a knock on my head yesterday, and it still aches a bit, that's all. It's the men who were injured. Adam, how are your ribs? And . . . Dad, how's your arm?"

"Fine," Taylor said, smiling at her having called him "Dad."

Come to me, or I will kill them.

The words were more clear with each syllable—and Darci knew who was speaking to her inside her head. *This is between you and me, isn't it?* Darci sent back to the voice in her head; then she looked at Adam to see if he'd heard her thoughts. But Adam was still looking at his sister, still contemplating what she'd told them.

The sound of laughter echoed inside Darci's head, making her temples throb and her eyes blink at the force of the sound. *Oh, yes,* the voice said. *You and me. No one else.* There was the laugh again. *Unless you want to lose them all, come to me.*

Darci said, "Excuse me, I need. . . ." She got off the bed and went into the bathroom. Once she was alone in the little room, she sat down on the lid of the toilet and closed her eyes. Through the door she could hear the low, flat tone of Boadicea's voice and guessed that she was telling the men something about her existence in captivity.

Now Darci sat in silence and listened, waiting for this person to tell her what she was to do. She was afraid to try to say more to the voice in her head for fear that Adam would hear her.

Darci wasn't practiced at doing this, but she put her head back against the porcelain tank, closed her eyes, and tried her best to listen.

This is between you and me, the voice said. *Between us two witches.*

No, Darci thought. No, no, no! I am not a witch. The power I have is *good.*

Even though Darci wasn't projecting her thoughts as she'd learned to do with Adam, it was as though the voice could hear what she was thinking. This person—this woman, as it seemed more like a female voice—could hear whatever Darci thought.

If you are good, then you will save them. Shall I show you what I have done?

"No!" Darci said out loud.

"Darci, baby, are you all right?" Adam called from the other side of the door.

"Fine," she answered. "Would it be all right if I got into the tub and soaked for a while?"

"Sure," Adam said, chuckling. "Take your time."

Darci turned on both tub taps full blast so the noise would disguise any sounds she made. *I want nothing to do with you,* she thought. *Nothing.*

But involuntarily, there came into her mind a vision. It was as though a video were playing inside her head. She saw the back of this woman, a tall, thin woman, wearing an elaborate headdress and a robe of what looked to be red velvet. In front of her was a tall stone altar and on it was a child being held down by three hooded men.

No, no, no, Darci said in her mind as she put her hands over her face. She would have recognized that face anywhere at any age. The child on the altar was Adam at three years old.

"Darci?" came Adam's voice again as he lightly tapped on the door.

"Can't a girl have a good cry in peace?" she snapped at him.

"All right," he said softly, "but if you need me, I'm here."

Darci's thoughts were on the vision that was playing inside her head. *Make it go away,* she thought. *Please, God, make it stop.* In a scary movie, you could close your eyes and not see the bloody parts, but now she couldn't block out the vision, for the video was inside her mind. *No, please.* She walked to the little bathroom window and looked out, but the view in front of her didn't stop what she was seeing inside her mind.

The thin woman took a knife and made deep cuts into the child's skin. Then she lifted a red-hot branding iron from a fire, and. . . . "Oh, God," Darci said, then went to her knees, her hands over her face. When the iron touched the delicate flesh of the child, Darci had to grab a towel and stuff it into her mouth to keep from screaming aloud. It was as if she were *there.* She could see everything. She could hear the child's screams. Oh, God. She could smell the burning flesh.

Abruptly, the sight of the room and the altar faded, and in its place was the vision of a man. His face was drawn, almost gray with worry and fatigue. Instantly, Darci knew she was seeing Adam's father. As Darci watched, the man got out of a small airplane and looked about him for a moment; then he turned and helped a pretty young woman out of the plane. As she stepped down, she put her hand on her belly in that protective way that pregnant women do. There seemed to be no one around them, just the landing strip and surrounding forest. But Darci could see shadows moving in the trees. Helplessly, she watched the man and woman walk toward the trees. She saw the man taken from behind, and while his wife watched, his throat was slit.

No more, Darci begged. *No more.*

But it wasn't over. There was another vision, this one of Adam's mother, heavily pregnant and tied to a bed. She was in labor and she was screaming, but not from the pain of the labor. No, she was screaming because the child was being cut from her.

Darci saw it all—and she felt the woman's pain. She felt the woman's life flowing from her with the blood that was pouring out of her body. No attempt was made to stanch the flow. "My babies," the woman was saying over and over as she bled to death. "My babies."

Shall I show you more? the voice said.

"No," Darci whispered. "No, please, no more." She was on the floor, her knees tucked into her chest, and she was trembling.

This is between you and me, not them. Do you under-stand me?

Darci nodded, holding herself tightly, feeling the cold-ness of the tile floor beneath her. She was so cold that she knew she'd never be warm again.

Put them asleep, the voice said. *Put them asleep, then leave. You will be brought to me. Do you understand?*

Yes. Darci nodded. *Yes.*

For a few moments there was blessed silence, and inside her head was only the memory of what Darci had seen. She was no longer in the middle of something too horrible to imagine; she was involved in something that she had no power to stop.

Slowly, her body feeling stiff and sore, Darci got up off the floor, went to the bathtub, and turned off the water. Then, again slowly, she walked to the sink and looked at herself in the mirror. There were deep, bloody scratches on her cheeks where she must have clawed herself during the visions. There was no need for her to look into a magic mirror now, she thought, because she could tell Adam what had happened to his parents.

But Darci didn't want to tell him. But, even more, she didn't want to see the same thing happen to *him.*

You can do this, she told herself. Maybe her father was right and Darci had spent her life trying to suppress what she could do with her "gift," as he called it. And maybe it was true that all her life she'd tried hard to be as normal as she could be, but, then again, she *had* been able to hold Adam and that armed man in place. She'd been able to freeze them so they couldn't move. If she could do that again. . . . If she could use every ounce of whatever power she possessed to hold this dreadful woman long enough to. . . .

Truthfully, Darci didn't know what she would do or could do, but her father's words came back to haunt her, "You didn't know you could do that, did you?" "That I can kill people with my mind?" she'd asked.

Could she kill someone? Darci wondered. But then the visions went through her head again, and she wiped at her face to make them go away. Her hand came away bloody from the scratches on her face.

The blood was on her left hand, the hand that had nine moles that formed a Tower, the same shape that had been cut and branded on Adam's chest when he was just a child.

Yes, she thought, she could kill. She could kill to save the man she'd come to love.

She took a few deep breaths to calm herself, then she sat down on the toilet lid and closed her eyes. Give me strength, God, she prayed. Guide me, watch over me, and give me the strength I need to make this horror end.

She said, "Amen," aloud, then focused her mind on making the three people in the next room go to sleep. It took time and it took concentration, for all three of them were nervous and alert and full of adrenaline, but she managed to do it. She felt them relax. She heard movements as they leaned back against furniture and went to sleep.

When all was quiet on the other side of the door, Darci heard the crunch of gravel from a car pulling up outside the motel. She knew that it was a car waiting for her. And she knew that she was to take the bag that Adam had carried out of the woman's house.

Silently, Darci left the bathroom and stood for a moment, looking at the people sleeping on the bed. Her father and Boadicea were curled together in the same way that she and Adam had been not long before. Slowly, Darci walked toward Adam. She stood there for a while, looking down at him. For the first time since she'd met him, there wasn't a deep furrow between his brow; even when he was laughing, he hadn't lost that look of worry.

But now it was gone, and she knew that that had come about because he had finally shared his story.

Smiling, she bent and kissed his forehead, then she placed her lips against his and held them there for a moment. "Whatever happens now," she whispered to him, "I will love you forever."

She touched his hair, then, turning away from him, she went toward the door. Hanging on the back of a chair was the leather bag that Adam had taken from the woman's house. Boadicea had said that the mirror Adam had taken was not the real one, not the magic mirror, so why was Darci to take it with her? She opened the bag, looked inside, and saw that there were two objects inside, both looking like picture frames. One was golden and beautiful, the other old and beat-up. Darci had no doubt whatever which one was the magic mirror.

As she left the room, she couldn't suppress a feeling of irony. They'd had Nostradamus's mirror with them all along.

18

ADAM AWOKE YAWNING, and the first thing he did was reach for Darci. With his eyes still closed, he remembered the way her little backside curved so perfectly up against him. Smiling, he reached his hand out farther. Maybe he *would* make love with her and to hell with reading any mirror, he thought.

It was the thought of the mirror that made him open his eyes. Since the room was dark and he could see nothing, at first he didn't know where he was. But, gradually, it all came back to him. Fumbling toward the bedside table, he turned on the light and looked about. Boadicea and Taylor were on the other bed, snuggled together like two puppies.

Rubbing his eyes, Adam felt as groggy as if he had a hangover. It seemed that Darci was still in the bathroom, soaking in the tub, and, maybe, crying. When she'd said that was what she was doing, Adam had reached for the doorknob, but Taylor had stopped him. "Let her have some time to herself," he'd whispered, then led Adam away from the door.

And that was the last thing Adam remembered. Now, blinking, trying to wake up, he glanced toward the bathroom. The door was just barely open and he could see a light on in the room. Was she *still* in the tub? he wondered, smiling at the vanity of women. That she could sit in a tub for. . . .

He looked at his watch. It was almost two P.M. and—

In the next moment he sat up in bed and rubbed his eyes. It was after *eight* P.M.!

He reached the bathroom in one long stride, flung open the door so that it hit the back wall with a loud thud. The bathroom was empty.

Turning back to the room, he saw that both Taylor and Boadicea were waking up.

"She's gone," Adam said flatly. "Darci is gone."

Taylor's face seemed to drain of blood as all that he'd learned in a lifetime of study flooded his mind. He knew without a doubt that Darci had put them to sleep. But why?

"Where is that bag?" Boadicea said, looking at the chair where the bag had hung.

"Who cares about that—" Adam began, then his eyes widened. "No," was all he could whisper.

"What was in it?" Boadicea asked, her voice rising.

"We don't have time for that now," Adam snapped at her. "We have to find Darci, and *you* have to show us the way."

"You found it, didn't you?" Boadicea said, her eyes wide. "Somehow, you found the true mirror."

Taylor put his hand out to Boadicea's arm, but she moved away from him.

"Why did you not show it to me? To her? One of us could have seen—"

"You?" Adam sneered at his sister. "And how do I trust *you?* I saw that room. How do I know what you have become?"

Boadicea looked at him with eyes full of fire. "If you saw the room, then you know that to survive I had to fight."

"Stop it!" Taylor shouted. "This is about Darci, about my daughter, not the two of you. Boadicea, how do we find her?"

"I do not know," Boadicea said as she calmed herself from her anger. "She is a good person; perhaps that will protect her. I know that only Darci can stop that woman. And if she does not, then the woman will gain more power than she has already. She has learned much over the years and has gained powers that even I know nothing of. And she controls many, many people. Now what she does is in secret, but if Darci is unable to stop her tonight, then I do not know what will happen."

"Get ready," Adam said. "We don't have time for more talk." With that, Adam left the motel room and went to the front desk to get the keys to the owner's car. While he was walking, he opened his cell phone and punched in a number he knew well.

"Mike?" he said. "This is Adam and, yes, I'm still in Camwell. Remember that I told you that I might need help? I do. I want you to get as many people here as possible as soon as possible. And, Mike? Bring an arsenal." He closed the phone and entered the motel office.

"I do not like this place," Boadicea said, looking about the dirt walls that were over, above, and beside them. "She could flood this place. She could send fire down it. Her minions could hide anywhere. She—"

"Stop it!" Adam ordered over his shoulder. *Darci,* he thought hard but received no answer. Why, oh, why hadn't they practiced sending thoughts back and forth instead of just from her to him? Now he wanted to shout for her, call her name. He wanted to know where to find her.

"Which way?" Adam asked as soon as they reached the big room with the vending machines. When he'd been here with Darci just a few days before, this room had seemed almost homey, now it—

"Even to me this place feels creepy," Taylor said. "Didn't Darci say that you two had visited here before?"

"Yes," Adam said, "but then it was. . . ." What could he say? That it had been a place of fun? Could he tell them about Darci stuffing candy bars down the front of her cat suit? Could he tell how she'd curled herself into a tiny ball on a shelf?

"Why is it different now?" he demanded of his sister. When he'd met her, he'd been hostile because he didn't trust her, but now he was beginning to realize that Darci had been right and he should have trusted this woman who had been through so much. If he had trusted his sister, if he'd told about the mirror that he'd found hidden under a cheap print, maybe they could have looked into it and seen what was going to happen to Darci. Adam had been told that the mirror showed what *could* happen; the predictions could be altered.

After they'd left the motel, Adam had driven back to the Grove. He'd skidded into the parking lot and jumped out of the car before the engine stopped. Taylor and Boadicea ran after him, and entered the guest house to see an empty room. But a crash from the bedroom that had been Darci's made them run to that room. Adam had thrown the bed over and was on his knees pulling up a trapdoor.

"This place was an icehouse, and a stream flowed under here," Adam said. "I requested this house because I needed a hiding place." Reaching into the darkness beneath the trapdoor, he pulled out a hoard of weapons, guns, rifles, pistols.

"What do you want?" he asked Taylor, looking up at him.

"I've never . . ." Taylor began, looking at the weapons in horror.

But Boadicea wasn't shy. She stepped forward, picked up a nine-millimeter Luger from the pile that Adam was bringing up, and chambered a round.

Both men were looking at her in speechlessness. "She likes anything that can be used to kill," she explained. "I did not have toys as a child."

Adam looked at his sister with respect. For the first time he thought that, possibly, her hatred of this woman was deeper than his.

"Show him what to do," Adam commanded his sister as he nodded toward Taylor; then Adam went to his room to pull on a black Lycra running suit that was very much like Darci's cat suit. Returning to the bedroom, he tossed a similar garment to Boadicea. "Put that on. You'll be able to move better in that. And do you have something you can put on?" he asked Taylor. The man's bags were heaped in a corner of the room.

"Yes," Taylor answered, and ten minutes later, the three of them were out the door.

And now they were in the tunnels. They didn't dare use flashlights but wore the night-vision goggles.

"Which way?" Adam asked his sister as they stood at the mouth of the three tunnels leading out of the main room.

"This one," she said, then led the way down the smallest tunnel. Adam's running suit fit her sleekly. She had on a wide leather belt that carried pouches of ammunition and three pistols. In her hands was a short rifle that was illegal in the U.S.

Adam carried the same weapons but, also, concealed inside his shirt was the dagger that he'd taken from the cage.

They had not gone far when Adam halted them. "I hear something," he said. Instantly, the three of them stopped and listened, but there was nothing. There was no light at either end of the space, no movement, nothing.

Adam signaled for them to move forward, but within a few steps, they reached a crossroads, and, once again, he stopped, again listening.

Adam? he heard.

For a moment, his eyes blurred with tears. She was alive! Darci's voice was faint, weak even, but she was alive. *Here! Here!* he wanted to shout to her, but he couldn't get a message to her. She just had to trust that he was near, and she *had* to keep talking.

"Are you hearing her?" Taylor asked.

"Yes, barely," Adam whispered, then leaned back against the wall and listened with all his might. *Talk, Darci baby, talk to me,* he tried to send her. *Let me know where you are.*

Adam? Are you there? came the words to him, if possible, even more faintly.

"This way," Adam said. "I think she's this way."

But Boadicea put her arm on his and stopped him. "That is not the way. Something is wrong. That is not the way to the chamber where she performs the sacrifices."

"Don't say that word again!" Adam snapped. "I heard Darci's voice and she's this way. Are you with me or not?"

For a long moment, Boadicea seemed to consider that question. "I want her reign of terror to end," she said. "And only Darci can do that."

Adam, I'm here. Can you hear me?

"Darci is talking to me," he whispered, then started walking faster.

Adam, come to me. I'm afraid.

"Something is wrong," Boadicea said from behind them. "Something is very wrong."

Adam stood still while he made a decision he knew would affect several lives. On one hand he didn't trust this tall woman, but on the other, he tried to imagine the hatred she must have inside her. "Lead us," he said at last, but his eyes held warning of what he'd do if she was lying to them.

Boadicea didn't hesitate as she led them through the tunnels, moving swiftly, never looking back to see if the two men were following her.

"She memorized the way," Taylor said to Adam when they paused for a moment to wait for Boadicea to see if a corridor was clear. "She's lived this escape in her mind for years and her belief in this escape—and us—is what's kept her from giving up hope."

When Boadicea motioned for them to follow her, Adam followed her, Taylor behind him. But he came up short when Boadicea stopped abruptly before a dark doorway. "I do not understand," she whispered. "This is the chamber. This is where they should be."

"Looks like she knew you were lying to her," Adam said, "and she did some lying of her own."

"But the mirror showed me that . . ." she began, but trailed off, puzzled.

"Didn't you tell me that the mirror shows what *could* happen and not necessarily what *does* happen?" Taylor asked as he reached into his pocket and pulled out a cigarette lighter. There was a candle on a brass holder attached to the wall. He lifted it and lit the candle, holding the torch in front of him as he walked through the doorway, Boadicea and Adam behind him. "Is it just me or does it seem strange to anyone else that these tunnels are empty of people? There aren't even any guards here."

"She has done something unexpected," Boadicea said as she stayed close behind Taylor.

He lit a couple more candles, enough to see the room they were in. Along the walls in the hollowed-out room had been placed tall, carved stone panels. Holding the candle aloft, Taylor examined one of them. "Someone has robbed some crypts. First century, I'd say."

"Yes. Many thieves work for her," Boadicea said, then turned back toward the doorway after only a moment's glance at the stone altar that stood in the middle of the room. The mirror had shown her what that altar had been used for, and she knew what had caused the dark stains on it.

Taylor followed Boadicea out of the room, but Adam hesitated as he stared at the altar in fascination. He remembered having seen a hideous pile of stone like this one. He remembered. . . .

"Come, brother," Boadicea said softly as she held out her hand to take his. She well knew what he was on the verge of remembering, for the mirror had shown her what had been done to her brother when he was a child.

Once they were outside the chamber, the three of them looked at each other. The question *Now what?* passed among them.

Boadicea shifted the heavy rifle she carried.

"How do we find where Darci is being held?" Taylor asked, and there was a bit of a tremble in his voice. He turned to Adam. "Can you hear her?"

"No," Adam said, his jaw rigid. "Her voice is silent."

"Or has been silenced," Boadicea said, but stopped when Adam glared at her.

"If we could find the mirror," Adam said, "it would tell us where she is."

Boadicea straightened her back. "The mirror would no longer be of use to us."

"But you could see—"

"No," she said. "I could not see. I am no longer a virgin."

All Adam could do was look at her in astonishment; then, slowly, he turned to look at Taylor.

For a moment Taylor didn't look up at Adam, and when he did, there was guilt in his eyes. "I thought Darci could see into the mirror when we found it. I—"

Adam wanted to blast the both of them, but there wasn't time. What was done was done. He took a deep, calming breath, then looked at his sister. "Didn't you say that she got other readers to check up on you? Maybe she has one of those readers with the mirror now."

Boadicea gave a bit of a smile at her brother, obviously

glad for his having thought of this. "There is a place where she goes to be private. Perhaps she has not had time to put the mirror in another hiding place. Come with me." With that, she turned and started running down the dimly lit corridor to their left, Taylor behind her, Adam in the rear.

Adam couldn't help but think about what he'd been told. When had it happened that Boadicea was no longer a virgin? Adam had slept for hours. Had Taylor and Boadicea stayed awake? Did they think that Darci was in the bathroom all those hours? Or perhaps the darkness of the room made them believe Darci was in bed, asleep beside a sleeping Adam.

Adam stepped close behind Taylor. "'You take her anywhere without marrying her first, and I will kill you,'" he said quietly, quoting what Taylor had said about Darci.

Taylor looked back with a smile, thinking Adam was teasing, but there was no laughter on Adam's face; he was dead serious. Taylor nodded, then hurried ahead to catch up with Boadicea.

She led them to an elaborately carved oak door that didn't appear to have a handle or lock on it. Boadicea touched the door in three places: on the left eye of an ugly little creature, on a leaf, and in the center of a carved medallion, and the door swung open.

Boadicea led the way inside and looked about for the mirror, but Taylor and Adam, holding their weapons at the ready, couldn't resist looking at the room. This room was as elaborate as the rooms in the house where they'd found Boadicea were barren. Here was an ornately carved bed that looked as though it should be in a museum. There were tables of carved and gilded wood. The walls and ceil-

ing were covered with what looked to be acres of rich bro-
cades and heavy silks—all of it in shades of red.

The magic mirror was on top of a mahogany dresser, in
plain sight. Boadicea grabbed it, glanced into it, and
looked at Adam. "Nothing," she whispered, and there was
pain in her voice.

Adam didn't like to think of the connection she must
have had with the mirror since she'd had a lifetime of looking into it. "Why the hell couldn't you two have waited?" he
said as he snatched the mirror out of his sister's hands and
tossed it onto the bed. "I can't even figure out *when*—"

"You have never been deprived in your life," Boadicea
said angrily, taking a step toward him, as though she meant
to fight him. "You have had everything given to you; nothing has been taken from you."

"You don't know what you're talking about. I lost everything. You have no idea what my life has been like. You
know nothing of—"

"There she is," Taylor said softly. While they had been
arguing, he'd stepped toward the bed to look at the mirror
that he'd read so much about.

Adam didn't pay attention to what Taylor said, but
Boadicea turned to look at him.

Taylor was holding the mirror up and looking at it in
wonder. "I see them," he said in a whisper. "I see a room
and people. Here, look." He held out the mirror, but when
Adam and Boadicea looked into it, they saw nothing, not
even their own reflections.

"What do you see?" Boadicea asked. "Describe it to me."

"The room is dark; I can't see much. There are people
there, all of them wearing black robes. Their faces are cov-

ered, so I can't see who anyone is. I don't see Darci, and I don't see anyone who might be the leader." There was awe in his voice, and his eyes were wide as he looked at the mirror.

"Do any of the people have on jewelry?" Boadicea asked.

"What the hell does that matter?" Adam asked but quieted when Boadicea put up her hand.

"Yes. I see a wedding ring on a hand. It's a man's hand, and he's older, as the hand has age spots on it. And I can see a birthmark on a man's throat." He looked up at Boadicea in wonder.

Boadicea turned to her brother. "He can see more clearly than I did. What I saw was hazy, with the details obscured. But he is not a virgin."

"I don't understand this," Taylor said. "In my family only the females have any powers of the occult. None of the men have ever had any power."

When Boadicea looked at him, her eyes were warm, caressing. "Perhaps God saw inside your heart and has given you what you deserve."

"Where is Darci?" Adam asked impatiently.

Taylor looked back at the mirror. "I don't know. I don't see her. I just see people walking about. The angle is from the back of the crowd. I can't see what's going on in the front."

"Ask the mirror," Boadicea said. "You must *ask* for what you want to see."

"Where is Darci?" Taylor asked; then with panic in his voice he said, "It's gone blank!"

"Wait," Boadicea said patiently, "but do not be disappointed. That creature has a mind of its own. It shows what it wants to."

In the next second, Taylor's body relaxed and, sitting down on the bed, he gazed into the mirror. "I see a woman. She isn't wearing robes. She has on a . . ."

"What?!" Adam asked, impatient. "Who is she? Where is she? Is Darci with her? Is she the witch?"

"I . . ." Taylor said, looking hard into the mirror. "I don't see Darci. I just see this woman. She has her back to me. She has on a short, white coat and black leggings, but the coat has a hood. She— Wait! She's pushing the hood back. She has—"

Taylor leaned back from the mirror and gaped at it, his face registering shock. "It's. . . ."

"Who?" Adam and Boadicea asked in unison.

Taylor took a deep breath. "This woman has long blonde hair," he said softly, "and I've seen her only once before."

"Who is she?" Boadicea asked.

"Darci's mother," Taylor answered, looking up at Adam.

For a moment, Adam could only blink at him. "Jerlene? But she's in Putnam."

"Why would the mother not come if her daughter needs her?" Boadicea said in dismissal of the two men's shock. "What else do you see? Is there an altar there?"

"Show me the place this woman is in," Taylor commanded the mirror, then his eyes widened as the "camera" drew back and he could see that Jerlene Monroe was standing in front of what looked to be a stone altar. "Yes, an altar is there," Taylor said softly.

"Are there markings in the stone?" Boadicea asked quickly.

"Yes. They . . . look like. . . ." Taylor looked up at her. "I think they're Egyptian hieroglyphics."

"I know where they are," Boadicea said as she started for the door. "Come. And bring that thing!" she ordered, already running.

Adam ran after her; Taylor put the mirror in his backpack and followed them. But the moment the men stepped outside the door, they were hit hard on the head and went down.

When Adam awoke, his head hurt, and when he tried to move his hand, he couldn't. Turning, he saw that both his wrists were chained to a wall, as were his ankles. He was immobile.

He was in a small underground room, and he was facing a heavy wooden door bound by iron. On the walls, on little shelves and stuck in niches, were hundreds of white candles. There was a small oak table in front of him, and on it was the dagger he'd taken from the storage room. Adam turned his attention to the iron cuffs around his wrists. If he could get one hand out. . . .

"Good evening," said a voice that made him turn. "Or should I say good morning? Oh, but no, it is not yet midnight, for I do believe your little one is still alive."

Blinking against the pain that roared inside his head— and with his arms raised, his ribs were excruciating— Adam looked at the woman in front of him. Since she was wearing a long dark robe that had been embroidered heavily with gold thread that glowed in the light of the many candles in the underground room, it took him a minute to recognize her.

"Sally," he said at last.

"That's one of my names, but, yes, I was once your waitress." This seemed to amuse her for a moment, but then her face turned serious. "I've worked at that demeaning job for nearly five years while I've waited for her to arrive." She spat the word *her* out as though it sickened her. "I knew her the moment she walked in the door. After all, I've had some practice looking for her, haven't I?" she said, smiling in a nasty way.

It seemed that Adam could see insanity in her eyes. Or was he just imagining what he saw? Did all evil people have to be insane? This woman had kept control of a growing empire of evilness for many years.

"Where is she?" Adam asked.

"Waiting for her hero to rescue her." Again, the woman seemed to be amused.

She walked toward Adam. They were alone in the room, just him and this woman. If he had been free, he could have broken her in half with one hand. Now, as she walked closer to him, he saw that she was older than he'd realized. There were tiny scars above her eyelids. In his research he'd found out that this coven in Camwell had been in existence for a long time, and since it was said that one woman had been its ruler from the beginning, he had been looking for someone older. But this woman had had the ultimate disguise: a face-lift.

"Where are the others?" he asked.

"Safe for now." Walking close to him, she held out a little stick that he hadn't seen, and she ran it down his rib cage. When she reached the place that was injured, she gave a little push.

Adam almost blacked out from the pain, but he willed himself to stay alert. "Where are they?" he asked again.

The woman, this "Sally," turned her back on him and walked away. There was a heavy oak table in the middle of the room, and she put her little stick on it. Adam could see that the thing was steel, and, like the dagger, it had markings on it. What manner of evil object was it? What had she used the thing for in the past?

"Did you know that I raised your sister as my own daughter?" she asked. "She never wanted for anything. She had the best that this worthless world could offer."

"Except freedom," Adam said, then cursed himself for being so stupid as to antagonize her.

"True," Sally said, turning to smile at him. "She didn't have that. And she had no men. Did you know that you and that other one are the first men she's seen up close? But it doesn't matter now. She'll be punished, just as she knew she would be. She knows she's not to defy me."

"How can you hurt someone who's been like a daughter to you?" Adam said, trying hard to think of something to say to reach her. "You must love her very much."

Sally seemed to consider that. "No, I don't think I do. But then, she's never loved me. If I told you what I've had to do to make her behave. . . . Well, perhaps I'll wait and show you. Yes, I'll let you *see* what I do to your sister." For a moment she cocked her head as though listening to something. "Now I must go. Something has come up."

"Darci's mother," Adam said, wanting to say or do anything to gain some time.

"Yes," Sally said, giving a little smile. "She says *she* is the source of her daughter's power, but she will not demonstrate it until I release the daughter. She is, of course, lying, but I must be sure. In another two hours it will be midnight and I must finish with this little witch who came with you. She—"

"No," Adam whispered, then his head came up. "Look, I'm rich. My family is very, very wealthy. We can pay you anything you want. You'd never have to work again. You could live in luxury and—"

He broke off because Sally was laughing at him. "Rich? You have no idea what wealth is. I could buy your entire family with the cash in my wallet. No, *power* is everything. Did you know that I can take her power from her and keep it for myself? I have a way. If the power she has doesn't leave the earth, then I can take it. You see, that's the key. I've read all the books that that man Taylor Raeburne wrote. Did he tell you that if the chain is broken, if there isn't a direct descendant, then the power goes to the person who *takes* it? At least that's the legend. I do hope it's true, because I plan to find out tonight."

With that she walked out of the room and shut the heavy oak door behind her. And when she'd gone, Adam let out a cry of agony that nearly brought the ceiling down on him. He pulled on the chains until his wrists and ankles were bleeding.

Adam? he heard, and calmed himself so he could listen to Darci's voice inside his head.

Adam, are you there? I wish I knew. Are you still alive? Can you forgive me for walking out without telling you?

"Yes, oh, yes, Darci, my love," Adam said. "I forgive you anything and everything. Don't think about it. Just get out of wherever you are."

Did you see who she was? Darci sent to him. *Remember that I told you that she reminded me of the witch in "Hansel and Gretel"?*

"Yes," Adam whispered as tears began to flow down his cheeks.

I'm in a room underground, and they've put me in a white gown. I look like I'm ready to go dancing and chanting around Stonehenge.

Pulling against his chains with all his might, Adam smiled through the tears that were flowing freely now. Jokes, Darci always could make jokes.

But I guess I'm in white because I'm a virgin. But I'm that way only in my body, she sent to him. *I can attest that my mind isn't virginal. Oh, Adam, are you there? Can you hear me? She hasn't killed you, has she?*

"No, my love, I'm here. I'm near you," he shouted as he pulled frantically on the chains.

I'm not going to think that anything bad has happened to you. You're going to burst into this room at any moment and save me. You'll be like one of your medieval ancestors and res-cue the fair maiden, won't you, my love?

With tears on his face, Adam tore at the chains until the cuffs had cut into his flesh. "No, no, no," was all that he could say.

Adam! Darci sent to him. *I hear them. They're coming. Oh, God, stay with me. Adam, I'm afraid. I want to— They're here! The door is opening. Oh, Adam, I love you. I love you with all my heart. I will love you always and forever. Whatever happens to me, I will love you forever. Remember that. Forever. I—*

"Noooooooooooooo," Adam screamed and tore at the

chains until there was no skin left on his ankles or wrists. But no matter how much he pulled, he couldn't get away.

When Adam awoke, he had a headache to end all headaches. Groggy, disoriented, he moved his hand to run it over his face.

"You okay?" an unfamiliar voice asked.

Adam had to work to sit up. His ribs hurt like hell and now his head was splitting; his ankles and wrists were raw and bloody. "Yeah," he managed to say, then looked into the deep blue eyes of a kid. A big kid. He was looking at a very large young man who had the freckled face and stick-up blond hair of a mischievous boy, but the body of a line-backer. "Who are you?" Adam rasped out, his hand on the back of his neck.

"Putnam," the young man said.

Adam's eyes opened wider. "You—" he began, then lunged at him. With all that Darci had told him about the Putnams—father, son, town—Adam wanted to destroy the lot of them.

"Hold on there, old man," the boy said, putting his hand on Adam's shoulder. "You're in no shape to be wrestlin' anybody."

"I'll show you—" Adam began as he pushed himself away from the wall.

"Your energy would be better spent elsewhere," came his sister's voice, and Adam had to bend sharply to look around Putnam. Boadicea and Taylor were sitting on the floor on the other side of the room.

Adam knew she was right. Slowly, testing to see how badly he was injured, he pushed himself up along the wall until he was standing. "Where are we? What happened?" he asked, looking around.

They were in a large, underground room that seemed to have no outlet. The room had dirt walls, but since it was egg-shaped, with a domed ceiling, they wouldn't be able to climb up the walls. Only when he looked upward did he see that far above their heads was an opening with an iron grate over it. When he looked back down, he saw that the room was bare, with just its dirt walls and floor. Boadicea was sitting on the floor, close beside Taylor, and he had the mirror on his lap.

"What are *you* doing here?" Adam said, looking back at Putnam.

"Jerlene wanted to come save her daughter so I came with her. Darci and I are gonna get married."

"Over my dead body," Adam said.

"According to the mirror," Taylor said dryly, "that is exactly what's going to happen."

Adam ran his hand over his face and tried to calm down. "I was chained to a wall. I saw the witch. And I heard Darci. But then I blacked out. What happened next?"

"You were thrown through that hole," Putnam said, looking up. "And I caught you. I'm not sure, but I think we're supposed to stay in here until we die."

"Nice thought," Adam said, turning his ankles and wrists to see how much damage had been done. He could still stand, still walk. "So how do we get out?"

"We make ourselves into a ladder," Boadicea said, looking upward, then back down at Putnam. "I believe he can hold all of us."

"Sure can," Putnam said, grinning and looking about twelve years old.

Adam turned to Taylor, who was gazing into the mirror in fascination. "Why didn't you see that we'd be captured? And why wasn't that mirror taken from you?"

Before he could answer, Boadicea said, "Because he did not ask the right questions, and I do not think she knows we have the mirror."

"What is that thing?" Putnam asked.

"It's a mirror that shows the future," Adam said.

"Cool. Can it tell us if we can get out?"

"Can we—" Taylor said, but Boadicea cut him off.

"It can hear your thoughts. Think your question and it will show what it wants to show you." There was bitterness in her voice and the tone of a woman who had had a great deal of experience with the magic mirror.

"Yes, we can get out," Taylor said softly.

"Can we save Darci?" Adam asked.

Taylor looked for a moment, then said, "No. We cannot. The witch is too powerful for us. All of us will be killed."

"Where is Darci?" Adam asked yet again.

"She is. . . ." Taylor looked into the mirror. "She is asleep. She's. . . ." He looked at Boadicea. "Now she's strapped to the altar. Before, it was empty, but now. . . ." He took a deep breath. "Now Darci's on that stone altar."

"Where's Jerlene?" Putnam asked. "Can *she* save Darci?"

"How could she save her if we can't?" Adam asked.

"She was gonna offer herself in Darci's place," Putnam said.

19

~

"OKAY, EVERYONE KNOWS what to do?" Adam asked and the other three people nodded. "You think you can hold us, kid?"

"Sure, *old man*," Putnam said pointedly.

Adam ignored the gibe as he looked at Taylor. "There's no lock on the grill in the ceiling?"

"No," Taylor said, looking into the mirror. "There wouldn't need to be that high up."

"We do this slowly," Boadicea said. "Taylor's arm. . . ." When she said this, she looked at Taylor and there passed between them a wave of feeling almost like an electrical current.

Smiling slightly, Taylor nodded in response. "Yes, slowly. We don't need more injuries. Adam is. . . ." He trailed off, not wanting to say how awful Adam looked, with his bleeding ankles and wrists. Taylor turned to Putnam. "Are you ready?"

"Yeah, sure," the young man said, positioning himself directly under the grate. Cupping his hands, he looked at Adam.

Slowly, Adam moved to climb onto Putnam's shoulders. He moved cautiously, fearful of putting one of his cracked ribs through a lung, and the places where the iron cuffs had cut into him hurt like hell.

"How did you hear of this?" Taylor asked Putnam as he helped Adam up. The boy was as solid as if he were a boulder.

"Darci's aunt Thelma called to brag that Darci had finally asked who her father was. Thelma's ugly, and sick with jealousy over Jerlene. I guess Jerlene always knew who Darci's father was because she called your office and they said you were researchin' in Camwell, Connecticut. So Jerlene came and got me and we drove all night to get here."

Putnam cupped his hands for Taylor to climb up. He was going to have to go up Putnam, then up Adam.

"I don't understand," Taylor said, wanting to talk to take his mind off the pain in his arm. He didn't think it was broken, but it was badly sprained. "I was under the impression that Darci's mother didn't know who fathered her child."

"That's what Thelma told everybody. She hates her sister real bad. On the way here, Jerlene told me the truth. She stole some papers out of your car, so she knew who you were."

"So why didn't she contact me when she found out she was pregnant?" Taylor asked. Truthfully, he had no idea what he would have done if a girl he hardly knew had told him she was carrying his child, but at least he would have known about his daughter all these years.

Putnam winced a bit when Adam's foot dug into his shoulder, but he didn't falter with the extra weight of Taylor. "Jerlene planned to have the kid, get her figure back, then show up at your house with a cute kid. But you got married." Putnam sounded as though he couldn't understand why Jerlene had ever wanted *him*.

"So Jerlene said she'd wait a couple of years until you got over the honeymoon part of your marriage, then she'd take Darci to meet you. But by the time Darci was four, she was already real weird, and Jerlene had read one of your books so she knew your whole family was a bunch of freaks. No offense. So Jerlene didn't let you know you had a daughter because she said she wanted her kid to grow up normal."

"Normal!" Adam said as he positioned Taylor on his shoulders. "Darci's been passed from one person to the next, while her mother went from man to man. What's 'normal' about that?"

If Putnam could have, he would have shrugged. "Yeah. Well. Jerlene ain't gonna win no prizes for bein' a good mother. Stayin' beautiful takes all her time. But she's real good at that beauty stuff."

"She—"Adam began, anger in his voice.

Taylor cut him off, as he steadied himself on Adam's shoulders. "So why is Jerlene here now?"

"To save her daughter," Putnam said, as though he should have known that. "Just because Jerlene never wanted to be around a strange little kid like Darci don't mean she don't love her. Darci is her own flesh and blood.

Jerlene said she figured that if you found out you had a daughter you'd turn her into a witch like your other relatives. So when she heard Darci was here and you were here and this was a town full of witches, it didn't take a genius to put it all together."

Putnam looked at Boadicea, standing before him, waiting to climb up the human ladder to the top. "Who are *you?*"

"It's too long a story to go into now," Adam said. Before they'd started forming this ladder, Taylor had consulted the mirror and found out that the *only* way they could defeat the witch was with Darci's help. But Taylor had seen that Darci had been drugged into a deep sleep so she couldn't use her power. "How do we wake Darci?" he murmured as he helped his sister climb up him and onto Taylor. He was trying to concentrate on what he was doing, but at the same time he knew that once they got out, there would be many problems to overcome.

"Stimulants," Taylor said. "If we had stimulants, we could wake her."

"You mean like diet pills?" Putnam asked, and his voice was strained from the weight he was holding up. "Jerlene's bag . . . filled with diet pills," he said. "Break them. Put in Darci's mouth."

"But they might react with whatever she's been given to put her asleep," Adam said. He was now holding both Taylor and Boadicea.

"You have . . . better idea?" Putnam said, then the next moment, Boadicea reached the top, pushed open the grate, and lifted herself up.

And once she was outside in the cool night air,

Boadicea saw about a dozen men, crouched low, running across the fields, and she knew in her heart that these were the men Adam had called. She had seen these men in the mirror long ago. She took a chance and shouted the one word that she knew would get their attention, "Montgomery!"

20

One Year Later

ADAM LOOKED AT HIS newborn daughter and couldn't help wondering what her future would be. She had a mother with an ability that hadn't yet been explored fully. Her grandfather, with his ability to see the future in a magic mirror, said that one never knew how much a child in his family had inherited until she was an adult. Now Adam wondered if his daughter was going to be as powerful as her mother, or if. . . .

Gently putting the baby back in her cradle, he stepped across the room to the other cradle. His sister and Taylor had produced a baby girl, and he wondered what powers that child had inherited.

When Taylor had been told that his wife was expecting a baby, he'd not believed it. Patiently, he'd explained to the doctor about his injury. "The ducts are fused shut," Taylor had told the man. The doctor had smiled and said, "So were the pipes on my kitchen sink, but they still sprung a leak."

Now, as Adam looked at the cradles holding the precious babies, he thought back to that night a year ago.

It had been his cousin Michael Taggert who'd lowered the rope and helped Taylor, Adam, and Putnam out of the Cell of Death, as they later learned the room was called. As requested, his cousin had arrived with many men and an arsenal of weapons, but not a shot had been fired because, by the time they got there, it was all over.

Based on the descriptions Taylor had given her, Boadicea knew exactly where Darci was being held, and she took off running before the others were out of the deep cell. Michael had sent two of their cousins to follow her while he stayed behind to help the others.

Adam began running as soon as he was up, and he'd caught up with his sister by the time she reached the chamber. It had taken all of them to break open the huge steel-covered doors at the end of the corridor.

And when the doors were open, Michael had tried to keep Adam from seeing what was in the room, because the absolute silence from within made him sure that there was no one left alive. But Adam broke away from them and slowly entered the room. Darci had walked into that room alone, and so would he.

To his left was a partition—some ancient thing covered with signs and symbols—that created a hallway. With his left hand on the hideous wall, although he hated to feel the indentations of the markings, he paused as his eyes adjusted to the dim light in the room.

Near the doorway was a cage, about four feet high and

six feet square, and in it were half a dozen children, all tod-dlers, the oldest not more than four.

Blinking, Adam stared at the cage, not fully understand-ing why the children were there, and for a moment he thought they were dead. They were heaped on top of each other, arms and legs askew.

But then, one of the children moved, and Adam realized that they were asleep. And he had no doubt that Darci had used her mind to put the children asleep.

A few more steps took Adam past the children, and as he stepped around the wall, he saw three people lying on the floor, two men and a woman. Each of them wore long, dark robes. And each of them had a pool of blood at the base of one nostril—just as Adam had on the day Darci blasted him with her power.

To his left was a stone altar—and when Adam looked at it, he remembered what had happened to him so long ago. He remembered the altar, the woman, and the knife—and the red-hot end of the branding iron coming toward him.

Adam had to stand still for a moment to overcome the hideous memory, then he took a step forward.

Around the edge of the altar he saw a woman's head, with her artificially blackened hair spread across the stone floor. Her face was turned away from him, but Adam knew who she was: She was Sally the waitress, the one who'd waited for him to bring Darci to her.

As Adam took another step forward, he could see about two-thirds of her body, and part of her face. Except for a tiny trickle of blood from one nostril, he could see no injury on her, but her body lay lifeless.

As he took another step, his heart was racing. Where was

Darci? Was she alive? The woman at his feet was clutching the knife, the one that he'd stolen from behind the iron bars. Adam realized that *he* had brought that knife back to her.

Now he was only one step away from her spread-out robes. Another step and he'd be able to see what was behind the altar.

Adam stepped across the dead woman. Behind the altar was Darci's pale body. Kneeling, tenderly, gently, Adam picked up Darci's body and cradled her to him. He couldn't tell if she was dead or alive.

It was Taylor who grabbed Darci's arm and found a pulse. "I think she's still alive," he said, "but we need to get her to a hospital immediately."

Michael said that he would carry Darci, since Adam was in no shape to carry anyone, but Adam wouldn't release her. At the door, he saw Putnam looking at Darci with lovesick eyes. A short time ago, Adam had wanted to hurt this young man for all that he'd done to Darci, but now he could see the love in Putnam's eyes. And he could see that the young man knew he'd lost the woman he loved.

When Putnam turned away, Adam said, "Where are you going?"

"To find Jerlene," he said.

It had been a moment of indecision for Adam. He didn't want to leave Darci, but he knew he owed a great deal to both Putnam and Jerlene. With reluctance, Adam slipped Darci into his cousin's arms, picked up a rifle, and followed Putnam. When he heard someone behind him, he turned, ready to shoot, but it was Taylor and Boadicea, rifles on their shoulders.

Adam started to tell them to stay with Darci, but he

didn't. If nothing else, it was Boadicea who knew the tunnels. Adam motioned to Putnam to tell him to let Boadicea lead, then the four of them crouched down and began to run.

With the woman who had led the coven dead, there was mass chaos all around them, as her followers fled for their lives—but they took time to loot the many rooms in the tunnels as they ran.

After an hour of fruitless searching, Putnam leaned back against a wall and there were tears in his eyes. "She's dead. I know she's dead. What kind of Putnam am I if I can't protect my own?" he said.

"You don't own—" Adam began, but when he looked at Putnam's face, he didn't have the heart to go on. Taylor was standing under a torch and had pulled the mirror out of his backpack. As Boadicea had warned him, the mirror was being uncooperative and, no matter how many ways he asked, he was not being shown Jerlene's whereabouts.

Adam turned to Putnam. "Why does Darci say that she owes you seven million dollars?" he asked softly.

"Oh," Putnam said, looking down at the floor. There were remnants of the mass desertion everywhere around them. A half-open box of paper cups was against one wall, a broken table against the other. "I told her that if she'd marry me I'd forgive all the debts of everyone in Putnam." He looked up at Adam. "You know, mortgages, car loans, that sort of thing."

Adam narrowed his eyes at the young man. "But you're going to forgive the debts anyway, even though Darci isn't going to marry you, aren't you?"

"Yeah, sure," he said. "But there ain't nobody else like Darci. I'll never find—"

"Oh!" Taylor said, looking at the mirror. "That's not true. You'll marry quite soon and I. . . ." He looked up at Adam. "Since the church in this vision is filled with what look to be your relatives, I think Putnam marries someone in your family."

At that Adam grimaced and Putnam grinned. "Can I call you 'Dad'?" Putnam asked.

"You do and you won't live very long," Adam said. "Now get moving."

An hour later, they found Jerlene—and her beauty was startling—so heavily drugged that, later, the doctor said it was amazing that she was still alive.

"All them diet pills," Putnam said. "Her body's so used to drugs that it can fight off anything."

When Jerlene recovered, she told how she'd talked to the witch enough that she'd given herself time to empty her coat pockets of the prescription diet pills, break the capsules apart, and gather about a tablespoonful of the powder. While pretending to make an incantation over her daughter, she'd put the powder in Darci's mouth. The stimulant had revived Darci enough that she was able to use her power to stop the witch and her four followers. There'd been four of them against Darci, but she'd won. She'd used her True Persuasion, her great and wondrous gift from God, to kill them. Later, autopsies showed that all four of them had died of massive cerebral hemorrhages.

It had taken Adam, Darci, Taylor, and Boadicea a long time to recover from what they'd been through. Darci had been in a comalike state for nearly a week. The doctor had said in wonder, "You're not going to believe this, but she's asleep. Could she be that exhausted?"

"Yes," Adam answered, looking at Darci sleeping peacefully in the hospital bed. He'd filled the room with yellow roses, and he'd sat by her, holding her hand, for all the days that she slept. The few times that he'd seen her use her power had exhausted her, so he couldn't imagine what it had taken from her body to kill four people.

While Adam waited for her to wake up, he had her hair that he'd secretly saved from when he'd cut it from the gate put into a little gold locket that he carried with him always.

The first time she awoke, she'd smiled at him, tried to sit up, but the exertion had been too much for her, so she went back to sleep. The next morning, the sun came through the big windows in the pretty hospital room that Adam had procured for her, and Darci opened her eyes to see Adam, Taylor, Boadicea, Putnam, and her mother standing there watching her.

Darci blinked at her mother, then clutched Adam's hand tightly.

"It's okay," he said. "She came to help."

Darci turned to Adam with eyes filled with disbelief.

"Weird kid," Jerlene said, then left the room.

An hour later Putnam asked Adam to come into the corridor, where he said that Jerlene wanted to go home.

"What does she want?" Adam asked.

Putnam looked confused. "To go home," he repeated.

"No, I mean, is there something in the world that she'd like to have? Something that I could give her?"

Putnam smiled. "Between you and me, I think Jerlene would like to be a movie star."

"I'll see what I can do," Adam said, smiling at Putnam. "And is there anything you want?"

"Naw, I got money. Lots of it. I wanted. . . ." He trailed off and glanced toward the door to Darci's room. "He said . . . I mean, Darci's dad said that. . . ." Putnam looked down at his shoe.

"That he saw in the mirror that you marry a relative of mine?" Adam asked, smiling. "Think you could stand to spend a few weeks at my cousins' house in Colorado? I'll make sure they invite every one of the Montgomerys and the Taggerts to meet you. A fine young man like you should find someone in that crowd."

"Think so?" Putnam asked, his face alight. "The girls back home just want me because I'm a Putnam. Darci was the only one that didn't want me."

"Darci is unique," Adam said softly, then held out his hand to shake Putnam's. "Thanks for what you did. If it hadn't been for you a lot of people wouldn't be alive now." He lowered his voice. "Including Darci and me."

Putnam shook Adam's hand, but he looked away because his face was red with embarrassment.

"Come back in an hour and I'll have made arrangements," Adam said. "And why don't you take Jerlene with you to Colorado? Hey! Maybe you should take her shopping in New York before you go."

"I thought you wanted to *thank* me. Now you wanta send me shopping with a woman?"

Adam laughed. "Sorry. They have stores in Colorado. I'll see that she gets to go shopping there."

Smiling, Putnam turned to leave.

"Wait a minute," Adam called after him. "What's your first name?"

"Don't have one," Putnam said over his shoulder. "Why bother with one, is what my dad said. Nobody ever used his so he didn't give me one."

"What does the *t* in Darci's name stand for?"

Putnam smiled. "Taylor. Looks like Jerlene named her after her dad."

The young man turned the corner, and Adam leaned back against the wall. Yet another secret that Darci had kept from him. When she'd seen the picture of her father on the computer screen, she hadn't told him that her middle name was Taylor.

Now Adam turned as he heard the door to the nursery open and Darci entered. Even when she was pregnant, she hadn't put on much weight. Her stomach had grown to enormous proportions, but she'd not added any fat to any of the rest of her body.

A year ago, as soon as Darci had been well enough, they'd flown to Colorado. She needed a place where she could be quiet and rest, and Boadicea wanted to meet her family.

But after the initial few days of chaos, with all the Montgomerys and Taggerts flying in from around the world to meet their long-lost relative, Boadicea couldn't stand it anymore. She'd had a lifetime of solitude, and she couldn't take the noise of her boisterous family. One afternoon, she and Taylor had quietly slipped away and been married; then they'd flown back to Virginia and Taylor's home.

"I wish we could do that," Darci said to Adam.

"What?" he'd asked. "Go to Virginia?"

"No. Get married quietly and have our own home. With a cook."

"Married quietly?" he asked, smiling and pulling her into his arms. "But you said you wanted to have the biggest wedding the United States had ever seen."

"I did until that woman—"

"The wedding planner?"

"Yes. Her. She asked me if I wanted pink doves or blue doves to fly out of the cake. Adam, I don't want any of those messy creatures at my wedding. I just want. . . ."

"What do you want?"

"*Our* family. You, me, your sister, my dad, and. . . ." She looked down.

Putting his hand under her chin, Adam lifted her face. "And your mother?"

"Yeah," Darci said. "Think she can find the time now that you got her in that movie with Russell Crowe?"

"She was there when you needed her before, so I think she'll probably be there when you need her this time."

"Yeah," Darci said softly, then pushed Adam's hand off her thigh. "Behave yourself!"

Adam removed his hand. "What happened to the girl who offered me her body at every opportunity?"

"That was before you loved me," Darci said, smiling. "My plan was to go to bed with you and make such wild, passionate love to you that you'd fall in love with me. But now you *are* in love with me so I don't have to debase myself with sex before marriage."

"Debase?" Adam said. "You do realize that this is the

twenty-first century, don't you?" Chuckling, he shook his head. "All right, so what is it you're dying to tell me? I can almost read your mind."

"Where are we going to live? I mean, neither you nor I have a job, so we can live anywhere we want to."

"And where do you want to live?"

When Darci looked at him, her eyes narrowed to pinpoints.

"Oh, no, you don't," he said, then he picked her up and threw her over his shoulder. "None of your True Persuasion on me! Where do you *want* to live?"

When Darci didn't answer, he put her down and looked into her eyes. This time, they were wide open. She was silently asking him something, but the silence didn't last long. When she did answer, she said it with her voice and her thoughts—and the resulting sound was so loud that Adam put his hands to his ears. *"Virginia!"* she shouted.

"Okay, okay," Adam said. "Your dad, my sister. I got it."

"Thank you," Darci said, leaping onto him, her legs around his waist, her arms encircling his neck.

And that's how they came to live in Virginia. Adam bought a big, old southern colonial house set on twenty-five acres, and two weeks after he and Darci were married, she asked him to allow her father and Boadicea to move in with them. At first Adam hadn't liked the idea. He'd grown up surrounded by too many people, so he wanted his privacy. But the four of them had shared so much that it was difficult for them to separate.

After they were all living in the big, old house, Adam became the one to introduce Boadicea to the world. And

Taylor and Darci began to work together to try to find out what she could do with her True Persuasion.

Darci gave birth to their daughter one week before their first wedding anniversary. And that's when Adam told her that his cousin Michael had purchased the Grove in Camwell, and had hired men with bulldozers to destroy the underground tunnels.

What Adam didn't tell his wife was what had been found inside some of the rooms in the tunnels. One week when Darci had been in bed with endless morning sickness, Taylor and Boadicea—who didn't have a sick day during her pregnancy—drove to Connecticut and went through the objects the workmen had found. Some of the things they buried—with prayers and a service—some things they destroyed, but a few they put into Taylor's new Range Rover and took back to Virginia. Most of the objects were put in a vault that was hidden inside the house in Virginia. But Taylor kept the mirror of Nostradamus in his bedroom and consulted it daily. He worked with his daughter to change or prevent what he saw.

Now, as Adam looked down at his wife, he smiled. "Happy?" he asked.

"Perfectly," she said, standing on tiptoe to kiss him.

"No regrets?"

"None," she answered; then, holding his hand, she walked to their daughter's cradle.

Epilogue

~

Three Years Later

THE TWO LITTLE GIRLS, Hallie Montgomery and Isabella Raeburne, were always into everything. Two women had been hired to look after them, but the toddlers still escaped.

"Where are you?" the frustrated nanny called, looking behind the chairs and doors. "When I catch you, you'll be sorry." But she knew it was an idle threat, because the girls had a way of making her anger dissolve as soon as they looked into her eyes. In a single ten-minute afternoon spree, they had taken six cartons of yoghurt out of the refrigerator, opened each carton, and poured the yoghurt into the flour bin. When they tossed a few dog biscuits into the concoction, the two Irish setter puppies had jumped in and out of the sticky goo and frolicked all over the kitchen.

When the nanny saw the mess, she was so angry she

decided then and there to quit. But when the girls looked up at her with their big eyes, she'd forgiven them everything. In the end, she hadn't even made the girls help her clean up. She gently washed them, while singing their favorite songs; then she'd given them cookies and milk while she set about scrubbing the kitchen.

But now she knew she'd *had* it. She loved the children madly, but she was tired of searching for them, tired of cleaning up horrendous messes. She was tired of—

The nanny stopped thinking because she'd found the girls. They were sitting on the carpeted floor of their playroom tossing a ball from one to the other.

The nanny didn't say a word, just backed out of the room until she hit the wall of the hallway, then she took off running. She'd been told that she was only to disturb the parents in the case of an emergency, but now she didn't hesitate. Without knocking, she threw open the office door.

"You have to come *now!*" she said, breathless.

"Who's hurt?" Darci asked, coming out of her chair. There were newspaper articles in front of her, and she'd been trying to solve the problems the articles told of.

"No one's hurt," the nanny said. "Your daughters are playing ball!"

"I hardly think that's a reason to interrupt us," Taylor said. "We—"

Boadicea looked at Darci, and the next moment the two women were running for the door, Adam and Taylor behind them.

In the nursery, the two little girls were indeed playing

ball. A bright red ball was floating through the air from one girl to the next.

The only thing unusual was that no hands were being used. The children were using their minds to toss the ball back and forth.

"Well, I'll be damned," Darci said.

The Mulberry Tree

JUDE DEVERAUX

Turn the page for a preview of
The Mulberry Tree. . . .

Chapter 1

He needed me.

Whenever anyone—usually a reporter—asked me how I coped with a man like Jimmie, I smiled and said nothing. I'd learned that whatever I said would be misquoted, so I simply kept quiet. Once, I made the mistake of telling the truth to a female reporter. She'd looked so young and so in need herself that for a moment I let my guard down. I said, "He needs me." That's all. Just those three words.

Who would have thought that a second of unguarded honesty could cause so much turmoil? The girl—she had certainly not attained the maturity of womanhood—parlayed my small sentence into international turmoil.

I was right in thinking she herself was needy. Oh yes, very needy. She needed a story so she fabricated one. Never mind that she had nothing on which to base her fable.

I must say that she was good at research. She couldn't have slept during the two weeks between my remark and the publication of her story. She consulted psychiatrists, self-help gurus, and clergy. She interviewed hordes of rampant feminists. Every famous woman who had ever hinted that she hated men was interviewed and quoted.

In the end Jimmie and I were portrayed as one sick couple. He was the domineering tyrant in public, but a whimpering child at home. And I was shown to be a cross between steel and an ever-flowing breast.

When the article came out and caused a sensation, I wanted to hide from the world. I wanted to retreat to the most remote of Jimmie's twelve houses and never leave. But Jimmie was afraid of nothing—which was the true secret of his success—and he met the questions, the derisive laughter and, worse, the pseudo-therapists who felt it was our "duty" to expose every private thought and feeling to the world head-on.

Jimmie just put his arm around me, smiled into the cameras, and laughed in answer to all of their questions. Whatever they asked, he had a joke for a reply.

"Is it true, Mr. Manville, that your wife is the power behind the throne?" The reporter asking this was smiling at me in a nasty way. Jimmie was six-foot-two and built like the bull some people said he was, and I am five-foot-two and round. I've never looked like the power behind anyone.

"She makes all the decisions. I'm just her front man," Jimmie said, his smile showing his famous teeth. But those of us who knew him saw the coldness in his eyes. Jimmie didn't like any disparagement of what he considered his. "I couldn't have done it without her," he said in that teasing way of his. Few people knew him well enough to know whether or not he was joking.

Three weeks later, by chance, I saw the cameraman who'd been with the reporter that day. He was a favorite of mine because he didn't delight in sending his editor the pictures of me that showed off my double chin at its most unflattering angle. "What happened to your friend who was so interested in my marriage?" I asked, trying to sound friendly. "Fired," the photographer said. "I beg your pardon?" He was pushing new batteries into his camera and didn't look up. "Fired," he said again, then looked up, not at me, but at Jimmie.

Wisely, the photographer said no more. And just as wisely, I didn't ask any more questions.

Jimmie and I had an unwritten, unspoken law: I didn't interfere in whatever Jimmie was doing.

"Like a Mafia wife," my sister said to me about a year after Jimmie and I were married.

"Jimmie doesn't murder people," I replied in anger.

That night I told Jimmie of the exchange with my sister and for a moment his eyes glittered in a way that, back then, I hadn't yet learned to be wary of.

A month later, my sister's husband received a fabulous job offer: double his salary, free housing, free cars. A full-time nanny for their daughter, three maids, and a country club membership were included. It was a job they couldn't refuse. It was in Morocco.

After Jimmie's plane crashed and left me a widow at thirty-two, all the media around the world wrote of only one thing: that Jimmie had willed me "nothing." None of his billions—two or twenty of them, I never could remember how many—none of it was left to me.

"Are we broke or rich today?" I'd often ask him because his net worth fluctuated from day to day, depending on what Jimmie was trying at the moment.

"Today we're broke," he'd say and he would laugh in the same way as when he'd tell me he'd made millions.

The money never mattered to Jimmie. No one understood that. To him it was just a by-product of the game. "It's like all those peels you throw away after you've made jam," he'd say. "Only in this case the world values the peel and not the jam." "Poor world," I said, then Jimmie laughed hard and carried me upstairs, where he made sweet love to me.

It's my opinion that Jimmie knew he wasn't going to

live to be an old man. "I've got to do what I can as fast as I can. You with me, Frecks?" he'd ask.

"Always," I'd answer, and mean it. "Always."

But I didn't follow him to the grave. I was left behind, just as Jimmie said I would be.

"I'll take care of you, Frecks," he said more than once. When he talked of such things, he always called me by the name he'd given me the first time we met: Frecks, for the freckles across my nose.

When he said, "I'll take care of you," I didn't give the words much thought. Jimmie had always "taken care" of me. Whatever I wanted, he gave me long before I knew I wanted it. Jimmie said, "I know you better than you know yourself."

And he did. But then, to be fair, I never had time to get to know much about myself. Following Jimmie all over the world didn't leave a person much time to sit and contemplate.

Jimmie knew me and he did take care of me. Not in the way the world thought was right, but in the way he knew I needed. He didn't leave me a rich widow with half the world's bachelors clamoring to profess love for me. No, he left the money and all twelve of the expensive houses to the only two people in the world he truly hated: his older sister and brother.

To me, Jimmie left a rundown, overgrown farm in the backwoods of Virginia, a place I didn't even know he owned, and a note. It said:

> Find out the truth about what happened, will
> you, Frecks? Do it for me. And remember that
> I love you. Wherever you are, whatever you do,
> remember that I love you.
>
> J.

Chapter 2

Phillip watched Lillian get out of the car and walk slowly toward the house. Though she'd had a quick burst of tears when she first saw the place, he thought she was holding up well. Considering what she'd been through, she was holding up extremely well. Shaking his head in disbelief, he remembered all he'd done to prevent this moment. He and three of his associates had spent two afternoons and one morning trying to persuade her to fight James Manville's will—a will Phillip had come to see as immoral and possibly illegal.

But he hadn't always felt that way. When James had told Phillip what he wanted to put in the will, Phillip had raised his eyebrows. He hadn't dared let James know what he was thinking—that, obviously, James had found out that his young wife didn't deserve his money; that she was probably having an affair. But instead of speaking his mind, Phillip had tried to talk James out of causing what would surely be years of court battles. It never crossed his mind that James's widow wouldn't contest the will. Phillip told James that if he wanted to leave his brother and sister money, then he should split the fortune three ways; there was enough for everyone.

But James didn't seem to hear Phillip. His only concern had been how to make sure that Lillian got some farmhouse in Virginia. "She'll love it there," James said in one of his rare self-revelatory moods. "I stole a lot from her and this is the way I can give it back."

To Phillip, cheating a woman out of billions of dollars didn't seem to be repaying her; it seemed more like a punishment. But he kept his mouth shut.

It wasn't until after James's death, when Phillip saw the true nature of Atlanta and Ray, that he wanted Lillian to fight. He wanted to head a team of the most clever, most conniving lawyers in the U.S., and he wanted to take every penny away from those two greedy worms. In the weeks since James's death, Phillip had never seen anything like what had been done to Lillian, both by the media and by people he'd thought of as James's friends.

But Lillian wouldn't budge. Nothing anyone said could make her file suit. Phillip and the other lawyers told her that she could give the money to charity after she won it, but that still didn't make her change her mind.

"Jimmie was very smart about business," she said, "and he did this for a reason. There's something he wants out of this, so I'm going to abide by the will."

"Manville is dead," one of the lawyers said, his face red with exasperation. His thoughts were written on his face: What kind of woman could turn down billions of dollars?

After the third meeting, Lillian had stood up from the table and said, "I've heard all your arguments, seen all your evidence that shows that I could win, and I still won't do it. I'm going to abide by my husband's will." She then turned around and walked away from them.

One of the lawyers, a man who hadn't known James, and certainly didn't know his wife, snickered and said softly, "Obviously, she's too simple to know what money means."

Lillian heard him. Slowly, she turned around and looked at the man in a way that was so like James Manville, Phillip drew in his breath. "What you don't understand," she said quietly, "is that there is more to life than money. Tell me, if *you* were a billionaire and *you* died and left your wife nothing, would she fight for it? Or would she love the memory of you more than the money?" She didn't wait for an answer, but turned and walked out of the room.

The other lawyers hid their faces from the man Lillian had just told off because they couldn't contain their laughter. He had, in fact, just been through his third very nasty divorce and his ex-wife had fought him down to who got the antique doorknobs.

In the end, Phillip had given up trying to persuade Lillian to fight. The night of the last meeting, he'd fallen into bed beside Carol and said, "I don't know what else to do."

"Help her," Carol said.

"What do you think this has all been about?" he'd snapped at his wife.

Carol was unfazed; she didn't even glance up from the magazine she was looking at. "You've been trying to make her into what she isn't. You're a worse tyrant than James was."

"Yes, and I can see that you're terribly intimidated by me," he said sarcastically. "So what's in that pretty little brain of yours?" After twelve years of marriage, he could almost read her mind, and he knew when she wanted to tell him something. As always, she'd waited for him to fail, and only then would she offer her help.

"You've got to help her do whatever it is that she wants to do," Carol said.

"Any ideas what that is?" he asked, looking at her with skepticism. "She stays alone in the guest room, and doesn't talk to anyone. All those so-called friends that James used to fill the house with haven't so much as called her to say they're sorry about his death." His voice was filled with disgust.

"I don't know her very well, but it seems to me that when she was with James, she tried very hard to have a normal life."

Phillip snorted. "Normal? With James Manville? Carol, did you have blinders on? They lived in vast houses all over the world; they were surrounded by servants. I took her into a department store right after James died, and I swear she'd never seen one before. Or at least not since she ran away from home and married him."

"That's all true, but what did Lillian do when she was in those houses? Give parties?"

Phillip put his hands behind his head and looked up at the ceiling. "No," he said thoughtfully. "James gave the parties and Lillian put in an appearance. I don't think I ever saw anyone more miserable than she was at those functions. She used to sit in a corner all by herself and eat. Poor kid."

"Did you ever see her happy?"

"No, not—" Phillip began, then stopped. "That's not true. One day I took some papers to James to sign, but after I left his house, I saw that he'd missed one, so I went back. When I got there, I could hear voices, so I went through the house toward the back and I saw them. They were alone, just the two of them, no guests, no servants and . . ."

He closed his eyes for a moment in memory. It had been one of James's multimillion-dollar houses, "all glass and steel," as Lillian had said, and the voices had come from a room Phillip had never seen before. It was off the kitchen, and since the door was open, he looked inside. As he was standing near some flowing drapery that some designer had put up, he knew they weren't likely to see him. He knew he was playing the voyeur, but he couldn't move as he looked in on the scene.

Lillian, wearing jeans and a sweatshirt, not the designer clothes that he'd always seen her in, was serving James dinner. They were in a small sitting room with a tiny, round table at one end. From the look of the room, no designer had touched it. The sofa was covered in a rose chintz; near it was a plaid chair. The table was pine and scratched; the two chairs with it looked like something from a country auction.

None of the furnishings had that fake look that designers managed to achieve. There was nothing "arranged" in this room. Instead, it looked like half the living rooms in America, and the couple in the room looked like what other American couples hoped to be. As Lillian filled James's plate from the food set out on a buffet, James was talking nonstop. And Lillian was listening closely. When she turned and put the plate in front of him, she laughed at what he was saying, and in that moment, Phillip thought she was beautiful. She wasn't just the billionaire's plump wife who never had a word to say, but a real beauty. As she began to fill her own plate, she started talking and Phillip was astonished to see James listening to her with an intensity he'd never seen in him before. James nodded as she talked and Phillip could see that he'd asked her opinion about something and she was giving it. "Partnership," was the word that came to his mind.

Silently, his paper unsigned, Phillip tiptoed away. How many times over the years had he heard people say, "Why doesn't Manville ditch the dumpling and get a woman who isn't afraid of her own shadow?" But, obviously, as in everything else, James Manville had known what he was doing.

On that day, as Phillip walked back to the car, he thought that in all the years he'd known James, he'd never been jealous of him. Thanks to James, Phillip had all the money he wanted, so he didn't envy James his billions. But Phillip realized that when he'd looked in on that scene, he'd felt a hot wave of jealousy. Carol hadn't looked at him like that or listened to him in that way since the first year they were married.

Phillip had looked at the unsigned paper and was glad he hadn't made his presence known. It would be better if James didn't know that his private moments with Lillian had been observed.

"Yes," Phillip said to Carol. "I've seen her happy."

"Oh?" Carol asked, her voice full of curiosity. "When was that?"

James might be dead, but Phillip still couldn't bring himself to betray his friend by telling what he'd seen. The memory of it, though, just made him more confused. If James loved his wife so much, why hadn't he at least left her enough money to protect herself from the press? "You have something you want to tell me," he said to his wife, "so why don't you spit it out?"

"On the way to James's funeral, Lillian asked me if I'd seen the farmhouse that James left her."

"So?" Phillip asked. "What does that mean? The place is a pig sty. It's horrible. The countryside around it is beautiful, but the house ought to be torn down, and only a bulldozer would help the landscaping."

"Hmmm," Carol said, closing her magazine. "Nobody made as much money as James did without being able to plan. What do you think his plan was for that farmhouse?"

"Insure it for millions then burn it down?"

Carol ignored him. "How can she ever live there in peace? She'll have reporters setting up camp in her front yard. She'll . . ." Trailing off, she looked hard at her husband, as though she expected him to figure out the rest of her idea.

Phillip was too tired to play guessing games. "What?" he asked.

And that's when Carol revealed her idea to change Lillian's looks, and even her name.

Now, as Phillip got out of the car and watched Lillian— no, Bailey, he reminded himself—look at the ugly old place, he had to admit that she certainly looked like a different person. He remembered one day when James had slammed a book down on a desk and said, "I can't concentrate. Lil's on one of those damned diets again." Then he'd yelled for his secretary to come into the office—no intercom system for James Manville. He'd ordered his secretary to send Lillian a pound of every kind of chocolate the nearest Godiva store had. "That should do it," he had said, smiling. "Now let's get back to work."

Without her husband's sabotage, Lillian had dropped a lot of weight in just a few weeks. When Phillip told his wife what James used to do to keep Lillian off her diets, she'd laughed and said, "So that's the secret to losing weight. I'll remember that the next time you get on a plane."

Between the weight loss and the removal of that big schnoz of hers, Phillip had to admit that Bailey was a looker. Pudginess had been replaced with slim curves, and without that nose, you could really see her beautiful eyes and small, full lips. One morning at breakfast, Carol, holding a metal spatula, had leaned close to his ear and said, "You keep on looking at her like that and I'll ram this . . ."

But Phillip did admit that Bailey looked good. "Do you think anyone will recognize me?" was the first thing Lillian had asked when the bandages were removed.

"No one," the doctor, Carol, and Phillip had all assured her, each trying not to say how much better she looked, because that would have been saying how bad she used to look.

Now, Phillip got out of the car and motioned to the man in the car behind him to remove the suitcases from the trunk and put them inside the house. He'd arranged for two cars to be waiting for them at the airport: the SUV he'd bought for Lillian, and a black sedan from a local car service to follow them and drive Phillip back to the airport.

On the plane to Dulles Airport in D.C., Lillian had put her head back against the seat and closed her eyes. When Phillip had spoken to her, she'd just nodded. He figured that she wasn't speaking to him because he'd taken the job with Atlanta and Ray. He wanted to explain to her why, but at the same time, the less she knew the better. If she wasn't going to fight for herself, then he was going to do it for her. And the only way he knew how to do that was from the inside.

It had been a three-hour drive from the airport to the tiny mountain town of Calburn, where the farmhouse was. On the drive Lillian had put aside her anger and had pumped him for everything he knew about the town and the house.

Unfortunately for Lillian, Phillip could honestly say that even though he'd been James Manville's friend for twenty years, he knew nothing about his childhood. Truthfully, he wasn't at all sure that this farmhouse was even connected to James's past.

"How can Jimmie be related to people like Atlanta and Ray?" she'd asked. "I can't understand that."

Phillip was tempted to say, "That's because you never saw James do business. If you had, you'd know that he was more like them than you realize." But he didn't say that. Let her have her dreamy-eyed visions about her dead husband, he thought.

Lillian—Bailey, he corrected himself again—had walked around the house to look at the back. The investigator Phillip had hired had taken photos of the property, so he knew that the back was more tangled than the front, and he dreaded when she saw it. Using the key that James had given him when he'd signed over the deed to the house, Phillip opened the front door.

The door fell off its rusty hinges and crashed onto the floor, taking the jamb with it. In astonishment, Phillip turned and looked at the man behind him, whose arms were loaded with suitcases. Turning back, Phillip stepped onto the fallen door and into the house.

The place was ghastly. Thick, dusty cobwebs hung down from the ceiling all the way to the floor. He could hear creatures—mice, rats, and whatever else they have in the country—scurrying about under the floor. The sunlight that came through the dirty windows showed years of dust floating through the air.

"Take the luggage back to the car," Phillip said over his shoulder to the man behind him. "She's not staying here." He waited until the man was gone, then he turned, stepped onto the door and out into the fresh air. He'd never thought of James Manville as evil until this moment. That he'd leave his wife this filthy place, and expect her to live here, was either insane or truly evil. Since he knew for a fact that James was not insane, that left . . .

Lips tight with anger, Phillip walked toward the back of the house to find Bailey.

The photos hadn't lied: the back really was worse than the front. Huge trees, vines that were covered with lethal-looking thorns, bushes that were as tall as trees, and weeds that were as big as something in a science fiction movie fought each other for space and light. The tangled mass of plants around him made Phillip shiver. To his right were stones set in the ground that made a narrow path through weeds as high as his head. The many bees buzzing around him made him quicken his step. "Lillian?" he called, then caught himself, and, like the lawyer he was, he looked around to see if anyone had heard him make the error of calling her by her former name. But as he looked at the tangle of weeds, he knew that an army could be hiding ten feet away and he'd not be able to see them. "Bailey?" he called louder as he quickened his pace. Still, there was no answer.

Immediately, his mind filled with all the horrors of the country: snakes, rabid skunks, deer that could kick a person to death. Were there wolves in these mountains? What about wild cats that hid high up in trees and jumped on people? What ... about ... *bears?*

If the jacket she was wearing hadn't been bright pink, he never would have seen her. She was entangled in the biggest, ugliest tree he'd ever seen, and all he could spy were her denim-clad legs and part of one pink sleeve. Oh, God, he thought, she's hanged herself. In despair over James and this hideous place, she'd somehow managed to commit suicide.

Heart pounding, he ran toward the tree, ducked under two low limbs, then saw her. She was alive and looking upward raptly as though she were seeing some heavenly vision. It's worse than suicide, she's lost her mind, he thought.

"Bailey?" he said softly, but when she didn't respond, he said, "Lillian?" She just kept looking upward. Slowly, carefully, he stepped toward her, but he also inspected the ground. Weren't people supposed to stand still if they saw rattlesnakes? Was a poisonous snake the reason she wasn't moving?

"Bailey?" he said softly when he got closer to her. "We can go now. You don't have to stay here. If you want a little house somewhere, I'll buy it for you. I'll—"

"Do you know what this is?" she whispered.

He looked up, but all he saw was an old tree that badly needed pruning—or better yet, removal. "I know," he said, "it's a horrible old thing. But you don't have to look at it." He put his hand on her arm to pull her away.

"It's a mulberry tree," she said softly, her voice sounding almost reverent. "And it's very old. It's a black mulberry tree."

"Nice," Phillip said, then pulled harder on her arm.

Bailey smiled. "The Chinese duped James the First."

At first he thought she meant James Manville, but then he realized she meant the English king, Elizabeth the First's incompetent successor. What did an English king have to do with a derelict farm in Virginia?

She spoke again. "James decided to grow mulberry trees in England so he could raise silkworms and make silk an industry in England. The silkworms feed on mulberry leaves, you know. So James imported thousands and thousands of mulberry trees from China. But—" She broke off and smiled as she touched a leaf of the big tree. "The Chinese tricked him. They sent the English king trees that bear black mulberry fruit instead of white. Black mulberries are great for eating, but silkworms won't touch them."

Phillip looked at his watch. It was two P.M. Three hours back to the airport, and his flight was at six. Of course he'd have to find a seat for Bailey on the same flight. "Look, why don't you tell me more about mulberry trees and the kings of England on the way back to the airport? You can—"

"I'm not leaving," she said.

It was Phillip's turn to want to burst into tears. Why did all women have to be contrary? "Bailey," he said firmly, "you haven't seen the inside of that house! It's falling down. The door collapsed when I opened it. How can you possibly spend the night here? The place is filthy! It's—"

"What's that?" she asked.

At the sound of a large truck on the rarely used gravel road in front of the house, Phillip started chanting, "No, no, no, no," even as Bailey leaped over two tree limbs and started running down the overgrown path.

The furniture had arrived.